MW00444283

THERE IS NO LOVELY END

There Is No Lovely End

PATTY TEMPLETON

ODD ROT · CHICAGO, IL

THERE IS NO LOVELY END
Copyright © 2014 by Patty Templeton
PattyTempleton.com

Cover design by Matthew Ryan Sharp
Carny.MidwestWorkEthic.com

Book design by Patty Templeton and Matthew Ryan Sharp

Author photo by C.S.E. Cooney
CSECooney.com

There Is No Lovely End is a work of historical fiction. Apart from the well-known actual people, events, and locales that figure in the narrative, all names, characters, places, and incidents are the products of the author's imagination or are used fictitiously. Any resemblance to current events or locales, or to living persons, is entirely coincidental.

Published in the United States by Odd Rot
Chicago, IL

Publisher's Cataloging-in-Publication-Data

Templeton, Patty.
   There is no lovely end / Patty Templeton ; illustrations by Matthew Ryan Sharp.
   452 pages cm
   ISBN: 978-0-692-23124-1 (pbk.)
   1. Winchester, Sarah Pardee, 1837-1922—Fiction. 2. Winchester Mystery House (San Jose, Calif.)—Fiction. 3. Mediums—Fiction. 4. Ghosts—Fiction. 5. Grief—Fiction.   I. Sharp, Matthew Ryan, ill. II. Title.
PS3620.E4675 T44 2014
813—dc23
                                                    [2014910223]

First Edition

For my mother—
I can't afford to buy you a castle, but I sure as hell can write you stories.

PROLOGUE

THE PATH ENDED in a clearing.

The clearing held one tree.

Anyone with an eye half open and a salt toss of thought could see the oak was old. It was a jagged woodcut against the ochre twilight. Rot wafted off it. Beetles skittered on westward-tilted branches. Sap coated the woodbine that climbed the trunk.

Sarah Pardee had no control over her hideously curly hair, how short she was, or the fact that even though she was eleven, her mother dressed her in frilly, floral frocks, but on these precariously nailed planks Sarah stood in control. She was the captain of the dread ship *Pandemonium*.

Captain Sarah Pardee was known throughout the eastern American seashore as the Belle Hellion. Her treeship housed a multitude of stolen jars, jugs, vases, and teacups. Was it not discovered by the Belle Hellion that 1,600 candlebugs generated the coequal propulsion of 1,600 pounds of coal? Radiating tableware dangled from branches and kept company with crows. Wine bottle pyramids glowed against the November gloaming. A mason jar chandelier hung over the center of the deck.

The figurehead barked.

"Aye Cort. The drear gains."

The puppy, a Lilliputian creature, turned a tight circle and scratched at its post three times. He was shaggy, the color of rain splashing stone, and floppy eared. An insubordinate but kindly mutt.

"No, it has not been three hours, dog. We are not yet called in for dinner."

Sarah inspected the clearing. Dead leaves knee-deep. The scrub overgrown. The uphill path through the trees toward home.

Cort snuffed a chunk of hair off his eyepatch, circled, and scratched thrice—this time marring the wood.

"Scoundrel! It has been but two hours and fifty-three minutes and you mark my *Pandemonium*? Be warned dog, I suffer fools foully. There are places, deep, flea-ridden, hexed locations for traitors." The captain leaned back at the helm and bumped into a shelf of teacups.

Cort hung his head and gnashed his teeth.

A rock cut the air in front of Sarah's nose.

"Cort! Prepare for hostilities."

The dog leapt from the forecastle to the main deck, nails clicking.

Isabelle Pardee was tall for her age and nearly the same height as Sarah, though she was four years younger. She rustled through the fallen leaves, attentive to avoid the Place of Traitors. It was a two-day-dig of a pit covered with shrubbery. It exuded the odor of rancid apples.

Isabelle peeked from behind a thicket.

"Sarah, come down. It is time for dinner."

"I will dine on my ship, gravel-lobber."

Sarah took in the sight of Isabelle. Thin, elegant for a child, always in a dress the color of cantaloupe. Of her five siblings, Isabelle was Sarah's favorite.

She was prim and polite in front of adults, but often stayed up late with Sarah to read adventure tales. They shared a secret. Both wanted to move to California. Sarah dreamt of prospecting and Isabelle wanted to marry a rich hardware store owner.

"No. Mama said come in and wash up."

Isabelle stepped outward, threw another rock upward, and knocked a jug off the deck. It landed with a shatter. The *Pandemonium* did not appreciate this.

Isabelle ran to the base of the oak and huddled against a pile of discarded jars.

"You there, Isabelle the Destroyer!" Sarah yelled. She knelt to sort through the armory basket. Honey trickle? Bean toss? Ant gush? "I told you what would become of you if you broke any more of my jars!"

"You wouldn't dare dirty me before dinner. Mother would punish you."

Cort nipped at Sarah. He pointed a drippy nose at the water pitcher.

Yes, recompense. Isabelle had recently put Sarah's hand in a warm glass of water as she slept. Sarah had peed all over her bedding.

"Sarah."

"It's Captain Pardee and I'll pit you for that indiscretion."

"Sarah, mama will knock a sensible woman into you if we are late. Not me. Only you."

Cort snapped at the air in Isabelle's direction.

"She knows you are not in the garden reading."

Sarah poked her head down the escape hatch. Cort followed suit. Isabelle lifted her head at the noise.

Sarah poured the water pitcher down the hatch.

Isabelle screeched the keen of a hoof-crushed kitten.

"Sarah!"

"Cort, we miscalculated."

The dog nodded. It had been a partial soaking.

Isabelle picked up several stones that had begun their lives as mountains.

"Sarah, mama noticed the missing dishes and I'm going to tell her what you and your mutt are doing out here."

Isabelle's stones soared skyward, arched around the deck, and landed on Cort. The dog careened and leveled a light tower. Jars crashed.

The *Pandemonium* wanted to crush Isabelle with a fallen branch but refrained its revenge out of respect for the Captain.

Sarah remained calm.

Losses were calculated.

Homeless candlebugs crept through Cort's fur.

Cort headbutted the armory basket. A cheesecloth ball filled with flour rolled out.

"Brilliant sir, you are brilliant!" Sarah picked it up and stepped to the edge of the deck.

"Fine. Stay here. I am telling." Isabelle turned toward the path to the Pardee house. There was plum pudding and hot tea to be had.

"Do we let her depart, Cort?"

Isabelle turned and tried one last time to bring her sister home. She stomped her foot. "Sarah, now. Come *now*."

"But Isabelle, I need help."

"With what?" Isabelle eyed her elder sister.

"I need help down."

Isabelle squinted at the ladder. It was intact.

"I am seven. Not stupid. Your ladder is whole, Sarah. I do not want to help you. I do not like you right now. I am sodden." Isabelle wrung water out of her skirt.

A red leaf fluttered against Sarah's neck. Then an orange one. Sarah grabbed the leaves with the palm of flour still behind her back.

"I didn't want to yell it to you all the way down there." Sarah lowered her voice. "But I have a secret."

Isabelle's eyes enlarged with interest. She went back to the treeship.

Sarah wound her arm back, affecting an itch.

Isabelle stopped.

Cort growled.

Sepia-colored clouds curtained the sky.

Mrs. Pardee looked at the hall clock. She tapped two fingers against its face and thought better of sending Isabelle after Sarah. Mischief-makers, the both of them.

"What sort of a secret?" Isabelle demanded.

"Quiet! You cannot go yelling about privacies in these parts."

That was the truth. An aggregation of ghosts, unseen by the sisters, promenaded the clearing, collecting ambiguous information.

"What sort of secret?" Isabelle whispered.

"A tremendous secret. A terrible secret. A very large and important secret."

Isabelle forgot about the plum pudding. She no longer noted her chilled person.

"Tell me, Sarah. Tell me, *please*."

"Come closer, sister."

"Tell me from here. I might know it already."

Sarah held up the red leaf. "I learned how to read leaves."

Isabelle was shocked.

"What does that mean?"

"I can see your future in this leaf. I won't say a word further until it is in hushed tones on the deck of the *Pandemonium*."

Cort shook a moth off his ear. Sarah passed him the flour ball. He edged to the escape hatch, ready for the drop.

Isabelle ran to the tree in awe.

Sarah sat at the edge of the deck. Her feet dangled off. She waved the leaves like fans.

"Sarah, will I marry someone handsome? Am I going to have a big house with lots of snapdragons and daisies? Will I leave New Haven?"

"This red leaf says you will marry a noble and handsome man and have at least one noble and handsome baby."

Sarah dropped the leaf on her sister.

Isabelle tried to catch the leaf as it fluttered downward. She missed and it tumbled to the thousands of other leaves at her feet. Isabelle's eyes narrowed. Her lips tightened.

"This leaf," Sarah said. She held up the orange leaf. "This one says you will live a glorious life with yearly holidays to European places, in the spring, of course. But it only counts if you keep the leaf forever."

"Give it to me, Sarah!"

Sarah swung herself back on deck and scuttled to the hatch. There she dropped the orange leaf.

It fluttered past the trunk.

Cort snorted. The flour ball had clotted his nose.

Isabelle ran to the base of the oak before the leaf could finish falling.

Cort dropped the flour ball.

Isabelle caught the leaf.

The missile struck Isabelle's head. She and the leaf became floured shades.

Isabelle shrieked.

Cort did a tail-wagging waltz with Sarah.

Isabelle sat on the ground, a hiccupping mess. She held the leaf in her hands.

"Oh come now," Sarah said. She grabbed Cort, put him in the armory basket, and dangled him over the edge of the deck. With a flick of a cord, Cort flitted downward. The basket landed with a yip and a thud. "You can't possibly be angry. You broke at least twelve of my propulsion jars."

Sarah climbed down the ladder. She sat next to Isabelle.

"You cannot be sore. Those candlebugs took three evenings to collect. Three!" Sarah elbowed Isabelle. Cort licked the younger girl's nose. It left a peach spot in the pale dust.

Isabelle wheezed. She stuffed the leaf into her skirt pocket.

The pale and pearl of late evening edged toward the children.

"Isabelle, we should go. You said so yourself."

Sarah stood.

Isabelle gave one final hiccup and focused. She grabbed Sarah's pantalettes and pulled.

Sarah yawped. She and her undersuches went to the dirt.

Isabelle gave a crow-stirring cry and the girls rolled, pulled, and generally thwarted one another in waves of leafage.

Cort nipped at the muslin of Isabelle's underskirt.

"You are bad, very bad, Sarah," Isabelle heaved.

"Little villain," Sarah countered with a tug on the ear.

"Dwarf." Isabelle kicked Sarah's shin.

"Corrupt child." Sarah pulled her sister's curls.

Cort pillaged the auguring, orange leaf from Isabelle's skirt and sat back with a growl. His ear smarted from a kick by an undecipherable foot. He would democratically chew on both of their special things later.

"Liar," Isabelle uttered. The laughter began to boil as Sarah tickled behind her knee.

"Street rat," Sarah said. She snorted as Isabelle poked her in the ribs.

"You are a horrible, horrible sister, Sarah Lockwood Pardee." Isabelle pulled her sister forward.

"And you are a fussy, upstanding civilian, Isabelle C. P."

They stood in the fallen leaves.

"In return for your horribleness, Sarah, you will have a terrible future. I will marry a nice man and have nice children and the world will be well for me."

Sarah nodded. "Duly noted."

Cort deposited the leaf in Sarah's palm, who put it in her own dress pocket.

"All of your paramours will depart, all of your children will die, and you will have a nasty, ugly widow's life. The world will be dark for you," Isabelle said brightly.

"Yes, yes. Noted as such. Shall we?"

"Yes."

"Darling Isabelle?"

"What?"

"I'll wager my pudding I reach the porch first."

Sarah bolted.

"Not fair!" Isabelle cried, running after her sister.

Cort disappeared under the leaves as he followed the girls.

The air was thin.

The apparitions wandering the wood frowned as the children passed.

The *Pandemonium* shuddered, but could not strike the girls' conversation from the clearing.

Sarah's leaves had held no meaning. It was the words. No matter the age of those that said them, no matter the intent—a person's words carried weight in the world.

CHAPTER ONE

NEAR CHICAGO, ILLINOIS, 1852

HENNET C. DANIELS required a pick.

What he had was a beggar, a drunk, and a Chinese fella watching as he stabbed at a keyhole with a stick from a busted chair.

The pins didn't shuffle. Didn't shift. Didn't click.

A guffaw came from the cell crosswise.

Hennet raised eyes to find a wild-haired woman in tattered flounces laughing at him. Likely seventeen to his twenty.

"Inapt width," the woman said.

Hester Garlan was her name, but she didn't give it out often.

"Thin enough," Hennet replied.

"Don't even have a tension wrench."

"Don't need one."

The sheriff grunted, cheek flat on his desk, arms hanging by his knees, hat slouched into a puddle of sleep-spit. His wheeze, wheeze, snore filled the two-cell jailhouse.

Hennet ran a hand through his dark hair. It came back bloody. He'd been pistol-whipped before he was thrown in his cell.

"Sweetmeat, you're the least able picker I ever witnessed," Hester said.

Hennet didn't abide offensive attentions.

He flicked his hand at the woman. Blood spattered Hester's chin and frayed lace collar. The cutpurses and evening women bunking with her scampered to the clapboard wall. Hester wiped the blood from her chin with her knuckles and sucked on them. She did this slowly.

There was vantage in owning your adversary's fluids.

Hennet watched the woman.

Her head tilted.

Hester's head tilted because a deceased, pink-faced woman paced the jail that only she could see. Hester was a medium. She saw and spoke to the dead.

Most ghosts were mumblers. There was no accounting for what confidentialities would tumble past their teeth. Hester sold these dead-uttered intimacies. She should have been propertied and prosperous, but for every coin that came to Hester, so did a curse.

"You're boil-brained if you think you're going to dub the jigger with a stick," she said after the pink-faced woman walked through a wall.

"Speak like you're learned on the matter."

Hennet loosened the kerchief on his throat. He thumbed the scar of a bullet graze under his ear.

Hester ferreted through her skirt folds. She emptied four hidden pockets. She searched the nest of curls behind her ear and pulled forth her picking kit.

"Tell you what I'm *learned on*," she said as she jiggled her own lock. "I'm *learned on* the certitude that a proper man doesn't throw blood at a lady. I'm *learned on* how to punch that sheriff dead. I'm *learned on* how to take his gun to your chipped ear for staining my time and dress."

Her lock clicked mightily.

Hennet turned to the men in his cell. "Whatday'all got?"

The beggar flipped him a button.

The drunk tossed in two ribbons of rabbit jerky.

The Chinese fella pitched a short knife into the ground by Hennet's boot.

Hennet nodded appreciation and picked up the knife.

His cellmates crossed their arms and backed away.

Hester had halted.

"Forget how?" Hennet sneered and took to the keyhole with the blade.

"Didn't want you sniveling I had excess time when I shoot you in the head while you're still diddling that hole."

Hennet shived to.

Hester's lock clinked louder.

"Think you'll prize this, little bird?"

"Look at the mud brick, outlaw, it's where you'll die."

Hennet frowned.

Both locks whined over their common assault.

Hester wanted to hit the man's lips. His chapped, thin lips. She hissed a fragrant whore out of one of her shoes, picked up the boot, and threw it. The leather sole smashed into Hennet's cheek.

"For Chrissakes!" Hennet yowled.

"Your face is a botheration," Hester replied.

This was a moderate lie. Hennet was a full, frontier fathom of handsome.

Hennet wiped the new sprung blood from under his eye and slung the boot at the sheriff.

A wham and a slam and the sheriff fell off his chair.

Hester kept at her keyhole.

Hennet stood with his fists on his hips.

"What's this?" The sheriff huffed on the short walk to the cells. He shook the boot at Hester.

"Pickin' a lock, sir," Hester said.

"You ain't picking a lock here."

Hester looked at him dead-on and kept tricking pins.

"Stop."

"No."

The sheriff dropped the boot, rolled his right cuff, directed his fist betwixt the bars, and boxed Hester in the eye.

Her head jerked back. The lock clicked. Hester rolled her neck and gazed lazily at him.

"Ain't you got sense? Stop," the sheriff told Hester.

There was a deep split in Hester's eyebrow from the sheriff's wedding band.

The sheriff's dead wife, she of the pink face and pacing, was present. Mrs. Lawman passed of heat stroke on an August afternoon, after she brought her lovely-dovely his lunch. Permanent perspiration dripped grey from her temples. Her husband did not ignore her. He did not see her. This did not stop Mrs. Lawman from chattering at him about church and the weather and washing his hands.

Hester kept at the lock.

It was Hennet's turn to guffaw.

The sheriff never beat on his delicate lovely-dovely—rest in the glorious Lord's peace, she'd been gone one year and one half. He woulda never beat on any decent woman, but this one, she was nabbed for roughing up a priest.

The sheriff picked up the boot and swung it at Hester's hands. Busted fingers would teach her to respect his warnings.

The pick went through the web of Hester's thumb and forefinger.

There was an intake of breath from the other prisoners.

Hester held up her hand with the pick still in it. She pulled it out, clinched the sheriff's collar, pulled him forward, and drove the pick into his hairy neck.

The deceased Mrs. Lawman screamed.

Only Hester heard it, but the scream caused a wind to rush through the jailhouse.

The sheriff fell to the floor yelling and squirting red.

The other prisoners grunted in satisfaction.

Hester's hand was five minutes from swollen, her eyeball felt slack, and the sheriff's late wife alternately crooned apologies for her husband's disreputable behavior and squealed ruination for Hester's untoward attempt on his life.

Hester looked at the brown-eyed outlaw.

He had the grin a wolf gave a rabbit half a second before innards become outters.

Hester ripped a strip of leather from the whore's shoddy boot. She rubbed it in the blood Brown Eyes had flung at her earlier. She pulled out a hair, lathered it in her own blood, and wrapped it around the leather with a dirge in her throat. Lace torn from her collar bound the bundle.

Hester threw it at the candle on the sheriff's desk.

A lick of fire exploded outward. Ate the bundle. Burnt quick. Disappeared.

The women behind Hester started a prayer circle.

The beggar, the drunk, and the Chinese fella did likewise, though they didn't join hands and not two of them prayed in the same way.

Hennet went back to lock picking.

Hester drew a line in the dirt with her hand. She walked over it three times then smoothed it out and said, "You will never once be satisfied in this life."

Those that take notice of such declarations took notice of Hester. The line in the dirt, the bloody bundle—that was stagecraft—but the words mattered.

"You curse me, little bird?"

Hester winked at him and blood reddened her eye.

"Damn you and your damning me."

Hester attempted to absolve herself, but the outlaw's curse was already marked by the world for later use.

Hennet huffed over his keyhole.

Hester concentrated on hers.

It took one minute more.

The locks sighed in defeat. Each opened.

Hester had to kick-shove the groaning sheriff from her path. By such time, Hennet had his haversack from a wall peg. Had his gun belt from the sheriff's drawer. Had his six-shooter trained on her.

What Hennet noticed was that there'd be a slight less beauty in the world when he shot this woman. Fetching, in spite of the split brow and puffed knuckles. Maybe it was because of the split brow and puffed knuckles. Hennet came from a line of half-crazed wildcats and appreciated vigor in his women.

The sheriff grunted. Felt like he was dying. Thought he heard his wife calling. (She was.) Reached out for mercy and found Hennet's pant leg.

Hennet kicked the sheriff in the armpit without looking at him.

Hester stomped her flat-heeled boot. A razor shifted out of the toe. She kicked Hennet in the neck, but she missed the main vein. The cut wasn't deep, but it bled flowingly and Hennet's footing faltered. His head hit the mud-brick.

His six-shooter went off.

The bullet brushed Hester's arm and found a home behind her in the guts of a thirteen-year-old vagrant who, a lifetime ago, was the spelling bee champion of Little Tick, Illinois.

The sheriff tried to drag himself from the fray.

Hennet got to his hands and knees. Hester kicked him in the ribs. There was a delightful crack.

The other prisoners eyed each other. Looked at the open cell doors. The near-dead sheriff. The brawl.

Hester swung her foot at the outlaw again, but this time Hennet grabbed her by the heel, wrenched it, and Hester fell. Her ample backside would bruise.

The women, the drunk, the beggar, and the Chinese fella exited their cells and ran from the jail. The Spelling Bee Champion of Little Tick, Illinois died. A straw bonnet was tipped over her blank eyes.

"Sonofabitch, you sonofabitch there is dirt on my dress." Hester elbowed Hennet in the face.

"Already was dirt on your dress." Hennet dragged her to him.

The sheriff moaned. Hester had fallen on his legs. Hennet punched the dying man, but it was Hester's follow-up thump that sent the sheriff into the final dark.

Hester and Hennet got to their knees.

"Sweetmeat, I will cut you." Hester grabbed a fistful of Hennet's hair and swung his head back. She searched her pockets left-handed for a blade.

"No, you won't." Hennet shived Hester in the shoulder instead. Twisted it.

Hester growled, extracted the blade, and lost her grip on the outlaw's hair.

Hennet dove forward and landed on top of the woman.

"Not so bad down here." Hennet eyed the low scoop of Hester's dress. The lace collar had fallen off.

"Not a here you're welcome to." Hester kneed Hennet in the particulars, grabbled at the sheriff's belt, and found his sad, little knife. She stabbed Hennet in the side and dragged a jagged pattern.

Hennet wailed every wrong-sided word he knew, pulled the short knife out, fell off the woman, and landed on his back. He clutched at a bow as he rolled and a hole appeared at the hip of her dress.

"Can't claw a woman's dress to flitters without her permission," Hester said as she climbed on Hennet's chest and strangled him with a broken chair leg.

It was sitting astride Brown Eyes that Hester noticed what a fine chest he had. The kind of chest that could stop a hammer, a train, or a whore walking a full room.

While grabbing at the chair leg, Hennet couldn't help but admire the woman's calves. They were traveling calves.

"I mean to tear something, it'll be imperative," he said. With a quick rip, Hester's scoop neck split. Her bosom spilled out.

"Never been a lonely, unclad lady, and I'm not starting now." Hester kept the chair leg at Hennet's neck and tore open his vest and shirt.

They bled onto each other from abundant wounds. Each raised an eyebrow.

"Temporary accord?" Hester asked.

"Com'ere," Hennet said.

Hester let the chair leg fall.

Hennet bunched the dress over her thighs. Being a man of the world, he attempted composure at Hester's lack of britches, but she felt him rise beneath her.

The dead blathered of Hester's vulgar talent for having sexual relations outside of bedrooms. The sheriff was now one of the blatherers.

Hester didn't give a fig what the dead thought of her.

She rocked her weight over the outlaw's waist.

Hennet undid his belt. Once again, he thought on the world losing a damn sight of beauty when he shot this woman.

Thirty minutes of biting, scratching, back curving, thrusting, bending, rolling, and Hester's hips moving up and down later, Hennet wouldn't have the chance to shoot her. The wound in his side bled through the fornicating. He passed out shortly after Hester wiped the inside of her thigh with his kerchief.

The dead said that Hester's lewd aptitudes appalled Hennet into a swoon.

When Hennet awoke, it was midmorning. He had no pants, his vest was in shreds, his neck had gummed up, his side wound had a rag shoved in it, and he was back in a locked cell. Be that as it may, there was a pick within spitting distance.

It wasn't his lowest start to a day.

Then, the screeching started.

"Net!"

Hennet's brother ran into the jailhouse.

"Mornin', Walleye."

"Net, you ain't got none pants on." Walleye leaned against the bars and gave them a shake.

"Do now." Hennet pulled on his pants.

"Why you the only one in jail, Net?"

"Because your sorry trigger finger couldn't coffin a sheriff."

"I was gonna pick you out, Net, pick you right outta here," Walleye said. And he could. Walleye could liberate any lock in less than eleven seconds.

Hennet thought he smelled marjoram. His neck smarted. Hell, his everything smarted.

"Why you hurt?" Walleye asked.

"None of your fool business."

Hennet thought on her brown hair, full of twigs and shivs. The curve of her neck. The way she tongued his ear. The weight of her legs. The extension of her arm before she stabbed him. Hadn't even got her name.

Hennet shook his head, then worked the keyhole. His brother poked at the pick.

"Quit."

"I'm helping."

Walleye poked Hennet's hand one more time.

"I'll bust you up, Wall."

But the lock clicked open.

Hennet sighed. It should've taken at least three more minutes.

Walleye stepped back and rubbed one of his feet. He didn't believe in shoes before eleven in the morning or after eleven at night.

Hennet washed out his side wound and stitched it up with a needle and thread from his haversack. How that little bird didn't puncture any of his guts, Hennet had no idea. He'd had worse but barely. He hoped her shoulder festered.

Walleye kicked the sheriff's cadaver.

Hennet took the dead man's boots, but his gun and billfold were already gone.

It wasn't the first time the Daniels Brothers walked out of a jailhouse and into the morning light.

Chapter Two

AS HESTER STOLE the sheriff's horse—a spotty fella whose teeth didn't fully fit in his mouth—she thought on death.

The heart beats. Beats. Aches. Then quits. This resignation was an unavoidable experience. That which lived died, but not everyone left the world when they died. She didn't understand how the world decided who stayed.

"Giddyup."

The horse ignored her. It was old. It was tired. It was in the middle of a shit and enjoyed the moonlight.

Hester counted to five to calm herself.

A reek arose. The horse moved.

They passed the jail tree and the general store. Two dead farmers played checkers on the porch. Each had a bullet hole in one eye. They had quarreled over cattle. One of them noticed Hester, balled his fists, but could not leave the porch to swing at her.

When and if the dead recognized Hester, they did not like her. She was not surprised. She killed them, often, for pay. She was the lone practitioner in all thirty-one states of sending a spirit to the Something After. Heaven, Hell—

wherever they went—they were gone from the living world after she met their eyes and said a few words she had learned from her mother.

Hester didn't like the puzzle of how some people stayed on as spirits and others didn't. Hester didn't like any puzzles or riddles. She didn't like thinking. She liked doing. She didn't like learning. She liked knowing.

From what Hester could parse, it came down to a person's last words and thoughts.

For example, the pick-stabbed sheriff.

His last words were "Not yet."

As such, he was destined to brood at the jailhouse, never to be noticed by anyone, except for the desperados whom his harping was experienced as piss cans spilled by no visible wind and the thumping of food tins out of steady hands.

If the sheriff's last words had been "Shit" or "Oh hell," he would have left the vale to the Something After. But no. His final reflection was that of self-preservation. Hester knew that because she heard him.

Something, or someone, heeled to the closing consideration of the living mind—especially if that thought was said aloud.

Thus the earthly province, inhabited by humans doing their breathing and living, was also populated by those that need not breathe, that went unseen. Specters, spirits, apparitions, ghosts—all words for the same damn thing—the dead.

Hester had seen them all her life. They did not age. They did not sicken. They wore the clothes of their last day and bore the marks of however they died.

Hester kicked her horse. It didn't move. It gnawed on a shrub in front of a booze tent. It savored the scent of whiskey-piss near the entry. Hester did not. She kicked harder. She wanted out of town before that brown-eyed outlaw awoke. She had taken a scuffed silver pocket watch and one-hundred-seventeen dollars from his billfold. The horse gave in, but it decided to chew on her when it had the chance.

A sleeping drunk was propped against the trunk of the last tree before town turned to flat land then forest. Hester leaned sideways to steal the rum cradled in his arms and winced. Her body was a patchwork of bruises and wounds. It'd been years since anyone had given to Hester as good as she gave, and she didn't even get the man's name. She sighed, tipped back the bottle, and forced herself to think.

Haints had limited ambulation. When somebody passed on, they affixed to an object, a place, or a person—but once attached, shit, there was no unhitchin'. Hester rummed her weary mind trying to figure why the hell a ghost had to attach to anything. She believed the dead were bound to what or who they wanted most. If they held no passions, their adherence was arbitrary.

Spirits splintered into one of three categories: idiocy, artifice, and aid. As you were in life, so you were in death.

Broad quantities of the dead were too dull to be anything other than pantry-opening-air-cooling-wind-whispering-wall-knocking nuisances.

Others shirked wickedly around and knit their anger into nets to cast over the living. Hester had found that the dead could harm humans. Animals for that matter. Plants, even.

But the dead were not completely atrocious. There were those spirits that found fulfillment in alleviating the living. They reinforced walls during earthquakes. Unobstructed jammed shop locks. Did the dusting. Set the tea to boiling. Opened holy books to encouraging passages. Assisted wheeled-chairs over breaks in the boardwalk. Frayed hangman's knots and snuffed fallen candles before fires caught.

These helpers believed that good deeds would quicken them to the Something After. Hester knew better. Her dead sight and words were the only unnatural carriage to other worlds.

She also thought that it was hardly appropriate that those who lived continually wished for something *more* and those that died continually wished for something *after*.

It all deepened Hester's headache and barely any of these were even her thoughts. Her great-grandmother had written *An Uncommon History of the Dead*. She took another drink. Knew that all she had were hunches and an old woman's speculations. Remembered that she had to pick up her wagon in Joliet, felt another brain shudder, and took a larger swallow.

The only surety Hester held, as she set off on her farting, unpleasant horse, was that all people—living and dead—were greedy and needy and never to be trusted.

Chapter Three

NATHAN GARLAN WAS a sixth-generation medium conceived by a ne'er-do-well and an outlaw.

He was not expected or desired.

In truth, Hester Garlan had several times drunk abortive teas. When these had no useful effect, she had the sincerest intention to lift the lid of the nearest garbage barrel and leave the sniveling babe for the mutts and maggots.

It was known among her people that unless you were done watching the dead, you didn't breed. Your dead sight would go to the child.

Hester had never had an accident breathe out of her before. In a candlelit moment of the child blinking dark eyes, she called him Nathan. Once. Then Hester thought better of becoming sentimental over a swaddled setback and hoped that when she killed him, she'd once again be able to see spirits. If not, she'd be fighting the dead blind-eyed all of her days.

But waste made woe.

Hester, lacking in delicate sensibilities, had a mind for money. Why drown in a trough that which might bring a grip of gold?

Solomon Nerebit's silver door knocker was a human fist hanging out of a lion's mouth. The fist was polished, but the porch step was in sad want of a scrubbing. Hester Garlan knocked, paused, then added two boot jolts to the bottom of the door.

She nudged a burlap sack with her foot. It, for Hester regarded her son, Nathan, as less engaging than an upturned beetle, chirped and rolled toward the edge of the stoop. She stepped on the child to halt Its progress.

Across the cobblestones, two gentlemen had silk top hats and base speculations. They could smell Hester. A stimulating cinnamon brine wafted from her.

She reached under her unbustled skirts, winked at the scattering, scandalized men, and produced a nub of chalk.

The child punched tiny fists at the burlap.

Hester sat on her heels and scribbled on the stoop.

The door creaked open. A cherrywood pegleg and an opal-buttoned leather shoe reflected the spiders in Hester's hair.

Mr. Solomon Nerebit, worth approximately 13,000 dollars a year, stood six foot four with greying temples and a cigar stub. The box the stub came from cost more than a housekeeper who'd properly open the door, but who was Hester to question a rich man's peculiarities?

Hester liked her men thoughtless bastards.

Solomon Nerebit was a thoughtless bastard.

The child wouldn't live long in Solly's hands. It'd be tupped at a mantel, starved, or dropped down the stairs in a month, maybe less—give it till the thing pissed on the parquet.

The infant had taken her dead sight, but Hester could still hear the departed mutter. Bothersome lot always warbling about something lost, lonesome, or undone. Much as Hester wanted to promptly hatchet the boy apart, if it meant a hoard of velvet and her hotel bill paid through the end of the year, she could endure a month without seeing the dead.

But it would give them time to scheme. Their hate had grown in the past nine months. They'd become more violent with her. All because of that churchyard of spirits Hester'd sent to the Something After.

Until Hester could get her dead sight back, she soaked her clothes in salt water. It repelled most of the bitter Bessies intent on her destruction. Her once deep burgundy walking dress was now a lackluster red.

"Darling, so pleasant of you to drop by unannounced." Nerebit flicked his cigar and grasped his lapels.

The cigar landed on the burlap sack.

The ghost of a three-year-old girl watched from a neighbor's chokeberry bush. She hoped the baby boy inside the burlap would burn. Then she would have a friend.

Nathan saw the rotted specter from the holes in the cloth. Ribbons sliced deep into the girl's throat and were tied into a neat bow at the back of her neck. She had been strangled by a coachman. She was a dense brume rather than a solid being.

Not every spirit was more fog than form, though most beclouded about the edges.

Nathan cried.

He was yet to understand that this was his lot in life—to be an agency of communication between the living and the dead.

"Hello, Solly." Hester dropped the chalk into her corset and stood. "I was leaving my remarks on the ownership of a certain tot to you and the missus."

Hester had outlined a baby discharging offensive liquids while Solomon attempted to change its bottom cloth.

The burlap smoldered.

The garden ghost smiled widely. Too widely.

Since Its birth Hester had felt empty. Somewhat less. Not even hot baths and room service could make up for more than one ghost-blind month. Too many dead things wanted her gone to grass, and how did one exchange blows with invisible enemies?

"Your illustration has missed my distinguished eyebrows, my pushing girl."

"But I left room for all that forehead."

"Utterly splendid yourself, precious. Are those, hmm, are those twigs in your hair? How festive."

Hester kicked the cigar off of It. Can't sell It if It was dead. Not for as much, anyhow.

The dead assembled in front of the Nerebit home. A mob of shufflers who'd perished on the thoroughfare.

Their murmurs headached Hester.

Solomon Nerebit heard nothing.

Nathan saw them. Heard them.

"You're the pa," Hester lied.

"Hester, my mischief, that child looks not a lick like me."

"Solly, it's in a bag."

"Still. Perhaps some embroidery would do agreeably?"

Solomon Nerebit was not a fool. He knew the infant did not commemorate his last association with Hester, a dolorous bout of itching did.

"You and the missus still want one?"

"Not that one, Hester-pet."

"I'd sell It for a just rate."

This time Solomon thoughtfully nudged the burlap with his toe.

"No."

"Fair enough."

"Hester, my pretty plague." Solomon placed peaked fingertips on an upturned lip. "My requirement of your affections has diminished. I am astounded and disappointed in your appearance at my private residence."

Hester leaned into Solomon.

Solomon's chest puffed out.

Hester raked her fingers across the piping of his jacket. Her left hand pilfered his pocket watch. "Solly, you're a hideous man with a terribly unimpressive requirement."

Hester thieved from Solomon.

He had never once caught her in the moment.

He tolerated it because the thought of one day seizing Hester in the act and beating the blue into her aroused him greatly.

But verily the itching was awful.

"Mister Nerebit, who is at the door? Come back to tea," beckoned Mrs. Nerebit from the parlor.

Mrs. Nerebit drank posh tea picked by trained monkeys.

She would not be pleased to learn that the monkeys did not delight in their trade and often relieved themselves on the tea leaves.

"Shortly, Missus Nerebit, I'll be there shortly. It is only a repellent solicitor."

Solomon pushed Hester back. Her shoulder blades stitched into the brick entry. He grabbed her ear and twisted.

Solomon Nerebit delighted in intimidating people.

"Hester-pet, toss it off a high precipice, perhaps the bank. That might be tall enough. As the awful, unfashionable creature falls toward Old Scratch, step after. Do what you will, but never come back to my home."

Solomon let go of Hester's ear, put his palm on her forehead, and cracked the back of her skull on the brick.

There are many bad decisions made each day.

Bill money goes to whiskey.

Tithes fund dog fights.

Little ones fib.

Large ones lie.

The thick-headed thieve, nimbly or not.

Sons of Cain kill and are only sometimes caught.

There are a mighty number of missteps man may take. None are as foolish as enraging Hester Garlan.

The dead knew this.

Solomon should have known this.

Hester squinted. Her lips tightened.

She took deep, steady breaths.

She put her hand to the back of her head to see how much blood was there. She frowned at her fingers.

Hester was not a woman of meditative pausation.

Nor was she a woman to be bullied.

The dead skittered several steps back.

The garden child hid and peered hollow eyes out of the chokeberry bush.

Solomon Nerebit should have known better.

Hester rummaged under her skirt. She plucked one of three knives tied to her thigh.

Solomon saw a distinguished eyebrow mirrored in the blade before it befriended his throat. Crimson soaked his tailored shirt.

Solomon fell onto Nathan.

A cheer came from the chokeberry bush.

A squall from the bag.

A sigh from the bush.

Nathan had not been broken.

With a practiced hand, Hester pillaged. "Gold watch, good for nothin', bullheaded, sonofabitch." She flipped over Solomon so that he was face up.

Solomon Nerebit's lips moved soundlessly.

"Where's the billfold, lover?" Hester popped the opals from his shoe. She tapped his pegleg until she heard an echo, tipped the knife into a slit, and found twenty dollars.

Solomon punched Hester with a loosely balled fist. Hester pushed his hand down.

"Repellent, Solly? Am I?" Hester took off his rings. "All I wanted was to sell the sprat, and look what you made me do."

Solomon Nerebit blinked one final time.

Mrs. Nerebit put down her tea and went to the door.

Nathan gibbered as Solomon's blood leaked into his burlap.

Hester reached inside Solomon's left cuff. Three more dollars. "And really Solly, toss myself off the bank, eh? Eh?" Hester smacked Solomon's cheek hard.

One of his eyelids fell shut.

Hester tugged It from under the formerly attractive Mr. Nerebit and shoved her findings into the sack. She kicked Solomon's neck and a spurt of blood fountained across the doorframe.

Mrs. Nerebit's plump silhouette screamed.

"Don't sham like he was a decent man," Hester said.

Mrs. Nerebit stepped into the light, a lace handkerchief to her puckered mouth.

Hester crossed the entry and took a silver dessert plate from the foyer table. Almond sticks and butter cookies dropped on Nathan. The plate put a minor, permanent dent on the side of his head.

"Don't suppose you'd purchase this chickadee from me?" Hester swung the sack. Nathan cried. Mrs. Nerebit demurred.

A bouquet of lilies and irises from a further entry table were fastened into Hester's hair for later sale.

Mrs. Nerebit's skirt hem soaked up Mr. Nerebit's blood.

A miniature painting, a lock of Solomon's hair, the silver door knocker, and a gold and blue damask pillow smothered Nathan.

Hester patted Mrs. Nerebit on the puffed sleeve. "Think of it as a wild, new beginning." Hester's other hand stole Mrs. Nerebit's amber earrings.

Mrs. Nerebit opened and closed her mouth like a decked fish.

"You'll have plenty to squawk about at bridge club, eh, pretty lady?" Hester took the now Widow Nerebit's scarab brooch.

The Widow Nerebit would tell the ladies. Only they played rummy, not bridge, and it would have to be after a brief mourning period. She would spread tears across the tablecloth and for at least three weeks she would win every hand. She would buy extravagantly beaded black gowns and never, ever again would the Widow Nerebit have to listen to Mr. Nerebit complain about her tea selection, or how he thought she was growing fat in the face, or how the violet brocade curtains (she absolutely adored) violently clashed with her "potato pallor."

Hester hopped down the steps with the sack over her shoulder.

The stoop would need a harsher scrubbing.

Solomon Nerebit did not join the dead milling about the cobblestones. Call it lack of ambition or luck, but sometimes, most of the time, dead was dead.

The garden ghost sat with her head on her knees in the chokeberry bush, yet again cold and all alone.

There are many ways to kill an infant.

Infants do not have the physical structure to run from you. Nor do they make a mewling if one has properly sealed their mouths.

Anybody could go about suffocating one of the things, but it's getting rid of the carcass that can be a trial. One mulling over murdering an infant should quietly inquire into close-at-hand pig sheds, riverbeds, rendering kettles, train tracks, soap boxes, and large manure heaps.

Since the meat-pie man wouldn't buy the babe, Hester thought to burn It. Were Hester not arrogant—and easily distracted by the scent of coffee—perhaps she would've lingered to watch Nathan roast, but Hester didn't stay and Nathan didn't burn, and it was ten damn years before she found the mishap again.

CHAPTER FOUR

WESTERLY, RHODE ISLAND, 1852

HESTER HAD A misconception. Slaying her son, by itself, would not return her dead sight. She needed a trick box.

The only living person aware of trick boxes was Enton Blake—better known as the Reverend Doctor Enton Blake, proprietor and mouthpiece of the Alleviating Theatre, a medicine wagon that toured New England, the Great Lake states, and once even made its way out West and back again.

Enton's prevailing position was Westerly, Rhode Island. There, he knew a woman named Sita who had a seaside shack, posed for his figure drawing, and made him laugh.

She lay before him in her purple parlor. It was also the foyer. And the kitchen. And her art studio. It was an intimate abode of dark wood and soft firelight.

"I want to see it."

"What?"

"Enton Blake, you show me what you keep fingering in your jacket pocket or you aren't getting meat and mashed potatoes tonight and you certainly aren't mashing mine."

Sita sat up from her pillow pile and set strong eyes on him. Enton straightened his posture in the hard-backed chair.

"My Aphrodite, might I show you your drawing instead?"

"Don't bother. It'll be smashing. I'm gorgeous and you illustrate gorgeously. What is in your pocket?"

Enton grimaced. He hadn't realized he had touched the trick box, let alone repeatedly. He placed his sketching pad on the floor.

"An heirloom obtained on my last tour."

"Show me."

Sita came to Enton and sat on his lap.

He pulled the box out of his pocket. It was small in his palm. Sita picked it up. It was elaborately carved and curiously heavy.

"What is it?"

"A trick box."

"Enton, you are unhelpful. What is it?"

"It is, as I said, a trick box."

Sita shook it next to her ear. It sounded as if there was a calm storm inside.

"What's in it?"

Enton stopped Sita from agitating the box.

"My father."

She raised her eyebrows and dropped the box in his hand.

"His ashes?"

"No."

"Then what?"

"His ghost."

"His soul?"

"That is uncertain. I am unschooled in these matters. Are spirits and souls the same? I prefer to think of it as his ghost."

"You carry your father's ghost in a box in your pocket?" There was a measure of disbelief in her voice.

"Indeed, I do."

"Why?"

"So that I may see and hear the dead."

Sita opened her mouth to argue.

Before she could speak, Enton placed the box back in her hand. He turned her so she looked through her open front door. He kept his palm on her back. Sita saw the sand and the sun setting over the sea and a blue-grey, vaporous skiff wrecked on the shore.

"Enton, is that a ghost ship?"

An equally blue-grey, vaporous man walked around the skiff. He was missing an arm and part of a thigh.

"Yes."

"How curious."

She gave him back the box and looked out the door again. No skiff. No man.

"I do not ever want to touch that again."

"Noted, my Sita."

Enton was appreciative that his entourage had hidden themselves from Sita. Six ghosts followed him on his travels. Too many dead things wouldn't have done her well.

"How'd your father enter that box?"

"I would prefer to forgo that conversation."

Enton had cut back the black skin of his father's chest, cracked the ribs with a medical hammer, and jostled the box into the heart as the beautiful, old man sweat and sputtered, "That's how it's done" and "Good man, Enton" and "A limp sapphire light will enter the box."

"Is he the only one that's in it?" Sita asked.

"It is a polite rule to never put more than one spirit in a trick box."

"Why?"

"It would be cramped."

Sita put on a robe and set a pot of water over the fire.

"Your father wanted to go in there?"

"It is within my family's tradition."

"Could you put an unwilling ghost in that box?"

"I would not, but there are legends of people using it that way."

"Why?"

"One, they did not realize the box was already employed. Two, they collected as many ghosts as they could, amenable or not, misguidedly thinking that more ghosts meant more power."

"Doesn't work that way?"

"No. One ghost from blood-tied kin. No more is needed."

"Can a ghost escape from the box?"

"No. It can only be opened from the outside through a flummoxing series of old words, subtle squeezes, and shifts."

"You can see and hear the dead. What good is that? I don't understand." She pulled several potatoes from a sack and scrubbed them clean.

"If you see and hear the dead, you can help them."

"Why in the howling world would you help them? Don't the living wear you out enough?" Sita dropped the potatoes in the pot.

"My father put it thus, that both the living and the dead contribute to the energy around us. If we want a balanced and better world, there should be no desistance to compassion. It has been my family's calling for over two centuries. Though that charge may be coming to an end."

"All my family ever did was tend bar."

"A fine calling."

Sita threw a hand over her shoulder to say she was no longer listening. The smell of fried meat and pepper filled the shack.

Enton took up his sketching pad and drew his lover.

Chapter Five

SAINT ANTHONY'S ACADEMY of Wayward Sons had official documents, received from the Night Watch, detailing that no one in the wide open world wanted Nathan Garlan. The sprat was come upon in a fox's maw under a harvest moon by an opium-eating dandy.

Or at least, that's what the Night Watch wrote down. They were wrong.

It wasn't a fox. It wasn't a mongrel, or a vagabond.

It was a ghost. With teeth.

Chauncy Edelstein, the aforementioned dandy, had seen this with his own blue eyes. He'd never seen a ghost before. He'd never see another one.

"You a soak throat? Been tippin' back?" A man of the Night Watch poked his pencil nub at Chauncy's thistle print waistcoat.

"No."

"Chasing the dragon? Seem sleepy, don't you?" The watchman put his scratch pad in a jacket pocket. No need to take notes if you're listening to a tar-tooth taker.

"I stand a sober man." Chauncy tapped the handle of his walking stick against his forehead. He was neither a drunk nor a poppy fiend. He was a teetotaler who owed his presence in the late lack of light to a visitation to the bed of a barrel-chested lover. This was not something he preferred to disclose to the Night Watch.

"I've communicated what I witnessed three times. We are an hour from morning. May I leave?"

"Tell it a time more," the watchman's partner directed. He held the abandoned infant. The child was remarkably quiet considering the burlap it had been wrapped in was covered in ants and excreta and an unknown villain had scratched the child's name onto its stomach.

"Quickly," the first watchman goaded.

Chauncy sighed and paused to collect his thoughts. "I heard a child mewling. I went to assist it. A ghost covered in an orange rag quilt was crawling on all fours and had the child in a burlap sack hanging from its mouth. I know it was a ghost because I could see through it. I know it was a dead woman because I knew her in life. Miss Jeanine. She had been my nanny. She passed thirteen years prior. Ran down by a carriage on this road. Probably why she crawled, her legs were chopped off. As a lad, I enjoyed Miss Jeanine's company and blueberry cobbler. I dislodged the child from her mouth with considerable difficulty. You will notice the dirt on my elbows, knees, and right shoulder. Those men witnessed this." Chauncy pointed his walking stick at a gaggle of factory workers smoking near the cotton mill's entrance.

"What'd ya see?" the first watchman called to the workers.

All of them shrugged their shoulders, flipped their fags, and marched inside. All but one, who took off his cap, scratched behind his ears, and said, "Saw the fella from forty yards wrestle someone for a baby. Didn't see who. It was dark." Then he followed his peers into the mill.

Nathan gave a small screech. He did not like the burly arms that closed around him.

The watchmen turned back to Chauncy. The one with free hands lifted them, palms up in a challenge. "Eh, ponce?"

"May I take my leave?" Chauncy was resigned to the watchmen believing him a lunatic.

"Yeah. Best not I see you none too soon, maybe ever," the watchman holding Nathan said. "Shouldn't be stealin' babes from vagrants."

It wasn't until he left that Chauncy considered that taking the child from Miss Jeanine might not have been a first-rate action. She had been a kind woman. But why would a wraith want an infant?

Miss Jeanine didn't hanker for a child. She'd wiped the snot from plenty'a bairns in her breathing years. What she wanted was to not see the pitiable thing melt down to fat and ash in the baker's oven where she found him. Jesus wept. There was an attractive family that lived on the edge of the wooded square who would've taken him in.

Communication among the dead worked somewhat like the telegraph. Miss Jeanine whispered to another spirit who whispered to another spirit who whispered. News circled round. It wasn't difficult for her to learn young Nathan's name or to divine that the waste of a womb that had left him in an oven, waiting for the grey-hour fire lighting, was the ghost murderer Hester Garlan.

There's power in a true name and Miss Jeanine had given the boy his due. Shallow scratches was all they was. He'd heal. That is, if he made it to manhood in a public home, seein' shades, without anyone there to explain him what for.

Miss Jeanine stood under a gaslight and hard-eyed Chauncy, the gallant busybody.

Chauncy walked past the gaslight. There was a fog about the pole. It made him uneasy. He turned back to the watchmen. "What are you to do with the infant?"

The watchmen didn't bother answering.

"I say, what's to become of the baby?"

The men of the Night Watch veered left, down Stone's Throw Road, toward Saint Anthony's Academy of Wayward Sons.

CHAPTER SIX

A BOOK SAT on Sarah's bed.

She untied the ribbon around it.

The Ladies' Book of Etiquette, and Manual of Politeness, A Complete Hand Book for the Use of the Lady in Polite Society. Oh, it didn't stop there. Florence Hartley made that title go on another fifty-three words or more. Sarah lost count. Phrases such as "deportment" and "morning receptions" perpetually revoked her focus.

Cort grunted from the bay window. He had seen Mrs. Pardee dust the book off, kiss the cover, tie the ribbon, and place it on her daughter's bed with a nod. He had known the book was useless by its weak stink of boiled cherries.

Sarah tossed Florence Hartley's advice onto a high dresser. It knocked a batch of sketches that depicted art glass windows of spider webs and daisies to the purpleheart flooring.

"Cort, move."

Cort jumped from the window seat to a small dresser. From there he leapt to the top of the tall dresser.

Sarah took the dog's place at the window and leaned her forehead on the glass.

The party would be like every other party. Tiresome. Half of the company would see her as ripe for matrimony and the other half would know better from previous acquaintance.

Cort gnawed on the etiquette book's edges.

"Admirable work, dear sir."

Mrs. Pardee walked in to see her daughter mussing her face on the window and Cort eating a book.

"Sarah! You will have a pig nose if you insist on mashing it into glass."

Mrs. Pardee reached to take the book from Cort.

He growled.

"Oh no, you do not you, you, beast." Mrs. Pardee swatted Cort's ear.

Cort gave a final growl, expelling a thick strain of slobber down the book's gutter.

Mrs. Pardee took it between two fingers and frowned.

Cort jumped down to Sarah and nosed her knee. Sarah scratched behind his ear.

"Sarah, you infuriate me." Mrs. Pardee's eyes welled up.

"Mother, calm yourself. Please."

"No, I will not calm myself. I am…" Mrs. Pardee looked to the crown molding in consideration. "*Fuming.*"

"It's barely any spit at all." Sarah took the book and brushed it off with the bottom of her skirt.

Mrs. Pardee's cheeks reddened.

"That is why I gave you this book! You cannot do things like *that.*"

Sarah looked at her gown. "What?"

"Daughter, you are progressing toward spinsterhood. Is that what you want? Do you want to grow old and ugly with only a foul dog to keep you company?"

Sarah stayed quiet. She did not dare say it aloud, but living a quiet life somewhere with a fine dog and a few friends would suit her.

A sob hawked out of Mrs. Pardee. She closed her eyes and placed her forefinger on one eyebrow, the rest of her fingers extended in exasperation. Tears flowed.

"You will never acquire an eligible bachelor sopping dog spittle off books with your dinner gown."

Cort licked the tears that splattered the floor.

"I'll read it, if it will cease your playacting."

Sarah's mother could sally forth a bucketful of tears in less than five seconds, and then the wailing would commence. Sarah could not abide her mother's wailing. No one could. It had caused a minor feud with the neighbors several years back.

"Playacting? Sarah, I, I, eeeee-ah-who-who-whooooo!"

The wailing. It was a gull cry with an owl call end.

Sarah pictured a faraway place. Somewhere warm. Somewhere not standing in front of her hooting mother. A wide open space. A place to build. She wanted creeping vines. Overhanging eaves. Turrets. Spindles. Acres of orchards.

Sarah crossed her arms and watched her kin.

Cort mimicked Sarah to the best he was able.

Mrs. Pardee abruptly stopped wailing. Her tears dried.

Isabelle leaned against the other side of the wall, listening from her room.

"If none of it works on you, I'll save the rest for your father." Mrs. Pardee gathered herself. She dabbed her nose with a lace handkerchief.

"I do not care if you read the book. I do not care if you clean it or buy a new copy or read all the books on etiquette that exist on this blessed and plentiful continent. What I concern my weak heart over is that you look a wreck and dinner guests arrive in less than one hour."

"Isabelle!" Mrs. Pardee rapped her knuckles on the wall next to a standing mirror.

A muffled "Yes, mother?" came from the next room.

"Come!"

A door squeaked. Heels clicked in the hallway. Sarah's door opened.

"Mother?" Isabelle tottered into the room. Her high-piled hair wavered, then steadied, as Isabelle straightened her posture. There was a blush of red on her temple where she had leaned into the wall to eavesdrop.

"The girl looks like a garden. Fix her."

"Yes, mother."

"Sarah," Mrs. Pardee continued, "After dinner, follow the women into the parlor for tea."

Sarah nodded.

"You've thought of proper conversational topics?"

Sarah nodded.

"Be down before guests arrive."

Sarah nodded.

Mrs. Pardee gave Cort a final scowl and left to make sure the cook had completed the rose water pound cake and the peach compote.

Sarah stared at herself in the mirror.

Cort barked.

"I know, dog. Tonight, I am beautiful."

"Wrong," Isabelle said.

"I look the picture of exquisite. Practically a Rossetti."

Sarah's hair was a heap of pinned curls and red flowers.

"Sister, there is a bouquet on your head and the Pre-Raphaelites paint lewd women."

"I like the Pre-Raphaelites and the flowers match my dress." Sarah wore a deep red gown with bronze trim.

"It doesn't matter, Sarah." Isabelle picked out all of the tulips and roses. "I am, once again, saving you from the wrath of our mother and sorrow of our father."

Cort stole one of the blooms Isabelle dropped and trotted down the stairs, passed the bustling kitchen staff, and snuck outside. He took the rose underneath the porch, put it in a tin on top of an orange leaf, and nosed the box shut.

He was met with resistance when reentering the Pardee home.

"No! Do not come back inside tonight! No!" Mrs. Pardee shrieked from the kitchen.

Sarah rolled her eyes.

"Isabelle, finish up. Cort needs safeguarding."

Isabelle left one blooming rose in Sarah's hair, in the back.

Sarah pinned a tiny cage, slightly larger than a matchbox, several inches above her hem on the inside of her gown.

"Ugh. Sarah. What was that?"

"A blessed cricket. Splendid what one can find down back alleys at clandestine midnight markets when your parents think you are asleep."

"You are an awful child," Isabelle said.

Sarah smirked and hurried from her room to assist Cort. Isabelle may have been her favorite family member, but Cort was her favorite friend.

"Husband!" Mrs. Pardee bellowed.

The kitchen staff kept close to the counters. The back door was wide open. Cort and Mrs. Pardee faced off before it.

Cort growled. It did not intimidate. He was a lap dog that thought himself a wolf or perhaps a member of a petite bear clan.

Sarah hurried down the stairs, skirts pulled high, and burst through the kitchen door. Isabelle was not far behind.

Mrs. Pardee had a lengthy curtain tassel tied to Cort's neck. Cort ran in circles. Both fell into a barooing, eeeee-ah-who-who-whoooooing jumble.

"Mister Pardee!" Mrs. Pardee entreated. Cort licked the inside of her ear.

"Nearby, Mrs. Pardee," said Mr. Pardee as he entered the kitchen.

Mrs. Pardee attempted to untangle her yellow ruffled skirts from the curtain tassel. She had the look of an upended turtle.

Cort nipped at her underskirt.

"It would do no good, say, no function at all to be shed upon," Mr. Pardee said into his whiskey glass, and then put it in the hands of a servant.

Cort ran another ring around Mrs. Pardee who shrieked, "Leonard!"

Sarah stifled a laugh.

"Present." Mr. Pardee took off his jacket and nodded at another servant who took it from him. Then with the agility of a much younger man, Mr. Pardee had purchase on the dog, threw Cort into the night, and slammed the door shut.

Mrs. Pardee rolled to her hands and knees.

Isabelle and Sarah watched in horror. Their mother had flour on her dress.

The four other Pardee offspring conversed in the parlor, uninterested in the kitchen fuss. Their mother's whooping was an almost daily occurrence and guaranteed on evenings the Pardees' entertained.

"My bonny love." Mr. Pardee put out one hand for Mrs. Pardee and one hand to the servant who held his whiskey.

Mrs. Pardee stood. Mr. Pardee sipped his drink.

Cort scratched at the door.

"Do not open that door, Sarah," warned Mrs. Pardee.

"But mother—"

"Do not," Mrs. Pardee interrupted, "open that door."

Mr. Pardee cleared his throat, "Er-hahrem." Obviously. Loudly. Again, "Er-hahrem."

"What is it, Mister Pardee, *what?*"

Mr. Pardee itched his nose and simultaneously pointed.

More scratching.

Mrs. Pardee followed the point of her husband's finger.

The curtain tassel was caught in the door.

"Leonard."

"Assuredly, Mrs. Pardee, taken care of."

Mr. Pardee fractionally opened the door and the curtain tassel disappeared.

Mrs. Pardee patted at her hair and puffed out her cheeks in large breaths.

The servant presented Mr. Pardee with his jacket.

Mr. Pardee shrugged it on and left the kitchen before he had to hear about the flour on Mrs. Pardee's dress.

Cort circled the house and sat in a dark corner of the front veranda. He contented himself on tearing apart one of Mrs. Pardee's catalogs. A clump that said THE REV. DOCTOR'S! EXOTIC! VIGOROUS! NATURAL! BRAIN CURE! wetly flopped from his mouth.

Carriages lined the street.

Soon the door would open.

Cort would find his Sarah.

William Wirt Winchester seized no delectation in soirees and society. He did not believe in sitting around parlors soaking in brandy, chatting about freeing blacks, fashion, and the weather. Desk work, not trivial talk, was his strong suit.

The gate was solid but not tall and the yard behind it freer than William would have allowed. The windows silhouetted time-fritterers.

William had forced himself to purchase a new suit and matching topper for the occasion. Miss Pardee was marriageable property and William was yet without a companion. He remembered her from his youth—a quiet, awkward, short girl who spoke French—but he had no recent opinion of her. It was the expense of the fresh formal wear that caused him to continue inside, rather than retreat into his carriage. William felt breathless in large rooms of people that did not involve board members. He screwed tight his courage, crossed the gate, and stepped over the Pardee threshold. He was promptly tripped by a scampering mutt that hustled down the front hall.

The only persons to note this blunder were the butler who opened the door and a ghost (a gentleman who wore a frock coat forty seasons out of taste, riddled with musket holes).

William Winchester saw only the butler. His knee smarted from smacking it on the doorframe.

"Why did you allow a mutt to run into the Pardee household?"

"Sir, I—"

"Rest assured, I will tell Mr. Pardee of this." William gave his gloves and hat to the butler.

"But, sir—"

"No excuses. Find it and drag it out of the house."

The butler nodded at the gentleman and ceased trying to explain. "This way, sir."

William did not give a whit about interior decorating. Though if he did, he would say that the dining room was overdone. Garish. A massive chandelier hung over the fourteen-person table and though Mrs. Pardee might be under a contrasting impression, William believed the true use of a sideboard was for table service, not towering intimidation.

A sturdy carrot-celery soup uplifted his mood, until something brushed his leg. William feigned dropping his handkerchief for a glance under the table. There were two elements of interest. One: Miss Sarah Pardee had kicked off a slipper. Unseemly of her to do so, but the foot did look a dainty, pleasant appendage. Two: the door-mutt was in attendance.

Upon sitting up, William said to Sarah—whom he had not yet spoken to, "Are you aware that there is a mutt under your table?"

"Cort," Sarah said.

"Beg your pardon?"

"The dog's name is Cort."

Sarah dropped a cracker.

Cort snuffed it up.

"You are feeding it?"

"Yes."

"Why?"

Cort sniffed at William's ankle.

William shook his foot.

Cort glared at the well-leathered affront.

Sarah dropped a thinly sliced, buttered piece of bread.

"I've known this particular mutt for ten years. Do you have any pets, Mr. Winchester?"

William frowned. "No. I am not overly fond of too many personalities in my home at any given time."

"Are you well this evening, Mr. Winchester? Until now, you have been uncommonly quiet," Sarah said, though she had not minded the silence.

"I am in robust health, only indifferent to these functions." William brought a napkin up to his mouth, as if he could cover the words.

Sarah barked a laugh and then shrouded her own lips.

William smiled.

Sarah smiled back.

"Mr. Winchester, I would have to agree. I, also, abhor these functions. Though don't tell it to my mother."

William looked up to find Mrs. Pardee staring at them.

Mrs. Pardee was pleased to see the young people talking. She was not pleased that she had to strategically carry a shawl to cover the floor grease that remained after she smacked the flour off her dress.

William nodded.

Mrs. Pardee sipped her wine, then nodded back.

"Mr. Winchester, if you smile too much longer at my mother, she will assume we are getting married."

William chuckled.

"I have no interest in such things." He did not know why he lied, but he did. William did not understand himself in regard to this woman. She made him nervous.

"Neither do I."

"But that is precisely the reason for this dinner."

"Frankly sir, I am exasperated with my continual reintroduction to society."

"Why are you unmarried?"

William saw before him a woman who, though diminutive, had dash. She didn't shy from his forthright inquiries. She made inquiries of her own. He liked that. She would be someone to speak with in the evenings. He liked the rose in the back of her hair. He liked the size of her hands and he wondered how soft they would be.

Cort growled. He did not like the way that Winchester leaned toward Sarah.

Sarah dropped a radish to the floor.

It did not satisfy Cort, but it kept his mouth busy.

"I am unmarried because I do not like most people and most do not like me after we've spoken at length."

Cort spit half the radish into William's pant cuff.

"That was a remarkably honest answer."

Sarah nodded at him.

William was scandalized by her. The candor. She would never lie to him.

"If your goal is not to be married, what is it?" William asked.

"To be happy. I see myself in California someday. San Francisco or somewhere where there is room to build and a city of great beauty near to me. I enjoy architecture."

"Miss Pardee, your veracity intrigues me."

"What about you, Mr. Winchester? What are your goals?"

"Previously, to run the day-to-day operations of Winchester and Davies Shirt Manufactory. More recently, to build the New Haven Arms Company into the most fashionable, leading gunmakers in the world."

Sarah's eyes widened. "You are ambitious, Mr. Winchester."

William nodded at her and felt pleased that she was impressed.

Cort chewed on the back of William's shoe, soft and slow enough to tear at the heel cap without being noticed.

The second course came. Grilled salmon with caper vinaigrette. Smoked mullet. Whitebait with lemon.

William hated fish but noticed Sarah pecking at the salmon. He followed her taste.

Sarah found herself pleased with Mr. Winchester. He was a starched and serious fellow, but he hadn't told her mother about Cort. It showed a trace of impropriety, and the way he blushed—only in his neck—it was endearing.

The conversation turned to Isabelle's blustering tablemate, a man with exquisite eyebrows. The initial pleasure Sarah had taken in the young man's cheekbones and deep voice diminished when he wouldn't stop rattling about the eight-years-unsolved murder of his financier, peg-legged uncle. The morbidity did not bother Sarah. It was the repetition and onion breath. It made a woman genuinely grateful to be forced to the parlor for tea.

William watched Sarah leave.

Mr. Pardee noticed William noticing Sarah.

"Young man," Mr. Pardee said.

"Yes, sir?"

"You want to marry my daughter, do you not?"

"I have only just met Miss Pardee, I—"

"Oh go on, take a little time, but I have seen that look."

"What look?"

"The look you gave my daughter's bustle."

William choked on cigar smoke.

"It's fine." Mr. Pardee slapped William's back. "I gave Mrs. Pardee that look, years ago. You'll marry. I have a feel for these things."

William nodded at Mr. Pardee and regularly sipped at his brandy to avoid speaking for the rest of the evening.

"Mrs. Pardee, a trice, please."

"Mr. Pardee, I am occupied with nightly ablutions."

She poured water into a bowl and splashed her face.

Leonard walked behind his wife before she patted her face with a towel, and grabbed her waist.

"Ooo! You, brute! Now I have water down my front. What is it?" Mrs. Pardee snapped the towel at her husband.

"We are soon to have a son-in-law," Leonard said.

"For Sarah?"

"For Sarah."

Mrs. Pardee puffed her cheeks in relief.

"William Wirt Winchester?"

"Winchester," Mr. Pardee confirmed.

"Is it an adequate match? He is the son of a clothing manufacturer."

"Bonny love, his family is in weaponry now. They own the New Haven Arms Company. He talked of nothing else. Did you not listen?"

"That is Sarah's responsibility."

Mrs. Pardee went to the bed. She brought back the corner of the sheets and patted the mattress. Mr. Pardee slipped under the covers. Mrs. Pardee climbed in after him.

"It is a strong company, Leonard?"

"Hmm?"

"The New Haven whatever it is."

"The New Haven Arms Company, chicky. Stronger than Samson. Their Henry rifle is becoming popular. If there's secession over all this slavery nonsense, I'd want that rifle by my side. That or a Spencer. Christopher Spencer. He's from Connecticut, isn't he?"

"Hmm? Yes. Go to sleep."

"If I'm not tired?"

Leonard rolled over and wrapped his arms around his wife.

"You strapping man! Get thee to your own side," Mrs. Pardee started, but her mouth was soon stopped by Leonard's.

Neither slept for an hour longer.

CHAPTER SEVEN

BESIDE A CREEK IN OHIO, 1862

TRIBULATION SAT WITH Hennet C. Daniels as he leaned his back against an oak on the edge of a creek. The sun had turned in ten minutes past. The stars shone between the branches.

His horse grunted nearby.

Hennet smacked a mosquito on his cheek, looked at the smear on his palm, and frowned.

Walleye was missing.

The wagon was there. The loot was there. Tracks on the road. Tracks by the water, but no mule and no brother. Hennet walked for a far-see well down the way. Walleye was nowhere to be found.

Hennet was a hair's breadth from drowning his brother as soon as he arrived. Maybe it'd teach the prick to stay put.

It'd been a small town and a large take and neither Hennet nor Walleye had been shot, caught, or suspected. They thieved in the night. Walleye picked the locks. Hennet had an eye for the valuables.

They took from houses on the high end of the street. They left be the banks. Too much trouble. They didn't drain the general store or appropriate from churches, hostlers, whores, or saloon owners. Any respectable thief didn't shit in paradise or steal horses.

Walleye left town before dawn with the wagon full of riches. Crated. Roped. Don't get on being fooled by the dust and mud shucked over it, you'll miss the ivory footstool, silver candlesticks, fabric bolts, billfolds, books, buffalo rugs, and jewel boxes tarped under.

Hennet stayed at the hotel through breakfast to ward off suspicion and watch which way the posse went.

The re-congregating point was at the creek oak half a day east. Walleye should've made it by midday. Hennet by early afternoon.

The black fist of night had curled completely.

If Walleye was out smacking a yellow-haired harlot's ass, leaving Hennet to sleep with a sack pillow and a breeze blanket, there was gonna be hell to pay.

Hennet'd bang-down anyone who exclaimed his brother an idiot, but that didn't stop him from thinking Walleye was a sonofabitch. Hennet swatted a mosquito away from his ear and pictured his brother's tongue swollen so he wouldn't have to hear excuses.

Hennet took off his boots. New boots. His boots never lasted. Always lost one in a mudhole, had 'em stolen, crapped in, something. Hennet thought his feet were cursed. He was correct. A few years back, Walleye'd heard a barber grumble, "Damn yer boots, too," after Hennet had missed a spittoon and splattered the man's new shoes in a saloon. Hennet wrapped his heels so they wouldn't bloody, put the boots back on, and thought on the should'ves.

Maybe it was the damn moon hanging low over the river making a lonesome soul disconsolate, but Hennet thought on Her. It'd been years. How many? Five? Ten? Hennet didn't want to be any woman's Casanova, but that lock-pickin' woman, hell. She was a curly-haired, sharp-tongued should've. He'd give twenty dollars for her name.

The clouds crowded the moon.

Walleye'd been tardy before but never half a day past plenty of time.

Hennet's exasperation turned into apprehension.

Across the creek, he heard a groan.

CHAPTER EIGHT

BOSTON, MASSACHUSETTS, 1862

IN THE TEN years of Nathan Garlan's confinement at Saint Anthony's Academy of Wayward Sons, he tried to escape no less than thirteen times. Who wouldn't? It was the only sensible thing to do, as Saint Ant's wasn't nearly as propitious an institution as its name declared. That, as much, was obvious from the building itself—a patchwork shack tower that swayed in strong winds with no sign stating to passersby its function.

Nothing said *Welcome Orphans of the World!* quite like Saint Ant's drooping eaves and entry. The building made old women cross the thoroughfare and horses shudder. Children fled from it as often as the paint chipped.

Saint Ant's punished the runaways. Leaks gushed above problematic children's dinner plates. Hammock nails pushed out of walls. The stairs shifted, causing trips and chipped teeth. The orphanage preferred to be feared and orphans did go guardedly through its halls.

Saint Ant's scowl was only outdone by that of the maw of Franwell Doogood, its round-backed mistress. Her lips were particularly wont to maliciously curl after handing off a burnt biscuit to an elder boy for hauling a runaway home.

Nathan's first memory was that of being grabbed by the back of the short pants as he ran to the glowing display window of Wester Brothers' Rare and Fine Bookshop. He often went to the bookshop. He'd never been inside, but looking in its large window gave him contentedness. A dead bookwoman with stunningly short blonde hair would often sneak him a penny dreadful from the sale stack.

Jimmy Doogood would find Nathan pining at the picture window as he watched Robert Wester pricing old tomes.

"Up and over, beetlehead," Jimmy said as he threw Nathan over his shoulder—Jimmy being the bastard son of Franwell Doogood.

"I want to live there. Not with you," little Nathan had said and pounded his fists on Jimmy's shoulder blades, "There. There. THERE."

"Ain't no matter what you want," Jimmy said as Wester Brothers' Rare and Fine receded in the blizzard.

The snow was thumb-dip thick on Nathan's rag shirt when they got back to Saint Ant's. Jimmy secured Nathan in a high-hanging net in a locked pantry.

Nathan shivered and festered near Reggie, his preeminent chum. If one can be preeminent chums with a boy five years older than you, two years dead whose chimney sweeping accident was described by the newspapers as "*Uncommonly Grotesque and Dreadfully Unusual.*"

Impalements always impressed the press.

But all of that was a minor falsification. Upon reflection, that was Nathan's second memory. His first was of being used as Franwell Doogood's doorstop.

At ten years old, his lot had not much changed. Nathan still hated Saint Anthony's, still hated Franwell Doogood, still tried to pound his fists on Jimmy at every available opportunity, and regularly found himself slammed against, locked behind, or slumped to the bottom of doors. Which is where he was on the night of the Great Rager of '62, lip bleeding, guts bruised, lying against the parlor pocket door with a crowd looking on.

All of the orphans of Saint Anthony's anxiously stood in a horseshoe around the parlor as Franwell Doogood sashayed about them.

"Boys," Franwell said and nipped a ginger's nose between her thumb and forefinger.

"Little children." She pinched the cheek of a scrapper almost as tall as she.

"Chicken-brained, idiot lovelies." She scratched the heads of a set of twins until dandruff sprinkled across their shoulders. She blew a puff of dead scalp from behind her fingernails.

Ancient drapes had been pulled across the cracked bay window to muffle the rain and wind.

"What's that filth on the floor?" Franwell flipped a poof of purple netting out of her face for a better look.

All the boys swiveled their gaze to Nathan.

Nathan, in turn, attempted not to bleed on anything he couldn't easily clean.

"Well, what is it?" Franwell Doogood said and kicked Nathan's shins.

Nathan wheezed.

Jimmy Doogood chuckled.

Saint Ant's orphans shifted their hundred eyes elsewhere.

Reggie snarled. He was unseen by all but Nathan.

There were other spirits agitated at the evening's discipline that even Nathan had not noticed.

"That," Franwell picked up the fire poker and jabbed Nathan, "is a thief"—poke—"and a liar"—poke—"and a betrayer. Tell them, Jimmy, what the contemptible toad did."

Jimmy stood taller and brought forth the full dignity of his eighteen years. "He acted the pinchpenny. Withheld funds from their rightful mistress."

"And who is mistress of all monies made in this household? Who gets you little scruffs the factory work? Who made you feral brutes educated enough to quit eating dirt and stand on your own two feet responsibly in the world?"

The orphans looked at the purple netting brushed back onto Franwell's hump. They looked at the rusted tin ceiling. They looked at Jimmy's shoes— the only shined leather in the room. They looked at gas lamps, mouse holes, cuticles, corner leaks, and at Franwell's seven-inch, hat scissors. They glittered in the firelight on the edge of a circular side table.

Saint Ant's perspired through newspapered walls.

"*Who* is mistress *here?*" Franwell shrieked.

"You, miss. You. Franwell Doogood. You. The missus," a chorus of small voices babbled.

"Have I not done right by you? Have I not given you food and work and a place out of the rain? Do you hear that? *Listen.*"

Thunder cracked. Lightning peeked through nicks and notches in the walls.

"How am I repaid, Jimmy?"

Nathan sighed. He was bored and sore.

"That beetlehead," Jimmy pitched a thumb at Nathan, "had a handkerchief-coin-bundle under a floorboard."

"What do we do with holder-outers, Jimmy?" Franwell smoothed the hair off her son's forehead.

"We put 'em in the wet room, ma."

The orphans groaned.

The parlor echoed the utterance as the wind flung itself against Saint Ant's.

The wet room was an open-air cage on the second floor that had been a bedroom before the roof caved in. It did not bother Nathan. His bloody lip did.

Franwell reached for Nathan's collar.

Reggie met her hand instead.

Franwell stumbled into the side table. Her scissors fell into her craft basket, blades up.

It was never a pleasant experience to collide with the dead. It put cramps in the living and made your guts give. There was a long-standing bargain between Nathan and the dead. They did not try to possess or claw at him for attention. In return, he would keep an orderly queue of their issues to resolve— no matter the neighborhood they lived in. Even when the dead did try to lash into or onto Nathan, he had enough experience with the convergence to convert it into a slight tremor and a hiccup.

Franwell held her hands to her stomach, almost retched, twitched from her toes to her hump, then recovered herself with a belch. Her triangular hat sat crooked over her ear.

Reggie smiled.

Nathan shook his head.

"You have the audacity to deny your hoard?" Franwell asked.

"Didn't make it at the factory. It's not yours."

Nathan was saving to once and for all leave Saint Ant's. He wanted to move somewhere warm. Somewhere with possibility. Somewhere like California.

"How'd you make the money?"

Nathan stared at Franwell.

He'd made the money from assisting the dead.

Franwell nodded at Jimmy.

Jimmy kicked Nathan in the ribs.

Nathan grunted.

Jimmy kicked him again.

Nathan spit blood.

Jimmy jerked Nathan up, ripping his sad tatter of a shirt.

Saint Anthony's thunder shuddered.

"Shake him up, Jimmy," Franwell said.

Jimmy thrashed Nathan from side to side.

The other boys in the room tried to press themselves back against the walls. None of 'em would ever hold out on Franwell Doogood. No, ma'am.

Nathan's head hurt. Blood speckled the door and floor.

The wind howled louder.

"Give him here," Franwell said. She held Nathan by the scruff of his neck. "Where'd the money come from?"

"Not you."

Ten cents had come from a gravestone rubbing. Another fifteen had come from burning a bundle of cheating love letters. Another ninety cents from an all-day sit-down with a spirit who "just wanted to talk." A whole dollar came from feeding a dead smithy's bird until he could find it a home. Another two dollars came from ferreting out used books and selling them to Wester over on Bookman's Row. It took a year of standing in front of Wester's window for the man to notice him, but once Robert Wester did, he said, "Boy, be useful. Find me books." And Nathan did. Made a good penny off it, too. The dead told him where to look.

Franwell smacked Nathan. He drooled. She grabbed him by his hair and hauled him toward the staircase. She'd put the boy in the wet room till morning and let Jimmy visit him with the woodblock for every loot-filled hidey hole he had.

A roar of wind hit the front of Saint Anthony's so fiercely that it shattered the cracked bay window and the curtains rushed parallel to the floor.

It was a wind that was not really a wind.

Saint Ant's did not welcome this intrusion.

The wind knocked Franwell Doogood across the room. She dragged Nathan with her.

The orphans scattered and yelped and fled. Jimmy was trapped in their milling.

The wind cycloned around the room.

Saint Ant's shuddered its walls in disapproval.

What Franwell did not know was that when a congregation of exasperated apparitions wanted to, they might tear down a building whether you believed in them or not. Whether you saw them do it or not.

The dead were not pleased that Nathan was being beaten. Again. It wasn't every day an effective medium was born with the ear and the eye for it. He was an advantageous, polite find. Gads better than his godforsaken, double-crossing, vainglorious mother. Nathan was no use to them as a cripple or a cadaver.

The gust of ghosts shoved Franwell Doogood face first onto her hat basket. When she lifted her head, her seven-inch scissors were stuck through her right eye at an upward angle.

Jimmy shrieked.

Reggie cheered.

Nathan debated removing the scissors. Then he threw up the half a potato he'd had for dinner.

Franwell sat with her head hovering over the hat basket. Not thinking. Not moving. Breathing.

Jimmy went into a rage.

The rustling dead pushed orphans into his path.

The rain poured in the front window.

Saint Ant's floorboards quaked.

Jimmy batted the boys aside. He took the scissors from his mother's eye.

Franwell did not have enough mind to mind. She breathed steadily. She stared distantly. She bled.

Nathan looked up from his pitched potato as Jimmy raised the scissors, but before Jimmy could hack into Nathan's head, Reggie inhaled a deep breath and stepped *into* Franwell's son.

Then Reggie threw Jimmy at the window.

On the window. A shard of the window.

Reggie raised Jimmy's head and slammed his neck down onto the broken glass, again and again. Reggie cut so severely that Jimmy's head hung sideways by muscle, not bone.

Reggie exhaled and exited Jimmy's body.

Possessing someone had been an altogether claustrophobic, uncomfortable, and unexpected experience, an experience that Reggie would endeavor to never undergo again. Most spirits could not possess anyone at all, but those that found the talent for it usually only did it once. It was a cumbersome enterprise.

Blood poured out of Jimmy's mouth and neck.

Nathan vomited anew.

The rotten and copper smell of blood and bile made every orphan that hadn't left or dashed themselves senseless against walls gag out their meager dinners. Whooping, choking, and unfortunate smells filled the air.

Jimmy thought, "I ain't going. I ain't leaving ma." He tried to say it out loud. Managed a half a word and a whisper. He twitched, gassed a leaky one, and then Jimmy stood over his body.

The view was angled as Jimmy's head now dangled.

Reggie frowned.

Nathan put a blanket around Franwell and tried not to look at her bloody face.

Franwell said nothing. Did nothing. Breathed. Bled.

Nathan gathered the orphans near the kitchen stove, heaved one more time in the alley, and limped through the rain for the Night Watch.

The gusting ghosts calmed, separated, and went back to their nearbys, some muttering that escaping ten feet from routine wasn't much of a holiday, but it had been somewhat refreshing.

Examining the black hole that formerly held his mother's green eye, Jimmy decided that he would destroy Nathan Garlan.

CHAPTER NINE

CLEVELAND, OHIO, 1862

GRAHAM JOHNSON HAD a desk to stand at. A quill and inkwell at the ready. A newspaper to write for. An assignment he didn't want. Graham was a town man. He was, by no means, going to the frontlines of the Southern rebellion. His friends were the facts and his lovers embellishments and both he could concoct on his indigo chaise. This did not please his editor, Kominsky.

"You're going," Kominsky said. He leaned over his thin desk.

"No."

"Don't you want to write of the momentous?"

"I want hot baths and fresh food." Graham picked the lint off his collar.

"Our readers want a truthful Army correspondent."

"Our readers want to know how fancy a shitter Robert E. Lee builds on the field and how many times—"

"Stop talking. Start packing." Kominsky tossed a packet of train fares into Graham's lap.

"If I say no again?"

"You're fired."

"You genuinely demand I go? That I write cold and stiff on a bloody field where cannonballs wang past my brain and Bowied-up Jeff Davis men wish to carve my blue Yankee belly? It's unnecessary endangerment. I could fabricate it all from here."

"Go or get gone. Wenspisle will take the train if you don't." Kominsky crossed his arms. Never before had Graham thought this short man to be formidable.

"Wenspisle couldn't hustle a story out of Mary Todd Lincoln clothed solely in a Confederate flag."

"So go."

"I'm not going."

"You're fired."

"I built this paper."

"You'll never work for another."

"You'd be that cruel?"

"You'd be that stubborn?"

The men stared each other down.

Graham Johnson conjured the image of himself being shot in the head by a Henry rifle underneath a Kentucky Tulip Poplar. A pencil fell from his hand and his papers scattered in the wind. Graham juxtaposed this gore with sipping Earl Grey on his indigo chaise, naked but for a silk kerchief, a book on his lap, and a paid woman sucking his toes.

"I'm not going."

"Wenspisle will have the word out in an hour that your spine is a yellow willow strap and you're unwilling to serve the Northern cause."

"You're histrionic."

"Get out." Kominsky pointed to his door.

Graham slammed it. He stole several inkwells, quills, and notepads from the supply shelves. Kominsky had him dragged out before he could secure the indigo chaise to his back.

Graham Johnson did not mind being a cur, but a cur without work was another matter entirely. He only had a month's worth of savings. He had a slight frame that was not built for huddling in doorways. Dark eyebrows and dimples did not receive handouts after you passed knee-high. When his savings were spent he would have nothing. He'd be hoveling and cold and pathetic with a ruined suit. No purpose. No prospects. No hot whiskey. He'd have to move. He didn't want to move. Where would he move to? He'd have to start fresh on some paper six states over, as if he were some trifling greenhorn. No. No. And no.

Several hours of walking, empty and insignificant, Graham Johnson began to fixate on the hooves and iron wheels of horsecars.

If Graham's mother had been living, she would've smacked him a good one and said, "Get out of it, boy. You're going downward." Through the continual supply of raspberry-smeared toast, *The Atlantic Monthly*, chores, and occasional wallops out of the fog, Graham would've unsunk himself. But his mother was dead and falling under a horsecar seemed justifiable for a man who had no friends, family, or work. His luck, he'd get conscripted if he didn't. Then he'd be paid even less for harder work.

Like a celestial reprieve breathed into the shape of a woman, Hester Garlan shoved Graham Johnson from his own shaky-legged destruction.

Lincoln could shit in his hat for all the care Hester had in the newspaperman getting hit by the horsecar. But if Hester'd learned anything from her mother's mother, it was that paper scraps to people, they all had their use. Hester saw the horsecar, saw the trim-suited man staring at the ruts in the road with hair in his eyes and hat in hand, and Hester picked a use. Easy money. She pushed the man into a mudhole.

"Well?" Hester said after the horses, wheels, and pointing passengers pressed on.

Mr. Graham Johnson raised his head from the muck-up.

"I'm waiting."

"Thank you?" Mr. Johnson said. He stepped up from what did not smell only of mud.

"And?"

"I am mildly pleased you have rescued my life?"

Misreckoning. That's what this was. It took less time to steal a dead man's wallet than talk a living one out of it. Hester felt unintelligent. She blamed it on the recent confrontation she'd had with three dead riverfront workers. One had knocked her ear hard enough her eyesight smudged around the edges.

"What's your name?"

"Mister Graham Frederic Johnson."

"What's your life worth, Mr. Graham Frederic Johnson?"

This was a question Graham had considered often.

"I am unsure."

"I would assume it's worth turning over whatever amount is on your person for my aid."

Hester tapped her toe. Slaps of mud daubed Graham Johnson's slacks.

"Yes. Of course. I apologize for inconveniencing you." Graham Johnson rifled through his pockets. No billfold. He looked past the woman's green skirt into the mud. With a pinched nose, he gathered his effects.

Graham tucked his hair under his soiled hat and tried to hand the woman a fistful of dollars. Bills poked between his fingers. He'd have to do better than a fool death in front of a horsecar if he wanted the papers to cover it.

The street was busy. Deliverymen crisscrossed the paths of carriages. Strays rooted about.

No one besides Hester heard the mob of muttering dead that flitted near shop fronts. None of them discussed Hester's niceties. (She had several. Three exactly: she was literate, she once saved a mole rat from drowning, and the third is unmentionable as it pertains to skills of the mouth that do not involve speaking.) Common phrases such as "swindling shrew," "get her," "kill her," "hack her apart," and "swallow her soul" badgered Hester incessantly. Hester frowned. She didn't relish hearing such gems as "burn her bones," "pike her," or "spit the bitch." Vindictive bastards. It'd been a decade of this.

Send a few apparitions to the Something After before they're good and ready and you had the whole Spectral Plane organizing your demise.

JOLIET, ILLINOIS, 1852

A man of the cloth came upon Hester as she unhitched a dead horse from her shuttered wagon.

Hester often had to unhitch dead horses from her wagon. This was not one of the numerous curses attached to Miss Garlan. It was a curse attached to the wagon. Hester won it in a poker game off a man whose heavy eyes lightened when he lost it.

"It is rumored that you can manage the dead," the priest said.

"Eh," Hester grunted.

The wagon tongue almost cracked as she kicked at the slumped horse. She couldn't push the wagon back and she couldn't manage to push the horse forward. Hester's new horse looked on this spectacle with critical, black eyes.

As did the washerwoman who now had eleven hundred pounds of stew and glue before her doorstep.

"Is it true?"

Hester wiped the dirt off her hands, smacked the side of the wagon, and leaned against it. She didn't speak to bureaucrats more than she had to.

Below Hester's smack, the wagon read:

MEDIUM FOR HIRE

NECROMANTIC COMMUNICATIONS AND CONSULTATIONS

If one walked to the opposite side, which the priest did, supplementary images such as water ripples, tea leaves, cloud configurations, fire, dice, smoke, glass, grave dirt, and a deck of cards outlined further (false) extrasensory skills. Hester wasn't a fortuneteller. She didn't read leaves. She didn't read cards. She didn't sense your future from your palm. She was a medium. She talked to the dead. That was all. That was enough. And when it wasn't, she was a thief.

"Do you number the banishment of phantoms in your proficiencies?"

"Sweatmeat, I'll do anything for a wage."

"But you are so young."

"And you are so fat."

The priest ignored her rude remark.

"You have accomplished this feat before?"

He folded his hands. He had tried to exorcise the spirits. He couldn't see them. The air felt thick. Several times imperceptible objects sashayed past him. He walked amongst the tombs performing the ritual and grave moss was smeared on his bald spot. Tree branches bent toward him on the path. His cassock was torn. His mouth was clamped shut by sources unknown.

Why the church couldn't build on a different lot, he didn't understand, but his was not to question God's will, only to carry it out.

"What are you looking to rid yourself of?"

"The church would like to build a new sanctuary."

"So?"

"Near and partially on a graveyard. A very old graveyard. Full of heretics."

"Uh-huh."

"There has been some concern."

"About?"

"Unseen beings have been interrupting the construction. Breaking ladders. Spilling bricks. Filling holes. Frightening workers. Strange winds through the scaffolding."

"And?"

"Are you able to banish them?"

"How much are you paying?"

"What is your rate?"

Hester pulled a pencil nub and a paper scrap from under a sash, scribbled down an amount, and handed it to the priest. His eyes went wide, his forehead wrinkled, and he nodded. They shook hands.

Hester had never before ambushed more than one spirit at a time. It was frenetic audacity that got the church's chore done. You had to sight a spirit to send it to the Something After. Look into its eyes, whisper several old words, and then endure its second death slipping through you, using your breath to waft it to another realm. If you couldn't see the dead, you couldn't send them off. If the dead didn't have at least one eye, well, Hester hadn't found a work-around for that, yet.

For the church, Hester compelled ten acres of spirits into the Something After. Apparitions of boys, girls, hogs, yellow birds, women, men, squirrels, an ox, those that'd been murdered, passed natural, accidentals, all of 'em—hastened into the light or the night, or whatever came next. It took the day entire, and then some.

The remaining dead on earth heard tell of the massacre. It was with the Church Purge of '52 that the departed decided that Hester was no longer a puerile bully but a pine box-deserving brute.

It surprised the hell out of Hester that she had the might to do such a thing, and then it felled her for a month with a case of pneumonia.

The church never paid.

Hester took issue with that after she recovered. Took issue by choking the priest with his rosary and beating two parishioners and one badgeman before she was dragged off to jail where she'd met a brown-eyed outlaw that'd given her a helluva ride and ruined her life.

Seeing the dead—there was riches in that game. But Hester hadn't seen a ghoul in a tenner, which left her twitching at the wind and throwing salt everywhere she walked.

Hester didn't work magic, only control, and she had lost most of it.

Graham Johnson did not mistake the momentary pause in the woman's conversation as concern for him. Nonetheless, she put a light in him. An interest. Graham Johnson hadn't been interested in anything other than the newspaper for what felt like an everlasting age.

Hester looked at the mud-soaked money.

"Give it to the inn, The Fancy Badger. Over there," Hester said and waved at lodgings that looked only somewhat disreputable and only half down an alley.

Graham Johnson was distracted by the woman's mouth. He was shocked by an abrupt notion of wanting to lick her teeth.

"Go on. Or is your life not worth a month's lodgings?"

Graham looked at the filthy money. He looked at the woman. She had unsullied hands. Her gloves were fingerless lace. He looked at The Fancy Badger. It had a number of balconies. A dingy red door and trim gave the place an atmosphere of harlotry.

"What designation should I state for the quarters?"

"Hester Garlan."

Hester. How very Hawthorne. Graham Johnson wondered on how long it would take before he could call Miss Garlan by her given name. If ever. Why should she bother to let him? Why should he bother to try? Perhaps he could find another horsecar. Not a horsecar. Horsecars were humdrum. Why was he fixating on horsecars? Ophelia shouldn't have a monopoly on rivers and Euripides shouldn't be the only writer mauled by wild dogs. Either would gain Graham a headline.

Hester had migrated to the boardwalk and leaned on a table of kerchiefs and scarves. She pilfered six narrow silk ties without thinking about it. She was on her way to search a poor house, a mill, two factories, and a few cafés that didn't chase the newsies from their trash piles.

After she'd searched all of New England for her son, she worked her way to Illinois and back now to Ohio.

"Thank you again, Miss Garlan. Thank you and good day."

Hester waved the man off and wandered the thoroughfare. No need to make an entrance at an inn with a man who she'd not see again. Mr. Johnson was a sad man and sad men did dangerous deeds like stand in front of horsecars, shoot presidents, and set fire to buildings. Hester did not need a sad man in her life.

Graham Johnson paid the inn for lodgings, food, and a daily bath for one month. It had taken all the currency Graham had on him and a there-and-back to the bank. He had closed his account. He would not need it. It was not unthinkable that if he swallowed a revolver in the reception office of the paper he'd receive a headline spread, hopefully break the front window with the bullet, and leave an exquisite stain for Kominsky to pass each day. He'd even write the story and leave it in his pocket. Title: *Forsaken Ink Slinger Self-Murders.* Word count: two hundred and fifty. No need to be greedy. The illustration's caption: *Note the shape of the stain—the silhouette of Saint Anthony of Padua can be seen in all that remains of Graham Frederic Johnson.*

It wouldn't be until the end of the day that shop owners noted the loss of six silk ties, two contemporary editions, one pair of vertically striped stockings, a set of elegant grey slippers, and a pound of coffee.

Graham Johnson had noticed all of these thefts. With no further horsecars available, and no pistols, rivers, or wild dogs to his name, Graham paid for the inn, then watched his new acquaintance. Killing himself could wait. Miss Garlan had a mouth he wanted to use.

Chapter Ten

New Haven, Connecticut, 1862

"Mr. Winchester, would you mind too terribly if we ladies followed you and father into the woods? I know you are shooting, but we will not get in your way."

Sarah tugged on her gloves. She was prepared to leave the house. Her mother had commanded it while babbling at great length about how showing interest in "masculine activities" was an attractive quality.

William took in the sight of Sarah, her mother, her sisters, and the mutt Cort nosing betwixt their grey, brown, and rose-colored skirts. Sarah stood out. She wore blue.

"Miss Pardee, first, may I say, teal plaid suits you?"

Sarah blushed and nodded at him.

Her sisters tittered.

"Secondly, the excursion is under your father's command," William said.

"Let them come, Winchester. They will find specimens for their pretty pressing books and we men will give them a thrill with each duck we bag."

"Huzzah!" came from behind the ladies as Sarah's brother, Leonard, pushed his way forward. "Let us hunt and gather our dinners like the ancients!"

Sarah rolled her eyes.

"Off we go," said Mrs. Pardee. She winked at Mr. Pardee as they crossed over their threshold. Sarah and William had been speaking through letters, dinners, carriage rides, and parlor visits for years—two to be exact. Mrs. Pardee was certain that today's outing could have no other purpose than to inquire after her daughter's hand.

William was pleased for an afternoon near Sarah, but he had intended this to be a business outing. He had a specific task—to query Mr. Pardee about direct investment in the Company.

He supposed he could add a secondary task. Sarah was an acceptable woman. She was responsible and read the newspaper and had delicate wrist bones and the several kisses he had stolen had been sweet. He thought marrying a doll-like woman would agree with him.

"Winchester, you're a devil of a shot," Mr. Pardee called out behind him. The Henry rifle at his shoulder fired. He missed a rabbit. "How did you achieve such gunning skill?"

William was concerned at Pardee's complete lack of aim. Sarah's father had missed three rabbits, six ducks, and a goose as fat as a mountain. Mr. Pardee would have better aim were he to look at the target, instead of the person he was conversing with.

"Years of polish, sir," William said, but his words were drowned in another report. "One has to experience and be expert with the products they produce. Have you had a chance to consider investing in the Company?"

"Not today, my man, not today. Today is for men to beat the forest with bullets. We will win our women by dominating smaller beasts."

"Speaking of women," William began, "I know you are aware that I am fond of your Sarah."

Mr. Pardee straightened his back, put a smile on, and lifted the Henry back up. He'd seen a deer across the creek.

William took Mr. Pardee's silence for a signal to continue. "I would be honored if you would acquiesce to my request to propose. Today. When I decide on a thing, I want it done quickly and correctly."

"Fine, that'll be fine, Winchester."

Mr. Pardee took his shot at the deer.

There was a squeal across the creek followed by the sound of Cort barking.

It was not a deer.

"Mister Pardee!" screeched Mrs. Pardee.

"Yes, darling?"

"You almost shot me!"

"Hmph. Sorry bonny love, I thought you were a hoofed beast. You shouldn't wear brown in the forest."

"I am not wearing brown, Mr. Pardee, it is *topaz*."

Mrs. Pardee stomped her foot, almost fell in the creek, and had to be steadied by Isabelle.

Mr. Pardee's attention had already moved to the sound of what he thought was a wild boar. It was a quail.

William bowed his head, rubbed between his eyes, and reassessed marrying into the Pardees.

Sarah walked up to him.

"I will show you something beautiful if you follow me," Sarah said to William.

"You know this forest?"

"Cort and I played here when I was young."

They walked for several minutes.

"Are we almost there? The rest of the party, they will wonder. I was not aware it would be this far," William said.

The path ended in a clearing.

The clearing held one tree.

"We are here. This is it." Sarah pointed to an oak.

To William it looked like the carcass of a tree. It tilted to the west and was surrounded by rotted boards and broken glass. "That is hideous."

"It's ancient."

"It's full of beetles."

"You don't like it?"

Sarah's smile dropped.

"We can go," She started walking back to her family, careful to avoid the Place of Traitors.

"Wait. Wait, Miss Pardee."

Sarah turned. William had the rifle tilted on his shoulder and the sun behind him. For all that she was unsure of, she knew he was beautiful.

"What is it, Mr. Winchester? As you said, our party might be wondering where we are. Additionally, I hear mother packed pudding in the picnic. I do not want Isabelle to eat my portion."

"I do not like pudding," William said.

"Of course you don't," Sarah said this to herself and sadly. For every right that she found William wonderful, there was a left that made her wary. She turned back to the picnic.

"Miss Pardee, wait. Please wait." William grabbed her shoulder. Could she not infer he had a confession for her? "What would it take to make you stay here with me a small while longer?"

Sarah thought on it. Mischief brightened her eyes.

"Teach me how to shoot that." Sarah said, pointing to the Henry rifle.

"I couldn't possibly."

"Then I couldn't possibly stay."

"It wouldn't be proper."

"It wouldn't be proper for me to stay."

Sarah decided that if William Winchester taught her how to shoot a gun, there'd be enough adventure in him to love him. To marry him.

William looked at the gun and at Sarah. His brow furrowed. His mustache moved as he bit his lip.

"Good day, Mr. Winchester," Sarah said and started away.

William let her walk.

Watched her walk.

Could not let her leave.

Thought on how a wife who knew his work, knew how to shoot, knew how to talk about firearms would be a useful thing. She could talk to other wives. Those wives could worry their husbands on having the best rifle. Sarah could help him attain an otherwise unreachable publicity path.

"I will do it."

Sarah turned.

"You'll teach me?"

"Yes."

"Excellent!" Sarah bounded back to him. "Show me, show me please."

"First, listen. There are rules."

Sarah nodded.

William said, "One: Treat every gun as if it is loaded. Two: Always be sure of your target."

"You should share these rules with my father."

William grimaced. "I was not going to mention your father."

"I will mention it unmercifully for the next five years at dinner parties so you won't have to."

William ignored the jest.

"Three: Keep your finger away from the trigger until you are consciously ready to shoot. Do you understand?"

Sarah nodded and brushed a stray curl off her forehead.

"I will now show you an apt stance. Repeat my movements." William squared his shoulders, had his feet shoulder width apart, then shuffled his strong foot six inches back for support. He lifted the rifle.

Sarah did the same with a phantom rifle in her hands.

William looked over her stance.

"Take my gloves."

"I am wearing gloves."

"I do not want yours to be smudged. You will grip the barrel with your left hand and lever it with your right. The barrel becomes hot depending on how many shots are fired."

Sarah put William's gloves on. It pleased her to do so. They were warm.

William tucked Sarah's gloves into his pocket. He liked their presence there.

"Take the Henry. It is loaded."

Sarah did.

"Now raise it as you saw me do."

Sarah did.

"Elbows down."

Sarah shifted.

"Buttstock should be close in to your right shoulder."

Sarah adjusted.

"Choose your target."

"I wish to hit the board hanging from the bottom branch of the oak."

"You may shoot."

Sarah pulled the trigger.

The Henry kicked her shoulder.

She didn't fall.

This surprised William.

There had been a crack. That surprised William more.

"You hit your board, Miss Pardee."

"I nicked the corner."

The decrepit *Pandemonium* was proud of its Belle Hellion.

"That is fine aim for a first run."

And for a woman, William thought.

"May I shoot again, Mr. Winchester?"

"Only if you answer one question for me, Miss Pardee."

Sarah waited to raise the rifle to her shoulder. "By all means."

"Will you take my hand in marriage? I am a busy man, but I believe I have time for a wife. I believe I want that wife to be you. I will make the most honest promise I can, and that is that I will never purposefully grieve you."

"Do you love me?"

"I am not sure I believe in that."

"What?"

"Love. I believe in fondness. I believe in not lying. I believe in honoring my partner in all things."

Sarah felt that he did love her, as much as he was able. That he cared. That he would be a fair man who let her maintain her own interests.

"I will, Mr. Winchester. I will marry you."

William nodded.

Sarah nodded.

"You may fire."

Sarah did.

She hit the board dead center. It split in half and fell from the branch.

The *Pandemonium* quivered its branches in approval. A shower of beetles fell to the ground.

"Excellent," William said.

"Thank you."

Sarah smiled and tipped her head. Her face was pink with pleasure. She safely handed the rifle back to William. Their hands brushed. William stepped closer. Sarah looked up into his eyes and touched his hunting jacket. William put his hand to the middle of Sarah's back and pulled her to him. He leaned down to her. She reached up to him. Their lips met. It was a deeper kiss than ever they had attained before. It made Sarah think of summer and skin and bathing with him and—

"There you are, Sarah. Mama says—oh! Excuse me, um, oh." Isabelle blushed and turned from the clearing. She did not need to bring Sarah in for pudding this instant. Isabelle narrowly missed the Place of Traitors, tottered on its edge, then went back to the Pardee picnic site.

William stepped away from Sarah.

"Pfff," Sarah sighed.

"That was, I'm sorry, I shouldn't have," William said.

"It was lovely."

"We should get back. But I, here, yes, first, will you have this?" William handed Sarah a black box. His hands shook.

Sarah opened it to find a silver and sapphire ring.

"Yes, Mr. Winchester. I will have it."

CHAPTER ELEVEN

BESIDE A CREEK IN OHIO, 1862

WALLEYE AND HIS mule cart rounded the wooded bend.

A medicine wagon was tucked into the trees on the side of the road. A paltry crowd of two rough men stood before it. Walleye was a quarter mile from the oak Net told him to set down at and held no intention of stopping.

"My good neighbor and noble sir, as the crow flies, you're right on time!" said the Reverend Doctor Enton Blake, a tall black man in a black suit with a red string tie. He stood on a shaky, foldout stage.

"Keep on, Mule," Walleye said and shook the reins.

The mule agreed with this assessment. It saw a smattering of curmudgeonly ghosts that paced before the Reverend Doctor.

"I can tell you are an intelligent man from the wide angle of your focus," shouted Enton Blake. "Though I cannot cure that roaming eye, and I wouldn't if I could, it makes your visage uncommon and attractive, I can cure many— other—ailments. Please join us for the next performance!"

Walleye was well aware of his incurable right eye. It danced a here-bit-there jig and Mama Daniels used to knock hard on his forehead and say, "Boy, focus. All you got to do is *focus* an' it'll fix itself." After years of trying real hard,

Walleye finally figured Mama Daniels could cram it 'n cough. Wasn't none fix for that peeper. He didn't need no snake oil man to tell him that.

"Don't got all day," muttered one in Enton Blake's crowd of two.

"So be it, so be it. Though it's a shame to see a third of my levelheaded audience pass by when the music's to start." Enton Blake waggled his hands behind his tailcoat to gather his compatriots. A woman, only about three and a half feet, dragged forward a washtub bass. A man with a banjo strapped to his back finished pissing in the woods and walked to the other side of the wagon.

Walleye slowed the cart. "Mule, they got a banjo man." He hadn't heard a banjo since, he couldn't 'member since when.

The Reverend Doctor Enton Blake snapped his fingers.

The banjo man quick picked and the woman climbed on her washtub bass and thumped a steady line.

"Mule, don't tell Net on me. Don't you none say I done this." He let the reins down and itched his stump. He'd lost his left arm, elbow down, in a drunken cactus brawl some years before.

"Excellent decision, my sophisticated assembler! Let us appreciate the dulcet musical stylings of the world's only healing jug band. So powerful's their sound that it has been proven to straighten tangled organs! If you feel the depths of your innards shift, note that it is for your betterment!"

Walleye walked to the medicine wagon and leaned on a sign stuck in the ground. He wasn't so dull he didn't know his letters. Net'd taught him.

THE REV. DR. ENTON BLAKE'S ALLEVIATING THEATRE

CURATIVE MEDICINE!

RESTORATIVE DELIGHTS!

Walleye took a gander. The road was empty. It paralleled the low creek, which primarily hid behind the trees. The sun was high. He had plenty'a time. The banjo man picked quicker. The washtub bass thrummed faster. Walleye set himself to a flatfoot jig. Only folks he cared for the conclusions of was Net, Mama Daniels, and Mule, so hell and fire he'd dance barefoot if he wanted to.

Enton Blake gathered five jars covered in rags and lined them up at the front of the stage.

"Ain't no jug," a sun-leathered crowd member yelled. "Ain't no jug band without a jug."

Enton Blake curled the tips of his white mustache. The band continued but softer.

"You are a cultured man! A man of expectations!" He said to the heckler. "Please excuse my misdirecting remarks. It is my utmost misfortune to inform you that our bottle blower is six weeks gone to Richmond and I have no aptitude for the melodic arts. You see, I am a healer. A doctor. I have a scientific brain. The Reverend Doctor Enton Blake's my name. It's my honor and glory to meet your acquaintances in this, the invigorating Ohio air. I have cured everything from congressmen their indecision to husbands' their private itchin'."

Walleye wanted on everyone shutting the hell up so he could full-hear the banjo. Man was good. Wasn't looking as he picked either. Closed his eyes. A cloud of dust rose to Walleye's knees.

"Cottonfingereds ain't got doctor know-how," hollered a man whose hat shaded most of his face.

Mule saw the Reverend Doctor's six ghosts surround the ill-mannered man.

"I can assure you, my patrician cohort, that I am schooled in—"

"How about we take your wagon, cotton boy?"

There was a dip on the inside of Enton Blake's bottom lip. It was the accumulation of over five decades of biting his mouth shut when someone called him *boy*.

The pack of six ghosts did not prefer their patron somber. One of them, an elderly woman who in her living years had been the swiftest quilter in six counties, stuck her hand, quilting needle and all, in the agitator's stomach.

The agitator hurked, stumbled, fell to his knees, and the contents of his stomach watered the road.

The music continued but hushed. It was hard for Walleye to hear it above his foot thudding. This chafed his patience.

"What's wrong with him? What'd you do? Where's your owner? Which one of them?" asked the sun-leathered heckler as he looked back and forth from the washtub bass to the banjo. He pulled his six-shooter.

The grounded agitator, though he continued to vomit, said "There'll be—HUHHUH—satisfaction—HUHHUH—for this."

The Reverend Doctor Enton Blake remained calm. "I assure you, I am a doctor and a free man. I have the papers to prove it. They are posted behind glass on the side of the wagon. I will gather them for display if that assists in the lowering of your weapon."

There was a loud BANG and the sound of a bullet ripping through something wet.

Everyone turned.

Walleye had shot the vomiting man.

His hurking had made the music hard to hear. When the sun-leathered man turned on Walleye with his piece raised, Walleye shot him too. Both men dead, quicker than a bird squirt.

The Reverend Doctor Enton Blake's six ghosts appreciated the expediency of these actions and the blunt force with which they were accomplished. They went back to pacing the front of the stage.

To the band's credit, neither the banjo nor the washtub stopped playing during the disturbance.

Walleye went back to dancing.

The Reverend Doctor Enton Blake thought it best to not interrupt his flailing constituent.

It took twenty-seven more minutes of hill music before Walleye sweated out all of his forward rocking, backward clogging, hands heavenward, spiral dances. While Walleye danced, the good doctor hid the two bodies in the creek reeds.

Walleye leaned on the stage in exhaustion. His head rested between two of the five jars the Reverend Doctor had earlier brought forward.

Enton Blake stood on stage and clasped his hands in a prayerful position. "Many blessings and much gracious recognition. I can tell you are an analytical and inquiring man—I can tell this because of your brown hat, coat, and trousers. Brown being a sturdy and scholarly hue."

Walleye didn't lift his head from between the jars. He had to be feeding Mule soon. Beansies for Mule and coffee for him. He was tired.

"As an analytical and inquiring man, perhaps you would like to know what's in these jars?"

Walleye didn't raise his head.

Enton Blake bent down. His knees creaked. He lifted the rags from the two jars bordering the man's skull. One jar contained a cleft human hand. In the other, a two-headed squirrel floated, long since furless.

Walleye hollered and jumped back.

Enton Blake took this as a sign of discomfort.

It was not.

When the Reverend Doctor went to conceal the jars, Walleye grabbed his hand and glared.

"Show me and Mule more," Walleye said and let go.

Walleye's mule brayed. It didn't like being dragged into conversations.

"Pardon my confusion. I believed I had caused unintentional apprehension. Onto the three remaining wonders of these thirty-four states!" He lifted one rag. "See the teeth of George Washington!"

Walleye yawped at a pile of grey, crumbly choppers.

The Reverend Doctor lifted another rag. "And the horned skull of a dog!"

Walleye clapped.

"Finally, see the vessel that's been banned by seventeen sheriffs! The pig-nosed, miniature mermaid! Alive and well! In the depths of the Pacific Ocean, she surfaces, naked from the navel up, only on nights of the full moon."

Walleye could've sworn the faded, cod-tailed thing winked at him from the murky water.

"And with that, my good friend and discerning defender, might there be a need I may fill for you? Are you well? Is your health high? Do you require doctorial aid for an ailment? I have detected that you are fatigued, debilitated even." Enton inquired because he sincerely wanted fair health for this good, albeit touched, Samaritan.

Walleye nodded. "Tired."

"I have a physic for your exhaustion," the Reverend Doctor said. He snapped his fingers. The washtub bass player brought forward a blue vial from the back of the wagon.

"Pff. Not the modest size!"

The woman frowned, her forehead creased only above each eyebrow. She retrieved a girthy, short bottle from the wagon.

"That's better. If you are weary. If you are downtrodden. If you are as now, sweating and worn down to your toes, I have something for you. Not even Jonah crawling from the whale could've had the glide in his stride that will follow when you inhale a fingerful of this sanative substance begat from the coca plant. Your heart will accelerate. Your blood will fleet-foot through your body. You will feel the full potential of the day unfold, with only but one sniff."

Walleye continued to watch the Reverend Doctor but didn't say anything.

"I wouldn't have you think of purchasing such a miracle without knowing it was more than melodrama. A fingerful, sir?" Enton Blake uncorked the bottle and passed it to Walleye.

"One finger?" Walleye asked.

Mule brayed. If there was one trait it had learned about Walleye, it was that he was never a one-dose fella.

"One fingerful and you'll have the vigor of twelve warriors blessed by the Lord."

Walleye sniffed the bottle and didn't smell anything. He dug his finger into the opening and snorted the white and brown powder.

The washtub bass player took back the bottle.

"Do you feel it? Do you feel power in your blood?"

Walleye did feel it. He felt his head disappear and had to put his hands on it to make sure it was still there. He felt his heart hit his ribs. He felt…fast.

"In thankfulness for your dramatic assistance earlier this morning, I am prepared to vend this colossal bottle, yes sir, this entire and oversized quantity for the price of not a large vial, not a medium-sized tin, but for the compensation of the smallest parchment packet sold within my stock. Is this a deal, shrewd sir, that you are prepared to close?"

Walleye blinked. Even his eyes felt fast.

"Give it over to Mule and me."

The Reverend Doctor nodded.

The washtub bass player walked back to Walleye. She tapped his remaining elbow. She whispered the price.

Net didn't need to know he bought nothin'. It was a deal. A bargain. Walleye dug for his billfold and handed over the agreed amount. The woman gave him the bottle.

"I absolutely guarantee you, upon my honor and profession, that you will in the very least have a stimulated step. If ever this does not occur, you may write me here for a full refund. I also advise not more than one snort per several hours, preferably limit your daily use to no more than two." Enton Blake handed the man his business card.

Everything was lost on Walleye after the business card was in his hand. The clouds moved fast. The water. He wanted his feet in the water. Beans. He was hungry. He'd have beansies with Mule. He'd read him some *Beadle's* till Net came. No, he'd swim. No. He felt like running. He'd run with Mule. He felt good. Doggone good. He'd unhitch Mule and they'd sit together and tap, tap, tap toes in the water and eat beansies and if he felt this fast now, bets be that he'd feel even better if he had another snort.

Which turned into another snort after that.

And another.

And another.

And another.

Who keeps track of the medicine they take? No such thing as too much good for you.

He had another snort.

And another.

Mule tried it too.

It had been a packed bottle when the tail end of the Reverend Doctor Enton Blake's wagon disappeared from view.

The bottle was more than two thirds empty by nightfall, but Walleye was past keeping track of the time. Past remembering how he got Mule to take him and the wagon to the meeting oak. Past summoning to mind how he ended up across the creek, cloaked in scrub with dirt up his nose, a wobbling head, and the moon shining in his eyes. There's such a thing as too fast. He scratched at his chest. Dug nails above his heart. Wanted to calm it. Shook his head back and forth and couldn't get clear.

Net wasn't nowhere and Walleye wanted him here.

He didn't feel long for the world.

His head moved fast.

His heart moved fast.

Why had he wanted to go fast?

He groaned.

It was on the third groan that Hennet found Walleye, half in the creek, more dead than not.

"What the goddamn red ass of the Devil you think you're doing?"

Walleye moaned, "Mule's dead."

"What now?"

Walleye convulsed. Cried. Vomited.

Hennet looked around. Sure enough, the mule had fallen over in a bush, dead. Its nose was caked in powder. As was his brother's face.

"Net—"

Hennet took his brother's hand and sat in the weeds.

"Yeah, you bastard?"

"Mule and me went fast."

"Ain't nowhere we couldn't have gone slow."

Hennet chipped white powder from Walleye's cheek.

"Don't feel right, Net."

"You ain't never been right."

"Don't go fast."

"I ain't goin' nowhere."

"I don't wanna go neither."

As Hennet watched his brother's chest still, Walleye thought, "Not going no place without Net. Without Mule."

Hennet brought his brother's body back across the creek. Then he dug a grave.

Walleye didn't want to leave this world without his brother. So he didn't. He went haint.

Walleye appreciated that it was a decent hole with true walls. Three feet dug straight down. There'd been a shovel in the wagon, but Walleye knew Hennet woulda used his hands if he had to.

"None need for the sad, Net."

Hennet didn't hear this, but the hairs on his neck stood on end.

"I'm here."

Hennet felt uneasy.

He looked at the hole in the ground, then at Walleye's body. A fat rabbit came out of the trees and sat next to Walleye's hand. Its chubby eyeballs reminded Hennet of Mama Daniels. The rabbit sniffed at Walleye's fingers.

"Rabbit, I like you," said Walleye.

The rabbit stared up at Walleye's ghost, chose to ignore it, and nibbled at the hand.

"Git." Hennet threw a rock at the critter.

"S'alright, Net," Walleye said as he walked back and forth by his grave.

The rabbit pulled Reverend Doctor Enton Blake's business card from between Walleye's fingers.

"Whatdya got?" Hennet stepped closer to the fat-eyed creature and it ran. It left a half-eaten card. Only the words *Blake* and *delights* were legible through the mud, powder, and bite marks. He pocketed it.

Hennet looked at the three-foot hole.

"Nice, nice hole," said Walleye.

It wasn't right. Probably the only thing worse than letting his brother die would be hearing the hollering hell from Mama Daniels about not seeing Walleye before the dirt hit his face.

Hennet wrapped up Walleye, tied him down as cargo, hitched his own horse to the wagon, and hoped the smell didn't come on too soon.

"Move on, horse," Hennet said. "It's a long ride home."

Hennet clicked his tongue and the horse got moving.

There was an invisible thread that bound the brothers.

Walleye followed.

So did Mule.

Chapter Twelve

CLEVELAND, OHIO, 1862

GRAHAM JOHNSON TRAILED Hester for six days.

On the first day, Graham decided he did not have the fortitude to trap Hester, let alone the wherewithal to keep her locked up until she adored him, though the thought of her chained to a tree made him mad with want. Her collar askew. Feeding her orange slices. Her tongue against his fingers. But this was beside the point. He was a writer. Thin. No talent for violence. He looked posh in a waistcoat, but he spent too much time working in dim rooms. He had weak eyes, small arms, small hands. She would eventually overpower him.

On the second day, Graham was felled by fancies. He leaned against the alley across from the inn for four hours. He wanted to make Hester toast. To smear it with raspberries. To give it to her as she awoke in a large birdcage. He wanted to carry her in a sack on his back and hide in a wheat field where he would lay down next to her sheathed, squirming form, feeling her head rub against his shoulder, her hands push against his chest, her own chest swelling through the fabric.

On the third day, Graham followed Hester everywhere. Watched her steal. Watched her talk to people of spirits. Watched her lips part and close as she ate. Watched her walk in and out of two orphanages and four churches. Watched her face turn stony as she threw salt several times an hour, everywhere she went. He thought himself sly spying from behind trees and carriages.

Graham decided that Hester Garlan was searching for someone. She would not have visited the orphanages if it wasn't a child. Graham did not like children. They had sticky hands. It lowered his assessment of Hester to realize she had a child and was concerned enough about it to look for it. Nonetheless, Graham wanted to help. Wanted those lips to thank him.

On the fourth day, Graham found Hester's shuttered wagon not far from the Fancy Badger. MEDIUM FOR HIRE was writ on the side. An assortment of future-telling elements were painted and faded on the other side. Her horse was recently dead. Someone had cut choice steak chunks from its side and rear.

Graham did not belong inside of the wagon. No one did. It was, after all, cursed. He did not know this. Hester didn't even know this. She assumed all curses were attached to her person. She could've shed ten percent of her bad luck and trouble if she'd sold the wagon and her favorite knee-high boots.

In Hester's wagon, Graham found candle-holding antlers bolted to the walls. Knives clinked in corners, international spiritualist magazines heaped precariously close to tapers, and an enormous amount of tea jars lined one wall. A stack of books on violent and disturbing themes gave Graham a stutter as he read their titles aloud.

All of this confirmed to Graham Johnson that Hester was a dangerous personality. Whereas Graham did not want to be bitten in the ass by vipers on the frontlines of the Southern rebellion, Hester could bite his ass any way she wanted to.

Graham took three things from the wagon: an extraordinarily long sash that smelled of cinnamon, a book tied together with a leather strip titled *An*

Uncommon History of the Dead, and the name of Miss Garlan's only child, Nathan. The boy's whereabouts were unknown but continuously searched for (as demonstrated by a voluminous collection of notes bound messily together by a brown braid of human hair).

On the fifth day, Graham Johnson finished reading *An Uncommon History of the Dead.* The book was penned in a cramped, tall-lettered style and at least one hundred years old. The author was Coal Garlan. Graham assumed her to be Hester's great-grandmother from the torrid, dark-haired author illustration on the title page.

After Graham had turned the last page and closed the flaking cover, he sat with the book on his lap and his eyes shut. He quieted himself. He thought. After a lengthy time, wherein the sun abandoned the sky and the moon strolled out, Graham decided to kill himself in front of Hester Garlan. He was not guaranteed to haunt her, but from what the *Uncommon History* said, he had a generous chance, so long as his last moments were of fervid yearning arrowed at existing by her side.

On the sixth day, Graham Johnson knocked on Hester's door.

Hester had decided to kill Graham Johnson when next she saw him.

She didn't need a sentinel. She didn't appreciate the mannish boot prints outside her door. She didn't want him installed five tables away from her at every meal or hovering around building edges and street corners thinking himself stealthy. She didn't take any pleasure from his worship, and the bastard had been meddling in her wagon. She didn't know what he took, but something was missing. She doubted he had killed her horse, but she'd still like to punch someone for the fuss.

After several glasses of hot courage and two cigarillos, Graham Johnson knocked on Hester's door.

"Who is it?"

"Mr. Graham Johnson."

"Mr. Graham Johnson stop following me."

Hester's mouth was against the door. Graham put his cheek where he thought her breath to be.

"Miss Garlan, I adore you. I could love you."

"Mr. Johnson, I will kill you when I open the door."

Hester perched on her bed. She ate sunflower seeds and spit the shells at a horsefly buzzing around her bread loaf. The room wasn't fancy. Lumpy bed. Window. Table. Chair. Hester's clothes were piled on the floor. Her knives lined the wall according to height. Her favorite had a knucklebuster grip.

"Miss Garlan, I think that you would love me if you learned the use of me." Graham Johnson stroked the door.

"Mr. Johnson, do you doubt that I could cut your head off?" Hester looked at the amputation kit that she'd taken as payment for a fraudulent palm reading.

Graham Johnson's cheeks flushed. He would not fail at this. He would not give up. He would not be eaten by a pack of wild dogs when he could be with her.

"Miss Garlan I have a ring for you."

"Slide it under the door," she said as she coughed out a sunflower seed.

Graham took a thin gold ring from his pocket, squatted near the gap of the door, and shoved it through. He picked a splinter out of his finger as he stood.

The ring bounced off of the bed pole. Hester picked it up.

"You nasty man, Mr. Johnson. This is warm."

"Its heat came from being neighbor to my heart." Graham lifted his hat from his head, dusted it off, and placed it on Hester's doorknob. He took the sash from inside his waistcoat. "There is an inscription, Miss Garlan."

Graham Johnson doubled the sash then looped it around the light above Hester's door. He'd done three chin lifts from the fixture the day before. It would hold.

Hester read the inscription, "'Even in death,' what in the—" Hester began, but the feel of a ship sinking in her stomach shut her up.

The horsefly beat itself against Hester's window. Painted on the brick wall past the glass was the advertisement THE REV. DR. ENTON BLAKE'S PARAMOUR PILL! ESOTERIC! SCIENTIFIC! BLISS!

How could he know? There was no way that Graham Johnson could know how to haunt her.

Graham tugged on the doubled sash. The light fixture did not creak.

"Mr. Johnson?" Hester asked through her door. No answer.

Graham Johnson slipped the sash around his neck.

"Mr. Johnson, you better not be doing what I think you're doing."

Graham raised his legs to his chest.

Hester swung open the door.

The sash tightened around Graham's throat. He kept his eyes open, coughed, and swayed. Perhaps if he swayed it would take less time to suffocate. He would die, but he did not want to be dead. The book had hinted about haints, but it was circuitous on the creation of such beings.

"NO. No, you don't. NO."

Hester dove at Graham Johnson. She tried to lift his body. Graham stood long enough to kick her away. Hester's feet tangled in a clothing pile and she fell against the bed.

Graham leapt upward. It was quite high. He had been practicing.

Hester yelled, "No. No. Damn it!"

A door opened at the far end of the hall. Floor boards ached in the wake of Penelope Drench.

Graham came down with a sickening crack.

Hester tried to lift Graham's body again.

"Hes, what's that man doin'?" She scratched a nail against pock-marked skin.

"Dying," Hester said.

"Why's he goin' and doin' it in front of you?"

"Sonofabitch says he wants to love me."

"He's stranglin' the wrong part."

Graham's last moment slowed enough for him to not appreciate the intrusion. He had planned this to be a secluded ceremony. A special commitment. A red-letter footnote in the history of affection. His imagining did not include a fleshy prostitute or piss running down his leg. It pooled in his left shoe.

Graham Johnson thought, *I will not go. It wasn't supposed to be drab. I will be with Hester.* Then he breathed his last.

"Pen, is he dead?"

"How can you tell?"

Hester struggled to hold Graham's body up against hers as she searched her skirts for a knife to cut the sash. She'd been looking for that damn sash.

"Eyes blank? Mouth hanging open? Bones popping odd from the neck?"

"All that," Penelope said.

"Shit." Hester let go of the body. She retreated back in her room. Her room was circled with salt. The dead couldn't enter. Or shouldn't be able to enter. She heard them in the hall. The ghost of a card cheat pushed Graham's body and went into Penelope's room.

Hester tried to distinguish Graham's voice through the clutter she heard.

Graham Johnson stood as an apparition in the hall.

"Never no one went killin' themselves over me."

"Shut up, Pen."

"What're you doing, Pen?" Penelope said and went back to her room.

Hester left her door open and retreated to a whiskey bottle she had under her pillow. She eyed the gold ring on the table. She didn't hear Mr. Johnson. She took another sip.

A floorboard creaked in the hall.

Hester looked.

So did Graham.

Penelope Drench had hands in Mr. Johnson's pockets.

"What're you doing, Pen?" Hester walked to her door.

"You left it alone."

"It's my dead body, Pen. My dead money. My dead everything. Trot your trench back down the hall."

"Hall's public rights."

Graham's cadaver pitched between the two women.

"I could cut you from lips to slit and take the three worthwhile necklaces you own out from the wall hole behind your dresser." Hester crossed her arms and nodded at the amputation kit. A saw poked out of it.

Penelope Drench uncrossed her arms. Her brother had lost his legs and then his life at Bull Run. She didn't want Hester cutting on her.

"You ain't decent people."

"Neither are you." Hester pointed down the hall.

Penelope walked back to her room in a trail of dander.

Graham Johnson stood behind Hester Garlan.

The horsefly lapped at the yellow shore Graham had left behind.

Hester put lithe hands into each of Mr. Johnson's pockets. Graham had left Hester treasures. A brooch. Two blackberry biscuits. Saltwater taffy—Pen had stolen that. A solid stack of bills thieved from the newspaper. A silver pocket watch that dangled by a chain and flipped open to an illustration of Graham sitting at his newspaper desk. Hester put Graham's never-used monocle on. Cufflinks. His hat on her head. No coins. A white blossom from his lapel. She even took his waistcoat.

Graham Johnson chewed on his pinky nail as he watched Hester pillage his body. There was a certain excitement building in his form.

Graham sighed in pleasure.

Hester did not feel well. Did not feel right. Thought she heard something.

"Hester," Graham whispered.

Hester recoiled like an army against boiling oil.

"Hester, I am with you."

Hester peered about. There was a blur in the hall, but only out of the corner of her eye. She had never seen a dead blur before. But she had never been personally haunted before.

"Mr. Johnson?"

"Yes?"

"You are terrible."

"And entirely yours."

Hester slammed the door on Graham, hoped that the salt held him out, and threw the gold ring out of her window.

It fell into the mouth of a yawning, brown-eyed outlaw.

CHAPTER THIRTEEN

NEW HAVEN, CONNECTICUT, 1862

"WAKE UP!" ISABELLE said. She pinched Sarah's arm.

"What?" Sarah shook her head. "Huh?"

"You have been staring past the mirror for ten minutes. As much as I adore helping you dress for the most important day of your life, I would like company while doing it."

"Sorry, Isabelle. I was thinking on William."

"William? *Ooooh.* Sarah is thinking about *William.* You finally call him William?"

"Only to myself. We have not yet crossed that bridge of familiarity."

Isabelle stopped lacing Sarah's corset.

"In seriousness?"

"Yes."

"You are to be married today and you don't call each other by your given names?"

"Rarely."

Sarah shimmied a hoop and a crinoline over her petticoat. She did not want to talk about it. She would rather focus on the good. He was a kind man.

He was a handsome man. He was a successful man. He could be inattentive, but she thought someday he would love her.

"How do Parisian lace and bunched fabric go together? They don't. My dress is hideous."

Sarah poked the wedding gown laid out on her bed.

"Why didn't you say so at the fittings?"

Isabelle picked up the gown and lowered it over her sister's upraised arms.

"I did. You were too busy cooing to listen. Same with mother. This dress has fifteen layers and even more ribbons," Sarah said through the fabric as it was lowered around her. "I look like I was birthed by a smarmy French cloud. I'm blinded by puffery."

"The word you meant was pretty." Isabelle straightened the skirts.

"It makes me appear even shorter."

"It does not."

"Does too."

"Don't be ridiculous. You would tower over Napoleon."

"Wrong. He was roughly eight inches taller than my four foot ten."

"Why do you know that?"

"What does it matter? I'm covered in lace and ribbons and I look like a giantess."

"You do not look fat. You look like a lady."

"Well, let's get on with it."

"As if I would let you leave this room without talking about those." Isabelle pointed to Sarah's legs.

"What are you pointing at?" Sarah asked.

"Under the dress."

"Whatever could you be talking about?"

"The garters! Sarah, you are wicked. You're going to stop that man's heart. Did you make them?"

Sarah nodded and gave a self-satisfied blush.

"Sarah, you look marvelous."

Isabelle smoothed her sister's dress a final time.

Mrs. Pardee stormed into the room.

"Lord, drop me from this unreasonable earth! Sarah your hair is only half curled!"

Mrs. Pardee took the curling rod from Isabelle and the task was done in moments. The women looked at their reflections in the mirror. Two out of three were satisfied.

At the church, William had arrived early to talk with the priest. To talk with family. To pass out business cards. He did this all throughout the reception.

"Mrs. Winchester," Mr. Winchester said as he scooped Sarah up and crossed the bedchamber door, "please wait for me here. I will be but a minute." He put Sarah on the bed and left the room.

Sarah started to unhook and untie and generally rearrange all of her clothing. She was glad William left. He didn't see her reaching and rolling and hopping out of her hoop. There were several rips. She did not care. She would never wear or look at the gown again.

When William reentered the room, Sarah sat on her knees in her chemise, corset, and two black garters (threaded with red ribbon) that held her white stockings above the knee.

William dropped the box he carried.

Sarah was more than pleased with his reaction.

"What are you doing?" William asked.

That question was not what Sarah had expected. She had expected a mad scene mimicked from *Fanny Hill*.

"What do you mean?"

"I said what the dickens are you doing?"

"Preparing for our wedding night," Sarah said. She didn't understand his distress. She had, with great difficulty, procured several books of intimate knowledge and from these gleaned that men often paid for women to wear fanciful bedclothes.

"How would you know how to do this? To undress yourself?"

"Excuse me?"

"You heard what I asked, Mrs. Winchester. How did you know to sit there bare to the world?" William was heated. This was not what was supposed to happen. A husband was to unwrap a shy bride. She would be shocked by his manhood. He would hurt her with his entrance. He had a soft apology planned for these eventualities and even a gentle kiss as he tucked her in. What sat on the bed was no shy bride.

William could not tell where the heat was coming from. He did not know if he was angry or excited.

"There is no need to be mean, William. I saw some charming fabric and I made myself something charming from it. Would you like me to take them off?"

"I think you've taken plenty off."

Sarah covered herself with a blanket. The way he looked at her made her feel indecent.

"Why are you angry?"

"This was not according to plan."

"What plan?"

"You are not supposed to know these things."

"What things?"

"I do not want to look at you."

"Then don't."

William collected the ribbon-wrapped box he had dropped earlier.

"Here is your wedding present, Mrs. Winchester."

He passed it to her and Sarah grabbed his hand. "William, please do not leave."

Her hand was soft and William shook it away.

Sarah pushed the present from her lap and grabbed William again.

A fire in the hearth cast their shadows on the wall.

Sarah leaned back and pulled William over her. "Please, William."

She thought that if she could only get him to begin this action that they would fold together. That the creases between them would straighten and that they would finally understand each other.

William looked at Sarah. All of her. The lace edge to her chemise, the line of her corset, her collarbone.

Sarah did not know what to say. She said nothing. She put her hand on his cheek.

William ripped the front of Sarah's corset open. The eyelets scattered. He held down her hands and thought on all the things she should not know.

William allowed Sarah's lips on his face, his neck, and only after he was inside her and heard her gasp with what he thought was pain, did he take off his jacket, waistcoat, and shirt.

When William was through, Sarah thought the night not a total loss. She had been told by her mother the first night of any married couple was full of fluster and discomfort. It would get better.

William pulled his trousers up and put his shirt on. He kissed Sarah on the forehead and departed to wash himself.

Sarah watched the fire and wondered if she was happy. She opened her wedding present.

It was Victor Hugo's latest novel, *Les Misérables.*

A note stated, "For my fine, French-reading wife."

Sarah sighed, leaned closer to the bedside candle, and let her mind sink into the novel.

CHAPTER FOURTEEN

CLEVELAND, OHIO, 1862

WHEN GRAHAM JOHNSON died, he was shocked by the sordid and romantic sight of himself hanging from Hester's doorframe. He looked the picture of a Poe poem with his hair draped over extruded eyes. He deserved a deep-colored painting and a ballad with a despairing cello. Graham would have fixated more, but he was overcome by the tide of notifications sent through his person his first phantasmic stride.

A titillating touch of semi-omniscience occurred when he separated from his fleshy tenement. Graham Johnson was briefly connected to all dead persons. It was a disagreeable head pounding. He noted to himself that if he didn't want to go mad from being jolted every second step when others died, he must learn to meditate.

Jimmy Doogood chose the madness. Mad was better than stupid. Nathan could snuff him out, cleave his neck, and turn his ma twit, but could Jimmy figure how to possess the Beetlehead? No. Couldn't even pass wind at the kid. But Jimmy could repeat a phrase over and over that would eventually get back to the Beetlehead's ma.

Oh, Jimmy Doogood knew about Hester Garlan, alright. The dead gossiped worse than the living. *Keep away from Hester Garlan. Hester Garlan is a dead murderer. We need Nathan. Keep Hester from Nathan.* On and on the dead talked about the Garlans. Something about the old lady sending a boneyard fulla ghosts to the abyss. Jimmy Doogood didn't give a nickel or a shit about getting Purgatory-murdered by the bitch so long as she killed Nathan first.

So he repeated his phrase over and over hoping that somewhere out there Hester Garlan would hear him.

In less than a blink, Graham heard thousands of secrets, the stories of thousands of deaths, the longings of thousands of spirits. Each one felt like a hot pinprick to his liver, but only one projection brought Graham to full attention. Graham Johnson distinctly heard:

"Nathan Garlan lives in Boston and I want him dead."

This was a lead Graham could use.

He visualized himself telling Hester, "My hazardous love, I know the location of your son."

Hester would put down her knives, bury her nose in his neck and say, "My rogue researcher!" then rip his shirt open. She'd continue, "My august informer," and rip her own dress open. She'd push him into a wingback chair saying, "My delectable detective," and an evening of snuffling one another's notches and nobs would unfold. Perhaps a recitation of Baudelaire would be in order.

How this was possible, Graham didn't know. He felt scant and vapid since his termination. There was a tinge of blue to his skin. His body was like a walk on a frozen creek, solid, but shifting not far from the surface. But if anyone knew how to delight in the pale form of a phantom, it'd be Hester Garlan.

"Hester," Graham said.

"Hester, I am here…"

Graham's introductory evening to deadhood and his love was not all he expected it to be.

Hester did not rip open Graham Johnson's suit. She did not rip off her own dress. She didn't want to hear any Baudelaire and she certainly wasn't going to spill Graham's grains in a wingback chair.

Every time Graham attempted to gain admittance to Hester's quarters, she pitched salt at the door. The salt was better than the iron rod she swung. Both temporarily dissipated him, but the iron made him disappear for longer. The salt tingled. The iron tortured.

"My come-hither Caligula," Graham began.

Hester threw salt at the voice.

Graham Johnson's left arm faded out, then itched back into existence.

"My vile gamine," Graham attempted.

Hester paced in front of her window. She opened it. She chewed off a nail. She shut the window and sat on her bed in a huff. She had earlier walked outside, hoping Mr. Johnson was tied to the building, but no. There was no way to undo this. Graham Johnson was bound to her. She couldn't see him. She couldn't send him on. She was stuck with the sonofabitch.

With much effort, Graham had made it through the protective salt circle into the room. An esoteric powder circumscribed the bed. Graham could not cross the line without combusting and taking half an hour to reconvene. There was some physicality to the wraith world, and Hester had learned to burn it.

"What do you want, Mr. Johnson?"

"In life, I was a newspaperman."

"Get on with it."

"As a newspaperman I was accustomed to thoroughly examining the world around me."

"Five seconds till I rod-knock you."

"And gathering information."

"Three seconds." Hester stood.

Hester stared where she thought Graham might be. She could not see it, but Graham alternately stared at her breasts and bellybutton. It was hard not to. She wore a thin shift.

"I know the location of your son," Graham Johnson said in a rush. He did not want the rod again.

"You what?" Hester asked. She got up from the bed and did not notice she had crossed over her protected circle.

"I know where Nathan is."

"No, you do not."

"Yes, I do."

"No, you do not. I searched ten years for the mutt. How would you even know his name?"

"I am a profoundly effective inquirer." Graham walked to Hester. He sniffed her collarbone.

"Back your blue guts up, Mr. Johnson. I can't see you, but I can feel you near me."

Graham moved several of Hester's curls and breathed in her ear. It was slightly larger than her other ear and it had a v-nick chip to the side. Graham wanted to preserve the ear in a Grecian urn and write an ode to it.

Hester hit him with the iron rod. It went through his stomach. Graham lurched forward, unbalanced, and fell through Hester. It was a shudder and grimace for both of them.

"Where is he, Mr. Johnson? Tell me or I'll bind you to an iron mine." Graham did not know it was an empty threat.

"Pussycat, I've pursued your edification all night."

"Tell me."

"What tit for tat will be exchanged?"

Hester raised the iron rod and her scarred eyebrow to where she thought he was.

"Fine, fine, you arousing and heinous beast."

"Where?"

"Boston."

"Pff."

"I tell you, he is in Boston."

"Mr. Johnson, I've searched Boston. All of it. Twice. Three times. Six times. Why do you think we are in Ohio? Because I left the boy in Boston and now the boy is not there. The boy is not in New York. The boy is not in Chicago. The boy is not in ten other states and six score of cities and the boy is most certainly not in goddamn Boston."

Hester put on what, at one point, might have been a stylish walking dress. It now consisted of moth holes, lace, and paisley.

"Hester, I can guarantee the information." Graham's torso rematerialized.

"How's that?"

"I heard it from a dead boy."

"Heard what?"

"'Nathan Garlan lives in Boston and I want him dead.'"

Hester rolled her stockings up and buttoned her knee-high boots.

Graham enjoyed this.

"What other eavesdropping have you done, Mr. Johnson?" Hester constantly collected information to sell. Ghosts circled around like orating tornadoes. It used to be the babbling bastards were useful. Hester sold her learnings to the living. But not one advantageous loose lip in the lot of them for a decade. Grudge holders. All Hester got in return for her headaches was slander.

"A thousand things."

"Like what?"

"I will tell you when you tell me why you want to find your son."

"Mr. Johnson, I still have an iron rod."

"I will train to luxuriate in the throbbing you cause me." Graham swayed his hips back and forth.

"Goddamn it."

"Which it?"

"You."

"Why would you curse me?" Graham crossed his fingers and hoped nothing held.

"Because I usually kill leeches and you're already dead."

"What makes the boy important?"

"Suck a stone, ragman," Hester said. She tucked the iron rod and her knives into the amputation kit and slung it over her shoulder.

"Where are you going?"

"Boston."

"I am coming with you."

"Eventually, I'll get rid of you."

"I will exalt you, even then."

Hester walked out of her room with a "Pff."

Graham followed.

In Boston, Jimmy Doogood kept repeating, "Nathan Garlan lives in Boston and I want him dead."

CHAPTER FIFTEEN

BOSTON, MASSACHUSETTS, 1862

"WHAT DO YOU have for me today, Mr. Nathan Garlan?" Robert Wester asked.

"Gogol's *Dead Souls* and Swift's *Modest Proposal*, the 1729." Nathan pulled each out of his satchel and laid them on the glass counter. Through the glass, a sizable weasel paw (used as a paperweight) caught his attention.

"1729 Swift's don't exist outside of private collections," Wester started, but he stopped after he picked up the pamphlet. His mouth hung open. He gently put it back on the counter worried that his hands were greasy from lunch. "How—where—boy, you brought me a 133-year-old political pamphlet."

Wester Brothers' Rare and Fine gave a reverential groan to the young book scout.

Nathan nodded his head, "Are you selling that paw? That's a weasel paw, yeah? I would like that paw."

A dead weasel sat on the floor by Nathan's feet. It was bound to its preserved appendage. It looked forlorn but friendly.

"Nathan, look at me."

Nathan looked across the counter at Robert Wester.

Wester was a tall man with a beard, spectacles, a distinguished ring of grey hair, and a holey sweater. He faintly smelled of tobacco though he had quit its usage.

"Yes, sir?"

"Where did you acquire this pamphlet?"

Nathan decided on a partial truth.

"It was in a locked box in the study of a dead rich man who had no children."

Nathan had been given the pamphlet as payment for finding homes for each of the dead man's seven cats.

"You stole this?"

"I do not steal, Mr. Wester. He had no family. He had no debts to pay except to me."

"Why would a rich dead man owe you?"

"I can't tell you."

Nathan nodded at Ronda, the blonde lady who had given him penny dreadfuls when he was young. She nodded back and continued to dust behind the counter.

Wester looked over his shoulder and saw nothing except the expensive display wall. He eyed Nathan suspiciously.

"Mr. Wester, on my honor, it was not stolen."

"If authorities come to this shop I will tell them who sold me this pamphlet." Wester tapped the counter by the Swift.

Nathan nodded.

"Understood. How much for the paw? Will the Swift and the Gogol cover the paw? What is it?"

Wester chuckled. "It is a weasel paw and you have more than enough to cover it. I don't know what to price the Swift at, Nathan. I will owe you on this one."

"See. Folks are indebted to me all the time."

Wester smiled. The boy was a good sort.

"How are things at Saint Anthony's?"

Wester pushed a pile of buttery string beans to Nathan. The child had a knack for selling Wester books during his dinner break.

The boy primly ate one string bean and said, "Oh. Things are. Well, not good. I don't like it there."

"Newspapers said Franwell killed Jimmy after he stabbed her in the face."

"Night Watch wrote that down, too."

"What's become of Franwell?"

"Night Watch took her. Me and the boys made her a velvet eye patch, but we didn't know where to send it. I think Saint Ant's misses her. I am saving money to leave. Trying to get the boys to do the same. They still have factory jobs. That place isn't safe."

Wester Brothers' Rare and Fine concurred with a creak of its boards. It had heard of Saint Anthony's Academy for Wayward Sons. It had not heard good things.

"You know where you're going?" Wester asked.

"California!"

Nathan chewed another string bean.

Wester took the paw out and slid it across the counter to Nathan. "This paw was from my friend Frank. He was a weasel that loved me greatly and I loved him, too. May it bring you blessings in your travels."

Frank the dead weasel stood on his hind paws and blinked kind eyes at Wester then Nathan. Then a smell caught him. He nudged Nathan with his nose. The air was not right. There were faraway sounds he didn't understand.

Nathan noticed Frank's unrest. It made him nervous.

"I have to go, Mr. Wester."

Nathan ate three string beans in quick succession and put the weasel paw in his grey satchel.

"I will research the Swift and have a fair price for you the next time you drop by."

"Thank you for the beans and paw and everything."

Robert nodded at the boy, but his attention was back on *A Modest Proposal*. It was pristine. No foxing. No stains.

The bell over the door rang as Nathan left. Frank followed him out into a roar of dead muttering. Wester Brothers' Rare and Fine was not at ease over this. The air should not be cluttered.

Robert Wester absentmindedly petted a nearby shelf as he pulled out a pricing index.

Nathan's walk became a run. The dead crowded the streets. The air was stale. A barber with no nose, a set of triplets with wide, green eyes, a woman with a caved-in chest, a man with enormous sideburns, a pair of waterlogged lovers in a horse trough. They all watched Nathan. Nathan had never seen so many ghosts at once. In windows, alleys, under carriages, on horses, crawling out from under porches—they were everywhere.

The dead murmured and congregated, but so many were murmuring that Nathan couldn't make out what any one of them said.

When Nathan arrived at Saint Anthony's, Reggie met him on the back stoop.

"What's happening? Why is everyone whispering and looking at me?" Nathan asked.

"Dunno. Something about someone coming to town," Reggie said.

"Why would a whole city of ghosts care that someone came to town?"

"Keep interrupting my ears and I won't find out."

It was dark for early evening. The sun was low over the crooked fence and a black cat ran across it. Fog blanketed the ankles of three boys who folded laundry off the drying line.

Jimmy Doogood paced the yard yelling, "Nathan Garlan lives in Boston and I want him dead."

Nathan Garlan didn't yet know how to bind a spirit to an object, but if he did, he would've tied Jimmy Doogood to a brick and thrown him into the harbor.

Nathan was used to chatter. To gloom. The dead talked as they walked the world. To each other. To him. They weren't a sunflower bunch. They doled out financial warnings, recipes, advice, false prophecy. Anything that came to mind to pass the time. A few wanted to chum up or mother him, more wanted assistance to the Something After (which Nathan couldn't give), and greater still the number that asked for an outline of families, businesses, and lost lovers since they'd been gone. But Jimmy, he didn't harmlessly yammer. He didn't want to oil Nathan's palm for aid. Jimmy wanted Nathan glass-eyed and dirt-faced.

It wore down the nerves.

The dead did not approve of Jimmy Doogood's grudge against Nathan. Nathan was an obliging, handsome lad responsive to their queries who held regular hours, kept an orderly request queue, and made house calls. Decent rates, too.

Frank circled Reggie and sniffed him. Reggie kicked at the critter. It skittered back.

"Why is a weasel following you?"

"Wester gave me its paw."

"You keeping it?"

"It's Frank and I like him. Now translate."

Neither could hear anything over Jimmy Doogood yelling by the laundry line.

The boys doing the laundry got the cold creeps, flicked and folded the last of the sheets, and headed inside.

The fog parted as they passed.

They nodded at Nathan on the way in.

"Does Jimmy think someone's gonna help kill me?" Nathan asked.

Reggie looked away from his friend.

"What aren't you telling me, Reg?"

"He's trying to reach your ma."

"My ma?"

"Hester Garlan."

"Why?"

"She wants you dead."

"My mother is alive?"

"And she wants you dead. Nathan, how do you not know this? Every dead thing in Boston knows your mother is a ghost murderer and she wants you dead."

Nathan's face dropped. "Why?"

"Dunno. Something to do with you seeing the dead and her not seeing the dead. Fog got thicker."

"Taller, too."

Neither of them said anything for a minute.

"Where'd Jimmy go?"

Nathan didn't see Jimmy anywhere.

"Hear that?" Reggie asked.

"What?"

"Ex-zactly. Nothing doin'."

Not a blue wisp of a babbling yard ghost anywhere. Horse hooves clopped by, a church bell tolled, and that was it.

"How could it go from a dead roar to nothing?" Nathan asked.

"Dunno. I'mna check out front."

Reggie disappeared through Saint Ant's back wall.

Saint Ant's gave a floorboard chortle. It had heard what the dead murmured. It knew who had come to town.

Nathan looked around for reassurance and only saw the fog.

CHAPTER SIXTEEN

BOSTON, MASSACHUSETTS, 1862

HESTER TOOK IT as a good omen that it was only twenty-one days of travel from Cleveland to Boston and not one dead horse on the way.

"We continue north, if we wish to locate whoever shrieks for your child's extinction," Graham said.

Hester secured the wagon and walked to an establishment whose sign depicted a two-headed, intoxicated weasel bathing in a beer stein.

"I want a hard drink and salty food."

"I nudge you to find an establishment better fitted to—"

"To what?" Hester cut him off. She didn't take guff from living men, let alone a rotted one.

Graham bowed and swept his arms out. He hoped she could at least feel his gallantry.

"Ahead then, you perverse daughter of Gomorrah."

Hester went in the beer house. The room had no windows. The fog followed her in. A fire blustered up the chimney. A gathering of men leaning on the bar turned around and stared. The only other woman present was bare-shouldered and on the lap of a shaggy-mustached man.

Hester reveled in proving her mettle.

She walked to the counter, shoved a bald man in a soiled jacket out of his spot, and put her elbows on the bar. He was the largest man in the room, ten inches taller and twice as thick as she.

"Whiskey," Hester said to the barkeep.

The barkeep didn't move. His sleeves were rolled. He had a rag on his shoulder and another tucked into his belt.

Hester put a coin on the bar.

Graham stood by the door.

"We should remove ourselves," he said.

What Graham meant was *Do something wicked, Madame Gladiator, that I might record it*, for he had his diary and a pencil nub in hand.

Every greasy face in the Two-Headed Weasel wore a frown. Two gin-oiled ghosts babbled in a corner about the years it'd been since they seen a brawl worth a neck bend and they ain't never seen one with a bitch in it.

"Whiskey," Hester repeated. She had one eye on the barkeep and one eye on the cracked mirror behind him. She took a shot glass from her neighbor and placed it square in front of her, close to the counter's edge.

The bald man flung Hester around to face him.

"Shed that dress and you'd be closer to belonging here."

He had hands firm on Hester's shoulders.

"Let go," Hester warned.

"Nail hard, are ya? So am I." The man bumped his crotch at her.

Hester grabbed his wrists, tightened her hold, and dropped to a sitting position on the floor. The momentum of her down-pull crashed him like a tree. His face hit the bar sideways. The shot glass pierced his cheek and broke the top row of what teeth he had. Hester kicked him backward. His blood and groans covered the floor.

The whore let out an appreciative whoop.

Graham's jaw dropped. He scribbled notes about dental fragments in firelight, red clashing with wool, an eroticized mention of Hester's imposing eyes, and there was a hasty sketch of her supposedly heaving bosom.

Hester wiped the blood off the counter with the bottom of her skirt and leaned on it.

"Whiskey."

The barkeep filled a tall glass.

"Eggs, too."

The barkeep put pickled eggs in a wooden bowl and passed it to her.

The two ghosts kicked the bald man for allowing a woman to down him. Each kick made his stomach seize. Its contents spilled out of his cheek wound.

The room knew when to mind its own affairs.

Hester bent her ear to what those affairs were.

Graham moved closer to Hester. He left a cold, shuddering wake in the crowded room. He tucked his diary away and put his fists on his hips.

Hester ate half a pickled egg.

"You never once bothered to repulsify my refined features," Graham said. He would've cherished a subtle facial scar. Perhaps on the left brow or temple.

The noise went from whisper to gale. The whore gave a fake giggle. The barkeep opened a fresh bottle. The fog crept through cracks in the corners.

Hester ate the other half of the egg.

Graham watched her suck the brine and blood from her nails. "My ardor, I'd approve thoroughly of applying that suction to my—"

Hester had several plain iron rings on. She put her fist through Graham's throat without looking. The newspaperman's red-ringed neck vanished.

Hester hadn't wanted a hard drink and salty food. She wanted information.

It came from a man two down on the bar to her left.

"Didn't close it down," said a short man with a creased forehead.

"My chum at the Night Watch says he told them runts they can keep Saint Ant's for now. Says he trusted this little'un to make sure the place don't burn down. Nate or something. Trusts him? After Jimmy gets his head nigh chopped off and Doogood stabbed in the eyeball? Said the kid had kind eyes! Who the hell has kind eyes these days, eh fellas?"

His audience grunted.

Hester was familiar with Franwell Doogood. She'd searched Saint Anthony's Academy of Wayward Sons six times, *six*, from the coal chute to the shitter, ten years past. Hester'd cuffed and shoved Franwell, even stole one of her plaid frocks, but she never found the boy.

If Hester had offered something more than bad language and bruises, Franwell would've traded for the child. Instead, Franwell tall-taled such an ignorance that Münchhausen grimaced green from the grave.

On each of Hester's searches, Nathan had been nailed into the hollow, third step of the staircase. Reggie was with him, and kept the boy quiet, even when Hester stepped over her son and the sawdust and mold rained upon the infant.

Franwell had played the part of sparkle-hatted rattle brain so thoroughly that Hester eventually believed her son was not at Saint Anthony's. She didn't burn down the orphanage or kill Miss Doogood.

That was a mistake.

Hester ate a second pickled egg, threw back her glass of whiskey, and put another coin on the bar. She stepped over the bald man as she walked out.

Graham stepped through him.

The man on the floor vomited again. The liquid that leaked from his cheek hole made his face burn. The brass and garlic belch smell did not bother the bar crowd. They breathed easier once Hester left.

"None of that was necessary," Graham said as he followed Hester.

Hester didn't answer.

"I could've tracked your boy child."

"How long would that've taken?"

"An afternoon."

"I was in there ten minutes."

"Hester, why do you want to kill him?"

"Mr. Johnson."

"Yes, Lady Azrael?"

"Do you know what I miss most about you being alive?"

"My robust and hardened physique?"

"The knowledge of where to point my withering glances."

"Hmph. I was sure it was my propensity to please women on vanilla-scented, velvet coverlets."

"You've no experience with velvet coverlets outside of crusting them in your sleep," Hester said over her shoulder. She dodged a horsecar.

"You think upon my sleeping manhood, do you?"

Hester threw a pinch of salt behind her.

Graham avoided it. He did note that she didn't answer his question. He wondered what killing the boy would accomplish for her.

Hester turned left, down Stone's Throw Road, toward Saint Anthony's Academy of Wayward Sons.

CHAPTER SEVENTEEN

BOSTON, MASSACHUSETTS, 1862

THE FOG THICKENED. Hester and Graham unknowingly stood across the road from Saint Anthony's Academy of Wayward Sons.

A sprig of rosemary fell from Hester's hair as she paced.

Graham leaned against a storefront. An advertisement for THE REVEREND DOCTOR ENTON BLAKE'S ENLIGHTENING ELIXIR, KNOWN TO ASCEND BRAIN FUNCTION AND SOOTHE MIGRAINES. IN TOWN! TWO DAYS! papered the window. Graham picked at it.

"The ghouls mutter that you have arrived in town," Graham said.

"I can hear, Mr. Johnson. What I can't cipher is where the boy is. The orphanage was a shack. It was on this road. Everything is taller now."

Saint Anthony's opened its door to the confused woman.

Jimmy Doogood extended a greeting.

"Psst. PSST. Psst."

Hester reached for her iron rod. It was slung over her shoulder like a bow.

"Was that you?" Hester asked.

"I do not psst," Graham said.

"PSST."

"It is a nauseating youth," Graham said.

Jimmy's head wobbled at him.

"Where?"

"Across the road."

"Nathan Garlan lives in Boston and I want him dead," Jimmy Doogood tittered.

The spirits of Stone's Throw Road disapproved. The fog deepened and rose to Hester's waist.

Reggie saw Hester. Saw Graham. Did not like that this was who had come to town. This woman had broad shoulders and big knives. Reggie whispered to the dead who whispered to Nathan.

"Run, Nathan, run," said the fog.

"Wester's, Nathan, Wester's," said the wind.

Nathan knew when to trust the dead. The way to the bookshop was from the front of Saint Ant's.

Two piglets and a swarm of innumerable insects surrounded Hester. All dead. A wind gusted against her.

"My Medea, you are beset by enemies," Graham warned. He chewed at a hangnail, then spit it out.

Hester saw confusingly small gaps in the fog.

The piglets and vermin lurched forward. All involved hoped Hester would panic, convulse, choke, and die.

Those that lived and breathed on Stone's Throw Road shuttered windows against the ground clouds, lit candles, and poked at fires. The evening was unexpectedly dark.

The fog was not only a fog. The wind not only a wind.

Nathan crept around the side of the orphanage.

Hester scattered salt in a spin that made her skirts shift and the fog lift. The raggedy piglets disappeared. The first rush of cadaverous cockroaches, arachnids, mites, and other molesters momentarily vanished. The second multitude formed a bridge over the salt. The third bevy crossed the bridge to Hester. Bitey, spidery, dead bastards cold-crawled up Hester's stockings. Her legs numbed. The pigs faded in and out of form.

Graham spit out another hangnail. He did not feel helpful. He was underappreciated anyway.

The insects thickened. Hester felt her throat seize, the bile rise. Her hands shook and the iron rod fell. Her legs moved not of her own decision.

Jimmy Doogood pouted. As did Saint Ant's.

Hester said several old words before her lips tightened and blanched from the chill. The words did nothing. Her blood felt full of nettles.

Reggie caught Nathan on the side of the house.

"Your mother is here."

"Maybe if I met her," Nathan started.

"She'd still want you dead."

"But—"

"Nathan, get to Wester Brothers' Rare and Fine. He will help you."

"But Wester's is that way." Nathan nodded to the front road.

"We have her taken care of."

Nathan reached in his pocket. He took out the paw and handed it to Reggie.

"What's this?"

"A friend till I can come get you."

Frank the weasel curled himself around Reggie's ankle.

"Get yer ugly head outta here," Reggie said as he held back a blue tear.

Nathan nodded. He peered around the side of the orphanage and readied himself to run.

Hester stomped in the thoroughfare.

Only the two-hundred-year-old horseshoes sewn onto the soles of Hester's boots kept her from a full possession.

Hester had boxed a furious elephant, endured a water trial, survived a New York City gang war—and now she would be felled by a plague of pests because she couldn't walk to the wagon for additional cinnamon and rowan wards.

Graham put his diary in his jacket pocket (possible timely headlines noted: *An Insect Execution!* and *A Sinner Swarmed!*).

The pigs regenerated themselves. They chewed on Hester's ankles.

Graham would demand satisfaction for this assistance. He dragged a discarded wooden washtub from an alley and placed it behind his darling. It contained rank rainwater. He hauled a burlap sack of salt and a smaller satchel of crushed cinnamon from the wagon. He threw it into the rotted washtub.

"Now or never," Nathan told himself and ran into the street.

Hester saw the boy. He had the eyes of an outlaw she often dreamed of.

She leapt at him as he passed.

The dead things inside her held her back, but she was able to grab a fistful of the boy's hair.

Nathan faltered. He pulled a small blade from his back pocket and jabbed at her hand. Hester yowled and let go. Nathan ran.

Graham shoved Hester into the washtub and stirred the cinnamon and saltwater with Hester's iron rod. It felt as if someone had taken a hammer to his hands and flayed each of his fingers.

Instant relief came to Hester.

The insect horde recoiled from the warded water. They skittered underground, through the washtub walls, away from the salt and cinnamon.

Hester stood. Soiled, sore, drenched but whole.

"You don't getta hurt my friend," Reggie said. He tried to run to the thoroughfare to stop Hester, but he couldn't leave Saint Ant's front porch. Jimmy Doogood laughed. Reggie punched him in the face.

Hester saw Nathan duck into an alley and ran after.

The dead wind couldn't shove her past four doors down.

In the alley, Nathan passed a broadside for THE REVEREND DOCTOR'S TOBACCO CURE, SURE TO WARM AND EXHILARATE THE MOUTH TO POSITIVE HEALTH!

Wester will help. Wester will help. Nathan repeated this to himself as he ran. He exited the alley and came out on Bookman's Row.

Hester loped after him. "Keep runnin', sweetmeat!"

Nathan did. Twenty more yards and he'd be at the bookshop. It loomed large at the end of Bookman's Row. A lit lantern hung near the door.

Hester stopped. She balanced her footing. She breathed deep. She threw a knife at the boy.

Nathan pounded on Wester's door.

The knife bit deep into his calf and Nathan yowled.

Hester had meant to hit the boy's spine. She was bloody and tired and wanted a wagon nap. Guns were artless, but if she'd had one this errand would've been done. There'd have been satisfaction in seeing the boy's head erupt.

Nathan pounded harder on Wester's door.

"What the ATROCIOUS HELL is going on?" Robert Wester bellowed from the floor above. Ronda peered out the second-floor window.

Hester threw another blade at Nathan. This one was a tease.

"Can't hide," Hester called.

She threw another blade. It landed next to Nathan's ear. That one hadn't been a tease. She had missed. She gave her hand a disappointed look.

Nathan often dreamt of having a mother. His reveries included tea and reassuring discussions of unnatural aptitudes, not knife fights.

A clatter of footsteps came from inside.

The door opened. Nathan fell against Robert Wester who tumbled back and tipped several stacks of sale stock.

"Nathan?" Wester asked.

"Shut the door!" Nathan yelled. He scurried into one of the reading nooks.

Wester slammed the door shut. He locked it and lit a lantern.

"You are bleeding on my chair."

"Apologies, I—"

Hester slammed a fist on the door.

The door did not appreciate the glut of attention.

"Come out, boy, or I'll burn you out."

"Burn you out?" Wester questioned Nathan.

Hester stood on her toes and peered in the small window at the top of the door. "That boy belongs to me."

"Nathan Garlan, who is that?"

"My mother."

"What does she want?"

"To murder me."

"She will burn this store to get you?"

"Yes, sir."

"Unacceptable."

"OPEN. UP." Hester kicked the door after each word.

The building shuddered.

It creaked.

It did not like this woman.

Nathan left the nook. It was too near the front door.

"I don't open the door for degenerates," Robert Wester said. "Leave now."

Nathan backed further into the shadows and bumped against a rolling ladder.

Wester Brothers' Rare and Fine decided it would hide Nathan. The pine boards the boy stood on throbbed and shuddered.

"Throat, collarbone, groin," Robert Wester muttered to himself. It had been a decade (or three) since he'd last boxed, but he could surely take on a limping woman.

Graham Johnson stepped through the door, unlatched it, and walked through Robert Wester.

A chill ran from Robert Wester's thighs to his eyes. He dropped his fists. Wester put his elbows on his knees and his head between his legs. He was reminded of seeing a speckled hawk frozen to death, hanging upside down from a branch.

Hester shoved the door. She battered books and Robert Wester in the process.

Nathan hid behind the glass ledger counter.

"Boy, it'll be less painful if you come out now," Hester yelled into the store. She looked around. "I won't have to hurt your friend if you come here immediately."

Nathan's head popped up from behind the counter.

"Found you," Hester said to herself.

Robert Wester raised his own head to see his assailant.

Graham Johnson looked around Wester Brothers' Rare and Fine. He loved bookshops. This one even had a rolling ladder across an entire wall.

Ronda Wester came downstairs to see Hester's boot meet her husband's nose. Robert Wester pitched against a table of costly anatomy folios.

"Don't hurt him!" Nathan yelled. He climbed over the counter and ran at his mother.

Hester grabbed the boy's neck. "Idiot child," she said and squeezed.

Nathan stabbed at the hands closed around his throat. Hester let go at the third jab.

The floorboards beneath them wobbled and looked like they wanted to peel apart.

Robert Wester stood, shook his head, then said, "Nathan, drop down."

Nathan did.

Wester jumped over Nathan and leapt at the woman. They crashed into a poetry basket perched on a silver pillar.

Graham ignored the fight. He tapped his fingers on all the spines of the books he wanted to read.

Ronda smacked at the woman fighting her husband. Hester twitched with each hit to the back of her head.

Graham did not care to defend Hester from the dead woman. He had found an illustrated edition of *Confessions of an English Opium Eater.*

Robert Wester's fist caught Hester in the side of the throat.

The force of it reeled her into a table of Egyptian travel memoirs.

"Yeah!" Nathan cheered. His new hiding spot was halfway down the literature hall.

Ronda threw mystery books at Hester's back.

Hester grabbed a table for support.

Wester kicked her in the stomach.

Ronda ran out of mysteries and threw an inkwell at Hester's head. The glass broke. Black covered Hester's hair. Ronda threw the quill. It stuck in Hester's neck.

Wester Brothers' Rare and Fine knew where Nathan would be safe. The floor shuffled itself beneath Nathan's feet.

Nathan looked at the pine. It bulged. Murmurs rose from under the boards.

"I'm going to eat your heart," Hester said. She tried to stab Wester's chest.

Robert Wester was a calm man. A fair man. He picked up centipedes and threw them outside. He swept rats from the store rather than poison them. Wester did not believe in violence. Except during moments of brutish necessity.

Wester barreled into Hester.

She had two knives.

He had an oversized book.

He raised the book.

She brought the knives down. They caught in the book instead of Wester's shoulders.

Wester Brothers' Rare and Fine took control of the situation. If safety was what the boy needed, safety is what it would provide. It tipped the floor. Nathan tumbled away from the fight.

There was a door at the end of the literature hall. It was a door that never opened. Wester had bricked it up and nailed it shut after failing to acquire the conjoining property for a store extension.

Graham heard an excessive amount of grunting, slamming, and screeching but was diligently reading and did not look up.

The hall's floor tipped further.

Nathan slid toward the door.

Wester Brothers' Rare and Fine pushed the nails out of the frame and the door flung open. The bricks at the bottom fell away. There was a Nathan-sized hole, but it did not go next door. It did not go outside. It went down. It went into the dark.

"No, no, NO," Nathan screamed as he slid.

Squeaks and creaks came from below.

Nathan grabbed for purchase but found none.

Novels fell from their shelves and slipped into the opening.

Nathan unwillingly followed them.

He had the distinct feeling he had been eaten.

Hester climbed the bookman's chest.

Ronda flung a bust of Saint Francis de Sales at the woman but missed. It landed by her husband's feet.

Graham Johnson admired a 1674 *Paradise Lost*.

Wester slammed Nathan's mother against a wall. A sconce knocked the back of her neck.

"Uff," Hester groaned.

Wester plunged his thumbs at Hester's eyes. She shifted her head, then arched her back, and pushed away from the wall.

Both tumbled to the floor.

Hester wrapped her hands around his throat.

"I'm sorry," Wester whispered.

He didn't want to kill anyone.

Hester didn't think the bookman had it in him.

Ronda Wester looked away.

Robert Wester picked up the bust of Saint Francis de Sales and brought it down on Nathan's mother's head.

Graham Johnson looked up from an illuminated page to see Hester slump under the bookman. A slice of scalp was stuck to the bust.

The literature hallway righted itself.

The door closed over the hole.

Robert Wester rolled away from the woman and tried to steady his breath.

Graham grabbed Hester by the boots and dragged her out of the store. He would find his hemlock heart the proper help. She would not die on him. He would not allow it.

"What in the fly bitten kidney…" Robert Wester said as he watched the woman's feet lift. The body dragged itself through the books and broken glass into the night.

Wester shook his head, but he knew of stranger. He often thought Ronda still inhabited the bookshop. He found fresh art that lifted his loneliness—in window dust, on ledger margins, everywhere. More fantastic than that, the Rare and Fine itself was…unusual.

"Where are you, boy?"

The store shifted and creaked.

Ronda petted one of the walls.

"Nathan? Nathan Garlan?" he shouted into the shadowed stacks.

Wester Brothers' Rare and Fine groaned.

Robert Wester looked at his shop disapprovingly. "You didn't," he said.

Upstairs, a window closed in confirmation.

"At least let me send him a note, you selfish barbarian." Robert Wester rubbed the blood off his head and hands, gathered his materials, and wrote the boy.

It wasn't the first time someone had been swallowed by Wester Brothers' Rare and Fine. The shop would spit the boy back out…eventually.

Chapter Eighteen

NATHAN PITCHED AND tumbled down an earthen shaft.

He fell longer than it should've taken to get to the cellar.

That's because Wester Brothers' Rare and Fine didn't have one.

Nathan leaned on the dirt wall and looked up.

"Anybody up there?"

The query echoed to his right.

"Anybody?" he yelled into the dark above him. Again, the echo.

Nathan turned around.

There was a tunnel.

It was dark. Water trickled in the distance.

"Deep dark tunnel," Nathan said. "Walk the deep dark tunnel or try to climb back up?"

Nathan looked into the dark. Something skittered.

"Climbing it is."

Nathan grabbed the wall and straight off was hewed with rock clods. He avoided a minor landslide. He tried to take a two-step run-jump, but he slid and fell when the wound in his leg throbbed worse than seventeen straight bootings by a Doogood. He felt around for roots, but there was nothing.

Nathan collapsed.

He inventoried the situation to avoid panic.

He had a mother.

For untold reasons, she wanted him dead.

Robert Wester defended him.

Wester's store had eaten him.

It was dark. The dark often held the dead and the dead were not always kind.

The ground was wet.

He was hungry.

He would probably get pus-poisoned, pass out, and die if he didn't patch his leg proper. The rest of his body was a heap of gashes, scrapes, and bruises.

There was a tunnel he didn't want to take.

He missed Reg.

Nathan pulled his knees to his chest, rested his head on them, and began to weep.

The tunnel before him brightened.

"Boy, why are you crying?"

An old woman with short, curly, grey hair stood before Nathan with a candle. She was balding and did not bother to conceal it. She wore men's trousers and her jacket had frayed elbows. Her manner was scholarly, matter of fact.

Her candle gave them a small sphere of light.

"I fell."

"From where?"

"Above."

"Inadequate angel, are you? Wouldn't be the first to fall."

"I came from the bookshop."

A rat sniffed Nathan's toes. An illogically immense rat. It was the stature of a small dog.

Nathan backed up against the wall. Rocks and cave crickets rained over him. He would be eaten alive in a wet tunnel by thick-bodied crawlies and a behemoth rat while a ghost watched. He flicked the bugs out of his hair and frowned.

"Skittish?" the woman asked.

"That thing looks like it could eat an entire cow," Nathan said. He wiped his eyes and only succeeded in smearing blood and dirt further across his cheeks.

Nathan awakened too many times to the sight of his toes bleeding and a pink tail slipping through a crack in the wall. When he kept his shoes on, he had bloody ankles instead. He didn't like rats.

"You're bothered by O'Neill?" the woman asked.

"O'Neill?"

The woman nodded at the rat.

Something was harnessed to its back.

O'Neill took a step forward. He sniffed Nathan's leg and opened his mouth. His teeth were orange.

Nathan chucked a rock at it before it could nibble.

The rat scurried back.

"It wants to eat me."

"You mentioned cows, he went for your calf. He lowered himself to your expectations."

"What's it wearing?"

"What does it look like, boy?"

O'Neill stared at Nathan with its head cocked to one side. Its whiskers twitched. The rat looked bemused.

Nathan leaned closer to it.

O'Neill backed up.

Nathan leaned closer.

O'Neill hissed.

A wooden serving tray was strapped to the rat's midsection. A book was knotted to the top of it.

"Is that a tray or a saddle?"

"Call it what you like, boy. O'Neill transports my *Dombey and Son.*"

The rat had silver and brown fur and a wizened face.

"Why train a rat to haul a book?"

"So goeth the book, so goeth I. I do not prefer a sedentary life."

"Can't you carry it? You're holding a candle."

"I can hold many books, but not *that* book. My, you are brimming with rude inquiries."

"Sorry," said Nathan.

"Why are you bloody and in the mud?"

"I fell."

"Har! No one enters an underworld for the simplistic reason of *I fell.*"

"I'm cold. I'm hungry. I want to go back, but if I do my ma will murder me."

"There is no back. Not until the shop lets you leave."

"Who are you?"

"The Professor."

"Professor who?"

"Not all of us have the luxury of young, recollecting minds, you ingrate." She rearranged her cravat.

"Beg your pardon, Professor."

"Halt your amends."

"But how did you get here?"

"Here?"

"Under Wester's."

"I know that this is shocking, and I am surprised that you have not noticed, but I am not of the living. My heart met with violence. I went through the white light silence. Died over a *Dombey and Son* at Wester's. Hence my proximity predicament."

"That doesn't answer how you came to be under the store," Nathan said.

"It doesn't matter and I no longer retain the specifics. Get up. Up. Up. Up. Why are you still in that muckabout?"

"Are you gonna help me find the way out?"

"Out? Har! I will say it again and slowly, there—is—no—out. Not until Wester's gives you up."

"But—"

"No buts."

A small flash of light came from the shaft above Nathan's head.

A piece of paper fluttered down. Nathan reached for it and missed. The paper fell to the mud.

O'Neill rushed forward and chewed on the edge.

"Give it here," Nathan said.

O'Neill hissed.

"Give it," Nathan insisted.

O'Neill looked to the Professor.

She nodded.

The rat reluctantly spit the paper out.

Nathan took it.

"How could a paper come from above if there's no up and out?"

"Read it before you finish that self-righteous huff, boy child."

"I could make climbing shoes and rope my way."

"I will say it one final occasion. There is no exit above. The store will not allow it. Read your paper."

Nathan read it. It was a letter from Robert Wester.

He finished, balled the paper up, threw it to the dirt, and punched the wall.

O'Neill scurried forward and snatched the letter. The book wobbled in the rat's haste.

The Professor clicked her tongue at the off-balanced rat.

"What did Wester write?" she asked.

"I don't wish to speak on it."

"I will assume it read as so:

DEAR BOY,

IT IS EXTREMELY UNFORTUNATE THAT MY BOOKSHOP ATE YOU. YOU ARE NOT THE FIRST. IT WAS FOR YOUR OWN GOOD. YOU WILL SEE THIS IN THE FUTURE. ALL EFFORTS TO LEAVE ARE FUTILE. WAIT. LEARN.

TRUST THE PROFESSOR.

KIND REGARDS,
~~*ROBERT WESTER*~~

"Yes?"

"Something like that," Nathan said.

"Let us go."

"Where?"

"Where? Somewhere not in the muck, boy. And what sort of name is *Boy* anyway? Is that German or Scotch?"

"My name is Nathan."

"Nathan? Much higher quality than Boy. 'God has given,' I believe it means."

"God has given what?" Nathan asked.

"I am sure you will let me know."

"I—"

"You."

"I—"

"Stutter, yes. It is not an issue. I will teach you how to deal with the affliction."

"I don't stutter."

"Then speak your mind."

"I want food."

"I will trade you food for books."

"I didn't bring any books."

"No books?"

"I—"

"Your name should be Useless, if you brought me no books."

"I—"

"You."

"I—"

"Yes, I know. You stutter. Stop your tongue and observe what's under your ugly feet."

Nathan looked. He had been crushing several volumes into the mud. His face went red.

"Follow or not, Nathan, follow or not, but if you do, bring the books."

The Professor and O'Neill turned around and went down the deep dark tunnel.

Nathan collected the books and followed the flicker of light.

He would not surface from Wester Brothers' Rare and Fine for five full years.

CHAPTER NINETEEN

NEAR CONNECTICUT, 1862

HESTER STILL BREATHED and Graham could think of only one person who, hypothetically, had the skills to assist her.

The Reverend Doctor Enton Blake.

Graham had seen broadsides for the Reverend Doctor everywhere he traveled for years on end. Anyone with that extensive of a budget had to know a thing or three about reviving those sitting in life's lobby of imminent departure.

It took a day entire to find the Reverend Doctor Enton Blake on the road. The man was halfway to Connecticut.

The medicine wagon was boarded up on the shaded side of the road.

Two horses sucked water from a creek.

A man with slicked-back hair and a strong jaw leaned against a wheel. He picked dirt off his banjo and elbowed a small, dark-eyed woman who drew in a notebook. They had been with the Doc for over a decade. Never did get around to replacing their jug player, either.

Graham stopped Hester's rig in front of the banjo man.

An unpleasant tang came from the wagon.

The banjo man looked up with a twitch on his lip but thought nothing of a wagon driving itself. The Doc didn't pay him to think.

"I require assistance," Graham Johnson yelled. He didn't know why. No one outside of Hester and her brat had ever heard him.

The banjo man didn't hear Graham.

The short woman didn't either. She had put her work down to alert the Doc of the wagon's arrival, but she didn't need to. The Reverend Doctor Enton Blake wiped his hands on his trousers and exited the back of his traveling apothecary.

His six ghosts circled Graham.

Graham especially did not like the black eyes of the old woman with the stained knitting needles.

"Hold your hollering, good citizen. I'm at your disposal. What be your need?" Enton Blake said.

The banjo man and the bass player looked at each other. They hadn't heard anyone hollering. It was going to be one of *those* days. They gathered their gear and walked away. They would camp away from the rig. When the Doc talked to himself, he usually talked all night.

It was a mighty wagon that Enton Blake saw before him. Covered. Livable. Painted. Bound to be valuables inside. A frail fellow in a worn suit was at the head of it. He had a red ring around a crooked neck. Strangled or hanged.

"What can I do for you, my sir of journalism? I can tell you are a man of the reporting profession by your inked finger edges, the cant of your hat, the notebook falling from your pocket, and the investigative level to your gaze." Blake tipped his hat and hooked his thumbs onto his red-lined jacket pockets.

Graham Johnson looked to the right, left, and back of where he stood. There was no one else there.

He asked the doctor, "You see me?"

Enton Blake laughed.

Enton Blake's six ghosts mimicked the laugh and continued to circle Graham and his wagon.

"I can see you, gentleman scribbler. The question is, what can I do for you?"

"I'm sorry. No. I cannot pass the first dubiety yet. You—you, can see me?"

"I have many talents and apparitional optics is one of them. Could say I was born with it, but it's more accurate to say I learned from a man who learned from a man who—well, you understand."

A set of twin farmers, part of Enton's pack of six spirits, pinched Graham. They poked at him. They tipped his hat off and walked circles around him. Graham swatted at them.

"Be civil," Enton Blake scolded.

The twins went back to their dead friends and revealed details of the newcomer in harsh whispers.

"Charming family you have," Graham said.

"Protective," Enton said and nodded at the glaring group. They stood under a tree. "I loathe to rain on an otherwise sunny confabulation, but what is the sour stench that rode in with you?"

Graham peeked between two wooden slats. Hester had messed herself. There was also pus. He was displeased to see Hester appear fragile.

Graham hadn't ever had to do as much manual labor as he'd done in the past two days. Wagon driving and nursemaiding. He stitched one of Hester's wounds and made a fine mess of it. She'd have a crooked scar she'd salt him for.

Velour. Graham's time was meant for naked buttocks on velour, not aromatic sickness and leaking lacerations.

"Is there someone in there that requires aid?" Blake asked.

"Apologies, truly. It has been a trying campaign. Yes. My Hester is dying. Or dead. I am unsure. Fix her."

"Dying is rectifiable. Dead is usually dead. Let me have a look, pen fellow. I'll appraise and declare the damages."

Graham escorted the doctor to the back of the wagon.

Enton Blake opened the door.

Hester was on her bedroll. A stack of books was strapped to the wall behind her. Bunched herbs were pinned to the ceiling above her. Graham had, at great pains, put a circle of salt around her.

"Who does she need salt screening from?" Blake asked.

"Everyone," Graham said.

Enton Blake had a feeling in his stomach. A green feeling. A gold feeling. The woman didn't stir under her patchwork quilt. Over the quilt was a black crocheted shawl. One eyebrow was a tad crooked and her lip had a curl, like she was irritated at a dream. Clean the head gash and the other bloody bits and she was still beautiful.

"Who is she?"

"Hester Garlan," Graham said. He did not feel like lying. He was tired. It didn't matter. Nothing mattered. Life without Hester didn't matter. Why should he lie to a living man?

The group of ghosts under the tree screeched. A dull man in a suit put his pinkies in his ears so he wouldn't have to hear anymore. It was well known that no good could come of that name.

Enton Blake fell off the wagon. A look of surprise smoothed the wrinkles on his forehead.

"Hester Garlan?" Enton asked.

"Yes."

"*The Hester Garlan?*"

"Yes."

"She who sank hundreds to the Something After in one go?" Listen to the dead long enough and you find out what they're afraid of and here she was.

"I would not know." Graham found his capacity for speech shortened. Why talk when the one he wanted to talk to was going to die? What was worth saying if it wasn't to Hester? He felt like he was drowning in a shallow puddle in a foggy moor.

"Do I have your permission to enter and attend to her?"

Graham nodded.

For the rest of the evening and well into night, the only time that Enton Blake exited the wagon was when there was need to find another plaster, capsule, vegetable remedy, or medical text.

The banjo man and the woman made a fire, then dinner, then fell asleep.

Graham and Enton's six spirits paced around the fire.

Enton Blake cleaned and stitched Hester back together. He administered teas, chalks, chants, needles, pills, prayers, scents, and therapeutic liquids.

Hester Garlan. Enton had heard stories about her for years. He had an ear and eye for the dead, he could bind and unbind ghosts from their attachments, but he'd never sent a one to the Something After. This woman, if what ghosts said were true, was singularly the most powerful medium of the past century and her aptitudes were natural.

Enton felt the trick box in his pocket and knew that there was much he could learn from Hester Garlan. If she didn't want to give the information away, he would buy it.

But Hester Garlan did not wake that night or in the nights to come.

She didn't die either.

The next town the Reverend Doctor Enton Blake rolled through was the first population to witness his second wagon. It drove itself. It was freshly painted black and gold. A partition of gauzy cloth covered a window cut into one side. *LA BELLE AU BOIS DORMANT* was written in flowing script above the window. Below it, *SLEEPING BEAUTY* was written in tall, leafy letters. Further below that, in red, small letters was written, MORE FORMIDABLE THAN SHE APPEARS.

Hester wouldn't appreciate all of the gawkers and gossips staring at her, especially when she wasn't awake for the take, but Graham didn't appreciate cleaning up bile. No, he didn't. He had a weak constitution. Besides, the doctor was necessary to keep Hester healthy during her slumber. If Hester wanted to step out of her sleep and kick Graham in the throat with an iron heel while simultaneously yelling about how he should've gone about her hibernation, fine. She was part of the medicine show because it was all Graham could think to do besides stare at walls and write.

CHAPTER TWENTY

NEW HAVEN, CONNECTICUT AND THE WHITE HOUSE, 1863

"I AM GOING with you."

"What possible purpose would you have, Sarah, at the White House? This is business, not a holiday."

"William, I tell you I am going."

"We are not having this discussion anew."

"I will stay out of the way. May chance, Mary Todd Lincoln and I will take tea."

"Mary Todd Lincoln? I am sure she is more than occupied. Stay here. Decorate another room. You are not coming."

Sarah put down her fork and looked at William across the lengthy dinner table. The past year had been…effortful. William was used to walking alone and Sarah often found herself nudging him to the side to demonstrate that his path could reasonably accommodate two.

"William," she said.

"Sarah."

She raised an eyebrow.

He raised his own. Then he snapped his newspaper open.

"I disfavor when you read at the table."

"I disfavor when you scribble."

Sarah pushed her sketchbook and pencil off the table. She was working on a complicated raised wallpaper design. She only drew because William rarely talked. He eternally had his nose in the news or company minutes.

William shuffled the paper.

Abraham Lincoln was on the front page.

Sarah frowned at the president.

"William, I am going. I am packed."

"Empty your trunks," William said. One side of the paper dipped as he grabbed a roll, took a bite, and dropped it to the table, missing his bread plate.

The roll rolled to the rug.

Before a servant could pick it up, Cort snatched the bread and retreated to his favored spot in front of the fireplace.

"If I don't attend, you'll fling bread across the first lady and tell the president one of your dreadful jests."

William put down his paper.

"You do not like my humor?"

He looked hurt.

Sarah rubbed the bridge of her nose with her thumb.

"I thought you thought me clever," William said.

"What I laugh at a quarter of an hour before bed is different than banter for polite company." Sarah didn't give a wink for pleasing polite company. She wanted to get out of the house.

"I could tell the president that whimsy about the girl and the soldier. It is a good one."

"No, it isn't."

"I will prove it."

"Impossible."

"I am certain it is a good one."

"How certain?"

"Completely."

"How about a wager?"

"What sort of a wager, wife?"

"Tell the jest to one person who's never heard it before. If a laugh occurs—you win. No laugh—I win. If I win, I am coming with to the White House."

William paused to contemplate. He silently told himself the joke and smirked. It was a flawless jest.

"You are on."

"Cort," Sarah said.

The dog raised his head.

"Dog, you are witness. If William goes back on this deal, you are allowed to eat all of his shoes and cuff links."

William grimaced. He had tried everything in his power, outside of shooting the beast or running it down with a horse, to get rid of that mutt.

"Who will you tell the joke, William?"

"You, you there," William said to the servant who had gone for the roll.

The servant, Rordin Wint, looked for someone else in the room. He pointed to his chest.

"Yes, you," William said.

"William, it is inappropriate to tell witless witticisms to the servants. You get one telling, are you sure you want to use it now?"

"Hang appropriate. This whole house is inappropriate. I will tell my jest. He is as good as any. Come here," said William.

Rordin Wint smoothed his jacket and his hair and took a step forward.

"Far enough," William said.

Wint stopped.

Cort sniffed at Wint's pant leg then went back to chewing his roll.

"Listen, and I allow you to laugh when apropos."

Wint nodded.

Sarah noticed that Rordin Wint's hands shook. She would add a gratuity to his month's wage.

"A soldier goes off to war," William said, "and he is leaving his sweetheart behind. He says to this woman…what did he say…he says…'I will write you every day!'…and then for the next six months he does. He stops writing when, at long last, he receives one letter back from her."

William paused.

Rordin Wint kept his eyes on William's plate.

Sarah could not refrain from giving the table a sly smile.

"Go ahead man, ask me what the woman's letter said!"

Rordin Wint gulped. "What, sir, did the letter say?"

"That she was marrying the postman!"

The servant looked up from the plate at his master.

"The postman!" William repeated. Then gave a snort of laughter.

"Very amusing, sir," said Wint. He stepped back to the wall with a nod.

"My dearest husband, my only husband," said Sarah, "you are not funny. Wint didn't even smile."

"Who is Wint?" William said after he collected himself.

Sarah bobbed her head at the servant.

"Ah, well, it was above his head," said William. "The postman! Ha!"

"You will make President Lincoln snort for all the wrong reasons."

"You are not coming, wife."

"William, we had a deal."

"Yes, but—"

Cort growled.

William looked at the dog. Then back at Sarah.

"Pack lightly," William said and snapped his newspaper back open.

"Look at them, out there," said Mary Todd Lincoln. She gestured to the window. "Mr. Lincoln is a cat in cream when he has something mechanical to contemplate."

Sarah looked onto the South Lawn.

President Lincoln and a gathering of men, all holding either Henry or Spencer rifles, walked across the manicured grass. They headed to a weedy woodpile.

"Who is in attendance?" Sarah asked.

Mary gave a glance to the window. "Mr. Stoddard is my husband's private secretary. Mr. Stanton—the one with the long beard—he is Secretary of War. I've not a clue who the other several are."

"Where are they fleeing to?"

"Treasury Park," Mary answered. "Shall we repair to the Red Room for tea?"

Sarah smiled. She refused to sulk. She would not disgrace herself, her family, and William by brooding because she didn't get to shoot a gun with an overly tall president who exacerbated his height by insisting on a stovepipe hat. But she had been practicing her shooting and she did want to show off and William was never home.

"Tea, Mrs. Winchester?" Mary Todd Lincoln repeated.

"Yes, splendid!"

Shortly after Mary and Sarah left the fresh blossoms of the Blue Room, the shooting began.

The men stood in a fenced-off section of Treasury Park, one hundred yards before a towering lumber pile.

Christopher Miner Spencer stepped to the president's side with a rifle.

Before Spencer could speak, William Winchester said, "Mr. President, let me present you with this token of appreciation from the New Haven Arms Company."

He handed a narrow rectangular carrying case to the president's secretary.

William Stoddard opened the case and held it out for the president.

"Mr. Winchester, that is a singularly august apparatus." Abraham Lincoln took the rifle out of the case. "Rosewood, is it not?"

"Nothing less than a gold-plated rosewood stock and a one-piece, forged-steel barrel would do you honor, sir."

The president smiled and the lines of his face deepened. "I am not more worthy than any other mother's son, Mr. Winchester, but I will accept your tribute."

"General Ripley believes the Henry rifle to be too heavy for general use, and beauty will not win victory for the Union," Christopher Spencer said.

William Winchester glared at his rival.

Christopher Spencer smiled in return.

"I have noted that sentiment, Mr. Spencer," Lincoln said. "Unfortunately, General Ripley likewise believes the Spencer rifle not adoptable for military service either."

"Were it up to Ripley, the Union would use Springfield '61s into the next century," Stanton said.

The cluster of men groaned.

"The future," Christopher Spencer said, "is in lever-action repeating rifles."

"What use is a higher caliber, if you can only shoot three, perhaps, five rounds a minute?" William added.

Spencer nodded in agreement. "Why should a soldier have five rounds a minute when he could have fifteen?"

"Or more! When used correctly, Henry rifles have fired up to twenty-eight rounds in one minute!" William said.

"It appears, gentlemen, that we hold the future in our hands," said Lincoln. "Mr. Stanton, will you do us the honor of setting up?"

Stanton propped up a plank on the lumber pile then placed a set of indigo glassware in front of it as individual targets.

"I ask your assistance, my refined friends. If Mrs. Lincoln asks what we shot at, present ambiguous answers."

Winchester, Spencer, and company gave a chuckle as the president tipped his head, tapped his forefinger to his nose, and winked.

"The first round will tell us whose aim is true," Lincoln said. "Then we shall each have a flurry, my fellows. We will begin with the Henry, for I have it in hand."

Christopher Spencer snorted and kicked gravel in William Winchester's general direction.

The men formed a parallel line before the target with the president at its center.

"You first, Mr. President," said Christopher Spencer.

"Twenty-five yards, gentlemen…I hope that I do not disappoint you." Lincoln steadied his stance, sighted the target, and fired.

He nicked the lumber pile directly under a goblet.

Stoddard went next.

The goblet above the president's nick shattered.

"I declare," Lincoln said after Stoddard fired. "I believe you are beating me." The president smiled.

The men gave a small round of applause.

Stanton shot at the bottle next to the shattered goblet and missed.

William Winchester sighted the same bottle and, to Christopher Spencer's amusement, also missed. Spencer was not gladdened long, as he missed his shot, too.

Three more of the president's men shot the Henry, only one bursting a glass or bottle.

When all had fired for accuracy, the president said, "Now for speed, gentlemen."

"Shall I hold your hat, Mr. President?" asked Secretary Stoddard.

"Thank you, Stoddard," the president said and relinquished his stovepipe. "Mindful of the notes, if you would."

Stoddard pushed the papers in the top of the president's hat further down so a passing wind would not catch them.

Lincoln squared his shoulders to the woodpile, picked the bottles he would aim for, and raised the Henry rifle.

"You there," came a voice from the South Lawn. "You there, stop that firing! It is illegal! There is no shooting near the White House." A passing sergeant and his four soldiers trotted to the group.

The soldiers shouted behind their sergeant, "Stop that firing!"

Lincoln lowered his rifle to his side, as did all the others.

The soldiers halted within ten yards of the president and his men.

Lincoln stood straighter than before

Every soldier, sergeant included, paled. They looked at one another. The President of the United States had a Henry rifle in his hands.

"Apologies, sir. Greatest apologies," the sergeant stuttered. He waved at the other soldiers and they disappeared more quickly than they had gathered.

Lincoln smiled and watched them leave. "Well, they might have stayed to see the shooting."

"How did it go, my husband?"

"I do not believe I would like to discuss it."

Sarah tugged at one of her curls. She sat in a parlor chair in their suite.

William hung his overcoat on a hook, sat down in a plush chair across from Sarah, and unbuttoned his afternoon jacket.

"That awful?"

"He liked the Spencer better. How could he like the Spencer better?"

"Did the Henry misfire?"

"No, the Henry did not misfire. The president's rifle was immaculate. As were all the other rifles I brought."

"You didn't tell him the postman jest, did you?" Sarah smiled.

William snorted. "No."

Sarah put down her sketchbook and massaged William's shoulders. "I'm sure it couldn't be that bad."

"It is. Spencer stayed on at the White House after I left. How did you get home? Why are you home? Did you abandon Mrs. Lincoln?"

"Oh," Sarah said, "Mrs. Lincoln had other duties. I excused myself after an hour as not to become cumbersome. I hired a carriage to the hotel. You do not mind, do you William?" She kneaded deeper, trying to undo a few of the day's knots.

"No, it shows good sense and more manners than I knew were in you."

Sarah pinched his neck.

William laughed and grabbed her hands. He brought one to his mouth for a kiss. Then sighed.

"The president is, apparently, a mechanical man. Spencer took apart and reassembled his gun faster than I after Lincoln asked to see, quote, 'the inwardness of the thing.' To eclipse that indignity, Christopher Spencer was a better shot than I."

"You think that the Union will not order any Henrys?"

"The president offered Spencer the wood plank we shot against all afternoon."

"Why would you want a bullet-riddled board?"

"Sarah, it was a sign of preference. Lincoln liked Spencer or his rifle better than me or my rifle."

"I love you and your rifle." Sarah kissed the top of his head.

William squeezed her hands and said, "Your love will not win the War of the Rebellion. It will not make me rich."

Sarah frowned at William's black hair. She sat down across from him.

"Surely Spencer is not the absolute victor. You said yourself that the Union was hellbent on buying Springfields."

"First, I do not care about the Springfield '61. It can only shoot two to three minie balls a minute. Atrocious. Absolutely atrocious. It will descend from popularity soon enough. Second, I do not care that Christopher Spencer is not an absolute victor, I care that he is more victorious than I. Third, do not say hell. How many times do I have to tell you not to curse? You could make a dead grandmother blush."

Sarah picked up her sketchbook.

"Do not do that."

"What?" Sarah asked.

"You picked up your little drawing book."

"So?"

"That means that you have ended our conversation."

"It does not."

"Then put it down."

Sarah put down her sketchbook, irritated. She'd much rather shade a staircase rosette than be scolded.

"Thank you," William said.

"Are you sure that Spencer will receive a Union order? All you know is that he received a plank."

"And that he stayed at the White House longer than I."

"How do you know?"

"Because I was eventually, politely, escorted to the door and he was escorted elsewhere. I do not know where. Not out."

"What now?"

"Now? Now the New Haven Arms Company has to individually convince soldiers that buying a Henry rifle is in their best interest."

"Is it?"

"Certainly! You could load that gun on Sunday and shoot it all week. I'd gladly trade that security against four months' pay, any day."

"How much is the Henry?"

"Forty-two, without the sling, Sarah."

"Our boys go to war for ten dollars a month?"

"Privates, yes. I think it's about thirteen, maybe sixteen."

"Are Spencer rifles that expensive?"

"I believe they are about thirty-five or forty. Perhaps, that's the way to go."

"What? Lowering the price to thirty-five?"

"No, Sarah. Roaming the countryside like Christopher Spencer did, selling rifles to individual commanders. Hmm. Burdensome, though, wouldn't it be?"

Sarah didn't mean to, but she smiled at the thought of William being gone for an extended business trip. There would be no one to admonish her daily habits.

"I can't imagine scurrying about Illinois and Indiana like that. It sounds like low work, traveling sales. Perhaps the Company can hire someone."

"No work is low work," Sarah said.

"You do not even wash your own clothes or make meals, do not tell me what you think of work," William said.

Sarah reopened her sketchbook.

"I glean that our conversation is over?"

Sarah kept her burning cheeks facing her sketch. "As I do not have any proper work experience, I do not know what I could further add to the dialogue."

"If you are going to turn into a sensitive matron I'll pop out to the club."

"Have a good evening, William," Sarah said, but she did not mean it.

"You as well, wife."

William put on his jacket and left the hotel suite.

Sarah did not look up from her drawing.

Chapter Twenty-One

Woodstock, New York, 1863

HENNET LED HIS near-empty wagon out of the forest and into the meadow of his youth. His mama's spread was straight ahead. The cabin and outbuildings looked like exactly what they were, a small homestead built by a widow who had no time for frills. The only extravagance was a shaded porch that wrapped around the front of the two-room cabin.

Cleveland to Woodstock was five hundred miles. Selling goods along the way, Hennet made it in two months. Last of them sunups and sundowns was foul. The waft of Walleye became kin to a crabapple stuffed with the Devil's own shit.

Hennet brought the wagon up the path. Hadn't been home in nine months. Not much changed. The roof needed redoin', the shed tilted, and his mama had the same older-than-Eve floppy hat.

Mama Daniels was on her hands and knees in the kale with her back to the path.

"Come here, you," she muttered as she plucked greens, "you too, you bug-eaten bastard." She put bunches in a basket.

Hennet thought his mama a right fine woman. Brown-eyed, industrious, good humored, couldn't even tell she was in her forties 'cept by the smile lines. Didn't need any one telling her how to work her land or family. Ten to one, her Kentucky pistol was tucked in that basket.

It'd never bothered Hennet that his mama shot his daddy dead. If the man didn't want to get gunned down and burnt in a chicken coop, he shouldn't have been drawers-dropped-necking with another woman in it. Again. If he hadn't of done what mama told him not to do, daddy'd still be breathing.

"Phew, boys, what's in there?" Mama Daniels called. She didn't have to look to know that the racket wagoning out of the woods was her family.

Hennet jumped off the rig, went to the garden, and scooped his mother out of the dirt.

Walleye went to the porch and sat down.

Mule nosed around in the greens.

"Ooof! Put me down you reeking child!" Mama Daniels said and batted her son on the shoulders.

Hennet put down his mama. He took off his gloves and tucked them into a pocket.

"Get on outta here, you're crushing lunch." Mama Daniels shoved Hennet. "Where's Walleye? He sleepin' back there?"

Hennet frowned. "Got some bad news."

"Ain't sleepin'?"

Hennet nodded.

"Gone?"

"Brought him home," Hennet said and flapped an arm toward the wagon bed.

"Thank you, Hen."

Mama Daniels held out her hand.

Hennet put his knife in it. It'd been his granddaddy's.

Mama Daniels took the knife and walked to the back of the wagon. She threw the dusty tarp back. A buffalo rug crowded the wrapped body of her son. Mama Daniels leaned over the side and slit a hole in the oilskin over Walleye's face.

He was long gone, but he was still her boy. Cheekbones showin' or not. She cut a lock of hair and covered his face. She walked back to her garden and picked up the kale basket.

"Stay out here and think on where he'd best like to be put in the ground. I'll call you when the biscuits and rest is ready."

Hennet watched his mama walk crooked up the porch. She closed the front door. Three seasons of the year, that door stayed open. It wasn't cold enough to close that door.

"Mama, wait on me," Walleye said.

Mama Daniels opened the door and looked at Hennet.

"You say something?"

"No, ma'am."

"It was me, I'm coming," Walleye said.

Mama Daniels looked around the porch. Something wasn't right. Her skin prickled.

"I'll whoop you and that horse if you let it near my garden," Mama Daniels said.

Hennet nodded.

Walleye went inside.

Mule kept at the kale patch.

Hennet's horse heeded Mama Daniels and kept to sniffing dirt.

Mama Daniels shut the door.

Hennet unhitched the horse and unloaded the wagon.

Mama Daniels took off her hat, went to the stewpot, and rubbed her eyes. She'd didn't feel alone.

Walleye looked at the carroty brown stew. Being a haint wasn't so bad, till he saw his favorite cookpot in the whole wide world.

Three willows stood on a hill to the back left of the cabin. Hennet and Walleye had climbed the cluster as boys. Hennet taught Wall how to read at their base. They'd dug a hole to see how far down they could go. Wall was convinced Hell was reachable, if they dug deep and all day. Hennet was persuaded to dig by the mention of buxom, long-tailed imp women with loose morals and long fingernails.

Mama Daniels had found the hole the next day and told them to fill it in or make a well.

They filled it in.

While his mother mourned, Hennet stripped down to the waist and dug out the long-gone hell-hole in the shade of the trees.

He wasn't alone. Walleye climbed in and out of the grave, pushing dirt and causing minor avalanches.

Hennet kept digging. When the digging was done, Hennet put Walleye in the hole.

The sun was orange and low in the sky.

"Hen, where you at?" his mama's voice cracked from the porch.

"Back here." Hennet trotted from the side of the house. He'd scrubbed up and put his shirt back on.

Mama Daniels took Hennet's hand. She looked to the hill and shook her head. The sunset outlined each tree and a wooden cross.

"We got words to say, ma'am."

"I don't want to."

"Mama."

"He was my baby."

"I know."

"You were supposed to watch him."

"I know."

They walked up the hill to the three trees.

Walleye walked behind them.

Mama Daniels stopped far enough from the grave that she couldn't see inside. The smell reached out.

"Mama, I—"

"I don't want to know."

"He died while—"

"Hen," she crossed her arms, "I don't want to know. I accept the life you boys led. I took its fruits and I didn't give you any other path."

"I'm sorry, ma'am."

"Ain't we all? Sorry doesn't bring my baby boy back." She picked up a handful of dirt from a mound. "What I want, is you mad. Mad enough to kill whatever pig-turd took my boy, if he ain't dead already."

"He's not."

"Know who did it?"

"Got a lead."

"Gonna be able to find him?"

"Not easily. Eventually."

"Good enough for your mama. Come here."

Hennet put his arm around her shoulder and she slipped her own around his waist.

Walleye climbed one of the trees and watched from above. Mule snorted a ladybug off the tree trunk. Walleye looked down into the grave. True walls in his hole. Hennet'd done good. Always did.

Mama Daniels threw the handful of dirt into the grave.

"Don't know what to say."

"What'd you say over daddy?"

"'Burn you lying bastard' don't fit."

Hennet smiled. So did his mama.

"How about 'goodnight'?"

Mama Daniels nodded and said to the ground, "Goodnight, boy. Mama loved you."

"So'd I," Hennet followed up.

Mama Daniels broke away. "Finish here and come eat." She wiped the corner of her eye with her dress sleeve.

"Yes, ma'am."

He picked up the shovel and fingered the worn grip.

Mama Daniels walked down the hill, cleared her throat, sniffed louder, and kept her calm till she got inside the cabin.

Hennet had had two months to mourn. Two months of Walleye rotting behind him. He saw his brother's eyes bulge and tongue loll before he wrapped him in oilskin. The silent wagon ride had skinned his heart, but it had leathered over.

As he filled Walleye's grave, Hennet thought on murder. He wasn't convinced that Walleye had been killed by anyone besides his own fool self.

There'd been small cuts and bruises from brambles and falls, not fists and shivs. Walleye'd been covered in powder and it was Hennet's opinion that Walleye died from it. The mule had. It hadn't had a single mark on it, only white and brown powder.

The Daniels brothers hadn't passed by a druggist.

They'd not stolen from a sawbones.

The only place Walleye could've gotten a physic powder was a traveling man.

Whoever it was, Hennet had his card.

Brown and white powder and a chewed-up card. Not much to go on.

He didn't think it fair to kill a traveling doctor for selling whatever cure he did to Walleye, but it was what Mama Daniels wanted, and like she said, life ain't fair.

If life was fair Hennet wouldn't be haunted.

It took Hennet the whole trip to decide the matter, but it was definite. Walleye's body was in the dirt, but he sure as hell wasn't gone.

Hennet had had two months of intermittent shivers.

Of breezes indoors.

Of cold hands pushing him at night.

Of campfires that smothered themselves.

Of poker cards fluttered out of his grip.

Of his haversack shuffled through, his boots thrown at him, his billfold missing money, his shoulder bumped while he was shitting, and petty thefts interrupted.

Hennet had almost been jailed three times—*three*—for bungled filches. Even when he was a scamp, Hennet had never botched a wallet grab, a widow cajoling, or a holdup. But recently, a frigid force jabbed his hands or knocked through him or caused something in the room to crash at exactly the wrong turn.

It wasn't dread that Hennet felt, but continual observation. He couldn't even piss on a sycamore without feeling eyes on him. More than once, Hennet had yelled at empty air for Walleye to show himself.

Walleye couldn't do this. The closest he could come to physical emergence was to knock something over. He did. Often. It was a game. He

would push the horse or jostle campfire logs or throw cans out of the wagon
and Hennet would yell blue ruin. Like old times.

Hennet didn't take it as a friendly action to be shoved out of his seat.
He didn't like his hat flipped off, his whores saying he pinched them when he
didn't, or strangers regularly vomiting near his new boots.

Walleye didn't mean to pull up people's insides. He didn't want to go
through people. He wanted to stay inside people. He didn't want to stain Net's
shoes. He wanted to talk to him.

Hennet finished filling the hole. The sky was as black as the grave when
he walked down the hill. He'd leave the next afternoon. Mama Daniels would
expect him to.

Walleye followed Hennet to the cabin.

Mule couldn't.

Mule brayed in dismay. A force stopped him short when he padded too
far from Walleye's remains. Mule shivered in the dark by the trees and wanted
to die. Again.

Chapter Twenty-Two

New Haven, Connecticut, 1866

Sarah and William wanted a family. They worked on this goal and, for a brief time, Sarah felt satiated in life.

Then everything changed.

The anxiety set in.

Sarah heard the neighbors talk. Heard her own sisters and mother whisper. Everyone said that they'd never heard of a pregnancy this difficult. Sarah felt sick all day for months on end. Her ankles had swollen. She was tired. Her mouth tasted like she licked iron. Her hips and bones felt stretched to breaking. She relieved herself constantly, not always at opportune moments. She felt like there was an eel in her belly.

Then there was the bed rest.

William and the doctors demanded it.

Family commented on how full and beautiful her hair looked. It was because there wasn't much else to compliment her on. Bags under her eyes. Fattened hands. Slow brain. Sarah wanted a child, but she hated being pregnant. She felt inadequate to the task and suspected that William was disappointed in her.

He was.

He'd once caught her out of bed, in the kitchen, licking muffin batter from her thumb.

"What are you doing, Sarah?"

"Eating."

"I meant out of bed. What are you doing out of bed?"

William put his satchel on a chair and slackened his necktie. Loose bows were all the rage. Fashionable appearances fared well with clients.

"I wanted apple cinnamon muffins."

"That's what she's for," William said with a flick of his wrist at a servant.

"Ruth is the housekeeper, not the cook," Sarah said.

Ruth continued to pour batter into tins. The mister and missus fought often. It was best to appear not to notice.

"Where is the cook?"

"I don't know, William, and I do not care. I wanted muffins. No. I wanted to make muffins. Why can't you let me make muffins?"

William picked up his satchel. He would work in his office.

"Good day to you too," Sarah said as William walked away without saying anything.

William stopped.

"What do you care of my day?"

"I care."

"What with all your sleeplessness and sweating, you've found time to notice the Company and me?"

"William, I am well aware of your father restructuring the Company."

"The New Haven Arms Company is soon to be the Winchester Repeating Arms Company. The Henry rifle, with modification, will be the Winchester Model 1866. I do not have time to coddle you."

"I don't need to be coddled."

"Then act like a grown woman. Go to bed before you ruin my child."

"*Our* child holds no grudges against muffins."

Sarah licked the spoon and batter bowl.

Ruth put the batch in to bake.

"Sarah, we have been assured by multiple physicians that the passage to motherhood is dependent on attitude. Your outward manifestations of terrible health are due to a bad outlook. Pray. Draw. Do whatever it takes to produce a healthy child."

"Go away, William."

"What?"

William did not understand his wife. If she didn't want him to be supportive why had she dragged him into the conversation in the first place?

"Leave me with my muffins."

"Fine." William looked at his timepiece. "You have ten minutes before I send for my mother to supervise you."

The thought of swooning in front of William or his despotic mother made Sarah want to pee. No. Maybe that was the baby. But William's mother was an awful thought. Sarah patted her stomach and left the kitchen before her ten minutes were up. Ruth agreed to bring her the completed apple cinnamon muffins.

William did not leave his study all evening.

Sarah did not want to hate William.

William did not want to hate Sarah.

They had good intentions in common.

When Sarah finally had the child, William was the first to hold it.

Her.

They had a girl.

Her name was Annie.

William looked at Sarah with pride.

She almost forgave him for being a tyrant for nine months.

Annie gave them satisfaction.

It was a contentedness that did not last.

CHAPTER TWENTY-THREE

LOWER NEW HAMPSHIRE, 1866

IN THE YEARS since Walleye went haint, Hennet murdered a number of people. Christians, heathens, men, women. He'd put bullet to a stone scryer, a mind reader, a dead speaker, a pastor, and a spiritualist. He'd grievously impaired an automatic writer, an auguring academic, a chalk-swallower, a coal diviner, a card spreader, and a bone-eater.

Every bullet he discharged, Hennet felt justified. The bastards vultured about. Said that they could see Walleye, that they could hear him, that they could get rid of him. Hennet's thieving was an honest living compared to these morally decrepit cocksuckers. You don't piss in a man's mouth and call it whiskey. You don't say you can get rid of a man's dead brother, if you ain't got the competences to do it.

They put on silk-swinging, table-shifting, sweaty palmed, candle-lit shows. They spoke in different tongues, wobbled, prayed, shook, twitched, and howled.

Hennet was not impressed.

He had two questions:

How do I get Walleye to stop haunting me?
Who's the man that killed him?

Not a one of the palmist perjurers and medium misleaders Hennet had met could answer the questions honest. Saying *I don't know*, that Hennet'd let pass, but lying, lying about a man's passed-on brother, now that was horse and shit. When he pulled his gun on each, they whimpered or roared, and he answered each with a bang.

Hennet could not abide liars.

Wink's wife, Ys, couldn't make coffee fit for a pig, but she wasn't a liar.

Wink's Tea was a cramped shop. Thin as three men shoulder to shoulder. It had an unexpectedly high ceiling that narrowed. Pots and crocks of dried leaves lined the walls all the way to the roof. It was dark. Its smell was confusing but comfortable—it reminded Hennet of the earthy musk that accompanied his clothes after he slept on a woodpile—which happened anytime he drank.

Hennet learned early in their acquaintance not to call Wink an oriental, celestial, or Chinaman. Learned by getting knocked on his ass. Wink had a right fist that could make an elephant attentive. The pair had met outside a gambling hall more years back than Hennet could recall. Walleye had been thrown out and smashed into Wink's traveling tea cart—tore the lantern garland off the edges with his flailing and vomited on a wheel. Two seconds later, Hennet was thrown out and landed on Walleye, still busy expelling his dinner on the side of Wink's cart. Hennet couldn't bring to mind how that shit of a beginning turned into a friendship, but he thought it included three stolen billfolds going to Wink.

Hennet was in Wink's storeroom. It was even smaller than the front of the shop. A chipmunk paced inside a birdcage set on a stack of crates. Afternoon light streamed in from the open back door.

Wink tended an herb box outside.

Hennet sat at an unbalanced wooden table. It and the high-stacked crates were all that could fit in the room. Ys sat across from him. Wink said she was from San Francisco. She looked it. Deep red lips and a fan covered in roses.

"Tell me about my brother," Hennet said before he got distracted by her curls.

"I will tell what is written on your palms," Ys said.

Hennet put his hand, palm up, on the table. It gave a scritch with the weight shift.

Ys took a stained cheesecloth from the scarves knotted around her red hair.

"Both hands," she said.

Hennet put his other hand on the table. It scritched again.

His duster hung over the chair. His guns were visible.

Ys put the cheesecloth over his hands. She poked at his left palm.

"Your brother is dead."

"I know that. What else?"

"You have killed many people in his name."

"True enough."

"Your brother is still with you."

"How do I get rid of him?"

"Your brother is not your worry."

Walleye watched over the woman's shoulder. Wink's wife had a high, tight-collared dress. He paced disappointedly at the lack of visible bosom.

"What is my worry?"

"There's a woman."

"Ain't there always?"

"She's never far from you. Dark hair. Disheveled. She carries knives and wears tall boots."

Wink's wife poked at the cheesecloth.

"Stay away from her. Everyone around her dies. Even her horses."

Hennet smiled.

He thought back to the last woman he knew that was ragged and a risk. How her foot fit right smart into the hollow of his cheek when she kicked it.

"Why's my brother haunting me?"

Wink's wife stared at the cloth. "I do not know."

"How do I kill him again?"

"That is not a skill I own."

"Where's the man that killed him?"

Wink's wife straightened the cloth over the outlaw's hands. "Not far."

"Not far from where? Here?" Hennet straightened in his chair.

"It does not say."

"What's his name?"

"Blake."

"I knew that."

"It is all the cloth says."

"You ain't useful."

"But I'm not a liar." She nodded at his guns.

"You ain't giving whole truth either. What're you holding back?"

"There's something else."

"Say it."

She looked at the cloth. "This last counsel will cost you." She had seen an unknown son. That was worth something. The shop was in its slow season.

Hennet pulled one hand from under the cheesecloth, plucked a gun from a holster, and put it on the table. "If you hold out."

"I deserve payment."

"You deserve a bullet for all the times you lied to folks when that rag gave you nothing."

"That has not happened."

Hennet stared her down.

Ys did not look away.

"What'd you see?"

Ys decided she should've kept her mouth shut. But she hadn't. She gave him half of what she knew. "You have a son."

Hennet sat up straight. "Come again? A what?"

"A son. His name is Nathan."

"How old?"

"Fourteen."

"Where is he?"

"The cloth does not say."

"By who?"

"The cloth does not say."

"Will I meet him?"

"It appears so."

"You ain't fibbing?"

Ys glared at the outlaw. "I catch glimpses. I piece them together." The threads in the cloth helped her frame what she saw. It wasn't much.

"That all you got?"

Wink's wife nodded. She took the cheesecloth and wound it back into her headscarves. What she did not mention to Hennet was that calamity would come if he sought out his son.

"Git," Hennet said.

Wink looked in the back door.

Hennet dipped his head at him.

"She see what you need?" Wink asked. He held a handful of mint.

"Not enough, Wink."

"Staying for supper?"

Ys frowned and went to the front of the shop. She did not want to feed the mongrel. He would likely see she held something back and slit her throat over the stew.

Walleye followed Wink's wife. He tried to grab loose scarves, but she was a step ahead of him.

"Can I hole up here for the night, Wink?"

"You buying tea?"

Hennet nodded.

"Dinner's in an hour. Bed in the shed out back."

"Much obliged."

Wink nodded.

"Got anything strong to drink?"

Wink pointed his mint hand at the chipmunk. There was a bottle of bourbon behind the cage. Wink took his basket of herbs to the front of the store.

Hennet took the bourbon from behind the chipmunk. He sat at the table.

A clatter and squeal sounded from the front of Wink's. Half a breath after, Walleye walked into the storeroom. He'd accomplished what he'd set out to do. Grabbed a handful of pretty lady titties and took purchase of her cheesecloth, too. Looked mighty powerful. Walleye wanted Net to have it.

Walleye dropped the cheesecloth. It floated down to the table as he sat across from his brother. This. Walleye missed this. Bourbon with his Net. But Net didn't need him no more and Walleye didn't know how to go. Didn't know where to go if he could go. Walleye didn't like life so much no more. He missed Mule.

Hennet chose to ignore the cheesecloth appearing at the table. It was dark. If he squinted, he could pretend it wasn't there and call to mind other matters.

He had a son. He never wanted a boy, but hell, it wouldn't be bad to own one. Could teach the fella to shoot and pilfer. It'd be like having Walleye back. They could go to Abilene. That cow town had the saltiest, toughest, most libidinous whores in the thirty-six states. Every man should go to Abilene.

But a disheveled woman being a worry on him? Hennet took off his hat. There was only one woman that'd ever gotten the best of him. One. Hennet rubbed inside the brim where a piece of grey, tattered lace was sewn. Black eye, bite marks, stitches, a bum knee, a broken rib, and the loveliest backache he'd ever had. Hennet wouldn't mind wrapping his hands around her neck again.

Wouldn't mind making it hard for her to breathe.

Doubt she could kill him, but Hennet wouldn't mind her coming for him.

Walleye climbed the crates. He was bored.

Hennet ignored the shaking crates. Fourteen years. His wildcat had had him a son. He didn't picture a woman like that to want a youngster. Pictured her more likely to tie it to a high tree branch to starve.

"Holy hellfire, I'm a daddy," Hennet said to himself.

Walleye hadn't wanted to dance in years. Not since he died. If Net was a daddy then he was an uncle. Walleye danced on the crates. The crates were full of tea. Pots toppled. Wood creaked. Walleye danced. He had himself a boy. Or Hennet did. Hennet had a boy and Walleye would play with him. Shoot at his feet and make him dance, too, like he used to do with Mule. Walleye flailed and more crates fell. Leaves spilled. Walleye hummed "Yankee Doodle." He kicked the leaves as they fluttered down. They looked like little bugs flying away from him. They'd be prettier as candlebugs. Walleye'd always liked candlebugs. He lit a match and blew fire on the tea leaves.

Hennet grimaced. He put his hat back on. He didn't know what the hell he did to deserve his brother hating him so hard that Hennet had to either empty his billfold or bullet someone every other day, due to the wreckage Walleye occasioned.

Wink ran into the back room.

Burning tea leaves rained around Hennet who was drinking and frowning at the table.

"What did you do?"

Hennet raised his hands, palms up, and shrugged.

Wink ran around to stomp out small fires.

Hennet smothered a clump of burning leaves that landed on his shoe. His new boots were ruined.

Walleye slumped in a tea pile that smelled of vanilla and almond. He was tired.

Hennet kept drinking. He knew what came next.

"You owe me big," Wink said.

"How big?"

Wink surveyed the damage.

"Eleven small pots multiplied by thirty-eight cents, plus three pots multiplied by five dollars, plus—"

"Whoa, Wink. Whoa. What the hell you got in here that costs five a pot? Gold tea? Five bills could near buy me a barrel of wheat."

"Monkey tea. You broke three pots of oolong picked by monkeys. From China."

"Can't you sweep it up and use it?"

"Burnt tea? No. You owe for the pots, labor, and cleanup. And the crates and the angry wife."

"How much is all that?"

Wink looked at the ceiling and paused. "$21.58."

The number gained Walleye's attention. He circled Wink. Thought on hurting him.

"You want me to pay you twenty whole dollars when you're gonna sweep this up and put it back in pots?"

"Can't use burnt tea."

"Ain't there a cohort's decrease?"

Wink didn't want trouble. "Give me fifteen and get the hell out."

Hennet pulled a gold piece out and flipped it to Wink.

He caught it.

Walleye punched Wink. It wasn't fair. Net coulda bought three acres with that fifteen. Or fifteen whores.

Hennet didn't know why Wink doubled over, but he had a good idea.

"Sorry 'bout that, Wink. My brother ain't got manners. I'm taking this and leaving," Hennet said and stooped to pick up the bourbon.

"No, you aren't," said Wink's wife. She had a rifle trained on Hennet. "You and your dead bastard brother are leaving out the back."

Hennet stood. He didn't argue with rifle ends.

"Missus," he said. He grabbed his effects—haversack, duster, guns—and went out the back door.

Wink stood with the help of his wife.

Hennet festered as he walked away. Goddamn Walleye. Costing him at every turn. Hennet threw his haversack over his shoulder, adjusted the strap. The whole town was jar-topped-full of railroad men. He'd be lucky if he could find a whore's room for an hour, let alone a bed for the night.

Chapter Twenty-Four

New Haven, Connecticut, 1866

SARAH AND ANNIE sat in the shade of the back garden.

William was at work. William was always at work.

"How's my little girl? How are you?" Sarah asked the baby in her arms.

Annie whined. She pushed at the yellow and white blanket that covered her.

"You look lovely, my little Annie." Sarah touched Annie's nose with her thumb.

The child frowned at her.

Clouds crowded the sky. Two blackberry pies cooled in a window. A crow's shadow passed over the mother and daughter.

"Let's try for a sugar cloth, yes? My little girl is hungry?" A wet nurse handed Sarah a small cloth secured over a sugar cube that had been soaked in milk.

Sarah brought the cloth to Annie's lips.

Annie cried.

"Shh, have a taste, Annie girl," Sarah said. She pushed the cloth slightly between her daughter's lips.

Annie's cries muffled. Annie's thoughts scattered to images of her father.

Sarah loved her child. She loved Annie. But Annie would cry and Sarah didn't know how to restore the child's calm. She didn't know what the baby wanted. It wasn't food. It wasn't a changing. Sarah felt conspired against.

"You must eat." Sarah kept the sugar cloth at Annie's lips. Sarah was careful. She did not push. A day earlier, Annie had a minor coughing fit when Sarah tried to force a nipple into Annie's mouth. Sarah was left holding one breast and an earful of howling as William whisked the tiny expectorator out of her hands.

Annie's fists hit the sides of the sugar cloth. She blinked her eyes. After each blink she hoped she would see her father. Blink. No father. Blink. No father. Blink. She wanted the tall one. Blink. The mutton-chopped one.

Sarah looked at the wet nurse, a woman of sturdy build and a red face. The wet nurse frowned.

"Have you ever witnessed a child this reluctant to eat?"

"No, ma'am. Heard of children like such, but never met one."

"What is it? Why won't she eat?"

"Don't know, ma'am."

"We've tried the bottle. We've tried my wares. We've tried yours. She doesn't want a sugar cloth. She doesn't want goat's milk, cow's milk, or milk-soaked bread. She won't take to any other wet nurse we hire. The only one who has any lucky feeding the child is Mr. Winchester, and even then in only a small portion of his feedings."

"Aye, ma'am."

"And he is rarely home to feed her."

"Yes, ma'am."

"What are we going to do?"

Annie kicked Sarah's hand. The sugar cloth fell to the ants and dirt. Annie was unhappy. Where was the tall one?

"I'll put some milk in a bowl, ma'am. We could soak her fingers and maybe she'll suck on them."

Sarah nodded. She didn't look at the wet nurse. She didn't look at Annie. She wanted to yell at the child. She wanted to weep.

Annie began her high-pitched, short-breathed wail.

Sarah thought about shaking Annie till she stopped.

Instead, she rocked the girl in her arms.

She was a bad mother. No other mother Sarah had ever met had a child that wouldn't eat. She could see it in William's face. William thought her a bad mother. Sarah could've brushed off his approval if she had Annie's, but the child felt disconnected from her. It felt like the child tolerated her. It was Sarah's belief that Annie didn't like her.

Sarah was right.

Annie didn't know why she didn't like her mother, but she didn't.

She waited for the wet nurse to come back with the bowl of milk as Annie emptied her energy into monotonous shrieks.

The crow flew over the yard again.

Sarah wiped the wet from the corners of her eyes.

CHAPTER TWENTY-FIVE

HESTER HADN'T OPENED her eyes since Saint Francis de Sales slammed into the side of her head. This made Graham Johnson's life difficult. The Reverend Doctor traveled from town to town with his two-wagon train. Graham acted as wagon master, protector, and nurse.

The legend of Hester Garlan expanded even as she slept. According to dead chatter it wasn't several city blocks she sent to the Something After more than a decade previous (when she was a sprat of seventeen), it was all the apparitions of Chicago.

The dead took this as a personal affront. Hester must be punished. Do you see the way she heinously lies there? Bet she sends a score of spirits to the Something After with one dream alone. How has she been allowed to live this long? Think of the havoc she could commit in your town.

Graham was the only unbreathing bastard who realized Hester hadn't been overly dangerous to the deceased since Nathan was born. Hester hadn't had more than swindling stored up her skirts for years. She couldn't keep a coin in her pocket, let alone kill all the pales on the Eastern seaboard.

The truth rarely halts gossip and grudges.

Graham had always thought himself more a Grendel than a Galahad. Chivalry bored him, and he wasn't good at it. He didn't know how much longer he could keep Hester unmolested. There'd been a tipped wagon. A fire. Strangulation attempts. Blunderbusses blasted. A sword dangled in a sensationally *Pit and the Pendulum* manner. Poison. Migraine-inducing mobs. It was tiring. Graham was now wise to why Hester had half-moons often under her eyes.

The Reverend Doctor Enton Blake assisted Graham whenever possible. He did this because he wanted Hester to awake and relinquish her old words. Enton was a firm believer that if someone, ghost or flesh, wanted to end their existence, they should be allowed to, and if they didn't know how to accomplish this, he would help. He knew how to do this for the living. Only Hester's old words would let him do this for the dead.

The Reverend Doctor Enton Blake tried to sway the spooks into seeing Hester as harmless in her slumberous state. It was of no use. They were of one mind. She was a murderer when awake and possibly more jeopardous in her dreams.

Graham Johnson did not think himself a nice man and he was being forced to be a nice man. A decent man. A wagon man. A nurse. A protector. A maid. He did not like it. The responsibility gave him a rash. At least once a year, he cracked like an eggshell.

"Mr. Johnson, what are you doing?" asked Enton Blake.

Thump.

"Mr. Johnson?"

Thump.

"Mr. Johnson! Control yourself!"

Graham Johnson stopped banging his head against the iron rail. He had waited for several hours and not one train had come by to crush his skull. He thought on horsecars and wild dogs. On Kominsky probably giving Wenspisle a raise for his war coverage. On the intelligence that it was unlikely that he would ever get a kiss from Hester Garlan, let alone nude gyrations in exorbitantly priced bedding. As such, Graham hit his forehead against the tracks until it disappeared. It hurt. It didn't matter. He wanted toast and jam and his mother and *The Atlantic Monthly*. Forget the indigo chaise, he deserved a royal purple one.

Enton Blake had stopped the wagons near the new tracks to pitch his stock to the railroad men. He hadn't noticed Graham Johnson's despair until after a crowd of thirty had dispersed. He had sold mostly tooth pain tinctures, tobacco, and cure-all brain calmers for the day after a hard-drinking night.

Graham no longer had a face for Enton to talk to. The iron had erased it.

"What are you doing to yourself?"

"What does it matter?" said the vacant area above Graham Johnson's neck.

Enton hooked his thumbs in his pockets. His right thumb touched the trick box.

"Do you want to die, Mr. Johnson?"

"Yes."

"I can't help you with that, yet."

"I am aware."

Enton's six ghosts looked on the situation with pity and walked away from the tracks. Two milling railroad workers saw the Doc talking to himself. The rest of the men were occupied by the jugless jug band that played a sad song in front of Hester's wagon. If a person put a coin in a collection bucket, the weight triggered a spring that pulled curtains open to a seven-second sight

into Sleeping Beauty's quarters before the curtains closed. Enton Blake was
bewildered by how much money this made.

"Graham, I will call you Graham, because Christian names should be
used in times of crisis, you have been of great assistance to me. You drive
Hester's wagon well. You keep her in health and handsomeness. You are
usually good conversation. I can pay you for your time, your efforts, these past
four years."

"I don't need money."

"I am not speaking of money."

Part of Graham's head flickered back into existence then washed out.

"I know that you have seen me disenthrall a haint, Mr. Johnson."

There had been more than one. The Reverend Doctor was widely
known for his ability to detach a ghost from whatever it was chained to. A
frazzled educator was released from his schoolhouse's bell. An enraged woman
was unhitched from her wedding ring that her widower had gifted to another
gal. A boy with an arm and shoulder that looked like red mud and bone was
loosened from a cotton mill. Almost every stop of the wagons, the Reverend
Doctor Enton Blake untied spirits from their binds. He did this without
sending them to the Something After. These spirits roamed wherever they
willed. Enton Blake had a sliding payment scale dependent on the energy he
had to exert and an apparition's capacity to pay. His ability to loosen even some
of them from their tethers endeared the Reverend Doctor to the dead.

"What are you saying? You would *disenthrall* me from Hester?" Graham
tried to put the scorn of an unpaid high court whore in his voice. His headless
body paced on a railroad tie. His cravat whipped back and forth, his shirt was
unrestricted about his throat, and his jacket lay on a pile of railroad spikes.

"Graham, I am capable of detaching you from Hester Garlan, and you
know this. Would not freedom be kinder to your disposition? You talk of

Cleveland often. When she dies, Graham, you will be tied to where her body lies. Would not going home be better? You do not have to play the forlorn custodian of another. I will watch over her."

Graham stopped pacing.

"I do not require your obscene service. I require death."

"I cannot give you that, Graham, but if your mind reverses, my labor is at your disposal. In the interim, I suggest you sit by the St. John's wort in my wagon, it may help your cheerlessness."

"I am not cheerless. I am a nihilist," Graham muttered as his head reappeared.

Enton Blake walked away. Another crowd had gathered before his wagon after the railroad belled a shift change. Enton went from walk to swagger as he neared the unshaven clusters that stood before his stage and Hester's window.

Graham overheard the doctor say, in a voice the whole crowd could ear on, "Gentlemen, fellows, and friends, how may I interest you this afternoon?"

Graham stretched himself across the iron tracks. He stayed there until his entire body disappeared and pain rolled from his ears to toes.

Then he went to look in on Hester. He did not like when large groups of men surrounded her wagon.

Chapter Twenty-Six

WILLIAM HAD BARELY set himself in his favored chair before Sarah started in on him.

"William, you have to feed the child," she said from the door to his office.

Annie whined in the parlor.

"I fed Annie last night."

"You will have to feed her again."

"Do you realize, Sarah, that this is what a mother does? Feed her child."

"Don't you say that."

"What?" William stood, took off his frock coat, and loosened his cravat. He remained standing.

"Do not insinuate that I do not try."

Annie's mewling passed between the joined parlor and office wall. William looked at the mahogany paneling.

The downturn of William's lip was slight, but the frown was there. Sarah saw it under his mustache. She was fatigued. She did not sleep. She vomited practically every meal she forced down for the remorse of eating when her child wouldn't. Her hands had a tremor so much so that Sarah wouldn't hold Annie unless she was sitting down, for fear of dropping her. In the brief snippets that the child slept, Sarah called on doctors and midwives, she wrote hospitals and healers—no matter how tenuous their reputations, she even asked the advice of her ever prattling, never admiring mother-in-law on how to bring health to her child. No one's advisements worked.

Annie wouldn't eat.

"You are being an awful husband." Sarah threw Annie's crib shawl at William and walked away. The shawl fluttered a foot then fell.

William stooped to pick it up and followed Sarah into the hall. It was decided. He would have no rest. None. Absolutely none. A sick child. A fraught wife. A mountain of paperwork and Company notes to make order of and none of it, precisely none of it would get accomplished this evening. William was overtaxed. He could not pass his days dressing to the sound of Annie's cries, spending ten hours at the Company worrying about her, and then coming home to employ four hours fighting with Sarah. He could not take it anymore. He did not eat well. He did not sleep well. Nothing was well within his soul.

"And you are an awful mother," William said to Sarah's back as she walked past the stairs. He didn't mean to say it. But he did. He stood by his words.

Annie's yowling turned softer. She had heard her father's voice.

Sarah stumbled into the parlor. Her skin felt empty and heavy at the same time.

William followed.

A new wet nurse, an older woman of greying pecan hair, rocked Annie's cradle while she sat in a chair by the fire. Annie would not be calmed. She was hungry. She was very, very hungry. She wanted her father and food and did not understand why she couldn't have either.

"Do not walk away from me, Mrs. Winchester," William said.

"Do not call me that," Sarah said.

"What?"

"*Mrs. Winchester.* As if we were strangers. Do not distance yourself from me."

"Everything is about you, isn't it? I am home after working ten hours, and all there is in the world to talk about is you. A late dinner sits cold in my office. I had not one bite—"

"Dine, William." Sarah did not look at him. She looked at the wet nurse. "Take Annie upstairs." She didn't want the child to hear them arguing. William was not finished. Sarah could feel a lecture coming.

Annie shrieked when she saw her father. The fat one took her away from him.

The wet nurse kept her head down, went out of the parlor, and up to the nursery. Annie wriggled and wailed against her chest.

William watched them leave.

Sarah stared at the empty cradle.

"William, go. Eat. I will try to feed her."

"Eat? How am I supposed to eat when I come home to a starving child? Did you see her? Do you give a damn at all? Because she is withering away. Twenty days old and she looks like she hasn't eaten once."

"It is not my fault."

Sarah said it, but she didn't believe it.

"You are blaming our infant? Me? Whose fault is it?"

"You heard Dr. Ives, William. You heard him as clear as I did. You heard the three other doctors we opinioned. Annie has marasmus."

William took a step toward Sarah. They stood two feet apart.

"You have given up on her?"

"William, she doesn't digest."

"You haven't found what she likes."

"She doesn't like anything."

"You don't know that."

"I can't do anything."

"Except let her starve."

"William, you are being foolish."

William's palm met Sarah's cheek. He had not meant to. He'd never hit her before. He was unsure of how it happened. He didn't pause to reflect.

"I am a fool? You can't feed a child and I am a fool?"

Annie's muffled worries echoed down the stairs.

Sarah and William looked at the ceiling.

"Calm down," Sarah said. She touched her reddened cheek.

"You took more time decorating the damnable nursery with moldings than trying to feed her."

"William, you have to accept it."

"No."

"She is starving."

William grabbed Sarah by the shoulders.

"Shut your mouth."

He shook her and shoved her away.

Cort wandered into the parlor. He had heard yelling. He barked at William.

William glared at the mutt.

"That dog," William said.

"Cort has nothing to do with this."

Cort looked from William back to Sarah. Sarah was crying. He did not like to see his Sarah cry.

"You love that damn dog more than anything else."

"What are you talking about? What does Cort—"

"I will not have that mutt in my house." William went to grab the dog's collar. It shifted out of his reach and hid behind Sarah's dress.

"You are not getting rid of Cort."

Annie bellowed. Were her voice water, the waves would've rampaged through the nursery door, down the stairs, and into the parlor. Annie was hungry. So, so hungry. She wanted her father to feed her.

"Do you hear that," William yelled at Sarah. "You stand here with that mutt when you should be with Annie."

William reached behind Sarah and grabbed Cort's collar.

"What are you doing?" Sarah lurched as he pulled the dog past her. Her feet fumbled in her skirts. She had to steady herself against the fireplace mantle.

William dragged the dog to the front hall.

Sarah grabbed William's arm.

Annie's squall continued. The wet nurse frowned. She had not ever met an angrier babe.

"Stop it, William, stop."

Cort snarled and planted his paws. His nails dug into the cherrywood floors.

"This idiotic creature is a distraction."

They tangled in the foyer.

Sarah pulled William's arm back. Cort pulled his neck forward. William almost lost his grip. Servants watched from the kitchen door at the other end of the hall.

"William, you are hurting him."

"I don't care." He yanked hard. Sarah held firm.

Cort yawped. His neck was too short to turn and bite William's hand. He gnashed his teeth. William punched Cort in the eye. Cort snapped. He couldn't see out of his left eye. Crooked lines marred the wood where he'd been dragged.

"Stop!" Sarah said and repeatedly pounded on William's shoulder blades.

William pushed Sarah back. She tripped on her skirt and her temple hit the banister.

"Go feed Annie," William said. He dragged Cort to the front door.

Cort lost his traction when the foyer rug bunched up underneath him. He growled a much younger dog's growl. He turned his head to snap again.

William smacked the mutt's snout.

Cort snapped and twisted. Snapped and twisted.

Annie cried louder.

"Mrs. Winchester, feed my child!" William turned to face his wife. He held Cort's collar with one hand. The dog was half lifted from the floor.

There was blood in Sarah's curls.

"She won't have anyone but you, William."

Cort had had enough. He twisted and snapped and this time, he caught William's wrist.

William gave a surprised shriek.

Cort locked his teeth tight and did not let go.

William shook his hand.

Cort held firm.

William swung Cort at the banister.

Sarah screamed.

Cort's ribs cracked, but he did not let go.

"Stop!"

William swung the mutt again. This time after it hit the spindles, it released his hand.

Cort fell to the bunched-up rug.

Cort heard his Belle Hellion cry out. He could not see her. His insides felt loose. Cort snapped at William's ankle.

The housekeeper ran to the foyer. She had never, would never, interrupt a fight between the mister and the missus, but this—this sounded like murder. What Ruth saw was Mrs. Winchester slumped on the floor with Cort in her lap.

"Clean this up," William said to the housekeeper.

"Yes, sir."

Sarah tried to stifle the noises coming from her. She did not want to attract William's attention.

William went upstairs. He felt uncertain and tired.

Annie stopped crying when her father entered the room.

Downstairs, Cort wheezed. A blood bubble came out of his nose. His last thought was of catching candlebugs on the dread ship *Pandemonium* with his captain.

Sarah wiped the blood from her friend's nose and struggled to breathe.

CHAPTER TWENTY-SEVEN

NEW HAVEN, CONNECTICUT, 1866

A CROCHETED SHAWL was wrapped around Annie's cotton dress and emaciated form. Her cheeks were sunken. Her eyes closed. She looked twiggish. Her breath came at constrained intervals.

She lay in her cradle by the window.

It was invasively sunny.

Annie's mother looked outside.

Her father sat away from the light. Away from her mother.

Annie was disinterested. She did not care to be carried. She did not care to lie down. She did not care for the out-of-doors. For milk. For the maid. For sugar. For stories. For rattles. For rag dolls. She did not care for anything. Except her father.

Annie had not eaten in an age. Or she ate constantly and not a thing stuck to her. She could not remember. It did not matter. Her breath was short. Her insides suffered. She would not eat anymore. She had tried. It did not work.

A flap of skin itched in Annie's armpit. Her bottom was concave. Her thighs banged together like sticks. She hated dry skin. Shedding. Her eyelids flaked. Her mother drenched her in remedies. Annie's skin continued to peel and pull. Her stomach stayed empty. Nothing worked. Why bother with any of it?

But she did not want to leave her father. She would not leave her father.

Annie stopped breathing.

Sarah turned from the window and watched Annie's delicate chest rise, fall, rise, fall—and then Annie's chest did not rise again.

"William…"

William went to the cradle.

He did not look at Sarah.

Sarah did not look at her husband. She watched Annie's chest. Sarah concentrated on the pattern of the shawl. She willed her daughter's chest to rise, to twitch, to shift. Sarah's breath left her in large bouts.

"William," Sarah repeated.

William put his hand on Annie.

Nothing stirred beneath his palm.

Sarah could not manage to swallow enough air. She gasped and gasped and noticed a noise in the nursery. Someone was yelling. Who was yelling? She was yelling. She didn't know what she was yelling.

William bit his fist. He felt dizzy. He should smack Sarah. She was hysterical. He held his breath. His baby girl. His baby Annie. He stared at his baby girl. There was blood in his mouth. His knuckles hurt. He didn't know why his knuckles hurt until Sarah pulled his fist from his mouth. Red fingerprints marred Sarah's navy sleeves where William pushed her back.

Annie was less than two months old.

She was also not concerned with her death.

She was a shadow on the wall above the window.

She watched her mother. The woman opened her eyes. Closed her eyes. Leaned on the wall. Gulped repeatedly and let her mouth hang open. Her knees gave out. She slumped under the window.

Her father picked her up from the cradle. He was gentle. She did not like to see him sob. She crawled down the window. Down the wall. To the floor.

Sarah felt something move past her. Move over her. She saw nothing. She felt cold even though the summer sun pooled around her. Sarah did not remember standing up. They had to tell the family. She could not think. She closed her eyes and saw Annie. Annie not eating in the garden. Annie not eating in the kitchen. Not eating in the parlor. Not eating in the hands of nursemaids, sisters, friends, other mothers, servants. Sarah felt a pit of failure wider than a coal town could have dug, and then the walls of her failure caved in and Sarah swooned. She fell to the floor, hard, in front of William's feet.

William sat in the rocking chair with Annie in his arms.

Annie crawled to him. Over her mother.

Sarah convulsed.

William did not notice.

Annie sat next to her father's feet and watched him. He was a fine man. A handsome man. An accomplished man. He held her kindly.

Sarah woke. She was on the floor. The room was darker. It was late afternoon. The light had shifted. Her wrist hurt.

William had Annie on his lap. He did not move. He did not cry. He stared blankly at his child.

Sarah sat up. She reached for William's leg.

He jerked away.

"William, I. William—" Sarah could not finish a sentence. She reached for him again. Reached for Annie.

"Do not take her," he hissed.

"I would not do that," Sarah said. She reached for William.

William recoiled. The chair creaked backward. His face was the color of a worn gravestone.

Sarah felt far from her body. She was cold. Her child, cold. Her husband, cold. There was a rag doll in Sarah's hand. She had made it for Annie. She did not remember picking it up.

Annie crawled around her father's chair three times, then curled back up by his feet. She wasn't hungry anymore.

William did not know why he felt a surge of comfort, but he did. He stood and left the nursery.

Annie felt a tug and followed her father.

A breeze swept into the room. Sarah didn't feel it. Sarah didn't feel anything. She sat in the chair William had vacated. She smoothed the fabric on her lap. And smoothed it. And smoothed it.

Annie thought the morbid trappings amusing.

A boxwood and black ribbon wreath adorned the Winchesters' front door.

People filled the house. They wore black. Dull black. Shiny black. They had black fans, black shoes, black lace, black jewels. They brought flowers. Salt splashed from their eyes. It hurt when it hit Annie.

Her father bought her a casket. White velvet lined white lacquered wood. Annie loved velvet.

Sarah had picked it.

William had wanted silk.

Annie was pulled to where her father went. This suited her.

William noticed that since the death of his daughter, a continual chill wrapped around him. It suited him. Warmth was not acceptable when his child remained cold.

Men in black armbands passed Annie's casket. It was in the parlor. It rested on a discreet block of ice. Black crepe covered the melting tray. Flowers, garlands, and wreaths crowded the walls.

The neighbors blew their noses into black-bordered handkerchiefs. They talked of Annie. How small she was. How pretty she would've been. How elegant her white gloves and dress were.

Annie enjoyed crawling through the people. Sometimes they stepped through her. It did not hurt her person, but it made them shiver. Their legs shook. They excused themselves. Collected their wits in private. Wondered how a July house was cold. Why their stomachs turned sour. Annie felt older. Felt stronger. She could crawl and grab and yell and understand and she knew now the names of things. She learned. She listened. She blew out the candles by her casket. Servants clothed in mourning relit them.

Sarah sat in a chair. It was near the casket. She wore a black gown. It had a high collar. It itched. Isabelle had bought it for her, brought it to her. She had no other adornments. She gripped her hands over a black lap blanket.

William sat next to her. Sarah could not look up from her hands. Did not want to see the crepe. The silver and black mourning cards mounted on placards. Someone was talking. They would take Annie from the house. They would bury her daughter. She would bury her daughter.

Annie crawled to Sarah and cried at her feet. Because she could. Because she had a complaint. The white gloves and dress were atrocious. It did not matter that she liked her coffin if she did not like how she looked in the coffin.

Sarah looked from her hands to her shoes.

Annie cried louder.

Sarah saw nothing there. Heard nothing except the shuffling and mumbling of mourners.

Annie cried louder.

Sarah's feet were freezing. She felt watched. The cracks in her sanity shifted into chasms.

"William," she whispered.

William had not slept. He did not register his wife's voice. There was a dust storm in his head and a drought in his mouth.

Sarah gripped the sides of the chair and forced herself to look around.

No one else appeared as distressed or cold as she.

Annie batted at and pulled the bottom of Sarah's dress.

Isabelle put a hand on Sarah's shaking shoulder.

Sarah smoothed her skirt.

Family watched her. Friends watched her. The neighbors watched her.

Annie pulled harder.

Sarah jerked her skirt back and smoothed it out again.

Those around Sarah wondered where the breeze came from and why they didn't feel it.

Annie tumbled backward. She fell through passing mourners and chair legs and landed against the cast iron fireplace. She howled and could not see herself.

Sarah sobbed. She thought she heard, in a faraway fashion, her daughter cry.

Isabelle put her arm around Sarah's shoulder.

"Isabelle," Sarah said under her breath, "she is not gone."

"Shh. Shh, sister," Isabel said and held Sarah tighter.

William heard nothing. Felt nothing. Looked at no one except his Annie in her box.

Someone spoke of Heaven. The audience was attentive.

The gathered pitied Sarah. To lose a child, and not even six weeks old. Such a little thing. Would've been prettier if Sarah could've made her eat. Oh, it wasn't Sarah's fault, no, no one was saying that, but did you see that child? Withered away, wasn't it? Like a stick doll lost in summer, found in fall. What sort of mother couldn't get her babe to take even a little milk? What nursemaid did they hire? Didn't they check the woman's references? Doctor Ives said they tried everything. Poor William. He loved that little girl. Doted on her. And did you see Sarah at the service? Sobbing and shaking. Couldn't blame the woman, but she could've at least worn a veil.

The pastor, the undertaker, Sarah did not know who it was that talked. He'd stopped. Someone else said a prayer. Heads bowed.

Annie crawled out of the fireplace and to her father. She mewled at his feet.

For the briefest of moments, William thought he heard his child. But Annie was in a casket. He breathed in sighs. His shoulders were tight as twine.

Annie crawled, tugged, and coughed her way into her father's lap. William did not shudder. Did not shake. It was an unusual lack of reaction to the dead touching you.

The prayer ended.

William refused to let anyone else carry Annie's casket. He took her to a black coach with glass sides that two black horses led. Then he entered the second coach in the procession. Sarah entered after him, and though they were alone and William did not look at her, Sarah felt watched.

Chapter Twenty-Eight

Boston, Massachusetts, 1867

NATHAN GARLAN'S STAY beneath Wester Brothers' Rare and Fine was academically industrious, however infuriating. After half a decade of book-lined caves, lack of sunlight, and the Professor's tutelage, Wester Brothers' belched out Nathan the way a dog hacks up a chicken bone, quick and bloody.

Nathan was in the common room—a capacious cave lit by a skull-and-candle chandelier. Due to its unusual dryness, the room was where the Professor stored her most precious volumes. Carved stone shelves were so tall that a ladder could not reach the topmost, only a rope-waisted scaling would do. Nathan had been on such an ascent. He returned a two-hundred-year-old anthology of moon poems to the shelf. It was written by a woman named Rios in a baffling language fashioned after moss formations. A section of the stone his shoe was fastened onto crumbled. The wall did not avalanche out so much as inhale itself inward, sucking Nathan into it. He fell on his stomach. There was a minor collapse behind him.

Nathan had been eaten again. He knew this and it infuriated him.

Nathan could not kneel. There was no retreat back to the book cave. He could scarcely squirm forward. The tunnel was an incommodious, stale-aired affair, but at least there was a forward. The route before Nathan was tenebrous.

Tenebrous? Since when did he use words like *tenebrous?* Nathan, at times, felt like a grandiloquent bastard. He blamed it on the Professor.

A forlorn cave cricket with only one antenna crawled over Nathan's shoulder.

"Cricket," Nathan rasped.

"Chirp."

"Where are we?"

"Chirp."

"Are you familiar with an exit?"

The cricket dropped off Nathan's shoulder and matter-of-factly hopped into the dark. It hoped Nathan saw the disappointment in its egress. A man who knew ten living languages and three dead ones should know how to squirm forward out of a hole.

Nathan could either let the cramped quarters quicken his breathing until he keeled over, wherein he was certain that O'Neill would sniff him out and swallow his remains, or he could crawl forward.

"Wait for me, Sir Cricket," Nathan said. He inched his way ahead.

He spent many hours scooting forward across the rock and dirt. It was at least four because he was able to recite all 3,183 lines of *Beowulf.* And it must have been more than four because he was a book into the delivery of *Paradise Lost.* His clothes felt filthy and torn. His stomach empty. Nathan wanted to fall over for a nap when his knuckles hit something hard. He hadn't realized his eyes had been closed until he opened them to see light streaming between what looked like floorboards.

Robert Wester scratched in one of his ledgers with a large-feathered quill. One customer all day, and the woman had wanted to sell books, not buy, which was a waste of time because the one book in the stack Wester would've bought, an 1861 *Silas Marner*—which wasn't so much rare as it was popular, had a grape-colored stain on the orange-brown binding and smelled of cat piss.

Three knocks echoed in the store.

Wester held his pen in the air and looked around.

"Hello?" he asked.

Three more knocks rang out.

Wester got up from his stool and opened the front door. No one. He still had his quill in hand.

Three more knocks. This time they were aggressive, and if Wester reasoned rightly, they came from beneath the nature display. Wester shoved the table with his hip. Ronda helped Wester push the display then retreated to lean on the front door. It had been painted a loud green.

Three shy knocks vibrated beneath Wester's feet. Wester smiled, rubbed his bald crown, and said, "That you, boy?"

"Wester?" Nathan said. His voice was muffled and hoarse.

Wester hooted. "Hold on. I will pry you out."

A creaking and banging later and Nathan shot forth from the floor and threw himself at the bookman.

Wester caught the embrace and gave in kind. He held the boy out by his shoulders and gave him an appraising look.

"Got grown, did you now?"

Nathan was fifteen. He was as tall as Wester. His hair was long enough to tuck behind his ears. It was dark and had soft curls, calmer than his mother's.

There was a squeak.

Wester looked down to view the largest rat he'd ever seen, sniffing at his knee. Perhaps it was because he hadn't had dinner and his constitution was weak, possibly because his heart had been sluggish since the death of his wife, or maybe it was because of a blurry childhood memory of a rat gnawing on his wrist as he lay in his crib—whatever the cause, Wester felt his insides clench and the pressure beneath his breastbone shift. An ardent discomfort radiated from his arm to his jaw. His heart puttered, stuttered, and before it stopped, Wester thought, "I cannot go. I have a bookshop to run."

Wester's sweater tore as Nathan struggled to hold him. They fell.

The Professor exited from the hole. She looked at the two men on the floor.

Nathan began to cry.

O'Neill sniffed at Wester's knee.

"Child, I always find you at moments of tragedy."

Nathan looked up. "This is horseshit," he said while gulping air.

"Do not cuss."

"Professor," Nathan said.

"Yes?"

"This. Is. Horseshit."

O'Neill nodded.

Wester was not gone. His apparition stood behind Nathan. He was about to touch Nathan's shoulder when the Professor said, "Ah! No, do not proceed, sir." She knew the discomfort it would cause.

Wester stopped.

Nathan looked over his shoulder to see a blue-tinged bookman.

"Wester!"

"Boy, you can see me?"

Nathan nodded. He felt a great responsibility for Wester's death. If he hadn't have popped out of the floor...

"I am sorry—" Nathan started.

"For what?" Wester said, "You didn't create a Herculean rat or my weak heart, son."

O'Neill eyed Wester's specter.

"Robert," Ronda said.

Wester searched for the source of his name. His wife stood by the front door.

"Ronda?"

Ronda nodded her head.

"You've been here…" Wester began.

"I could not leave the books," she smiled and added, "…or you."

The two wrapped arms around one another.

Nathan wiped his nose on his sleeve. His clothes held the grime of his climb and he only muddied his face.

"Thought you would leave without a goodbye? Hmm?" the Professor said.

"I fell."

"Again?"

"Again."

"Inconsiderate to fall away from people. Take care to fall into someone, sometime. More enjoyable."

"I—"

"Still stutter. Unfortunate, isn't it?" The Professor smiled.

"What do I do now?"

"Anything you want, boy. Anything you want, but if you would have the advice of an old Professor, ask Robert Wester about his brother and make your way to his business."

"His brother?"

The Professor nodded. "Do not parrot. Be bold, Nathan. Be wild. Live fully."

"I will miss you."

"I demand you busy yourself with an educated life of aid and renown instead. Here."

The Professor handed Nathan two silver toads.

"What are these?"

"I taught you twelve languages and you would have me explain binding toads? Pointer: they are diagramed in an oversized leather tome you will not own until you are thirty. Page one hundred and eleven."

O'Neill chewed on Wester's knee through his trousers.

"You there!" Wester shouted.

"It's only a body, darling," said Ronda.

"O'Neill," the Professor said, "we must be going."

O'Neill snorted at this, but he stopped chewing. He trotted behind the Professor as she went down the hole.

"I will bury you properly," Nathan told Wester as he set the floorboards back in place.

"Much obliged, boy, much obliged."

"If I leave, what will happen to the store?" Nathan asked and looked around at all the beautiful books.

"Oh, this ship hasn't sunk," Ronda said, command filling her voice.

Wester looked at his wife. "The dead do not tend tills."

"Do not tell me what I can or cannot do. I have thought this through and through. We will run Wester Brothers' Rare and Fine as mail-order only."

A smile broke over Wester's face.

"It is a viable, profitable option," Ronda continued.

"I will assist in any way possible," Nathan said.

"Do not bother, Nathan," Wester said. "You've done all that was needed."

"But I killed you."

"Don't go softbrained," Ronda said. "You brought me back my husband."

"I should do more."

"You should make yourself scarce," Wester said.

"I—" Nathan started, but stopped as Wester and his wife began a furious kiss.

Wester Brothers' Rare and Fine shuddered a shushing floorboard at Nathan.

Perhaps, he would see what was in the pantry.

Chapter Twenty-Nine

New Haven, Connecticut, 1867

THE NAILS HAD cost Sarah a week's grocery money. William did not know and would not approve of the expenditure.

Annie was buried, but she was not gone. Sarah had tried to talk to William about this complication. The conversation was held before he left for work. Sarah thought well on William working. When he left the house, it felt as if Annie was gone, too. It made Sarah contemplate separation.

The conversation started with Sarah stuttering about besiegement and ended with William shouting, "*You would kill my child again?*" It was the closest they came to agreeing that Annie was still with them. They never spoke of their daughter's afterlife—even when Sarah woke with a pillow pressed onto her face, when scratches ripped through her stockings and into her calves, or when she tripped over an unseen barrier before the stairs.

Sarah did not want to hurt Annie. She wanted sanctuary. To this end, Sarah collected information on superstitions, charms, folklore, and the hereafter.

A visiting cleric mentioned the traditional belief that iron nails barred spectral entry to a room. The cleric had attended a house of worship in outer

Dublin whose entries were so cluttered with iron that the doorways and windows looked like rusted maws. The cleric assured Sarah that this was a ridiculously backwater belief. Everybody knew that it took only one iron nail per entryway to keep spirits at bay.

The day after Annie slammed the piano fallboard on Sarah's hands, Sarah bought iron nails.

Sarah watched as Evergreen's caretaker dug up the grave of a young man, a teacher. His mother sniffed on a bench. Sarah had paid for permission from the man's mother for the impropriety of harvesting nails from her son's coffin. Three nails were taken. Three iron nails from the recent grave of an honest man.

Sarah hammered the nails in the three entry points of her room—in the floor before the door and in both window frames. She set her hammer on her bureau and heard the front door open.

"I am home," William called out to no one in particular. A servant met him to take his jacket. Annie immediately crawled upstairs to see what her mother was doing.

Annie tried to enter her mother's room and screeched. She could not. She tried again. She thumped into an unseen wall.

Sarah wiped her hands on her skirts. Her room felt gloriously empty.

Annie was angry. She tried to cross the doorway a third time. Again, she could not enter. Annie chirped and hollered. It was insulting. A wall of nothing held her back.

Sarah was pleased.

Annie took her mother's slight smile as a challenge. She was not a silly child. She was not a stupid child. There were other ways. She tried to crawl through the wall. It did not work. She tried to crawl in the window. It did not work.

Sarah luxuriated in the solitude. She lay across her bed in relief.

Annie could not enter the room, but she could make noise around the room.

Sarah startled up from her pillow pile at a crash from the adjoining room. She ran to the guest room.

Her architectural journals fluttered to the floor. Fat gashes appeared in the bedpost. The fishbone fern was torn to flitters. Drawers were heaved out of place. A candle on a hall table near Sarah's hand sparked a blue flame and tipped itself over.

Sarah did not cry. She did not shout. The child could no longer shock her. She stomped out the flames. She'd have to nail every entry in the house.

A week later, Sarah had bought three buckets of iron nails. They weren't from graves. Perhaps they didn't need to be from graves. Sarah sealed the guest room and the kitchen. She did not believe she could do more than that without William's notice.

Annie did not need to be in the rooms to cause havoc. It was better to be inside the walls. That way she wouldn't have to look at her mother. The servants believed there were raccoons. Probably three families of them with all that warbling.

Sarah ordered every spiritualist weekly available, no matter if it was from Boston, Chicago, or London.

There had to be a way to communicate and force common decency upon her daughter.

CHAPTER THIRTY

BOSTON, MASSACHUSETTS, 1867

THE THEATER HAD blood in its mortar. Eyes plucked from the corpses of celebrated thespians were wrapped in stone and set into moldings at regular intervals. The cracked hearts of thirteen ingenious, unknown playwrights were buried in the foundation. The cornerstone was of Portland Brownstone, carved from the Connecticut earth by no less than three orators, one of which was crushed during transport. Chicken-footed gargoyles lounged on ledges. A relief of braided arms and pointing fingers bordered a sign that read:

WATCHBIRD THEATER

The letters had been carved by a small woman from a small country blessed with small nails hard as petrified wood. She made her way in the world by chiseling.

Nathan looked at the theater admiringly. There was a morbid elegance to the building. It intimidated and intrigued.

Before Nathan left Wester Brothers' Rare and Fine, Wester mumbled, "Arrol wouldn't give you a kick in the rear with your wardrobe, let alone a vocation. Buy a suit." He had shown Nathan the cashbox under the counter. Nathan patted the inside chest pocket of his new midnight blue frock coat. A crinkle alleviated his concern. Wester's letters were secure.

Nathan stood between two mismatched Corinthian columns and pulled the day rope. The rope was attached to a bell. The bell awoke Arrol Wester.

Nathan paced between the columns. The ghost of a fruit seller watched in appreciation. He'd not ever seen a frock coat that vibrant. Set off the young sir's dark eyes and hair, right it did.

Arrol Wester yawningly rolled his chair down a ramp, through a hall, took a left, and was at the Watchbird's front doors. If it wasn't hideous enough for his forty winks to be regularly disrupted by the living statue ladies bellowing at each other on what their next theme would be—*The Limber Jackals of Hades* or *The Winged Vixens of Fairyland* (personally he hoped for the former)—he was being woken up at the nonsensical hour of—Arrol pulled his watch from the vest he had unintentionally slept in—seven. He looked at the watch again. Who in the depraved palm of the Devil would get him up at seven in the morning? Arrol turned his chair around. He was not answering the door at seven. Back to bed. Three rolls down the way, the bell rang again. Then again. Then one more time.

"Don't ring that bell again," Arrol yelled.

The bell did not ring again. Nathan paced before the door.

Arrol tapped twice next to the entry. A five-inch panel dropped open and a small set of opal-plated opera glasses protruded. As Arrol pulled these to the bridge of his nose, a corresponding set of glasses dropped outside in front of the dark wood doors. The glasses were attached to inwardly mirrored pipettes. The ongoings out front could be seen without unlocking the doors.

Nathan stumbled back, startled by the sudden appearance of opera spectacles in front of him, far enough over his head that he could not touch them. The spectacles swiveled around Nathan, capturing a full view of his person.

A conical horn placed at the upper right corner of the doors verbalized. "What sort of rogue wears midnight blue and calls on a man at seven in the morning?"

The opera spectacles rotated to Nathan's right side and nodded up and down at him. Arrol admired the frock coat. The black buttons down the front and on the wide cuffs in combination with a subdued grey and black plaid vest gave the young man the appearance of a piratical, lunatic scholar.

Nathan blinked.

"You mute?" Arrol asked through the door horn.

Nathan opened his mouth to answer, but before he could, the spectacles pivoted to Nathan's left and the horn said, "No matter. Watchbird's not open. Come back this evening."

The spectacles lifted back to the ceiling.

"Is Arrol Wester available?" Nathan said before the spectacles completely tucked themselves away.

They dropped down, lower this time, eye level with Nathan.

Nathan stepped forward with a practiced, serious smile.

"Why do you want Mr. Wester?"

"His brother sent me."

"Who?"

"Robert, Robert Wester."

"How would you know Robert Wester?"

"It is a long account."

"What does Robert Wester want?"

"I would rather only discuss that with Mr. Arrol Wester."

"Mr. Arrol Wester is not available."

"When will he become available?"

"When he feels like it."

"Are you Mr. Wester?"

"Are you a debt collector?"

"No."

"Government man?"

"No."

"Ruffian?"

"No."

"You bring bad news."

"Yes."

"My brother ill?"

"No."

"My brother is dead."

"Yes."

"I am Arrol Wester. I do not wish to talk anymore."

The spectacles retracted.

"Sir, there's more," Nathan began, but stopped and rubbed the bridge of his nose. How do you tell someone that you carry two letters—one of recommendation, one of family news—penned by a dead man.

Nathan sat on his trunk.

Arrol Wester had his head in his hands.

"Who's at the door at seven in the morning?" Grimm asked. Grimm was near seven feet tall and the Watchbird's strongman.

Arrol blanched. "How do you walk that quiet with those elephant feet?"

"Sorry, darling. Who's out there."

"A young man."

"A young man?"

"From my brother."

"Why don't you let him in?"

"I am feeling cruel."

"You mad at Robert?"

"Yes."

"Why?"

"Bastard lives three miles off, hasn't been to visit in a year, then he sends this pup to tell me he's dead."

Grimm put a palm of concern on Arrol's shoulder.

Arrol petted Grimm's fingertips.

"He was a good man," Grimm said.

"That young man had the look of a secondary purpose."

"Ask him what it was?"

"I feel unwell."

"I could."

"No," Wester said and rolled away. He wanted his room. His pillows. Some tea. Sleep. His dishtub-dull brother to be alive. "I already know what he wants."

Grimm let his callused hand be tugged off of Arrol's shoulder. "What does he want?"

"A job."

"Eh?"

"Nobody is to feed or speak to him. No one is to acknowledge he is there. I will confront him in three days."

"Why three days?"

"If he's still here, he's desperate or talented enough to belong at the Watchbird," Arrol said and turned the corner.

For the rest of the first day, Nathan pushed his trunk to the corner of the recessed entry, sat on it, and did hand magic. People walked past. Occasionally, someone would stop and watch the young man in the shadowy entryway. Once every great while, someone would drop a coin into Nathan's bowler, which sat upturned in front of him.

Nathan flipped a shiny button from hand to hand. He caught the button. He disappeared the button from midair. Brought the button back, made two buttons appear in his hand. He opened and closed his palm and then there were three buttons. He shook the buttons in a closed fist, threw them to the ground, and it was three mice that hit the stones.

The Professor had kept him industrious, but five years under Wester's had also given him plenty of time to learn sleight of hand.

A dead man reading the paper on a nearby bench nodded appreciation for the demonstration.

Nathan smiled at him.

"Keep waiting, son, it'll be worth your while," the dead man said. He had dark circles under his eyes and the puckered appearance of someone who swallowed poison.

"Thank you, sir, I will."

By the end of the day, Nathan had three dollars in his hat. Double an honest laborer's wage.

The second day was not profitable. Nathan tired of gaining attentions for his dexterous hands.

He attempted entry to the theater like a normal patron, by payment for one of the twice-daily shows.

The woman who opened the doors and directed the line of persons to the ticket sales window in the foyer held her hand up to Nathan's chest.

"What you think you're doing?" asked a woman who barely came to his chin and looked older than Moses.

"Attending the theater."

"No."

"I will pay."

"No."

"I—"

"Will sit your fine fettle back in the corner."

"But—"

"Sit," she said with such force that Nathan did so immediately.

As people entered the theater, Nathan strove to contain his rage. He lost himself in *Essays: First Series* by Emerson, taking particular note of the passage entitled "Self Reliance." Wester had shoved it in his hands before he left the shop.

On the second day, Nathan learned that if he wrapped his legs tight underneath him and leaned on the wall, he could sleep tolerably well on his trunk. It was childish but comfortable.

On the third day, Nathan felt foul over being avoided. He felt foolish. He understood that Arrol Wester was a man in mourning. He understood that his own person was an unknown commodity to said proprietor. Nathan understood much, but he no longer had any patience with the situation. He was a serious man in a serious jacket. Aside from this, he had run out of apples and other foodstuffs pilfered from Wester's pantry.

He would make Arrol Wester take notice of him.

Midday, Nathan dragged his trunk to the edge of the cobblestone road. It was full of ladies on errands and men on their way back from lunch. An assiduous stream strode along with no intention to stop or attention to spare.

The opera glasses dropped in front of the door. Arrol swiveled them around until he found the young man near the road. He was remarkably clean for having spent much time in the out of doors.

Nathan stepped atop of his trunk.

"You, sir," Nathan shouted at a man in a brown double-breasted jacket.

The man kept walking.

A dead woman with broken fingers following the man muttered something to Nathan.

Nathan smiled at her. She smiled back, revealing broken teeth.

Nathan shared what the woman told him. "You, sir, stole laudanum from your pastor's quarters."

The man turned on his heel and rushed back at Nathan.

Nathan took off his hat and swooped it in the direction of his crowd of three. The barreling man observed the crowd, stopped short before he could push Nathan from his trunk, then slunk away.

Nathan turned to a woman coming down the road.

"Miss," Nathan said.

He reached into the ether and found a chittering whisper.

"Miss, you are the most beautiful man I have ever met," Nathan finished.

More people joined the crowd before Nathan. So did a carriage. All looked at the woman.

Her eyebrows raised and she put a surprised hand to her collarbone.

A man in the crowd winked at her. He added a nod to the hat shop. She ducked inside. The man followed. They would be married in the fall.

"Sir," Nathan said to the carriage driver, "may I have your hand?"

"I dunno about this," said the carriage driver, but he gave his hand anyways.

Nathan took off the man's glove and read his lifeline. It was long. He had not had much practice outside of the Professor and Wester.

"You will live until you are ninety-seven years old."

"How will I die?" asked the man.

Arrol counted a crowd of twenty standing around the young man. Twenty people stopped in less than three minutes. The young man had his consideration.

Nathan did not know how to read the future. He spoke with the dead and most of them only knew of what had already past. But it never hurt to ask.

Nathan brought his hands over his face and whispered to no dead person in particular, "Good friends, do any of you know how his life ends?"

Someone did, or said they did, and that was good enough for the here and now. Nathan heard the whisper but did not see from whence it came. He said to the man in the carriage, "You will steal a squash from your neighbor's garden. Her husband will hit you with a shovel. He will not mean to kill you."

The man put his glove back on. "Forty years left? Hit by a shovel?" The man didn't know what else to say. He left.

The crowd pushed forward to take up the empty space. The young man spoke with authority. Why, even his jacket popped with confidence.

Arrol's spectacles reached as far as their piping would allow.

"Who among you wishes to know of the dead?"

The crowd muttered loudly.

Business owners stood in doorways to see what all the fuss was about. The crowd was over fifty now.

"Do you have troubles?" Nathan continued.

The crowd murmured.

"Agitation, sorrow, tribulations?"

Ladies nodded at one another. Men mirrored the women. All mumbled congruently.

"Do you have inconveniences from this world or the shade beyond?"

A few street children stamped their feet in assent.

"Would you fix them?"

The crowd shouted, "YES."

People hung out of windows to see what was happening in the street.

"Come to the Watchbird Theater next week," squawked Arrol from the conical horn at the Watchbird's door.

Nathan bowed.

He stepped down and dragged the trunk back to the double doors. People looked at him warily, once he was eye level with them.

"Bring in your own things," said Arrol.

The spectacles cranked back up.

The crowd dissipated.

The Watchbird Theater's doors creaked open.

Nathan had the help of the dead to shift his trunk into the theater.

Arrol watched. "You move those with your mind?"

"No."

"How?"

"Apparitional assistance." He nodded gratitude to the two ghosts who had lifted the trunk into the theater.

"Fancy," said Arrol Wester. He was not much impressed by anything anymore.

"What exactly do you do?" Arrol asked.

"I talk to the dead."

"And?"

"Card tricks, sleight of hand, miscellaneous bits."

Arrol rolled back and forth before Nathan. The hall was wide enough for two strokes of his wheels each way.

"What do you mean when you say you talk to the dead?"

"I mean, I talk to the dead."

"You do not pretend to talk to the dead?"

"No. I talk to the dead."

"Would you call yourself a showman?"

"Not yet."

"What are you?"

"Highly skilled, unengaged, and willing to learn."

"You would work here?"

"Yes."

"What is your name?"

"Nathan Garlan."

"How long did you know my brother, Nathan Garlan?"

"I've loved his bookshop longer than I can remember."

"How did you know him?"

"I lived underneath the Rare and Fine."

"Underneath?"

"Underneath."

"The Rare and Fine let you leave?"

"Pushed me out after five years."

"Your first performance will be in one week. From then on you will have one or two shows a day from Thursday through Sunday, usually in a variety act setting. Sufficient time to advertise and organize yourself, yes?"

"Yes," Nathan said, terrified. A performance. A performance in one week. Then many more. He had no idea what he would do on stage, let alone how to beat the drum for it.

"All those that perform at the Watchbird are guaranteed a room in her. If you find a space, you can have it. There are more rooms than meet the eye. If you have other arrangements that is fine."

Nathan nodded. "I will stay here, Mr. Wester."

Nathan pulled the letters out of his pocket and handed them over.

Arrol took them without looking at what they were and tucked them inside his vest.

"Get to know the walls," Arrol said. "They'll want to know you." Arrol petted the stained wood and the wallpaper above it.

He rolled down the hall and Nathan was left alone.

Nathan looked around. There was a door in the wall somewhere. A door and a hidden room, the dead talked about it.

Nathan walked the opposite direction that Arrol Wester rolled. He touched every lamp, chandelier, and door knob. Broadsides of upcoming performances lined the hall in gilded frames.

BALLAD OF THE GRAVEDIGGER, A ONE ACT PLAY IN SONG!

THE WANTON WOMAN'S REVUE: LYSISTRATA REDISCOVERED!

ATHLETICISM FOR HEALTH AND SPORT: LECTURES BY THE WORLD'S STRONGEST MAN ACCOMPANIED BY THE FATTEST FIDDLER ON THE EASTERN SEASHORE!

Every step in the Watchbird brought astonishment. Ghosts were high and low, but none of them were frenzied. They acknowledged Nathan as he passed by and told him of the theater. The brassy screws that held firm skeleton-armed lighting sconces were stolen from a disreputable undertaker.

Nathan turned down another hall and an Egyptian stone of questionable cabalistic import displayed a vase whose roses never died. Velvet curtains that deluxified archways were filched from a French scientist's laboratory.

Nathan stopped by a sconce. He felt an itch. The dead whispered more powerfully at him. He pressed his foot against a worn wood panel that lined the lower half of the wall.

A door sprang open.

The Watchbird Theater sighed a breeze of approval at Nathan. The door opened wider.

Nathan looked inside. Two small rooms connected to each other by a small hall. Each had high, barred windows. It was practically a suite.

The dead at the Watchbird Theater whispered to Nathan that he was home.

Chapter Thirty-One

Boston, Massachusetts, 1869

HENNET WAS A sorry sonofabitch, sitting on a wood cot in the Suffolk County Jail. He was twenty days into fifteen years. Twenty days. It was the longest he'd ever spent behind steel. Wasn't no small-town stockade either. No backwater Bastille. No jail tree. It was eight by ten steps of granite in a Massachusetts fortress. Hennet'd heard tell on penitentiaries. Big-time holders with elegant locks, thick bars.

He'd have to sort out at least ten guards, five doors, and a wall taller than Goliath to get out. Impossible.

Not that any of that stopped Hennet from trying.

His efforts hadn't worked worth a piss-soaked bread loaf. Hennet's hands were cracked and callused. His back was sore. He hated Walleye more than ever before.

His predicament was Walleye's doing. Hennet didn't make a custom of faulting others for his own flaws, but he would've gotten out of the First Holy Temple of Spiritual Discourse without the fire and five deaths if it hadn't been for Walleye.

Hennet heard about the First Holy Temple through *The Boston Recorder*. Paper said that there was a tiny gal there named Nida Nay. Black hair. Big eyes. She had the power to talk to God or the dead or whoever. People built a church around her in Massachusetts.

Hennet hadn't arranged for a meeting. He wasn't good on planning. He was good on showing up. When Hennet appeared at the First Holy Temple of Spiritual Discourse, the last meeting of the day had recently let out. A small lady and a small crowd prayed by an altar.

Hennet walked into the room and candles lit themselves in the sanctuary. Rather, Walleye lit them. It gathered the gal's attention. Her congregants stood protectively around her. They did not like this striding fellow.

"May we help you?" asked a woman with secrets. She had tattoos on her shoulder, wrist, and foot.

"That the lady from the *Recorder*?"

"Yes, but you will have to make an appointment. It is late," the woman with secrets said.

Nida Nay gave Hennet a formidable glare. She had a schedule. She did not care he could light candles mysteriously. It clearly said on the sign out front to make an appointment. It was always men who thought she'd make an exception for them. She turned to a door. She'd wait in the office until he left. The group stood as a shield.

"I didn't come all the way here to be told to come back later," Hennet said.

The group of four congregants didn't acknowledge him. The office door shut. Hennet pulled out his six-shooter and shot the ceiling. The congregants gasped. Nida Nay opened the door.

"Sir, what do you expect to accomplish here?" she asked.

"You will sit down with me. You will answer my questions and then I will leave."

"Why should I?"

"Who do you want me to shoot first?" Hennet pointed the gun at the woman with secrets.

"That is unnecessary, you brute. Sit down."

The sanctuary was small. It held a table fit for about ten. Rings of pews surrounded it. Hennet sat down at the table. So did Nida Nay's four followers. They joined hands. Miss Nay walked around the table. Walleye strutted after her.

"Can you get rid of my dead brother?" Hennet asked. He refused to hold the hand of the person next to him.

"We communicate, not exterminate."

"What the hell does he want?" Hennet asked. "I've been trying to shake him off for years."

"What is his name?"

"Walleye."

Nida Nay wanted to go to bed. It had been a long day.

"Walleye?" she questioned the room.

Walleye walked up to her.

The group of spiritualists felt the air cool.

Hennet noticed several gold-plated candlesticks to take on the way out.

"Walleye?" she repeated.

"What?" Walleye asked.

Nida Nay didn't hear a response so much as feel ants crawl in her bones.

"Why are you following this man?" Nida looked at the ceiling while she talked.

"Stuck," Walleye said.

She shook her head. She didn't hear anything.

Walleye tried a different route. He took Hennet's knife, cut Nida Nay's hand, dipped his finger into her blood, and wrote "STUCK" on the tabletop. His "k" was backward.

The followers fell away from the table.

Nida Nay wrapped her hand. She remained calm.

"Says he's stuck. Get out."

"My dirty ass, he is," Hennet mumbled. "Can you send him away?"

"No."

Sounded to Hennet like she was truth-tellin'.

Walleye was bored. He juggled two candles in one hand.

Nida Nay's followers fled. It wasn't right that they'd bolt when he was juggling for 'em. Walleye dropped the candles and ran to shut the doors.

The flame spread wild when it hit several bunches of dried herbs and silk. Nida Nay unsuccessfully tried to smother the fire. Hennet knew when a fire'd go big. He kicked out a black-curtained window and was gone before it grew.

As Hennet rode away, he looked back to see the silhouette of the First Holy Temple of Spiritual Discourse fully aflame under the moon. It wasn't far from the main thoroughfare. A bucket brigade stood before it. A smaller batch ran the direction of the sheriff.

Hennet clicked at his horse to move faster.

The posse caught him two hours later as he stopped to piss on a pine.

Goddamn everything, was what Hennet had come to realize while sitting in his cell at Suffolk. Goddamn everything. Well, almost everything. The judge could've hanged him, but he hated spiritualists. Seeing the church burn made the judge smile and he gave Hennet fifteen years of labor instead.

Chapter Thirty-Two

New Haven, Connecticut, 1870

SARAH STOOD IN the parlor by the lit fireplace. She held a box. It fit in the palm of the hand and was wrapped in brown paper. It was a wonder the post carrier could read the minuscule print. It smelled of forest. Rain. A tinge of decay. The return address listed THE REVEREND! DOCTOR! ENTON! BLAKE! The back said GUARANTEED! across the fold.

Sarah felt the betrayer. She wanted Annie confirmedly expired. Gone away. Departed. It had been four years of the breathless, bloodless child tormenting her. Four. Dunkings were common in the bath. Knives, pins, needles, forks, fireplace pokers, and paperweights had been flung at her person. All of her clothing was torn or stained near the hems. She trained herself to hold handrails. It was expected that she would wake with bruises, cuts, and bite marks.

William barely spoke to her.

The dark circles under her eyes and wisps of grey in her brown curls made her appear further than her thirty.

The whole of the family thought her unhinged. There were wary looks and whispers, but they had not yet sent her to a home, and Sarah counted that as a victory. The child would have her dead within days if she went to an asylum that did not allow her salt.

Salt was Sarah's respite. Salt in her pockets, salt around her bed, salt-soaked ribbons tied about her head. The salt made Annie feel distant, less forceful. The salt worked when Annie forced herself through the iron.

The box in Sarah's hand made her feel wild. She was emboldened but held reasonable expectations. Many fixes had previously failed her. Blessed nails, exorcists of five different faiths, six distinctive prayer languages, sage spread by spiritualists, shining bright candles to ill-lit corners while declaring in a firm voice of her expectations of an unearthly egress. None of it worked.

But still, this might. Sarah had read of Enton Blake for decades. There were always positive testimonials about him in the paper. She even had an aunt, no, it was a cousin, yes, a cousin whose asthma had been relieved by one of his health cures.

Sarah tore the brown paper off the box.

William walked into the room. Annie followed him. Sarah saw only her husband. A wind furrowed his trousers at the shins. Sarah looked at the window. It was closed. She looked at the fire. The flames did not stir. She looked at her copy of *The Subjection of Women* lying open on Barnum's new autobiography, *Struggles and Triumphs*. The pages did not stir. Annie was in the room.

Sarah moved her hand behind her back. She tried to step on the packaging paper.

Annie crawled to it and blew it upward.

"What is that?" William asked and pointed to the paper floating down to Sarah's feet.

"What?" Sarah asked.

Annie watched her mother. The woman's shoulders slouched and she scratched her nose. The woman was about to lie.

"Mrs. Winchester, the paper. What is it?"

"I received a small package from Isabelle," Sarah lied.

"And?" William did not look at Sarah. He scanned the Company papers in his left hand.

Annie circled to the back of her mother. She pawed the woman's dress. Sarah felt something push her calves. She had been attacked so often by Annie that she no longer felt an immediate revulsion at the child touching her. Annie climbed. Sarah stumbled forward. Annie bit into Sarah's shoulder.

Sarah gave a small screech and fell into William. He dropped his papers and caught his wife. His eyes went to the box in her hand, not the rip at her collar. The outside of the box had a carving of a delicate specter with X's for eyes.

He shoved Sarah away.

Sarah caught herself on a mustard and mahogany armchair.

"Again? Again you would do this?" William growled.

Annie climbed up the chair and batted at her mother's hands.

William noticed his wife's hands shake.

Sarah stepped away from the chair. Away from Annie.

"Yes," she said. Sarah felt her purpose fully. She would survive her child's death with or without William's help.

Annie climbed from the sitting chair to the fireplace mantle.

William grabbed the box from Sarah's hand.

"Give it back."

William held the box to his shoulder's height and examined the ugly thing. It smelled like a pond.

Sarah reached for it. She was aggravated with her abbreviated stature.

"William, give me that box or I will ask for a divorce. See how well the Company does then," Sarah said and tried to reach higher.

Annie crawled around the mantel and into the fire. The flames whooshed upward when Annie rolled in.

Sarah glanced at the fireplace. Maybe she would wall it up. She had never liked it. Perhaps smash it to bits and put a door there. A door to the garden. It would be unusual, but what did she care of what the neighbors thought? She was already mad in everyone's eyes. She might as well be able to view her daisies while she read.

"I will not allow you a divorce and I will not allow this in my house," William said. He looked at the tiny, immoral box. He and Sarah had been given a gift. He could not see Annie. He could not hear her, but he knew she was there. Annie was with him and William wanted her to stay.

"If this works—" William started.

"Annie will be banished for hours on end," Sarah finished.

Annie blew embers at her mother's dress. None caused more than a scattered ash patch.

"Why would you have her gone?"

"William, don't play the fool."

"It is only ever minor harm."

"Minor harm," Sarah said. "Minor harm? Does this look like *minor harm*?" Sarah rolled her sleeves. There were contusions and mouth marks from wrist to elbow of her left arm. Scabbed scratches on the right.

"You could have done that yourself."

Sarah's breath caught. She didn't know what to say. She didn't say anything. She threw the decorative pillows from the mustard chair at William. She threw *The Subjection of Women*, then a framed portrait of their wedding day. Then she threw her wedding ring.

William ducked at the assault and dropped the box in shock.

A servant poked her head in the parlor, saw the fireplace over-flaming and the mister and missus in combat and ducked back out. It would be best to clean after the disturbance was over.

Annie crawled for the box. Sarah lunged for it first. William tried to boot it away and only succeeded in kicking her hand. Sarah cried out. Annie rolled onto her stomach and laughed. Sarah grabbed the box then crab-walked backward into the corner.

"I cannot care for you if you force her to leave," William said.

Sarah did not look at him. "You have not cared for me since she died."

Annie crawled up the chimney and slid back down. She landed at her father's feet.

Sarah opened the box. There were three smooth stones. She was to concurrently burn them in the three rooms of most disturbance. One for the parlor. One for her bedroom. One for the garden. A garden could count as a room, could it not? Preferably, the three locations would form a triangle.

"You will not do this, Sarah."

"Tie me to a chair and shove me in the fireplace if you want to stop me," Sarah said and got to her knees.

Annie thought on her mother burning in a fire. It was a pleasing thought.

William towered over Sarah. He would have those stones. They looked cultic. It would hurt Annie.

Sarah scrambled between his legs. She threw one stone in the fireplace. The flames licked forward. Annie did not scream. Did not feel a thing.

Sarah tried for the door.

William grabbed her dress from behind and halted her progress.

The servants on call listened from the kitchen door.

"You would not make me do this," William said.

"What? Would not make you do what?"

William grabbed Sarah's wrist. Idiotic, magic rocks. Ludicrous. But still William grabbed Sarah's wrist. Her hand tightened around the two remaining stones.

Annie grabbed her mother's dress and shook it.

The bottom of Sarah's dress tore.

"Give them to me," William said to his wife.

"No."

"Give them to me, Mrs. Winchester." He tried to pry her fingers apart.

It was Sarah's kicked hand. It began to swell.

Annie climbed up Sarah's fraying dress.

"You will not hurt her," William said.

"She is already dead."

Annie hugged her mother's belly. She melted through it and fell out of Sarah's back. If any other life could have come from Sarah, it would not now. Sarah violently gasped.

William let go and pushed her away. Sarah hit the banister in the front hall. The two remaining stones spilled from her fist.

"You would lose me, Sarah."

William looked at his wife and the two stones.

"You would lose me," he repeated.

Sarah nodded and bent over to pick up the stones.

William pictured keeping his child and disappearing his wife. He could bury the woman with her precious stones in the garden. But this, too, was ludicrous. He was not a murderer.

"I will not take part in this," William said.

"I wouldn't ask you to."

William walked out of the parlor. Annie followed.

Sarah limped up the stairs to burn a stone in her bedroom. She would go to the garden last. Perhaps there would still be a breeze and light to read by.

The next day the stones were burnt to char. The air in the parlor, Sarah's bedroom, and the garden held an alley stench that the servants didn't know how to clear.

Sarah peered out of her doorway. The house was quiet. William was in his study. She looked up and down the hall. She saw and felt no harbingers of Annie. No breeze, no gashes appeared along the walls, no stains on the floorboards, no weight at her waist or on her shoulder. Sarah allowed herself the briefest of smiles. She allowed herself to contemplate a glowing note to the Reverend Doctor Enton Blake for making her life, once again, livable. She would plan a banquet. It had been ages since she'd entertained. There would be lace cookies and apple custard tarts and she would hire musicians and—

The hair on the back of Sarah's neck stood up.

A crash came from behind her. Sarah turned in time to see her copy of *Struggles and Triumphs* be flung at a vase.

Sarah put salt around her bed and climbed in. She would have to remind the servants not to sweep the salt away.

Annie repeatedly hit her face against a bed table. If she could not climb to her mother, she would shake the world around her.

Enton Blake sat on his wagon and looked through his prescription logs. "Mr. Johnson," Blake called.

Graham Johnson walked to Enton's wagon and leaned on it. "Yes?"

"Mr. Johnson, I wholeheartedly appreciate your efforts to my business."

"You're welcome."

"I was not done, Mr. Johnson."

"Huh?"

"Did you fill this order?"

Graham Johnson looked to where Enton Blake pointed.

"Yes."

"And why did you send Stink Stones to a patron requesting Fade-Away Stones?"

Graham scratched his chin. "I, uh, I was not paying attention."

Enton Blake's smile became strained.

"Mr. Johnson, you are hereby banned from helping me fulfill orders until you are otherwise noted. The only order you may fulfill is if this woman writes us again requesting a full refund, which you will give her, in addition to the stones that will decrease whatever spectral disturbance she is encountering. Is that clear?"

"You don't have to get high and mighty about it."

Enton Blake stared down from his wagon seat at Graham Johnson.

Graham Johnson blushed.

Enton closed his prescription log.

Several states away, Sarah despaired. She was done. It was done. There was no way to get rid of her child. She did not want to be a disheveled hysterical woman, but she did not see much choice in the matter. She would exist as cleanly and quietly as she could, doing good where she could.

Sarah put a pillow over her head and tried to ignore the bed shaking.

CHAPTER THIRTY-THREE

BOSTON, MASSACHUSETTS, 1870

WITHIN THREE YEARS of Nathan's first appearance at the Watchbird Theater, he became the most exalted medium in Boston. He was popular with the posh and the proletariat. The mayor, Nathaniel B. Shurtleff, scheduled a private encounter with Nathan. The meeting was brief and held in the theatrical hall of the Watchbird. It redoubled the renown of each individual.

"Young man," the Democrat said to Nathan as he climbed the stairs to the stage.

"Sir," Nathan said and stood up to shake hands.

"Sit down, man, sit down."

The two retreated to a table in the middle of the stage. A thick candle, two glasses of water, and a small plate of sandwiches dominated the space.

Nathan brushed off his velvet lapels. He had bought a black velvet jacket for the mayor's visit. He wore it with a shirt he imagined Keats would've longed for.

The mayor lit a cigar and did not notice Nathan's shirt or jacket.

"Don't mind, do you?" the mayor said as he blew the first breath of smoke out.

"Not at all," Nathan said as he watched the smoke drift through an unnoticed, deceased lackey at the mayor's elbow. He did mind, but he didn't care to argue.

"What is it you do?" the mayor asked.

"I bring satisfaction to quandaries concerning the dead."

"Christ and the tree, Garlan, I don't want to contact the dratted dead. Ghosts, gods, augury, all of it—hogwash. You, Mr. Garlan, have your name in the paper. I want my name in the paper. Constant publicity, that's my motto."

The mayor leaned back in his chair and tapped his cigar.

The Watchbird did not appreciate the ashes between its boards.

"Is there anyone you've lost, Mayor Shurtleff? Anyone you wish to talk to, no matter how long gone?" Nathan had other things to do. A meeting at the bank. A lunch engagement. Two evening shows. He did not have time for hobnobbing, but Arrol had been adamant. If Nathan did not want to find his closet in tatters or smoldering, he would befriend and impress the mayor.

"Anyone?" the mayor asked.

"Anyone."

Nathan wiped ashes off the table.

The usual horde of Watchbird spirits puttered about. Two dead bawdy dancers sat with their dirty stockinged legs dangling over the stage. A gaggle of expired actors sat at tables on the checkered floor. More roamed the balcony seating. The living workers of the Watchbird spied from the balcony and didn't notice anything more than the occasional draft. Old buildings and whatnot.

The mayor made a show of thinking. He tilted his head back and looked at the silver tin ceiling. He scratched his beard and sucked on his teeth.

"Well, Garlan, I can think of no one. I am not a man of other worlds, other ways. I have barely enough time to fix here and now."

The spirit behind the mayor was a man round-abouts forty with a large belly and an expensive suit. He tipped a bloody bowler at Nathan. He looked like he'd been kicked in the face by a horse. He had. Nathan nodded at him.

"Sir," Nathan said to the mayor.

"Yes, Garlan?"

"I will not waste your day. We are here to be photographed together. You to appear with an open mind and ideologically fashionable. I to appear in good company. Let us smile at the cameraman."

"I admire your enlightened appreciation of time," the mayor said.

Nathan and Shurtleff turned with serious, friendly faces toward the camera. The camera was erected far enough back to capture not only the men but the foot lamps and stage curtains.

"Gentlemen, on the count of two," the cameraman said.

The mayor and Nathan nodded in unison.

"One. Two." A light flashed. Something popped. "Thank you. I will reset the plates for a second exposure."

"Always with a second. Never let the first one be," the mayor muttered to no one in particular. He was not fond of photographing sessions.

The fat, dead man wondered if he would be in the picture. He would but as an unexplainable luminous column behind the medium and the mayor.

"Mayor, did you know, or have in your employ, a rotund gentleman fond of bowler hats?"

Shurtleff cocked an eyebrow at Nathan. "What if I did?"

Nathan looked at the fat, dead man.

"Tell 'im it's Handie," the large man said.

"Was his name Handie?"

The mayor went white.

"Sir, are you alright?"

"Tell 'im ain't to worry, Handie's at his back."

Nathan said, "Handie would like you to know he is 'at your back.'"

The mayor's eyes went large.

"Gentlemen," the photographer called out. "At the call of two."

The mayor, Nathan, and Handie looked forward.

There was a flash of light and a pop.

"Garlan," the mayor said.

"Yes, mister mayor?"

"You are not a charlatan, are you?"

Nathan shook his head. "No, sir."

"Noted. Respected. Tell Handie I appreciate his assistance, as usual, in all things. That I miss his Saturday-evening humor over a pint."

Handie nodded.

"He heard you, mister mayor."

"I'll be off then," the mayor began.

"I would like one more plate," the photographer called out as the mayor stood.

"No."

"I believe the mayor is late for another appointment," Nathan said. "I am sure one of those two prints will be sufficient."

The photographer nodded. Frowned. Did not collect his materials.

"Garlan," the mayor said.

"Yes, mister mayor, sir?"

"I appreciate your talents. I appreciate Handie. But I have time only for the things of here. The problems of now. I do not have time for chickenheartedness and horror—both of which I feel in your presence. We will not meet again."

"Understood, mister mayor."

"Good day," the mayor said as he clomped down the stage stairs. Handie followed.

"Mister Garlan," said the photographer, a man of spectacles and plaid.

"Yes?"

"May I have another plate of you alone? Perhaps a relaxed pose? For a carte de visite?"

Garlan nodded. Arrol would want a cut of the proceeds from the photographic calling card, but some capital was better than none. He sat on the edge of the stage between two lit foot lamps. The dead whispered to him to raise his hands. He did.

When the photographer developed the plates there was a small orb glowing above Nathan's right hand and a large one glowing above his left. The medium had tousled hair and a beguiling smile.

It did not take long for Nathan Garlan to become the most well-known medium in America. As Nathan's fame grew, so did his worry. There was always someone out there who wanted more than he could give.

Nathan took up boxing, fencing, and better cultivated his friendships with the dead. He doubted that his mother was still alive, but if she was, this time he would be stronger than her and have more violent friends.

Nathan became prepared for every occasion. Every occasion except falling in love.

Chapter Thirty-Four
Eastern Rhode Island, 1872

HESTER SLEPT FOR ten years. During this decade, Graham Johnson abhorred life. His time was evenly divided between three exertions: nursemaid, white knight, and self-slaughter.

Hester's complexion was waxy. She had sores on her heels, backside, and shoulders. The skin had thinned, pinkened, and rolled back to form small, red flesh ponds. Graham could do nothing about these, but he moved Hester's limbs daily so that they would not atrophy completely. He shifted her into different positions so none of the sores ever rubbed the pallet long enough to reach bone. He touched her with such frequency that her body no longer got the dead shivers. She'd lost her curves. She emitted a rain-rotted bread smell.

The Doc thought Hester never able to walk again, if she woke at all.

"It's only with your daily administrations that she might have the use of her upper body," Blake had said. Graham knew these words exactly because he had written them down. Transcribing them did not make him feel any better or miss Hester any less.

For ten years, Graham waited. Sopping wounds and waste was not the arousing afterlife he had anticipated.

When not attending to Hester's unspoken needs or averting disasters to her person (such as a near beheading, an iron mask, and a handkerchief choking), Graham drank arsenic and gin from a tin cup stolen from a Baptist exorcist.

Self-destruction was a habit Graham started five years into Hester's dormancy.

He was lonely.

He was bored.

He didn't want to spend the next fifty years as Hester's wall of Jericho. He had failures enough notched into his belt without adding the seven-day walk around and trumpet sound that would eventually knock her out. She would die. Who had an inkling what would happen to him when she did? He couldn't envision haunting an atrocious, provincial churchyard filled with posies and prudes or dawdling about a rock pile protecting the remains of his rotting rose. It was equally inconceivable to live without the minimum of her bones to argue with.

He wanted everything over with. He wanted the Something After.

Graham ate rattlesnakes found on the graves of holy wanderers. He stood before trains, but he quickly recovered. He lay in the way of carriages. He finally found a pack of wild dogs, but they refused to aggress against him. A supernatural strongman agreed to break his neck, but Graham's head righted itself in a day. He stepped off rooftops. He slept in painful salt wraps. He set himself aflame on altars while judgmental, white doves shat through him from the rafters. He hung himself from a bridge with rope stolen from a riverboat revival. No matter how he tried—banshee brawl, trough drowning, iron saw— Graham Johnson could not kill himself. Yes, he was already dead, but he wanted to be irrefutably, authentically departed.

He missed his domineering Delilah.

Wilting. Vulnerable. Sweating. She would not have wanted him to toss her urine pots. She would not have wanted him to bathe her daily. She would not have wanted food poured down a tube in her neck. Yet here he was, and there she was, and there the Doc was deriving dollars off it all.

Graham sat in Hester's wagon with his journal on his knees. He had almost finished his autobiography, *The Astonishing, Absurd, and Romantic Adventures of the Mad Medium Hester Garlan and her Allegiant, Apparitional Adonis Graham Johnson*, but his fortitude was lacking. No one would read it. Most likely, it would disappear with him.

His last entry was short its last sentence. Graham held a quill. His memoirs wouldn't rival Defoe's *Plague Year* or even Pepys, but they would be done, and when they were, he'd murder his love. Then he'd search for his second death. Graham would allow the Doc to unclasp him from Hester's form. He'd drag himself across the world to find someone who could give him a true death. Before they did, he would write volume two of his recollections, *The Lamentable Crusade of a Melancholy Specter: Essayist, Libertine, and Cosmopolitan, Graham Johnson's Quest to Attain his Authentic End*.

Graham put the nib to parchment. He wrote the last sentence. He closed his journal, wrapped it in a sash smelling of cinnamon, and laid it to the side of Hester's bedroll.

Graham grabbed a ten-inch Bowie knife by its amber stag handle.

Hester lay on her back. Her eyes were closed. Her chest rose and fell. There was a slight sneer on her lips.

Graham sat with his knees astride Hester's chest. He debated stabbing her in the bosom. He could slash her throat. He could cut deep her wrists. He could slash the vein in her upper thigh. Graham tried to cipher what way Hester would most want to die. Fast. No fuss. That's what she'd want.

Graham leveled the blade to Hester's throat.

And almost pissed himself.

It was a function he no longer had, but nonetheless he felt a pelvic pressure.

At the first nip of the blade, Hester blinked.

The Bowie fell from Graham's hand into the space between Hester's arm and ribs.

Hester's shoulders twitched.

"You ugly button," Graham said. "Flutter those lashes again." He was crying. They were bluish tears with the consistency of sap.

A din kin to wet wood busting wheezed from Hester.

She felt worse than the morning after a seven-bottle-six-sailor Yorktown spree. She tried to roll onto her side but could not. There was a weight on her chest. There was pain in her everything. She couldn't open her eyes. She couldn't do a damn thing. It felt like she'd been asleep for a horse piss of an age.

Graham leaned his face an inch from hers.

She felt something above her. For a moment, Hester thought when she opened her eyes she would see a strong-shouldered, brown-eyed outlaw.

"Wake up," Graham said.

Hester did nothing. The voice was not his voice. She would still know that cocksure bastard's voice. She made no sound. She kept her eyes closed.

"Wake up, you pallid, pretty meatlump."

With considerable effort, Hester opened her eyes.

Graham startled back.

"I am up," Hester said to the air. Her voice was husky and cracked.

"Hester?"

"Get off me."

"You are awake. I told you to arise, and thereby you have risen."

"Off. Shove off," Hester said in a whisper. The low tone was all she could expel. She tried, unsuccessfully, to lean on her elbows. "I can't feel my legs."

Graham rearranged himself to Hester's right side.

"They are still attached, darling, but assumably useless. Apologies." Graham felt each limb a deficiency to his tenacity.

"How long did I nod off?"

"Ten years."

Hester blinked at approximately where Graham sat.

"Ten years?"

"Yes."

"It's 1872?"

"Yes."

"Goddamn."

Graham nodded for no one to see.

"Where are we?"

"Oh, no, no you don't. I have questions of my own. I have kept you breathing for ten, silent, taxing years. I want answers."

"I want coffee."

"You can't have any. The Reverend Doctor says it dehydrates the body."

Graham shoved a water jug at her.

"The Reverend Doctor?"

"Yes, the Reverend Doctor—"

"Enton Blake," Hester finished.

"How did you know? No. Annul that request. I have more pertinent quandaries."

"Do you, Mr. Johnson? Prop me up."

Graham propped Hester against the wagon wall.

Hester tried to lift the water jug and failed. She glared at it.

Graham lifted it and gave Hester a swig.

"Speak your piece."

"For five years I've wanted to die."

"You're already dead."

"I want the Something After."

"Not my problem."

"I could become a problem," Graham said. He made what he thought was a menacing face, but he only appeared bowel-blocked. Regardless, Hester was blind to it.

"Not any problem I couldn't get rid of." The end words choked out of Hester. Her throat felt like a fire ruin.

"Ding. That was the liar's bell. I rang it for you."

"That was obnoxious."

Hester gave the air in her wagon a dull look.

"Answer me, Hester Garlan. Can you give me a second, true death?"

"If I wanted to."

"Ding."

"Why ask if you don't believe me?"

"I want to believe you. I want to be dead. Even with you awake again, I want to be dead. This is what you do to people, my scabby harlot. You make people want to die."

"Go away, Mr. Johnson."

"I will shove you in an apple barrel and sing to you," Graham said.

"Eh?"

"If you do not answer my questions with truth, I will grab you by the bandages, shove you in an apple barrel, nail it closed, and sing. Incessantly. Until you die."

Hester wet her lips, coughed, and fell flat on her back. She chose not to show her terror at not being able to control her movements.

"I have three songs committed to memory," Graham said, "'Battle Hymn of the Republic'..."

Hester groaned.

"'Buffalo Gals'..."

Hester groaned louder.

"...and 'Oh! Susanna'"

Hester guffawed.

"I will, Hester. I will stuff you into a barrel and sing to you until your ears bleed, unless you tell me what I want to know."

Hester thought on going to the bathroom. On brawling. On falling. On picking herself back up again. On swinging her leg over the side of a man and circling her hips over his. On walking. On kicking down a door. On feeling threatened by Graham Johnson. He could. He could drag her to a goddamn apple barrel and nail her in. Hester did not know who she was without the use of her legs. With arms that felt the wet rag rather than iron rod.

"Ask before I find a salt bag to stuff you in, Mr. Johnson."

"You've killed hundreds of the dead."

"And?"

"How?"

"Ask something else."

"*Mine eyes have seen the glory of the coming of the Lord: He is trampling out the vintage where the grapes of wrath are stored,*" Graham sang. His voice was flat and loud.

Hester immediately felt a pain behind her eyes.

"If you can look a dead thing in the face, Mr. Johnson, you can hasten it from a place. I saw the dead. A sight, the right set of words—and a ghost is gone from this world."

"To where?"

"The Something After. The Great Unknown. Hell. Heaven. Purgatory. I don't know. The Not Here."

Light streamed in the back window of the wagon. It was late evening.

"So you can't send me off?"

"Not currently."

"And the boy?"

"I don't want to talk about the boy."

"*Glory, glory, hallelujah! Glory, glory, hallelujah! Glory, glory, hallelujah!*" Graham sang.

Hester looked for salt to throw. She found none. Graham had run out the previous morning when two roadside specters had started spitting at Hester's wagon.

"*His truth is marching on*," Graham finished the chorus.

"You missed half a verse."

"I'll still put you in an apple barrel."

Hester hurt all over. But her skin didn't creep. Nothing inside of her crawled. Nothing bled. Her forehead felt a regular warmth. She couldn't move her legs, but she could at least feel her arms. She would not be intimidated by a dead newspaperman.

"The boy is twenty now. Do you still want to kill him?"

"I'll have to think on that."

"He can kill me, can't he?"

"He's got the sight. Don't know if he's got the words."

"That was honest. Will you let him kill me before you kill him?"

"I want to sleep, Mr. Johnson. Shoot the birds when you leave."

"We aren't done. You think if you kill him, you'll get your dead sight back? Even after all these years?"

Hester nodded. She felt the canyon of a scar that dragged from her left temple to the back of her neck.

"Why?"

"Hunch."

"You'd be wrong," someone said from outside the wagon.

"Reverend Doctor, come in and meet Hester," Graham said.

"Enton Blake?" Hester asked before the Reverend Doctor could pull the curtains back on Sleeping Beauty's wagon window.

"You know each other?" Graham asked.

"It is more apt to say that we know of each other," Enton said and put his arms on the windowsill.

"How?" Graham insisted.

"I talk to the dead, the dead talk of Hester," Enton replied.

"Bastard has a hell of an advertising budget," Hester said. She'd seen broadsides for Blake since before she could read his name.

"Killing your son without the proper accoutrements won't bring back your sight," Blake said.

"What materials do I need?"

"I may tell you in time."

"I may steal them before you can tell me."

"You can't even walk, Miss Garlan, let alone thieve and flee."

"You'd be surprised at her accomplishments," Graham interjected.

Hester wanted to hit Enton in the teeth. She wanted to salt Graham for defending her to a man over sixty. She wanted to walk her ass out of the wagon. She needed crutches.

"You should rest," Enton said.

"Don't tell me what to do."

"We can discuss the exchange of information when you are more fully recovered."

"How do you know I won't bash your head in and take your information when I am fully recovered?" Hester asked.

"I believe I would be able to hear your approach, Miss Garlan, and if I did not, they would," Enton nodded his head to the side and though Hester did not see the six ghosts stirring behind his back, she heard them muttering.

Enton walked away. He patted his watch pocket as he left.

"Will you kill me?" Graham asked after Enton had departed.

"When I have the 'proper accoutrements' and am goddamn able, I promise, Mr. Johnson, I will murder the hell out of you," Hester said.

Graham had the urge to continue singing "The Battle Hymn of the Republic." He did. Loudly.

Enton groaned by the campfire.

Hester pulled a pillow over her face. She made a list of what to accomplish in the coming days.

She would gain arm strength. She would learn to use crutches, if possible, or get one of those wheeled chairs she'd seen while skulking about health sanitariums for gilded suitors. She would take from Enton whatever he knew about seeing the dead. She would find her son. She would kill him as a matter of accomplishment. As a matter of not counting the last ten years as wasted.

Then she would massacre that jackass, Graham Johnson.

Chapter Thirty-Five

Boston, Massachusetts, 1879

IF YOU OVERHEARD the warden, Suffolk contained a congregation of matriculates in diverse stages of rehabilitation. If you overheard the guards, Suffolk was a buncha cussed killers, rapists, and pricks not worth the bricks they were stored under. If you overheard Walleye, Suffolk was paradise.

Walleye liked the long halls. The grip-thick bars. The grey stone. The moss and mold that grew between. Scratching notes on Net's wall, the rest of him unseen. The slight damp. The kitchen and yard ghosts. The locks. He supremely admired the locks. Ain't never seen locks like Suffolk got. Walleye hadn't never before met a hole he couldn't fiddle open in a moment, but Suffolk's took tens of moments. Walleye wanted what learnin' Suffolk locks would lend. He opened dang near every lock at Suff—from the hole they kept the hardcases in while the governor toured the premises to the warden's scotch-and-gun drawer. Wherever Net went, Walleye followed, opening doors and drawers. Then he shoved them closed before Net'd get in trouble for them being open.

Is your brother still your brother if he's dead? Is family still family if your kin ain't got a bat's lick of blood wetting their withins?

Whatever breathless grey Walleye lived in, it had changed him. The Walleye Hennet knew would've, for a far sight of never, kept him in jail. Let alone be the red ass enough to open every other door around him and close them just as quickly. Hennet didn't know Wall's purpose for doing so, but he didn't like it.

On certain occasions, when the prison was at its darkest and the guards were at their drunkest and Hennet was assured that no hurdle could hinder him as that last pin was about to trigger, he'd feel cold surround him.

Walleye patted his brother's back. Tellin' Net he was doing good. That the lock was about to split.

Hennet's hands would jerk and jolt. His guts would give. He'd lurch back and forth, shivering and shitting and knowing it was his brother's damn fault.

Hennet had stopped loving Walleye.

The emptiness in Hennet's chest made him feel uneven.

So did the letter in his hand. It was a letter from his ma. She had died three months previous. He'd been informed of her passing by a hotel man looking for someone to redress a bill. Beneath the hotel man's letter was a page written in his mother's hand. The hotel man had found it when cleaning out her drawers.

Hennet stood. He leaned his forehead on the cool stone. He tapped the letter on his thigh.

A guard walked by and clubbed Hennet's cell.

Hennet raised his head with what he hoped was silent reverence and made sure the letter was hidden behind his leg. Hennet didn't like this particular guard. Fillpin was the breed of man that made injury of everything. Open your mouth around him and your day ended in the hole, leaking blood, with another boot print on your soul. Hennet thought on grabbing Fillpin by the collar and slamming his head into the bars until his nose disappeared. The image reminded Hennet of the long-gone gal with the twigs in her hair and the busted collar. Hennet's thoughts left Fillpin. Been over twenty years and he could smell her still. Cinnamon, dirt, and sweat. Goddamn. His shoulders loosened. He sighed.

His hand slipped from behind his thigh.

Fillpin saw the letter.

It shouldn't have mattered. It wasn't contraband.

It did matter. Fillpin saw it and Fillpin was a cocksucker.

"Whataya got?" Fillpin pointed the club at Hennet's thigh.

"Letter."

"Give her here."

Hennet collected his options. Give Fillpin the letter. Smash Fillpin's skull when Fillpin grabbed the letter. Hennet had five years left on his stretch. He didn't want to add more.

Fillpin hit the bars with his club again. "Give her over."

Hennet looked at the letter. His mother's large, curling handwriting took up the majority of the front.

Walleye'd been in Nock's cell. Nock was a bastard. Walleye didn't like him. He heard the greasy shitheart drowned a sack of kittens to hear the caterwauling that'd come of it. Walleye liked to poke at Nock until the man's eyes bugged out of their sockets and he was sobbing from a migraine.

Walleye left Nock alone and walked up to Fillpin.

"Not askin' again," Fillpin said. No warning was left in his voice.

Hennet didn't move.

Fillpin did.

Walleye had shoved him.

Fillpin fell abruptly forward and smacked his face on Hennet's cell door.

Walleye cackled and kicked the man in the back.

Hennet tried not to smile.

Fillpin stood quickly. It was a struggle. His organs felt chilled and loose and his legs weak as feathers. He didn't want to shit in front of the prisoners.

Hennet didn't look as Fillpin stood.

Walleye hissed at Fillpin.

Five years is what Hennet thought. That's all he had to wait out. Five years.

Fillpin was flushed. His cheek would bruise. He dusted his jacket off and quickly walked on.

Walleye went back down to Nock's quieted cell. It was not time for the sorrowing to stop. Not for Nock.

Hennet sat down on his bed and tore open his mother's letter.

MY DEAREST CHILD,

I WAS INFORMED BY A CHAIN OF MEN, OF WHOM YOU SHOULDN'T CONCERN YOURSELF, THAT YOU ARE IN PRISON. HOW? YOU WERE ALWAYS MY CAUTIOUS ONE. REGARDLESS, THERE YOU ARE IN SUFFOLK. HELL, HENNET. DO BETTER. GET CAUGHT LESS. YOU AIN'T GETTING YOUNGER. I HOPE THE ENCLOSED HELPS.

MAMA

Somewhere down the line someone snored. Somewhere down the line someone yelled at someone else. Somewhere down the line some inconsiderate cocksucker raked a cup against his bars and sang. Suffolk didn't speak the way a house did, but it wheezed in water trickles and groaned in boot scrapes. There was a constant feeling of the walls finding you unworthy—an assessment Hennet agreed with.

The enclosed was a thin packet. Hennet rolled his thumb across it. It was filled with a fine powder. On the front it stated:

REV. DR. ENTON BLAKE'S
40 WINKS LEISURE DRINK
1 SPOON PER SNIFTER GLASS

The back said:

THE REVEREND DOCTOR ENTON BLAKE
CURATIVE MEDICINE
RESTORATIVE DELIGHTS
FOR OUR CATALOG PLEASE WRITE AT...

The address was smudged and illegible.
Restorative delights.
Blake.
Restorative delights.
Blake.
"Goddamn," Hennet muttered.
Hennet frowned at the letter.
No mother left.
No brother, so to speak.
An old debt to collect that he no longer felt tribulation over, and the woman who did was dead herself.

Hennet didn't know what he was without his family. Some kind of asshole, alone in the world, taking from other people. That's what. Suff gave him time to think about himself and all of it made Hennet feel like a rotted log—hollow, crumbling. He was hungry for something better.

He'd always be a sonofabitch, and he might could become a word-breaker, but he didn't have to be alone. When Suff spit him up and tripped him out the door, Hennet was going to find his son, and damn everything else.

CHAPTER THIRTY-SIX

ISABELLE AND SARAH played cards in the parlor. It was dusk. The last light of day fell through the window across a portrait of Sarah and William above the fireplace. Neither of them smiled. They stood six inches apart. Each wore black.

"Sarah, you need to get out of the house."

"I do, on occasion."

"Going to the market and fabric shop do not count, and you shouldn't be doing that. It is what you have Ruth and the other servants for."

"I fancy the market."

"It looks like you would fancy sleep more. You appear positively haggard, sister."

Sarah had had hollowed eyes for half her life.

"Here I was thinking my little sister wanted to play cards, but no, she is here to badger. Please, Isabelle, can we not play faro? Bridge is tedious."

"No, faro is played by buffoons who spit on floors. I am here, Sarah, to make sure you do not turn into an unsociable troll. You never do anything anymore, or if you do, it is alone. You haven't been to or held a soirée in years."

"I do not like such entertainments any longer."

"Why not?" Isabelle shuffled the cards.

"They all talk about me," Sarah said.

"Who all?"

"Do not pretend not to know what I know you do."

"Maybe society wouldn't talk crudely if you would participate in it. The lace club ladies would love to have you attend a dinner."

"I do not want to converse with those snippety women."

"They are not snippety."

"They talk of me. They write of me. They say that I am cracked and daft."

"The lace club ladies do not gossip of you," Isabelle said. She dealt the bridge hand.

"They do."

"No, they do not. That is the poetry and garden clubs."

Isabelle and Sarah frowned at their cards.

"All of them talk of me and only some of them speak badly, but all I want is for none of them to notice me at all."

Sarah shuffled her hand. She organized her cards.

Isabelle watched her sister's tics. Sarah bit her bottom lip.

"Sister, throw a gathering and they will see how sane and stale you are and then no one will talk of you at all."

"I'd prefer not to."

"Sarah, your isolation concerns me. Your obstinacy gives me weekly migraines. You cannot collapse and give up on life."

"I have not. I have my books. I have my drawing. I have my piano."

"You don't let me call often. You attend functions at my abode maybe three times a year. You barely make it to funerals and almost never to weddings. That is not being good family. You have been a recluse since her death."

"Do not talk of her."

Sarah did not allow people over often because William had to be at work, thus Annie gone, or she had to salt the dickens out of the house to try and trap the child. Annie was clever. She had learned ways around salt.

Annie, having heard people talk of her, crawled into the room.

"Sarah, throw a party. I will assist. It will be like old times. You will play the piano. People will dance. You will speak French and impress everyone. Look at how much you and William have! Family will come by. You have nieces and nephews that adore you. Interesting people will populate your parlor. The neighborhood could use a gathering."

"No."

"It has been fourteen years. Fourteen. I will not even broach the topic of why you never had another child. You must move on from her. This is supremely unhealthy."

Annie crawled next to her mother and the card table.

"Please, do not talk of her. I have moved on as much as I am able."

"You cannot keep punishing yourself."

"Isabelle, I assure you, I am not punishing myself. The child is."

"You really still believe Annie exists as a spirit?"

"We are here to play cards, are we not? Look at that!" Sarah laid her cards flat on the table.

Isabelle frowned. Her sister had won.

"But you do, don't you? You believe the child haunts your home? Why would a child that you loved dearly terrorize you? And for so long?" Isabelle gathered the cards on the table and folded them back into the deck. She did

not believe in ghosts. She had never seen a whiff of an apparition at Sarah's
lovely home.

This was because of Sarah's exertions before her sister visited. Sage.
Iron. Salt. Prayers. Traps. Tricks. Usually, Sarah could hold Annie off for up
to four hours.

Annie contemplated her aunt's question. She did not know why she felt
empty to her mother.

"Sister, she does not haunt the house, she haunts William and plagues
me. We discussed this years ago. I refuse to talk about it again. I have no
answers, only one catastrophe after another."

"You cheated. I don't know how you did, but you cheated."

"I did not cheat at bridge. What would be the point? You will not play
me for money."

The table shook as Isabelle shuffled the deck.

"Sarah, quit kicking the table."

"I am doing no such thing."

The table shook again.

"Sarah, stop it."

The table shook harder.

"You should leave, Isabelle."

Annie laughed.

Sarah grabbed the cards from her sister's hand. The table jolted in front
of them.

"Sarah, this is not funny. Not one bit funny."

"Sister, I am not doing it. I adore you, but go now."

Sarah was not alarmed. Annoyed, yes. Bothered, completely.

Isabelle stood. She gathered her skirts and looked underneath the table.

Ruth, the housekeeper, came into the room to light the oil lamps. She saw the oak table shaking with Mrs. Merriman peering under it. Ruth finished her business. If she didn't leave quickly the thing would follow her out. Ruth was used to Annie, though Ruth thought of the child not as Annie, but the thing. She could not imagine any Christian child being that cruel.

William rang a bell for tea to be brought to his study.

Isabelle watched the table shake and Sarah's lower skirt flap. Sarah sat motionless.

"Sarah," Isabelle said from under the table. "You are not kicking the table."

"I am aware of that, Isabelle."

"Sarah, your skirt is flapping about."

"It is."

"Why?"

"You know why."

Annie turned her attention to Isabelle. She crawled over to the crouching woman and blew in her face. Isabelle's eyelashes fluttered. Her nose itched.

"Sarah, is there a draft in here?"

"Isabelle, if you don't leave her alone she will get worse."

"Who?"

"You know who."

"You can't possibly mean—"

Annie was bothered. This crouching woman looked like her mother. The mother who bothered her father. Annie did not like the crouching woman. Annie jumped onto Isabelle.

Isabelle shrieked and tipped backward.

Sarah vaulted out of her chair at her sister's cries.

Ruth prayed in the hallway.

William rolled his eyes and continued reading Company notes.

"Sarah, help!"

Isabelle rolled on the rug and grabbed at her skirts and chest.

Annie climbed Isabelle's dress.

"Annie, stop!" Sarah said.

"Sarah!" Isabelle cried. Tiny bruises appeared on her hands and neck.

"Annie, stop!" Sarah yelled at what she could not see. She took salt from her dress pocket and threw it on her sister.

Annie bit buttons off Isabelle's cuff. She screeched when the salt hit her.

Isabelle spit the salt off her lips and scrambled to her feet. Ruth peeked in the door.

William rang the bell again.

Annie thumped her head against a corner chair. These women. They made her hurt all over.

William gave up on being served. He left his study to find his own damn tea. When he crossed before the parlor, he saw Isabelle whirling around the room. The floor had a scattering of cards. Sarah had her back to the door. The housekeeper steadied a potted plant.

Annie crawled to her father and attached herself to his leg. The salt made her feel thin. William felt a weight on his left foot. Her presence no longer made him palpitate. It was a comfort.

Isabelle dabbed the corners of her eyes with a lace handkerchief. Her chest heaved.

"Sister-in-law, are you leaving?" William asked.

Isabelle hiccupped and nodded. Isabelle gathered her clutch. "Sarah, please call on me soon."

Sarah nodded.

"Goodnight, Isabelle," William said.

Annie petted her father's knee. Isabelle saw the fabric of William's pants shift though he stood still.

"Good night, William," Isabelle said and hurried past him.

"Goodnight, Sarah." Isabelle kissed Sarah on the cheek.

Ruth escorted Isabelle to the foyer and helped her with her wrap.

Annie bounced on her father's leg.

"I do not feel like sharing dinner with a woman who goads my child into terrorizing our guests. I am going to the club," William said.

Sarah was tired of this argument.

"I did not goad her."

"You tell me that our child leapt upon your sister for no reason?"

"I am tired of this argument," Sarah confirmed out loud.

"I am going to the club," William repeated. This time he said it to the floor, rather than to Sarah.

Sarah went to the dining room where dinner for three was set. She would eat with the latest Jules Verne to keep her company.

Isabelle sat in her carriage and thought on Sarah and the child who had never left. No wonder her sister didn't want to have a party.

Chapter Thirty-Seven

IT TOOK THREATS of murder. It took threats of suicide. It took threats of writing editorials to the paper that finally did it. Sarah told William she would write the *New Haven Register.* She would recount her entire life to the world. She'd write a column that would turn into a serial that would turn into a book that would turn into all of New Haven, and more, thinking that his little wife, Sarah Lockwood Pardee Winchester, was not only a hermit, but a lunatic hermit and oh, poor William Wirt Winchester to be stuck with such a deranged woman.

"I will," Sarah said.

"You will not," William threw down his folder of correspondence.

"You could cut off my hands and I would still write the *Register* with my feet."

Annie put her father's papers in a stack.

"It is ridiculous, Sarah. A séance? Didn't you have one back in the '70s?"

"It is an opportunity," Sarah said.

"It is your sister."

Spiritualism had grabbed Isabelle's attention after Annie had grabbed her dress. She'd read several books and scattered journals. She'd been to see a famous medium in Boston. She would share her learning with Sarah.

"She thinks she can assist us and I don't mind her attempting."

"If I do this for you, you must promise to quit with the trinkets. Quit with the salt. The iron. I know what you do. You make this house a living hell for that child. You may do whatever you want to your room, but do not continue to corrupt the rest of my home."

William wiped his brow.

"I will not bother the child so long as you live, William."

"Fine, then."

William picked up his neatly stacked letters. He nodded at the ground, hoping Annie would see his appreciation.

She did.

Annie kicked over Sarah's stack of architectural journals, a foot high and packed full of sketches, as she left the room.

Sarah ignored the spreading papers and drafted a letter to Isabelle.

They would hold the séance.

It would be at Isabelle's house.

They would attempt to understand Annie.

Sarah and William sat in Isabelle's parlor. It was midnight. Light came from candles on the table.

"What do you hope to accomplish, Sarah?" William asked. He sat with a straight back and his hands folded in his lap.

"To learn what the child wants. To give it to her. To make her leave," Sarah said. She tugged on her cuffs to smooth out her lace dress sleeves.

Isabelle, who wore black velvet and an absurdly high collar for purposes of impressing the dead, did not want the servants to hear this conversation. She hissed them out of the room. They left. They would still listen from the hall.

Annie spit up on her mother's shoe.

Sarah's right foot grew cold.

"Could you not ask Annie without your sister present?" William asked.

"William, I have asked the child thousands of times over. I have cried out my queries. I have begged. I have bribed. I have threatened. It does not work."

"We should get on with the ceremony," Isabelle offered. She wanted to change out of the velvet gown as soon as possible. It made her sweat. Ladies did not sweat.

"My hindrance is that this is a private matter or, if not a private matter, at least one for a professional. No offense to you, Isabelle."

"None taken, William," Isabelle said. Her tone told anyone within earshot—the housekeeper, the kitchen maid, and the scullery girl—that Isabelle did not like William. Isabelle had made her own family go to her mother-in-law's home. She did not want them present if the child came into her house.

"I have tried Baptist preachers, Catholic priests, missionaries, and more, William. A representative of every known religion has crossed our door. I have had mediums, fortunetellers, and one professed witch to our home. None of them could rid me of the child or even gather why she did not cross over."

"This will not work, wife."

William leaned back in his chair as the sisters gathered closer to the table.

Annie crawled underneath her father's chair.

"What now, Isabelle?" Sarah asked. There was an allotment of hope in the inquiry.

"We ask the spirits to come forward," Isabelle said.

"Oh no, we don't," William said. He leaned forward. He'd never held a séance, but he was sure he could do it better than Isabelle.

"Oh no, is right. We don't ask the 'spirits' to come forward, Isabelle, I don't want to deal with any devil I don't know," Sarah said.

"Only Annie," William said. "Only my evil daughter, is that it, Sarah?"

Sarah did not bother with the comment. She looked at her sister.

"You are both correct. Calm down. I have read plenty on how to do this and attended one successful séance by a charming Boston medium. We shall ask for Annie to appear," Isabelle said.

"She is already here. Move this forward. I could be smoking a cigar and eating steak at the club, or sleeping. It is midnight, an unsuitable hour for decent ladies."

"Join hands," Isabelle said.

The three joined hands.

"Annie Winchester, please come forward," Isabelle said.

Annie trotted out from under William's chair and climbed on top of the circular table.

"Annie, if you are here, give us a sign."

With the séance's start, Isabelle's confidence faltered. It felt as if a buffalo stampeded in her stomach.

"She is here. The child is here," Sarah said. She could always feel when Annie was near.

"That she is," William agreed.

"Annie, give us a sign," Isabelle repeated.

There was a slate on the table and a piece of chalk.

Annie stared at these. Oh, she could talk. She could play smash. But she did not know letters.

"Annie, do something for God's sake so I can leave your aunt's home," William said.

Annie took the piece of chalk.

The chalk shimmered and lifted in the candlelight. It drew a line on the slate.

Isabelle gasped. Sarah was proud. It was a fairly straight line.

"Annie, we have affirmed you are present. Tell us why you remain," Isabelle said.

This irked Annie. She didn't know how to speak. She didn't know how to write. She didn't know what they wanted of her.

"Annie, come now girl, I have a meeting early in the morning," William said. A meeting with scotch and water, he thought.

"Child, why do you remain?" Isabelle repeated.

Sarah said nothing.

Annie did not know the answer they wanted. She did not like being called upon. She pushed the slate at her father and hoped he would take her home.

"You stay for your father?" Isabelle interpreted.

Annie threw the chalk at Isabelle in response.

The chalk marked the front of Isabelle's gown.

"It is no use, Isabelle," Sarah said.

"Is there anyone with you to speak for you, if you cannot?" Isabelle asked.

Annie knocked over a pillar candle. She was not pleased. She did not like feeling stupid.

"We should stop this," Sarah said. "She is agitated." Sarah righted the candle. Annie swatted her hand. The air was colder than before.

"I agree with my wife. This is a farce," William said. He pulled his hands away from the circle.

Annie climbed into his lap. William felt the cold weight of her.

"But we did not find out anything," Isabelle said.

Sarah patted her sister's hand. "All is well, my darling Isabelle. We should leave."

Isabelle reluctantly nodded. She had the distinct impression that if her sister did not leave the room would be ripped apart.

Sarah and William left. Annie sat on her father's shoulder as they walked out the door.

Isabelle blew out the candles around her table. She had bought it specifically for the séance.

In the carriage, William thought on how warm his wife's hand had been when he held it during the séance. Small and delicate. Even after all these years.

Sarah cradled the hand that William had held and tried to ignore the scratching cold on her calf. She dropped salt. The scratching stopped. Ten more minutes from the relative safety of her room.

As Isabelle took off the awful velvet gown that had not helped one bit in allowing her to communicate with the spirit world, she grew determined. She would take Sarah and William to meet Nathan Garlan. It would not be in an auditorium full of people either. It would be a private session. Cost wasn't an issue, but William was. How would she convince him to take off time from the Company?

Chapter Thirty-Eight

Eastern Pennsylvania, 1881

HESTER WAS A vain woman. Always had been. Granted, her aesthetic vision was not of Sarah Bernhardt standards. Instead, it listed to lace, glass beads, gauzy fabrics, things that glistened—from baubles to blades—attached to her person (especially her thighs) and arbitrary amusing objects shoved into her voluminous curls, but she'd always thought herself pleasing to look upon.

And now.

And now.

Now, it had taken Hester almost ten years—after she'd already wasted a damn decade to sleep—to accept and assert herself again. To acclimate herself to the permanent discolorations where the red sores were. To find the large scar that went from her brow to the back of her neck piratical and pleasing. To soothe herself out of the dreams where she was eyeball-burstingly bludgeoned. To find a way to dip her hair into fabric dye so that an intimidating black with hints of blue could coat the abundance of grey that now gathered there. To develop arm exertions to build strength. To not loathe her limp, brace-bound legs. To have crutches constructed with retractable razors. To charm rattlesnakes to live in the shelf under the seat of her wheeled chair. To admit to herself when she was past the point of tired, it was time to sit in the damn wheeled chair. To learn that Enton Blake kept a trick box in his pocket filled with the ghost of his father and as long as it was on his person he could see and speak to the dead. To learn that it would not work for her unless a blood-tied ghost of her own was within it. It had taken Hester almost ten years to pull her scattered parts together.

But she had.

Because if she could no longer be a fetching and formidable girl she fully intended to be an exquisitely odd and dangerous woman. Because she was not one to give up. And though her mind had subtly changed—some might say matured—over the years, her charge did not.

Hester Garlan still wanted to kill her son.

Because a person can handle only so much metamorphosis. Because a person needed a calling. Because goddamn it, that boy—now man—had ruined her life. Because the past twenty years had to mean something and if she couldn't rack that boy—man—full of even a quarter of the pain that'd she'd felt, Hester would lose her tenuous grip on the rope of self she'd braided together.

"Beetlebug, darling dear," Graham said to Hester as she reclined in the nook of an apple tree. "You do intend to take action tonight, do you not?"

"Yes," Hester said. She bit into an apple.

The crunch of her teeth bursting through the skin was loud enough to cause the Doc to glare their way. Blake was angry at Hester. They had had another confrontation that morning. She had once again refused to give him the old words that would send a spirit to the Something After. Nine years she'd held out, even after he'd made her the leg braces. The old man put up the old argument that he could do great good with such a language. Hester told him to shove his great good in a great pile of pig shit. Bastard even tried to hypnotize it outta her, but Hester had not let him.

The Doc had salve in one hand and a small girl with bee stings all over her neck in the other. He was finishing sales over a crowd he'd crowed over.

The Reverend Doctor Enton Blake's Alleviating Theater was in a well-off and rather gorgeous town named Buzbee or Binton or Branhollow or some such, somewhere in eastern Pennsylvania.

There was an apple fair. The whole town was bedecked with red apples, green apples, apple seeds, and apple garlands. The gloaming was illuminated by apple branch bonfires, apple-shaped lanterns that hung from trees, and hollowed-out, flame-filled apple candles. Shops and scattered tables along the thoroughfare sold, traded, or gave away apple pies, apple tarts, apple puddings, apple cider, strudels, jams, butters, cobblers—Hester had even seen a jaunty apple and beet salad that she might have thought a passable meal if it had had pork in it.

"You are prepared for the night's exertions?" Graham asked.

"I am. Are you?"

Graham scoffed. "Of course."

"Fine. We are in accord."

"Hester," Graham said.

"What, Mr. Johnson?" She took the last bite of her apple then threw the core over her shoulder. It landed before one of Enton Blake's ghosts, she of the knitting needles, who appeared displeased to have something that touched Hester fall into her path.

"Once we acquire the trick box, we shall find your son, and soon thereafter, you will let me die, correct?"

"Mr. Johnson, as I have said before, as soon as I am able, I will kill you."

"I will take something from you now, in celebration of all of our approaching accomplishments."

Graham sank to his knees in front of her, knotted his fist in her hair, and pulled her mouth to his.

Three townies saw the strange woman trembling alone under the apple tree on the outskirts of the fair by the traveling doctor's stage wagon. They thought she was having a seizure. They knew she belonged to the Reverend Doctor and if he wasn't worried, neither would they be.

For a half shake, Hester closed her eyes and thought on the one man who had ever properly pulled her close, who'd bitten her lips and ripped her dress and made her shudder, and not for the first time, Hester wondered if her brown-eyed outlaw was alive. Then Hester hissed and threw salt at Graham Johnson.

Graham didn't mind. Once his hand was tangible he'd record the evening for his memoirs.

Hester stood gracelessly with braced legs and the tree's support. She had to steal a faster horse. She had to create a satchel of only the most useful texts, herbs, and charms. She had to convince herself that she was up to this. That she could creep into the Doc's wagon while he slept, that she could reach into his vest, that she could take his trick box without him waking.

Hester walked crooked and away from Graham.

Hester said, "I am dangerous."

Hester said, "I am strong."

Hester said, "I can be silent."

Hester said, "Graham will distract the others."

Graham sat bliss-eyed by the tree. Titles to write in his journal included: *My Darling, Her Lips Taste of Honey, Apples, and Arsenic* and *Now Death May Come.*

When he sketched the scene in his journal, two tangled hearts were formed by branches in the tree above them.

"I cannot swallow the situation," Hester said.

"Devour it down," Graham said. He rode behind her on a horse she'd thieved from the mayor of the apple town.

"That's it. It is done."

"It is."

Hester gripped tight the reins and held the box up to see it better. The horse didn't like the feel of her braced legs against its ribs.

"Do not drop it, Hester pet."

Hester ignored him.

"Nine years. Nine years of wondering if I could take the damn box from him and all I had to do was poison a pie so the codger'd sweat so hard he stripped to his long johns and passed out while you scared away his spirits and musicians by juggling flaming apples and singing."

"We, my beautiful blight, did it."

"It should've been harder."

"I will give you something hard, if you demand it," Graham said.

Hester had sewn sage into her clothes. She appropriately elbowed Graham into a fit of wheezing. She tucked the trick box into a pocket in the lining of her jacket.

The medium and her newspaperman rode into the moonlight, attempting to outrun those living and dead that would do them harm.

CHAPTER THIRTY-NINE

BOSTON, MASSACHUSETTS, 1881

ARROL AND GRIMM searched the boneyard.

Nathan was, in some ways, a predictable man. Whenever he was fretful, whenever worriment and desolation clutched him, Nathan went to one of three places.

Arrol and Grimm had not discovered Nathan at the Green Dragon Tavern.

He had not been at Brattle Book Shop.

Thus, Grimm wheeled Arrol through the tombstones at the Granary. They discovered Nathan talking to an unseen while pouring whiskey on Paul Revere's grave. Arrol had found it best not to interrupt Nathan when he spoke to spirits. Nathan did not mind disruptions, but the dead did.

"Revere. Paul. Sir. If you be nearby, I'd have your opinions on women."

Revere was not near, but the spirit of a stabbed wig maker was. "What is your trouble?" he asked Nathan in a voice nasal and aloof.

Nathan grunted. "I have been jilted. Tossed aside. My heart ripped from my breast and left to the crows."

The wig maker rectified his crypt-sullied, curled and plaited hairpiece.

"It could not be that bad. You still have your trousers on and money enough to buy refreshment. Who was the strumpet?"

"Caitlyn, oh Caitlyn. She was a can-can dancer who studied folklore."

"Caitlyn of the Watchbird-way? She's been dead sixty years!" The wig maker stepped into a whiskey puddle. He gave a contented sigh.

"Mmm, but she had a way with her hands," Nathan began, blushed, and silenced himself with another swallow.

"You degenerate! You bedded an ethereal tart?"

"Watch your words, sir."

"I'd watch her curls and wide eyes instead. You dolt. She is dead. If you feel the need to pole a hole, find a warm one. It is for the best."

Nathan pointed at the wig maker with the same hand he held the bottle. He paused. The wig maker scratched his bloody collarbone and lifted his eyebrows in expectation. Nathan had forgotten what he was going to say. He made do by scornfully stating, "She left me for an *artist*."

The wig maker made a swipe for the bottle.

"Muttonhead. Find a living woman. They have soft mouths and are made of more than mist."

Nathan did not give up the bottle. "I am too busy for the living." He took a drink.

"I second that," the wig maker said and walked away. He would find more generous company.

Nathan thought himself alone. He took another drink. He was tired of being the one that everyone needed, but none loved deeply.

Arrol had had enough. He flitted his hand over his shoulder at Grimm. Grimm let go of the chair and crossed his arms. If you deal with a drunk for enough years, the cord of concern that connects your heart to theirs burns. The heat frays the fibers and when the fire reaches your breast, concern shifts to rage as you realize that they are not the only one that is hurting. Arrol was past devoted distress. He was angry. He put himself into motion and wheeled into Nathan. Hard. It was not difficult to knock the man over.

Nathan yowled as he fell. He did not know if it was a ghost or a man who'd pushed him. He spryly turned his fall into a roll and arrived on his hands and knees looking at his persecutors.

"You bastard son of Puck, it is two in the afternoon. I can smell the whiskey from three feet away," Arrol said.

Grimm shook his head in disapproval.

"Arrol," Nathan said as he used Paul Revere's stone to stand. "My cherished patron and manager, I did pour a significant quantity on the ground, and now the ground is all over my person. That may account for part of the stench." Nathan's voice held an amusement that only boozers and lunatics could achieve.

"Pity," Grimm muttered, but even he was unsure if his commiseration was with the wasted whiskey or ruined suit.

Nathan did not count the spillage as a waste. He often poured good liquor on certain graves to goad spirits into helpfulness. Time and again, it worked.

"And Nathan, a burgundy suit for daily wear?" Arrol inquired.

Nathan straightened the silver stickpin in his cobalt cravat. A protection rune was carved on the back.

"I assure you, sir, I will be top notch by my evening performance," Nathan said, then belched.

A black cat crossed Nathan's path, lapped a lick of whiskey from the dirt, then continued on.

"Grimm, call him something nasty," Arrol requested.

"Damned fool."

Nathan nodded in agreement. Then stopped. The world had much too much spin for his liking. He leaned on the grave. For exactly two blinks, Nathan believed he had made it through. He had not.

"Excuse me," Nathan whispered. He leaned behind the stone and retched.

Grimm frowned again.

The black cat looked back, shook its head, and walked on.

Arrol's chin sank to his chest in reproach as Nathan's head raised. Nathan wiped his mouth with a cobalt handkerchief. He took a swill of whiskey to swish around and spit out.

"Apologies."

"I am tired of your apologies," Arrol said.

"I am otherwise empty of utterance."

"And full-up of liquor."

"This does not happen often," Nathan said.

"But often enough."

Grimm walked several aisles down and sat on the tombstone of a lesser-known. Two dead women followed. They were elderly sisters who passed on in their sleep minutes apart during a thunderstorm.

Nathan was paler than usual. He pushed the hair from his brow, but he deemed the depth incorrectly and jabbed his eye with his thumb. He put his hands in his pockets and decided sitting was better than standing. His eye reddened.

"Leave me be, Arrol."

Were misery to expel fog, Nathan would've been obscured from sight.

"You will kill yourself. Is that what you want? I didn't take in my brother's almost-son to see the idiot die of brown bottle flu."

Nathan winced at the Wester reference. What would he think of him? It wouldn't be hard to find out. All he had to do was walk to the Rare and Fine, but Nathan wouldn't. Nathan went to Brattle instead. Better selection, higher prices, no one to judge him.

"What do you want from me?" Nathan sat with his legs crossed, his elbows on his knees, and his head in his hands. "My duties are attended to. I make my private meetings. I keep up with my correspondence. I sincerely listen to and assist those that seek me out. I have never missed a theatrical performance or parley. I have made you money and myself well-off."

"I don't care a continental about the money and you know it."

Nathan did know it. The Watchbird was full of those that could pay for their lodging through their stagecraft and those that could not.

"Let me be," Nathan whispered. He felt as if a large stone sat in his lungs. He could not breathe as well as one should.

"I have seen your form of indulgence before, Nathan Garlan. I know it. It is not of merriment."

"What variety is it, brother of my almost-father?"

"You are not as alone as you presume."

Nathan said nothing.

"I will see you for the seven o'clock," Arrol said. It sounded like a warning.

"Punctual and polished." Nathan flicked a bug off his dirty knee.

"I swear upon the holy knickers of those I've wooed, nephew Nathan, if you die of liver destruction or choking on your own sick while you sleep, I won't pour whiskey on your grave. I'll piss on it. I'll hire entire taverns to piss on it. You will suffer from all the iron. Then I'll salt it with blessed seawater every Sunday."

Nathan nodded.

Arrol rolled to Grimm.

"Eat something," Grimm yelled as he stood. "It will help."

Nathan nodded again. He waited until their backs were turned. He took a long pull from the bottle. Easy for Arrol, he who had Grimm to hold him at the end of the day. He hadn't been left by a beautiful Caitlyn for a paltry still life painter who specialized in squat vases.

Nathan didn't drink for mirth. Right or wrong, he drank to drown out his only constant companions. The kind dead. The needy deed. The cruel, sentimental, vicious, and talkative dead.

Chapter Forty

THE REVEREND DOCTOR Enton Blake blinked and sweat rolled into his eye.

"It is about time you awakened. I was beginning to think I put on this old thing for naught."

Sita lounged in a chair. She wore a gauzy, gay dress of silver that matched her hair.

"My lovely Sita, I am pleased to behold you, but how, may I inquire, did I get here?" Enton wiped his brow and burrowed further into the pillow pile that surrounded him.

"A quiet man with a banjo and a little woman with a steely gaze dropped you off. You were thrashing around like a poisoned man."

Sita went to an easel. She turned it to Enton.

"What do you think?"

In Sita's charcoal drawing, Enton lay dead in the purple parlor's pillow pile. His shirt was ripped open. His legs tangled in the sheets. One arm was flung above his head, the other clutched at his heart. The wrinkles near his eyes and the lines around his mouth were deeper than in life. The look on his face was that of dread.

"I have titled it, 'An Unwilling Expiration,'" Sita said.

"Darling, you have turned into a realist! Look at that shading."

"Yes, I am talented, aren't I?"

They smiled at each other and Sita came to sit next to Enton.

"How long have I been here?"

"Two weeks."

"Did the man with the banjo and his silent compatriot mention where I may send their severance?"

Sita soaked the sweat from Enton's brow with her dress sleeve. She slid her cold feet under the covers and Enton made an exaggerated grimace at their contact.

"The Fiddle and Whistle. They said that you knew where it was. I had them write it down in case the fever broke your brain." Sita paused. "Enton, I am cheerful that the fever did not break your brain."

"But I am lesser," Enton said.

"You have your wits about you."

"But not an heirloom."

Sita recalled the weighty, complicated box. She shivered.

"Stolen?"

"Stolen."

"You will go after it?"

"I will."

"You are not well, yet. You will stay a little longer."

Enton nodded and buried his face in Sita's neck. His skull felt like it had been carved about with a butter knife.

He had never trusted Hester Garlan, but he had trusted that he, Enton Blake, and his dead friends were smarter than she. That she was more brutish than clever. Now she had his trick box.

He would find her.

He would take his trick box back.

He would release all that were in it.

Before Enton swam the waves of slumber that crashed against him, he wondered if he had it in him to end Hester Garlan.

One week later, he sold his medicine wagon to a credentialed doctor in Westerly. He kept two saddlebags of stock. He gave a portion of the sale proceeds to Sita, forwarded a portion to the Fiddle and Whistle, and kept enough to travel on. Then, because he could not hear or see them, the Reverend Doctor Enton Blake's phantom friends guided his way to Hester through tilted tree branches, dead winds, and lines in the dirt.

It was not an easy journey. Enton's eyes were not strong. He could not sit on a horse for long. He did not understand how it happened, but somehow, he had gotten old. He was eighty-one and tired of the road.

CHAPTER FORTY-ONE

TUBERCULOSIS WALKED ITS way into the Winchester household. It began with the flower delivery boy. He visited every other week with the hydrangeas. One sweating stop was all that was necessary to infect Ruth. Ruth did not mean to infect the master of the house, but she did, and she died before she could apologize.

William Wirt Winchester lay crooked over ledgers and cotton sheets. Papers were stacked in piles along the edge of the bed. Brown spatters and bloody fingerprints occasioned their edges. What was once an orderly floor of signed memorandums and calling cards was now a muck-about of used handkerchiefs, soiled quilts, and business diaries.

The drapes were tied aside and an abundant light filled the room.

It was unacceptable. A man could not attain optimum health without sleep and William could not sleep with the sun's hot fingers upon him. It was awful enough he had lost so much weight that his clothes hung slack. He refused to be muddy-headed due to sleep deprivation.

Annie liked her father's fine new figure. He was thinner. He looked more like her.

William turned his head to Sarah. His eyelids were heavy. He sweated profusely. His neck was not strong. Sarah sat in front of the window. She was a nuisance. He would have to erase hundreds of scribbled door frames, potted plants, and lamp fixtures she'd doodled on his documents.

"Too much light," William said.

Sarah looked up from her drawing.

"Doctor's instructions," she said and continued her sketch.

"Too much light," William repeated.

"You may wear the sleeping mask."

Sarah shaded the crown molding on her page.

William's throat was fatigued.

"Close the curtains."

"No."

The doctor had been clear. Light was beneficial to tuberculosis patients.

William couldn't feel his toes. They were curled. His legs bent. He wanted to straighten his limbs. He wanted to throw the sheets off, walk to the curtains, and pull them closed. He wanted to scrub himself clean, put on a suit, and go to the office. He rolled to the bed's edge.

"What are you doing?" Sarah asked.

"Rising." He shoved one of his legs off the bed.

"William, no. You will harm yourself." Sarah stood from her chair. Papers and scraps scattered from her lap.

William pushed himself up.

"William, wait! I will help."

Notebooks and inkwells spilled to the floor. A quill jabbed him in the thigh. He grabbed it and threw it.

The doctor sat outside the door in a comfortable pin-striped chair.

The quill speared Sarah's slipper. It stuck straight up. The feather waved at her. She did not know what to do. She hadn't for some time. Her marriage had devolved into her regarding William as she did politicians—necessary but uncomfortable to be around.

The doctor left his chair to explore the smell of rhubarb pie wafting up the stairs. The same smell struck William as absurd. He was dying and someone made pie. He would sack whoever baked that pie.

Sarah could not catch William as he fell to the floor with the ink and ledgers.

Annie saw her father struggle. Watched him cough. Wondered if she should have smothered him. It would have been quicker. She crawled to the ceiling. She tucked herself into the modest chandelier above the bed and cried.

William went wide-eyed.

"Do you hear that?"

"What?" Sarah asked. She worked to untangle the sheet around William so she might pick him up and place him back in bed. He was not as heavy as he once was.

"You do not hear that?"

"What, William?"

William frantically scanned the room for the source of the sorrowing. His eyes found Annie. She was in that hideously cheerful chandelier that Sarah bought years ago.

Annie noticed her father noticing her. He did not look through her. He looked at her. He smiled for her.

"Annie," William whispered.

"Annie?" Sarah repeated.

Annie crawled out of the chandelier, across the ceiling, down the wall under the sheets, and onto William's chest.

Sarah saw the blankets shift and moved away from the bed.

William saw his child. Held his child. His thin arms wrapped around her shrunken form.

"William?"

A cough forced its way through him and William rocked with spasms. Annie giggled.

"Doctor!" Sarah yelled as she ran to the door.

It was too cold in the room.

"Doctor!" Sarah yelled again and went back to the bed.

Bile crept through William's stomach and climbed up his throat. Another fit of coughing seized him. The blood leaked down his chin as his bottom lip deeply split. He looked like a canvas marionette stretched too thin. His chest caved in. Underneath the blanket his feet twitched. He didn't notice.

It was unfortunate that the sheets were white.

Sarah grabbed William's hand. Annie batted at their fingers. A small shiver went through Sarah, but she did not let go of William.

William closed his eyes. A chuffing shoved from his stomach and up his throat.

Annie mewed happily.

William's lungs labored. His eyes closed. His eyebrows lifted.

Sarah rubbed his hand across her cheek.

William wanted Sarah to cry.

Sarah did not cry.

Annie pawed at her father's chin. She nuzzled into his neck. This made William happy, but William did not have time to die.

Sarah saw her husband gasp. She saw his throat seize. His breaths were too far apart. Where the dickens was the doctor?

William's office was likely covered in dust. His files in ill order. His assistant on too long a leave. He had much to do.

William's legs numbed. As did his organs.

The doctor wiped rhubarb from the corner of his mouth, rubbed his stomach, and walked up the stairs.

"William," Sarah started, but she could think of nothing else to say. She kneeled by the bedside. She gave wide berth to the lump under the covers she assumed to be Annie.

William decided he was not ready to die.

"Company," William said.

"I am here," Sarah said.

"Not you."

"I am certainly not leaving."

"Do not ruin the Company."

Sarah's ears went red.

William's arms went cold. It was distasteful. This would not do. He would not go. He could not leave Sarah and extended relatives to run the Company. It would be bankrupt in a fortnight.

Annie tugged her father's ear.

William had a child to look after.

He had a Company to run.

This would not do. He would not go.

Sarah did not notice that she held her breath until a gasp came out of her.

Annie sniffed at her father's mustache.

William stopped breathing.

William could school Sarah in the art of business after the funeral.

Sarah sobbed exactly once when she saw that William's chest did not rise again.

The doctor stuck his head in the room.

"Do you need assistance?"

Sarah stared at him from the floor.

The doctor rushed in.

William stepped out of his body.

Annie crawled up his person to perch on his shoulder.

Sarah sat down in a chair and did not know what to do with herself.

Chapter Forty-Two

THE NEIGHBORS STROLLED past the Winchester home almost daily. Up and down, up and down, directly before Sarah's property. Hours of it. They should have packed triangle sandwiches, sitting stools, and parasols, as their walks were extensive and all that exertion could cause a swoon.

It started midway through Sarah's mourning. It worsened after she came out of her widow's weeds.

When it began, Sarah watched them watch her. After the first month of it, Sarah ignored them. She had her own business to attend to. She read books. Wester Brothers' Rare and Fine, out of Boston, had a particularly fine mail-order, occult collection. She sketched. She dreamed of a house with hundreds of windows but no way for busybodies to see in. She avoided William and Annie.

Sarah found notes in William's hand. To-do lists about the Company. She burnt them. The Company had a new direction and was doing fine without help from the beyond. William broke things when Sarah ignored his notes. Annie helped. Sarah did not care. She had more money than was moral. The rifle business was profitable. She had nearly fifty percent ownership in the

Company. William could break any table he wanted. She could buy a hundred new tables in one day. Probably more than that. Sarah didn't give a fig if the Neighbors heard the racket.

The Neighbors did.

"Did you hear that?

"It sounded like a bookcase tipped over!"

"Dishes breaking."

"Did you know she is forty-five?"

"Not too old to have parties."

"Too old to marry again."

They shaded their eyes with gloved hands. The more daring of them leaned on the iron fence Sarah had erected.

"Why would you attend a party there?"

"How horrible."

"She should at least ask."

"That house is a disgrace."

"That house is beautiful. That woman is a disgrace."

The group talked quickly and together so no one could remember who said what and no one person was ever accused of gossip.

A new Neighbor, one who didn't know any better, said, "But the poor woman."

"Poor woman?"

"Did she not lose a child?"

"Twenty years previous."

"And a husband?"

"A year past."

"She should at least invite us over for cards."

"But a year is not all that long."

"She didn't even like her husband."

"He was successful!"

"Wasted on her."

They strolled, up and down, up and down. They nodded at other Neighbors who passed them in carriages or on foot.

"She doesn't go to church."

"Terrible."

"Still dresses in grey."

"Overdoing it, wouldn't you say?"

The Sunday sun retreated home.

"No one could be alone that much of the time."

"Not natural."

"Absolutely."

Annie sat on the porch and watched the women. The child did not know how fortunate her freedom was. She had not had to follow William's remains to the graveyard. She was tied to his spirit instead.

The women saw the porch swing sway and thought it the wind.

"Perhaps we should invite her over instead."

"Oh, no, no."

"I would not invite that woman to my home."

"Why not?"

"Same reasons you wouldn't."

William sat next to Annie. They admired the Neighbors' walking dresses.

"My cousin's scullery girl knows a shopkeeper's daughter who knows the daughter of Sarah Winchester's head servant."

"Oh dear."

"She says that the head servant's daughter told the shopkeeper's daughter who told my cousin's scullery girl that Sarah Winchester believes William and Annie—her deceased husband and child—haunt her."

Annie crawled onto William's lap.

He stroked her back.

It was not raining, but the sky looked like it wanted to turn. Sarah shut her bedroom window.

"Look!" a Neighbor said and pointed.

Sarah backed away from the window.

"She was right there."

"That window there."

Sarah shut the curtains.

"Who?"

"Sarah Winchester."

"Right there!"

"I did not see her!"

"Oh!"

Annie left her father's lap, crawled across the front walk, and went to the women in the fancy walking dresses.

"Did you see what she was wearing?"

"No."

"Silk!"

"You could not tell that."

"I could so."

"Orange!"

"Not grey."

"But this day is turning bad."

"The clouds."

"The sky."

They gathered their clutches and prepared to leave.

The Neighbors did not notice that Annie crawled between them. She dragged sharp fingernails across the bottoms of their skirts.

The new Neighbor asked, "What if she is haunted?"

The others laughed.

"In a house that beautiful?"

"Not possible."

"Ghosts like dark, horrible places."

"Like your house!"

"You're terrible."

"But you laughed."

They all laughed and walked away.

Each would later wonder how the bottoms of their skirts became torn.

It had taken her half a lifetime, but Sarah decided that she did not care what the Neighbors thought or talked about or editorialized in the newspaper. Not here. Not wherever she moved—and oh, she was moving. Soon. New Haven was too full of bad memories for beautiful ones to bloom. Sarah wanted to live somewhere warm. She wanted to live somewhere with possibility. Somewhere like California.

Chapter Forty-Three

Boston, Massachusetts, 1882

HENNET C. DANIELS walked out of prison on a day when the sky was the color of a bird snake's underbelly.

His back was crooked from work. His mind tired.

He wrote a letter.

The letter was to the Reverend Doctor Enton Blake. It read:

MISTER –

YOU KILLED MY BROTHER, ONE WALLEYE DANIELS, WITH A WHITE POWDER. THIS WAS TWENTY YEARS BACK. PROBABLY AN ACCIDENT. HIS HAINT IS A PAIN IN MY ASS. I WAS GONNA KILL YOU. BUT I AIN'T NOW. I'M TIRED. I DON'T WANT TO FIND YOU. I WANT TO FIND WORK. I WANT TO FIND MY SON. IF YOU GOT A WAY TO GET RID OF A GHOST, I'D BE MUCH OBLIGED.

HENNET C. DANIELS

Hennet posted the letter to a Rhode Island address he'd found on a more recent advertisement by the Doc.

He didn't know what good the letter'd do, but it felt right to make his intentions known to the world. Felt like there was power in the words.

Chapter Forty-Four

New Haven, Connecticut, 1882

WILLIAM FOUND THAT living the dead life agreed with him. The only shortcoming being that he was tied to Sarah. He could not leave the house unless she did and, try as he might, he could not influence the Company through her.

Annie tugged on William's pant leg. He looked at his pocket watch. The child was correct. It was their appointed togetherness time.

Annie and William walked down the hall and past the kitchen. Annie crawled up the walls and onto the ceiling. The cook ignored the pattering of feet.

Sarah found that older women better handled the hazards of her house. Women that wore Saints on chains, left milk out for fairies, or kept lucky stones tucked inside their stockings.

William tapped his knuckles on the wall as he walked. It was habit. At each rapping, a picture frame would shake. Some fell. That is what servants were for.

William and Annie came to where Sarah and Isabelle sat together.

Sarah played the piano, lightly, not attentively.

Isabelle knit a shawl that was terribly long.

"I'm thinking of leaving here," Sarah said.

"Mmmhmm," Isabelle said.

"I mean it."

"Theater? Fabric shop? Market?"

"No, leaving New Haven. I don't want to be here."

Isabelle put down her knitting needles.

"Perhaps, if I move they won't be able to find me," Sarah said.

Something Beethoven and fantastic came from the piano, and Sarah barely looked at the keys.

"Where would you go?" Isabelle asked. She examined her shawl. "Do you think this is too long?"

The shawl curled on Isabelle's lap. It wrapped around one leg and lay in a pile on the floor.

"Not for Atlas," Sarah said.

Isabelle frowned.

"Perhaps New York, but all those people…and then I thought New Orleans…but that didn't seem right either…I've decided…I shall go West."

"West?"

"West. California."

"Mmmhmm."

Annie sat on William's shoulder. She petted the edge of his mustache and his right eyebrow.

Sarah felt distracted. Sarah felt anxious. Sarah tried to control her breathing, but the air went cold when they came around. She coughed when it was cold.

"Isabelle, you should go."

Isabelle was used to this ritual.

"No."

Isabelle was used to Annie, but what unpleasantness that William haunted Sarah, too.

Sarah stopped playing the piano.

Annie rolled down William and into Isabelle's shawl. This did not please Isabelle. She kicked at the bundle on the floor. Annie bit through Isabelle's slipper. Isabelle's foot twitched, but she'd been bitten by the girl so many times now that she no longer felt the need to empty her stomach. Isabelle kicked harder at the empty air.

Annie whined.

William stroked Sarah's hands as they rested on the piano keys. He had always wanted to learn. Sarah had wanted to teach him. He had never made time.

Sarah was convinced that all this dead touching led her more quickly down an arthritic path.

"Salt is on the side table, sister," Sarah said as she took some herself from a skirt pocket.

Isabelle tugged at the shawl pile. When Annie would not exit from the pile, Isabelle flicked salt over the yarn.

Annie howled and crawled away.

Sarah threw salt over her shoulder.

William felt a burn. In his distraction, his hand went not through Sarah's hand but into it.

Sarah repeated Annie's howl and stumbled from her piano bench. William's hand was attached to hers. She could not see this, but she felt it. It was as if there were centipedes crawling inside her skin.

"Sarah! What is it?" Isabelle held up her knitting needles like weapons.

Annie smiled at her father's accomplishment. The closest she'd ever come to entering anyone was a dormouse. It had exploded.

"One of them is in my hand."

William was amused and slightly aroused at holding his wife's hand from the inside.

Sarah shook her hand. She yanked her hand. She twisted this way and that. Her skirt flared from the twirling.

Isabelle prayed loudly.

"Isabelle, quit that and help me," Sarah said.

Isabelle got on her feet, but she continued to pray.

Annie clapped her hands to a simple tune.

William had not danced in ages. He took his wife in his arms then spun her away from him and Sarah tripped over a settee.

"My hand, Isabelle, how is he in my hand? It feels too big to be the baby."

Annie crawled up to the piano and over its keys.

William pulled his wife up and to his chest.

Annie saw her father and thought him stylish.

"Quit moving, Sarah. Quit!" Isabelle said, "What do I do?"

"I don't know," Sarah said. "Get salt. Get it. Get the salt. And iron shavings. In the side table's drawer."

Annie left the piano to tip over the side table. The salt and the iron shavings spilled to the floor along with a can of Sarah's drawing pencils. A clear vase filled with cicada shells broke. Annie howled at her own blunder. She'd collected those. Sarah thought it macabre, but lovely, and had kept it.

William inhaled the smell of his wife. He wondered why he had never noticed it before.

Isabelle went to her knees and scooped up the salt in her skirts.

Annie shook it back out.

Isabelle scooped.

Annie shook.

William dragged and dragged his wife around the room by her hand.

Sarah was no longer accustomed to feeling helpless, but she'd never been partially possessed and had read nothing useful on the subject. She had not a clue what to do. She surveyed the room for weapons.

Isabelle gave up on the salt.

"Sarah, she won't let me."

"The fire poker, Isabelle."

William admired the strong fire.

Annie tugged on her father's pant leg to let go. It was time to go. But William enjoyed dancing with his wife.

The piano shook when Sarah fell against it. The carpet shifted. She was on the tips of her toes.

Isabelle handed the poker to Sarah. It was sharp. It was iron.

"Throw the sage on the mantel in the flames," Sarah said. She took a breath, forced her right hand against the new, velvet-flocked wallpaper, and stabbed her palm with the poker.

Isabelle screamed.

William howled.

Sarah shrieked the loudest of them all.

Isabelle fainted.

Annie bit Sarah's foot.

The poker held Sarah's hand to the wall, but William no longer held his wife's hand.

William teared up and his hand disappeared. He did not understand women. She complained all his living days that they never went to waltzes.

Sarah could not loosen the poker from the wall. She tore the hole in her hand bigger by trying. She fainted. Her body slouched down with her hand held above her head. Blood streaked the wall and collected in her hair.

Annie pushed her father down the hall.

The cook and a maidservant ran to the sitting room. The maidservant fainted. The cook shook her head, crossed the room, pulled the poker from the mistress's hand, and sent for the doctor.

Sarah woke while the cook wrapped her hand in a rag.

"I am moving to California," Sarah said and then vomited in the fireplace.

The cook nodded. "I'd follow, missus."

"That'd be fine," Sarah said and looked over at Isabelle.

Isabelle did not try to stand. With her gown piled about her in a tangle on the floor, she said, "Sarah, we are going to Boston to see Nathan Garlan."

"I don't need a spiritualist to rap on a table and let me know that my dead husband and child hate me. I don't want to talk to Annie and William. I want them gone. No spell has been able to do that. No medium. No preacher. No prayer. No dust. No nails. No salt. No iron. No anything. Nothing and no one will make them go away, Isabelle."

"We will try one last time."

Sweat dripped from Isabelle's brow. There was grey in her hair where an hour ago none had been.

"Alright, Isabelle. Alright," Sarah said. She leaned her head on the cook's wide shoulder.

Isabelle sighed in relief.

Down the hall, a painting fell as William rapped on the wall.

CHAPTER FORTY-FIVE

NORTHERN MARYLAND, 1882

THE REVEREND DOCTOR Enton Blake was not well.

Whatever Hester poisoned him with ailed him still. His breath was ragged. He walked with a cane. He rode short distances. His sight was dim. His stamina fleeting. He often shook convulsively.

Hester was a maddening person to track. All Enton Blake had to do was watch the newspapers for peculiar murders and irregular robberies. When her activity calmed, Enton's dead friends would spook his horse the fitting turn at forks in the road. There'd be a nudge of wind. A trail of leaves. All of this, and he still did not have her. He felt cursed.

He was.

By Hester, of course.

He would have had her by now—for truly the Reverend Doctor Enton Blake was a man of brilliant scouting technique—but he had to pause frequently. When the convulsions came, it was better to be on the ground.

For each fit that the Reverend Doctor went through, his dead friends whispered along the line for whoever was nearest to Hester Garlan to murder her, or, in the very least, to murder her horse. If the good doctor wasn't moving, she shouldn't be either.

Chapter Forty-Six

SARAH AND ISABELLE stood before a blue door embedded in a red brick home.

"What if it doesn't work?" Sarah asked Isabelle.

"It will work. Knock."

"Why should I knock?"

"I refuse to touch a whale door knocker."

"What is wrong with whales?"

"I dislike elephantine creatures."

William leaned on the handrail. Annie crawled in the ivy above the door. William was leashed to Sarah and Annie was tied to William—a foul family on holiday.

Sarah seized the sea creature and knocked.

The door opened.

Nathan Garlan stood before them. He wore a dark grey suit with a deep purple vest and no tie. His hair was longer than the fashion and he wore it tucked behind his ears. His shoes were the same deep purple. He was hungover.

Sarah looked away to conceal her blush.

"I am Mrs. Isabelle Merriman and this is my sister, Mrs. Sarah Winchester."

The talking woman did not take Nathan's attention. The woman in black, trimmed with spring green, did. Her bodice was covered in baroque beading, her hair in tight curls. Nathan stared at her too long.

"Invite them in," said an old servant who poked Nathan in the arm.

"Ah, yes, do come in," Nathan said. He opened the door wider.

The sisters entered the foyer. The old woman took their wraps. William and Annie followed.

"This way, ladies. We shall converse in the library," Nathan said and strode off. He did not acknowledge the dead child or man. Sarah and Isabelle took quick steps to keep up with Mr. Garlan.

The library was a circular room. Old tomes covered the wall that faced the entry. A rolling ladder and rail spanned the collection. There were reading nooks and a desk fit for a titan, sprawled with book stacks, inkwells, and papers. Sarah's eyes followed a brass spiral staircase to a loft with a stained glass dome and a lounging couch.

William could not read the book spines; they were all in foreign tongues.

The library was Nathan's office and respite. Apparitional affiliates knew not to enter, unless specifically called upon.

Nathan led the women and ghosts to five chairs that loosely surrounded a low table. A carpet woven to resemble creeping myrtle lay beneath the furniture. All took a seat, even Annie, who chewed on a weasel's paw she had dragged off a low shelf.

Sarah could not look away from the chandelier.

"Isabelle," Sarah said and nodded upward.

Isabelle gasped.

It was as if Bosch took up silversmithing.

"You have exquisite taste, Mrs. Winchester," Nathan said.

Isabelle noted that Nathan's smile was reserved for Sarah and that Sarah's smile was shyly reserved for the floor. William noticed this, as well.

The servant brought in a tea tray and placed it on the table next to two silver toads, each the width of a gold coin.

William was distracted. There was something different about these toads. They were charming. If you looked in their mouths you saw your reflection.

Annie scratched herself. The rug had made her itch.

Nathan poured the tea. He said, "Please, tell me of your situation."

Isabelle began, "My sister is haunted by her child and husband."

"William and Annie," Sarah said. She found her steel and looked at Nathan Garlan.

"We want you to exorcise them," Isabelle finished.

"I am not a man of the cloth. I do not exorcise spirits. I communicate with them."

William looked at the medium. Men of style were rarely good conversation. He crossed his arms.

Nathan still gave no notice that he saw William and Annie.

"I do not want to talk to them. I want them gone from me," Sarah said.

Nathan noticed bruises on Sarah Winchester's neck.

"Are they cruel to you?"

Sarah lifted her collar higher and ignored Nathan Garlan's inquiry. "I would pay you well for their disappearance."

"Very well," Isabelle added. She took a sip of tea.

"I cannot send them on from the world, but I can trap them."

"Trap them?" Sarah and Isabelle said together.

"In the toads." Nathan nodded at the table.

William and Annie looked at the toads.

Sarah and Isabelle did likewise.

All thought the possibility absurd.

Annie scratched and scratched. Her skin had turned grey where the carpet touched it.

"I have been through many of these situations, Mr. Garlan."

"She has," added Isabelle.

"Oh?" asked Nathan.

"Priests in the house, holy water in rooms, iron around the neck, covering mirrors, getting rid of them entirely, chanting over the foundation stone, the laying of hands, swallowing silver, praying at crossroads. I even put pins in the gateposts and coffin nails around the house. Nothing, but salt, works."

"You will allow me to try, will you not, Mrs. Winchester?"

Sarah nodded.

Nathan put his teacup down and took up the toads. They fit easily in one hand.

William's feet itched. His legs itched. He had never in his living or dead years felt such a prickling.

"Ladies, I request that you please leave your seats and step onto the hardwood floor. You will be safe from whatever proceeds as long as you do not return to the carpet."

Sarah and Isabelle did as Nathan requested.

It was from standing afar that Sarah saw how young the man was. Maybe thirty. She had never cared that she was in her forties until right then. That discomposure dissipated when Nathan smiled at her.

William did not like the way that this man looked at his wife.

Annie did not like that after she floated off her chair, she could not leave the carpeted area. She reached its edge and hit her head on an invisible wall. Repeatedly.

A rug sewn by the dead could snare the dead.

"Do you have anything to say to your wife?" Nathan asked William.

William uncrossed his arms and pondered the dandy. The man had made no sign that he had seen him or Annie earlier. "You can look upon me, Mr. Garlan?"

"Indeed, sir."

"He is faking," Sarah whispered to Isabelle.

"Your husband died in bloody bedclothes," Nathan said over his shoulder to shush his client.

Sarah put one hand to her mouth. Isabelle held Sarah's other hand tightly.

"I do not want you speaking to my wife," William said.

"The dead do not keep living wives."

"I am here. She is mine."

"You will drive her mad."

"That is not your concern."

William leaned forward in his chair with his elbows on his knees.

Annie chewed at Nathan's shoe. She did not like him. He angered her father.

Nathan would not have Venetian boots gnawed through by an infant. He nudged Annie away with the iron tip of his shoe. The child howled. Sarah's skin prickled.

William leapt up and shook Nathan by the lapels.

"Do not touch my child," William growled. He tossed Nathan onto a chair.

Isabelle shrieked.

Sarah reached in her dress pocket for salt.

Annie wavered in and out of form.

Nathan Garlan frowned at the broken chair. The set of five had come from a blind carver in Savannah. He stood and began to chant. He sprinkled salt around himself in a tight circle.

"What are you doing?" William asked.

Nathan continued with his old words. He did not engage with violent entities. He removed them.

Annie crossed the salt and chewed on the medium's ankle.

Nathan kicked the child away again.

"Do not touch her," William said. He slugged Nathan in the nose. Blood spurted from Nathan's face.

Sarah rushed to the edge of the carpet, but Isabelle held her back.

"We should help," Sarah said.

Isabelle dragged Sarah a step further back from the carpet. "No."

Nathan continued chanting. The toads warmed in his palm. He wanted this over quickly. He wanted to impress Sarah Winchester.

William reached for the toads Nathan Garlan possessed.

William's hand reached into Nathan's.

Nathan chanted louder. It would take more than a dead chill to get him to stumble.

Annie rammed herself at his legs. Through his legs. Into Nathan's legs.

Isabelle prayed silently.

"Do you need assistance, Mr. Garlan?" Sarah called.

Nathan did, in fact, need help, but he could not stop his ancient soliloquy or else he'd have to start it again.

William felt gloriously sturdy. The toads were hot in Garlan's palm. He was up to the medium's elbow. He'd soon be to his shoulder.

Nathan breathed deeply. He should not have gone so far into the rum last night. His head was muddy. His arm, shoulder, and neck had gone completely cold.

Sarah threw salt. It caught Annie. Sarah saw the rug bunch where the child shrieked and shook.

If William could completely enter this man, he could get rehired by the Company. Nathan's arm was stiff before him and William wrenched it this way and that.

"We should help."

"We do as Mr. Garlan said and keep off the carpet."

Isabelle put her arms around Sarah. She would tumble Sarah to a pile of skirts on the hardwood, if she had to. They would not go back on that carpet.

Nathan's old words went to a whisper. It was not only proper pronunciation that mattered. Volume was key.

William could not feel his hand.

Annie bashed her head against Nathan's shin.

"Shut up. Shut up. Shut up. You give me a headache," William said.

Nathan looked the dead man in the eyes and smiled. His words went lower than a whisper.

William felt a tug.

Nathan winked at him.

William felt a pull.

Nathan recited one last line.

William was hauled into a toad.

Annie saw her father disappear. She stilled. She looked at Nathan with wide, helpless eyes.

Nathan kneeled down to the withered child.

"Would you like to be near your father?"

Annie nodded.

Nathan offered his hand.

Annie looked at the toads with suspicion and then pressed her head to his palm.

Nathan said what was needed.

Sarah knew why the medium knelt.

Annie felt a cramp and a shove. She looked at her mother in confusion. Annie took a step forward.

Nathan said one last word.

The child was gone and the toad was heavier.

Sarah slumped to the floor. The room no longer felt crowded or cold. There was a glorious stillness around her.

Nathan stood. His knees wobbled.

He deposited the toads in a vest pocket and turned to Sarah.

Isabelle held Sarah as she wept on the floor.

Nathan walked over to the women. He had seen many tears in his profession, but Sarah Winchester's mattered more than all the others.

"Annie and William are gone?" Sarah asked. She looked into his face. It wasn't really a question.

Nathan sat with the women. He nodded. He could not feel the arm William had tugged himself into and his shoulder was tar-hot.

Sarah took his hand.

He used it to help her stand.

"Will you meet me at the Indolent Café tomorrow for brunch?" Nathan asked. Her fingers still touched his.

Sarah looked at Isabelle. Isabelle nodded.

"For the toads. You should have them, but I must watch them overnight for irregularities," Nathan clarified.

Sarah's face settled slightly. She had hoped it wouldn't be for business. Every man in her life only ever thought about business.

"I have no obligations tomorrow, Mr. Garlan. I will meet you."

Isabelle gave Nathan a disappointed look.

Nathan inwardly railed at himself. By trying not to embarrass her with his blunt request, Nathan had made it sound like his interest was purely professional. He was a cretin.

Margery, his old servant, came into the library. She gathered the ladies and soothed Isabelle. There was primping done in the hall mirror, proper goodbyes, and an envelope of payment left on the calling card tray.

After Nathan had closed the front door, Margery said, "You want to love that woman, don't you?"

"I wouldn't know about love, but she is kind to the eyes."

"She wants to love you, too."

Nathan flushed. "How can you tell, friend?"

Margery smiled. "I got my chores. Market don't wait forever. Tidy this mess, ya hear?"

"Is that not what I pay you to do?" Nathan asked. He did not mean it.

"Shush," she said. She grabbed a basket and put on her shawl.

Nathan went to the library with a bucket and a scrub-brush. He knelt on the myrtle rug. He thought on Sarah Winchester's face as he cleaned.

Chapter Forty-Seven

Boston, Massachusetts, 1882

THE INDOLENT CAFÉ appealed to the reckless, the restless, and the theatrical. It was out of the way and outstanding for closed-curtain conversations. The tables were made of stained glass reclaimed from a charred chapel. The floor was cobbled from broken headstones. Who was to say that there weren't corresponding bodies residing underneath?

Nathan sat at a round table, his white teacup a beacon in the dark corner. It was a small restaurant. Three attendants busied themselves creating coffees and tidying tables.

Should he have gotten flowers? Truffles? Should someone say "I want to love you" to a woman he barely knows? Because he did. Sarah Winchester had fox eyes and a mouth that would've made Zeus stoop.

Neighboring bawdy houses and all-night theaters added to the brunch crowd. A tattooed woman with a sheer-backed dress sat at the bar. EFFICACIOUS! INFLATION! OF! STIMULATED! SATISFACTIONS! GRATIFICATION! GUSTO! THE REV. DOCTOR SAYS…But Nathan could see no more. The print became too delicate and Nathan had not his reading glasses. He did not understand why someone would permanently affix an advertisement to their person—and now it was out of date. The Reverend Doctor's catalog had not been current for several years.

A man in heeled shoes with opals sewn onto the backs of his hands waved at Nathan. Nathan gave a polite nod. The man gave a blush. Nathan pictured Sarah Winchester licking the man's opals and felt himself warm. Nathan turned his attentions out the window.

"Mister Garlan," Sarah said. "You are flushed."

"You're late, Mrs. Winchester," Nathan said as he pulled out her chair.

"Perhaps you should choose cafés that don't call for odd turns, a concealed staircase into the underbelly of the city, an iron stomach, and a pistol to find," Sarah countered. She'd have no lip from this whelp after she stepped in God knows what filth through those alleys. Her spats were ruined. Though it was a lively bistro.

Sarah began the conversation.

"How is it decided who may question you during Watchbird Theater performances?" Sarah asked.

"The first fifty people who enter who have inquiries put their names into a box," Nathan said. He was caught off guard. "I pull at random and attempt to answer as many as possible."

"How many do you average a performance?"

"Forty-two."

Sarah thought on this. Forty-two people whose lives were better for having known Mr. Garlan. Forty-two. Sarah could not think of forty-two people she had helped in the past twenty years let alone in three hours four times a week.

The man with the opals watched their table. He liked the light that spilled out of their eyes.

"There are more pressing matters to discuss," Nathan said.

"The toads?"

Nathan nodded. He pulled a small, embroidered pouch from his jacket. He put it on the table. Sarah took it, looked inside, and tucked it in her clutch.

"They are secure. They cannot escape. You may hear them clank against one another, but they are less formidable than a blind, two-legged lion."

"You didn't bring me here for the toads, did you, Mr. Garlan?" Sarah wanted to know Garlan's intentions. Isabelle had told her it wasn't for business. His dark eyes made Sarah inclined to agree. She flagged an elderly man down and ordered a fizzy drink.

"I want to make love to you. I believe us to be a hard-lived, glamorous match," Nathan said. He sipped his tea.

Sarah stared at him.

The capped old man brought her beverage. Sarah tucked a tip onto his tray.

The man with the opals petted each of his jewels. He would give one away.

Sarah did not look amused.

Nathan did not shift his gaze. He looked directly into Sarah's eyes as he pictured fingering open her high collar.

Sarah felt an itch. She scratched near her neck buttons.

"Did I mishear you?" she asked.

"You, Miss Sarah, '…walk in beauty, like the night. Of cloudless climes and—'"

"Thief! I know my Byron."

Sarah took another sip. She kept Nathan's gaze.

"I was going to attribute him."

Sarah gave Nathan an unimpressed glance. She said, "You cannot possibly want woo me. You hardly know me."

"But I do. You are a remarkable creature. There is a wild nature under that proper façade."

A pause. A wisp of a woman refilled Nathan's tea. The wisp let her hand linger on Nathan's shoulder. Then she swayed away.

Sarah wanted to hit this woman in the face. Sarah had never hit anyone outside of the dead let alone an urchin of public service pouring hot water for a man she felt no feelings for. A man who, of all the things, worked in a theater. A man who had dark hair and steady eyes who dressed like a mad poet and had a fine library.

"I don't know you," Sarah said.

"But you want to," Nathan said.

"You are mildly captivating," Sarah said.

"You think I am more than that, Sarah."

He had used her name. Again.

"Mr. Garlan, you are inappropriate."

"And you are more the Belle Hellion than the world knows." The dead had given him this name, had told him about her tree.

"How could you…"

The man with the opals passed by. He left a silk rag on the table and exited the café. Neither Sarah nor Nathan noticed.

"I do not know everything about you, but I know enough, and I am decided. I could never again care for anyone else."

Sarah stared at Nathan as if he were an invalid with mashed scone all over his face.

"You are too young. I have been married. I have had a child. I have had a lifetime before you."

Nathan smiled.

Sarah said nothing.

Nathan smiled at her still.

Sarah said nothing.

Nathan reached for Sarah's hand.

Sarah smacked a crumb-ridden fork at it.

Nathan's hand went red.

Sarah sat with tense shoulders.

Diners tilted heads their way.

"Manners?" Sarah reminded them. Everyone turned back around.

"You are not a normal woman," Nathan said.

"I do not know if that is for a stranger to say," Sarah said.

"A normal woman would not have met me here."

Sarah did not respond. She wiped off the fork.

"Or smacked my hand with a fork."

"You reached for something that wasn't yours."

"You are meant for mine, Sarah."

"One: I am meant to live my life. I am not owned by anyone. I had one husband and I have no intention of marrying myself off to another one. Two: my name to you, is not Sarah. It is Mrs. Winchester."

"I will not use his name." The tendons on Nathan's neck stood out.

"He was a good man."

"He had you. He ignored you. He gave you a child. Blamed you for its death. He cared more for guns than he did for love. He cared more about a departed infant than he did for a living wife, he—"

Sarah smacked him.

Surprisingly, no one turned to gawk at their table.

Sarah got up.

Nathan grabbed her hand before she could go.

"He was a quiet man. A busy man. And once, long ago, he was a good man," she said.

"I am the better man for you," Nathan said. He stood and let her go. The look he gave her made her feel naked and needed.

She did not walk away from him. She allowed her heart to riot and her hands to follow. Sarah pulled on Nathan's lapels. His head dipped to hers. Their lips met.

Sarah tasted of blackberries.

Nathan of Earl Grey.

Nathan reached to wrap his arms around her and Sarah shoved him away. There were over ten damn years between the two of them. She couldn't go falling for someone so young. She couldn't go falling for anyone. She was not someone meant to be loved.

Sarah walked out of Indolent Café into the midafternoon sun.

Nathan touched his lips with his fingertips. He felt an absurd grin on his face. He ignored the disapproving looks from tables around him. He noticed the silk rag and opened it. A fiery opal glinted back at him.

Sarah's hand was in a dress fold that held a .50-caliber percussion boot pistol. It was a dreg of a gun with too much kick, but Sarah could shoot the button off a cuff at fifteen yards with it. She could certainly shoot a young man in the shoe from three steps. Because if Nathan followed, Sarah would either have to shoot the man or immediately bed him.

Nathan did not follow Sarah.

He finished his tea.

A few apparitions chattered around him.

Nathan threw down salt in a circle. He did not want their company. He wanted Sarah's.

Since she no longer had a child to tear it or a husband to stain it with inked memos, Sarah decided to buy a new frock. She convinced herself that this decision had nothing to do with impressing Nathan Garlan.

CHAPTER FORTY-EIGHT

INSIDE TWO TOADS, 1882

ANNIE DID NOT like her new home. It was too shiny. She could not crawl out of the toad's mouth. She could not crawl out of the eyes. She could not crawl out any which side. It hurt to try.

Annie decided she would sit and wait.

William was equally ill pleased with being sucked into a toad. A toad? It was undignified.

He could not talk to or touch Annie. He had tried. They heard each other as if talking through a feather mattress. He was alone with himself as his image reflected around him more times than he cared to count.

There was no way out.

That man, that Nathan Garlan, that eccentric snob would make a harlot of his wife.

In Annie's waiting, she did cry. She missed her father.

William heard these soft sobs.

The toads were not a problem. They were a challenge. William beat death. He thought he could certainly find his way out of a toad.

He was mistaken.

CHAPTER FORTY-NINE

BOSTON, MASSACHUSETTS, 1882

SARAH FELL FOR him. She had no business falling in love, but she'd never met someone so fantastically odd and absolutely gorgeous. She'd spent her entire life surviving and now wanted to do better. She wanted to live and she wanted to live with Nathan Garlan.

Over the months, she visited him at the theater, at his home, in public, anywhere. She wanted to be near him. Her reading had suffered from the knowing of him, but her lips, they were well exercised.

For six months, Sarah collected Nathan after every performance at the Watchbird, and in her waiting, she made friends. Sarah had never had friends before.

The Steel Man found Sarah's handshake impressive.

The Illustrated Woman liked that Sarah didn't flinch at the hieroglyphics on the backs of her hands or the depiction of Athena on her neck.

Fence, a small man, adored that Sarah never petted his head.

The burlesque troupe, the jugglers, the magician, the mathematician, the hypnotist, the comedians, the Shakespearean actor—all of the Watchbird loved

Sarah. She often brought muffins, fresh fruit, and pickled delights with her good humor.

But not Arrol. It was selfish. Jealous. Juvenile. Arrol knew this, but he did not like Sarah Winchester. She would steal Nathan away from him. Grimm—who loved that Sarah could quote more Byron than Nathan—assured Arrol that the Watchbird would manage. Arrol did not want the Watchbird to manage. He wanted it to thrive.

Even the Watchbird itself loved Sarah. What free time she had away from Nathan she spent sketching its curved arches, filigreed lamps, crooked halls, and shadowy catwalks.

Nathan found Sarah sitting on the floor before a sconce and a framed poster that stated:

THE MASKED JEROME! HE WHO JUGGLES SIX SINGING CATS!

across a painting of a tall man in a thin, red mask. Cats sat on his hands, shoulders, and head.

"What are you doing, darling?"

"Wishing I could juggle," she said. She put the finishing smudges to a drawing of the sconce.

"Stunning," Nathan said.

Sarah was pleased. She liked that he liked her art.

"It is an oddity that you found yourself at the end of this particular hall," Nathan said.

"Why?"

"When I first arrived at the Watchbird, I lived here."

"Did Grimm keep you up with his snoring? That man, when he naps in the box office, they hear him backstage," Sarah said and smiled.

"I had secluded quarters. Nobody bothered me."

"Where did you sleep?"

Nathan smiled at her, walked to the sconce, and tapped his foot to a worn wood panel. A hidden door popped open. "In here."

Sarah's eyes opened wide.

Sarah and Nathan stepped through the door.

A modest iron-rimmed bed stood in the middle of a small room lined with books and boxes.

The door closed behind them. Light bled in through a high, small window. A thin hall led to another room.

Sarah should have blushed. A lady would've blushed. Sarah did not want to be a lady. She decided she could be whoever she wanted with this man. Someone entirely new. She took off her gloves and said, "On your knees, Mr. Garlan."

Nathan went to his knees in front of Sarah. He took her hands and traced his thumb on her poker scar.

They had never been this alone.

"Take off your jacket and waistcoat," she commanded.

Nathan shed what he was told.

"And your cravat," she said.

Slowly, he untied his crimson cravat.

"Your shirt, sir."

In one motion, the shirt was over his head.

Sarah gasped.

A maze of symbols and script crossed Nathan's shoulders in precise columns.

"What is it?" Sarah asked.

"Blessings, curses, wards to help a man through the day."

Nathan reached for Sarah. She smacked his hands.

"I did not tell you to do that."

Nathan knew when to let a lady have her way.

Sarah sat. Her frock pooled on the floor around her. She placed Nathan's hands on her thighs.

He held her stare. This was something William would never have done. Would never look at her when they were together. Would never even look at her when he was on top of her.

Sarah placed Nathan's hands on the buttons down the front of her dress.

As Nathan undid each button, he watched the mirrors in his room. They reflected Sarah trying to read languages few had ever seen.

"Teach me everything you know," Sarah said as her nails traced the symbols.

Nathan took her in his arms and did exactly as he was told.

CHAPTER FIFTY

SEVERAL HOURS OUTSIDE OF BOSTON, MASSACHUSETTS, 1884

GRAHAM WOKE HESTER by throwing a pudgy beetle at her forehead. Hester did not like insects. A few thousand creepies possessing you and a woman got cautious. She wore a ward ring on her left pinky that protected her from deceased vermin.

This beetle was living and it crawled in her nose.

Hester flailed and smacked herself in the face. The beetle reversed out of her nostril with a broken back. Its eyes locked on Hester's and its second-to-last thought was "Oh, but I've peed." Its last thought was "I will not die while excreting." The beetle stepped out of itself as its body fell to the ground.

"Wakey, wakey," Graham said.

Hester did not want to get out of her bedroll. It was barely light and she had had a dream about toads. She was not particularly fond of toads. Frogs had a pleasant demeanor. Toads were cantankerous creatures that barked, left stains on the floor, and chewed loudly.

Yet, Hester dreamt of two silver toads.

"Woman, AWAKE. I command it," Graham said. He toed Hester in the ribs.

"Why are you not constrained to the willow?" Hester asked. She rubbed her sore nose.

"No matter. Get up. Read," Graham said. He was thoroughly adept in pain management and escape techniques.

Hester grabbed the newspaper that floated over her head.

"Where'd you get this?"

"Blew out of town. Being a man who thinks ahead, I plucked it from the air for your morning ablutions."

Graham paced back and forth. After all these years, he still planned his day in accordance to pleasing Hester Garlan, and if not pleasing her, then at least being noticed by her. Graham did not know what to think of himself. He had gathered her a shit towel. This was not a romantic life.

"You may thank me by finally killing me, my golden calf."

Hester grunted.

The newspaper had begun its day in the callused hands of the Reverend Doctor Enton Blake. A gust had taken it from his grasp as he bought breakfast from a Chinese noodle shack.

"Sleep," Hester said and curtained her head with it.

"Get up, up, UP," said Graham as he stomped around Hester. He grabbed the paper before another breeze did.

Hester kept her eyes closed. She took a match from beneath her pillow and flicked it to flame with her thumbnail. She set the newspaper corner on fire.

Graham Johnson poured coffee on it. "It is news of your boy."

Hester's eyes opened and she grabbed the sodden paper.

"Look at the man's picture, Hester. Look at his name."

Hester took a handful of iron tacks from her pocket and threw them in Graham's direction for being a know-it-all. Graham dodged, but a tack hit the newly dead beetle and it screamed in fresh pain.

There was an oval illustration, front page even, of a man with dark hair and deep eyes.

"Damn him," Hester muttered.

In Boston, Nathan felt a chill behind his ears.

"Mr. Johnson, you are a treasure. What would I do without you?" Graham said in a high-pitched voice. He used a twig to lift the iron tack off the beetle.

"Shut your mouth or I will sew it shut," Hester said.

"If you were able to do that, my swagger and fuss, you'd have done it years ago."

Hester read.

NATHAN GARLAN! AN AGENT OF THE AFTERLIFE!

EMISSARY OF FINAL ENDINGS!

BROKER OF BEREAVEMENT!

Her son was Very Important. His feats included everything from treasure finding to séances with Mary Todd Lincoln.

The paper reported that Nathan Garlan could not only hear the dead, he could see them. He had the world's premier library of eerie and esoteric materials. A popular magic-lantern show in Boston demonstrated him dominating a mischievous spirit. And oh, he was strong. And oh, he was dashing. And ladies, he was unmarried—though a mysterious, widowed heiress had recently taken his attention! They called him the greatest medium ever known. No query was too small or too large. He had sold out every performance at the Watchbird Theater for over a decade.

Hester farted in distaste.

"I *again* present you the location of your son," Graham said. He petted the beetle that Hester had harmed.

"We were already headed to Boston and the bastard will still be there in a coupla hours," Hester responded. She fell back to sleep for forty-five more minutes.

Graham Johnson felt profoundly underappreciated.

Chapter Fifty-One

THE REVEREND DOCTOR Enton Blake did not feel well. As was his standard. The spicy noodles he had were rot and bother in his guts. They spilled onto the narrow path next to the exorbitantly priced inn that held his effects.

He had a vision of Sita stroking his forehead. Of sitting by the sea. Of growing old with someone rather than looking for someone.

He'd read of Nathan Garlan in the paper.

He knew Hester would be on her way to her boy.

This errand would be over soon. He would be in the artistic arms of an intelligent beauty within a month. He would save Nathan from his mother. He'd save his own father from a cramped and strenuous afterlife. Then he'd save the rest of his life for Sita, if she'd have him.

First, he would nap.

CHAPTER FIFTY-TWO

BOSTON, MASSACHUSETTS, 1884

THE PUPPY WAS a menace.

It was an unwieldy scamp with more dirt and devilry spilling off it than hell's back door.

Nathan bought it from a spoonmaker.

"Good day, sir." Nathan tipped his hat to the cart driver outside the Watchbird Theater.

A quick nod was all the regard the spoonmaker could spare.

The cart was a tempest. Wooden spoons knocked silver spoons knocked the sides of the cart. Yellow flags jutted from its corners.

The street held a Friday evening hustle.

Euri, the Watchbird's belly dancer, laid a hat down and moved to the music of the spoonmaker's cart. He was old and his hand-sewn bells now missed their clappers. He did not glitter as much as he greyed.

A sandwich board man passed. His clapboards read:

REVIVIFY! REFINE!

REINSTATE! RESHAPE!

Healthful! Wholity!

The Scientific! Doctor! Says:

But the rest was marred by a carriage splash and what looked like mustard. Another charlatan who chose a name close to Enton Blake's.

The sandwich board man heard this:

"Man, your cart is shaking."

"It is not," said the spoonmaker who watched a pendant shimmy across Euri's chest.

There was a bark inside the cart.

"You, sir, have a dog in that cart. And I want it." Nathan had never wanted a dog before, but having a dog with Sarah was pleasing to him.

"I do not," said the spoonmaker who now watched the sandwich board round the corner.

A happier bark came from inside the cart.

"What do you want for the pup?"

The spoonmaker's daughter, a dead little thing of five, tried to grab her father's hand. Nathan saw this.

The spoonmaker felt a cold itch on his hand and an ache in his heart.

The puppy was his daughter's. He didn't like the mutt, but she had, and she was gone.

"I will tell you of your daughter," Nathan said.

The spoonmaker met his gaze.

"Is there something to know?"

The spoonmaker's daughter nodded.

"Yes," said Nathan.

The little girl wandered up to Nathan. One leg was longer than the other.

The puppy pitched itself against the cart walls.

Nathan bent to listen to the girl.

A pink nose peeked between the cart's wood slats.

The girl pointed at her father.

Nathan whispered the girl's message to her father.

The man went to the back of the cart and returned with the puppy. He handed it over to Nathan.

The spoonmaker's daughter may or may not have forgiven her father for forcing her to collect coins in the carriageway on a hurly-burly afternoon.

Nathan met Sarah for dinner and brought the dog.

"What am I going to do with it?" Sarah asked.

The puppy ate from a dish by her foot.

"Name it," Nathan said.

"I can't keep it."

The puppy switched its nose from the dish of stew to Sarah's boots.

"He likes you."

"I don't know if I like him."

The puppy sat up and looked at Sarah.

Sarah looked down at him.

The dog blinked.

"It's a fluffy mutt," Sarah said.

She thought on Cort.

"You like fluffy mutts," Nathan said.

The puppy nodded.

Sarah found that she nodded back at the dog.

"He noticed that," Nathan said.

The puppy held out a paw. He gave her three more shakes of a tail before he liked the man more.

"He is filthy."

"Yes."

One shake.

"He's got black eyes."

"Indeed."

Two shakes.

"He will probably eat the kitchen staff when he gets done with the pantry."

Three shakes.

Sarah grabbed the paw and pulled the puppy into her arms.

"Name?" Nathan asked.

The puppy raced across Sarah's lap.

"Zip."

Zip stopped and looked at her.

"What?" Sarah asked.

He jumped up and rammed himself into her face for a lick. Thereby hitting the dinner table. Other diners looked at their table, unamused.

"My work here is done," Nathan said.

Sarah wasn't listening.

She talked to Zip. In a whisper. Under the ledge of fur that covered his ear.

Nathan smiled. He ordered enough crab for all three of them.

It was during dessert that dinner became serious.

"What do you mean you want to travel?" Nathan asked.

"Well, not travel. I want to leave. I want to go somewhere warm."

Zip nuzzled Sarah under the table.

"Where?"

"I think I would like to live in San Jose," Sarah said. "You can buy or build a house on a world of land."

"What would you do with it, the land?" Nathan had a spoon of chocolate pudding midway to his mouth.

Sarah dropped a cracker down to Zip.

"Orchards. I've read that California is full of orchards."

"Such as?"

"Plums. Apricots. Perhaps walnut trees."

"Who would do all this farming?"

Sarah frowned at Nathan.

Nathan gave an exaggerated frown back.

"I have a mind for business, you do know."

"Oh, I know. I hear you tapping about the telegraph all hours of the day talking to the Company."

"There are finances to keep track of."

"Quite," Nathan said. "Millions of them."

Zip nodded.

"Would you have me go with you?" Nathan asked. He said this quietly and while he watched his pudding drop from the spoon to the plate.

"You would go with me?" Sarah asked.

Nathan put down the spoon and reached for his pocket. In it was a silver chain with a single opal.

"If you'd have me," Nathan said.

"A thousand times yes, Nathan Garlan. In fact, I demand your presence."

Nathan stood. He went behind Sarah, he fingered a stray curl, and clasped the necklace.

Sarah turned the opal over and knew there would be a protection rune carved into the silver that cased the stone.

"You are my favorite," she told Nathan.

"Favorite what?" he breathed in her ear.

"Everything. My favorite everything."

Zip nodded and nuzzled their shoes.

"Shall we leave on Friday?" Nathan asked.

"So soon? A week from now? What about the Watchbird? What about your home? What about mine in New Haven? Isabelle could hire movers to crate it all...I haven't been there in an age. Arrol will absolutely hate me."

Nathan sat back down at the table.

Zip licked his ankle.

"Arrol will be annoyed, but the Watchbird will be fine. Our houses will be crated. They will be sold. We will buy one together in California."

Sarah did not know how, but in one year, her entire life had changed.

She kissed Nathan's hands across the table.

Chapter Fifty-Three

Boston, Massachusetts, 1884

HENNET C. DANIELS never thought he would see the day that he attained a straight vocation. Yet here he was at four in the goddamned morning preparing the fires at a bakery.

Suff had spit him out.

He felt old.

He felt Walleye near. Saw the messes his brother made with the flour and eggs.

Hennet was tired and alone and wanted a son to hear his stories. He had thought about hiring the Pinkertons, but they costed more than a queen's corset, and he damnwell hated Pinkertons. Nosey lawdog sonsabitches always in other people's business.

Instead, Hennet worked. He rebuilt some of the strength he'd lost sitting in a cage for fifteen years. He stacked his cash. He waited. When you don't know how to begin, you wait. You watch. Mama Daniels had taught him that and it had stood true in the past.

It was a cold morning. He hadn't lit the oven. He had his coffee first. He was going to sweat all damn day. He let the morning chill him and the coffee counter it.

He drained the last sip.

He sighed.

Working. Working was awful. How did people do this their entire lives?

Hennet lit the lamps. Swept the dregs that he'd left the day before. He tossed a stack of newspapers into the oven to begin the fire. He snapped a match and threw it in.

Hennet did not know that his son had been dragged from this self-same oven over thirty years before. What Hennet did know is that something caught his eye—a picture on the front page of a man with his eyes and a wildcat woman's impish mouth.

"Shit. Sheesh," Hennet muttered as he reached in to grab the flaming page.

The headline read:

NATHAN GARLAN! AN AGENT OF THE AFTERLIFE!

EMISSARY OF FINAL ENDINGS!

BROKER OF BEREAVEMENT!

"Well, goddamn," Hennet said.

He caught the phrase Watchbird Theater before the paper went to ash in his hands. Hennet smiled.

His son was down the damned street.

CHAPTER FIFTY-FOUR

"IT IS FRIDAY," Arrol said.

"It is," Nathan answered.

They were in the side hall of the Watchbird in front of Nathan's former residence, now prop room.

"You are packed?"

"We leave on the midnight train."

Nathan dragged his fingertips across the decorative wallpaper. His thumb grazed the frame of a painting depicting the whole round earth in Arrol's hands. The first Watchbird rat Nathan'd ever met fell on his head from behind that frame while he sat in a booze gloom beneath it. Arrol had taught him how to train the rat to stand on its back paws, squeak out speech, and bring an audience member a flower.

"I am angry with you," Arrol said.

"I know it."

"You are costing me thousands of dollars." Arrol spoke in a stern drawl. It was what he thought a banker to sound like. One part stick in puckerhole, one part posh pudding-eater.

Nathan nodded.

"But I am happy for you."

"I know it." Nathan did know it, but there was a cock to Arrol's eyebrow that he did not trust. He girded himself.

Arrol threw a handful of powder on the floorboards. This was not unusual for Arrol. A billowing of smoke surrounded them.

"Arrol! Remove your thieving hand from my person."

"None shall stop Wester the Great and Powerful!" Arrol cackled.

Through the smoke, Nathan's swatting hands could be glimpsed, as well as the shining brass corners of Arrol's chair as it circled and screeched around his nephew. Three dead actors dove in and danced around them. Their forms were visible in the gritty puff.

"Brute!" Arrol cried as his chair rolled out of the dissipating cloud. He employed a sword cane (ordinarily used to gesture threateningly at creditors) to grasp a door handle and stop himself.

Nathan coughed, dusted off his black velvet tailcoat, and said, "It is not proper to pickpocket family and it is especially gauche under such obvious circumstances."

"I did not find your train ticket. Do not lord it over me."

"I should thrash you, uncle."

"Not unless you would deal with Grimm."

On cue, Grimm walked from the other end of the hall toward Arrol and Nathan.

"You are truly leaving?" Grimm asked. He took up his accustomed position behind Arrol's wheeled chair with his arms crossed.

Nathan nodded.

Grimm sniffed and cringed at the ashy odor. "You used a smoke burster on the man?"

Arrol picked his cuticles in a huff. "If you had let me out of bed to lock him in a cage or pillage his personal effects last night, this awkwardness wouldn't have ensued."

Grimm's eyebrows were long and curled at the ends to match his mustache. He looked at Nathan. "It's a hard pass, him letting you go."

"I will write."

"Imbeciles. I am fine. The Watchbird will be fine. We got along before the marvelous Mr. Garlan. We will be fine after."

Grimm petted Arrol's shoulder. Arrol took his hand.

"Do not be angry with me, uncle. I am in love."

Arrol and Grimm squawked out a laugh at the same time.

Nathan colored.

"Calm down, nephew. We know you are sincere in your affections," Grimm said.

"Bloody right, I am."

"You sound like a melodrama even I wouldn't put on stage," Arrol teased.

"You let one on back in '64," Grimm reminded Arrol.

"Ye gods, and it was the last. The crowd cried so hard they couldn't see their wallets. Souvenir sales were dismal. Never again."

Grimm nodded.

Arrol said, "This Winchester woman is a good woman, but the air around her is not always right."

Grimm smoothed Arrol's collar down. It was embroidered with flowers.

"How do you know it's not me? How does the air feel around me?"

This was a fair question. Nathan was followed by so many apparitions that there was, at times, a wake of cold around him, and depending on the needs of said spirits, an ambience of despair.

Arrol did not mean to, but he shuddered. "The air has never been right around you either."

"However the air, Sarah and I leave tonight for San Jose by way of train, coach, and train again."

Arrol opened his mouth to say something and closed it again. He took a moment. "Be wary, Nathan, my adored and only nephew. The Watchbird is excessively expressive tonight." Arrol did not want to speak anymore. His heart would fall out of his mouth. He felt as if nothing would be well ever again.

Arrol tapped Grimm's hand. Grimm rolled him down the hall.

They would check on the ticket takers. They had to be clear with patrons that there would be only a fraction of the variety acts Friday usually held. There would be a *Faust* monologue by noted actor Claire Suzanne Elizabeth Peabody while the orchestra played Saint-Saëns and the living statues posed about the edges of the stage. There would be a brief interlude of acrobatics by Fence the Small Man and Rarely the Willow Man. Grimm would perform a short bout of feats of strength in front of the drawn curtain as the stage was cleared. Then Nathan would take the spotlight for the last time.

Nathan watched Grimm and Arrol leave. There was something final about their forms receding down the hall. He turned his attention to his prop room. He did not need much for the evening. Mostly, he wanted to leave the room in a habitable state for whomever the Watchbird led there next.

The room was dark but for a lamp and the meek evening light that crowded in the high, barred window. The window was open. A blackbird sat on the outer ledge.

"Hello, friend." Nathan crossed the room, took a few sunflower seeds from his pocket and fed them to the bird. The bird brayed a thankful caw after each seed.

"I know, I know. It is time. It is always about that time. But this is the last time."

The blackbird blinked. It wanted more seeds.

Nathan tugged a cravat from a pile on his desk and folded it about his neck.

The blackbird scratched at the windowsill and bobbed its head between the bars. There was a whole pocket full of seeds this man was not giving over.

"I appreciate your enthusiasm and approval. It is a new cravat. At first, I thought the color choice too bold. Who wears paisley the color of the sea?"

The bird cawed again.

"Correct. If my suit is black, why the dickens shouldn't I wear a teal paisley cravat. Momentous evenings require exceptional ensembles."

Several dead mice, regulars to Nathan's prop room, crawled up his pant leg. Nathan ignored them, checked his visage in a looking glass, and appraised the room.

"It will have to do," Nathan said to himself. The bed was made. The shelves free of clutter. His most important books and collections had long since been packed, here and at his private residence.

The dead mice dropped off Nathan and burrowed into the cravat pile instead.

The blackbird cawed. It did not think it right for a man to have such a full pocket of seeds and give so few.

"I'm going. I'm going."

Nathan pushed aside a tasseled curtain and left his prop quarters through a clandestine door. It led down a long, narrow hall and exited backstage.

Sarah was to watch him from the wings. They would leave together after his last show.

Only the blackbird heard the sound of the crates and the soapboxes being stacked outside the window.

CHAPTER FIFTY-FIVE

BOSTON, MASSACHUSETTS, 1884

SARAH SAT AT the Indolent Café. She would leave for the theater in quarter of an hour. She wanted to give Nathan time alone to grieve the leaving of his home. She realized she had never ached over New Haven. But what did it hold for her? Family, yes, but mostly only demanding memories and dreary neighbors.

She opened her journal. "Wide unclasp the table of their thoughts" was writ in a stained glass window outline. Her reading had turned to Shakespeare and it had influenced her architectural drawings.

A woman passed the window of the Indolent Café in a wheeled chair. The chair pushed itself down the thoroughfare. Sarah, intent on her sketch, did not notice.

The apparitions of Boston did.

A dead rumbling made its way toward the Watchbird Theater.

CHAPTER FIFTY-SIX

BOSTON, MASSACHUSETTS, 1884

THE LINE OUTSIDE the Watchbird Theater extended blocks upon blocks. Lavishly dressed women mingled with droop-eared old folks. Investment-seeking businessmen stood with forlorn grievers. Local apparitions wandered the crowd. A dead owl, missing its legs, tilted against the knee of a long-nosed man who wondered what was wrong with his circulation. It felt like there were pins in his calf.

A magician from a rival theater worked the line with a hat full of doves and tinsel tucked in his sleeves. He was run off by a bald man in a yellow vest. The yellow-vested man then went to a soapbox in front of the doors and yelled, "Pardon me, my good people. If you don't have a ticket, you ain't getting one. Kindly leave the line if you ain't got a ticket."

At this, a small crowd grumbled and left the line and the yellow-vested man picked up his soapbox. He repeated his message further down the road.

Near the theater doors, Hennet took note of a ten-foot-tall poster.

THE GUILELESS NATHAN GARLAN!!!

A CANDID AND CORRECT! RELIABLE AND RIGHTEOUS! MEDIUM!

The Last Appearance of the Most Renowned
Spirit Meeter and Dead Reader!!!

Someone had painted "SOLD OUT" over it.

The paint ran and looked like blood.

Waiting in line was waiting for death. Hennet did not wait in line. He walked past the line. He nodded at folks as he picked their pockets. The bakery barely made him boot money, let alone coin to throw at whiskey. If he was to meet his son tonight, surely he'd buy the first few rounds.

Hennet pardoned his way through the line. He could hear Walleye gaining on him by the "OOF"s, "Watch where you're going"s, and retching sounds not far behind. Hennet found the tight alley alongside the Watchbird. He was a master of secondary entrances. Side doors. Windows. Busting holes in flimsy walls. He would get in the theater.

For a man near fifty, Hennet didn't look it. He had borrowed a formal jacket off an equally long-shouldered, narrow-waisted man. By borrowed, Hennet reflected on his knuckles itching. The man he had punched had had a greasy face. What kind of man doesn't take the time to wash his face before going to the theater?

The theater's side door was crowded with workers. An illustrated woman with bangled ankles winked at him and continued to smoke. A man sat on a stack of crates. His legs rested behind his head while he drank from a bottle of bourbon. A baby bear chased a garbage picker's ghost back and forth between the alley walls.

Hennet searched for other points of entry.

Hennet would've walked past the high, barred window, but a blackbird's caw made him look up. Mama Daniels had taught him to take note of birds and rats. They knew more than they let on.

It didn't take much effort for Hennet to stack crates, grab hold the bars, then knife-dig 'em out of the wood frame. It took more effort not to gun down the blackbird that pecked at him the whole way. Hennet swatted at it and the bird pecked harder. Walleye swatted at it, but he only succeeded in toppling Hennet and his crates on two occasions. Hennet settled on twisting the bird's neck after it flapped his hat to the garbage pile.

The blackbird did not want to leave the garbage alley. It chose to sit with a permanently tilted head amongst the other feathered dead on the washline behind the Watchbird Theater.

Hennet busted the last bar from the window as a cheer and tussle came from the front of the theater. The doors had opened. The line moved. Hennet elbowed his way into the window, had a worrisome wink where he thought himself stuck, then felt Walleye's cold hands shove his ass forward. He fell in a bad topple.

"Popping a shoulder from joint from a four-foot fall..." Hennet muttered to himself. Aging was one mortification after another.

Walleye agreed. But he didn't say anything. He barely talked these days. It was not worth his time. Nothing was worth his time. He was tired of Hennet. He was tired of being dead. He missed Mule.

With a grunt and a grimace, Hennet budged his shoulder back into place, navigated his way out of the prop room, and joined the crowd.

CHAPTER FIFTY-SEVEN

BOSTON, MASSACHUSETTS, 1884

HESTER FOLLOWED THE crowd into the theater.

There was a dead roar when she entered.

Nathan thought this roar was the living crowd.

Hester had a ticket. Three in fact. One for each clutch she cutpursed as Graham rolled her to the front of the line.

Hester muttered a prayer. It released the rigidity from her shoulders. She did not pray to God. She did not pray to Lucifer. She prayed to herself.

Graham Johnson knew that by the end of the night, Nathan would be dead. He did not care. He'd never met the man. By morning, he would be dead, too. There was a peace in him—a warmth akin to what he imagined heating his hands on a fire made of Kominsky's bones would feel like.

The Watchbird's murmurs of Hester's entrance could not be heard over the living crowd.

Dead performers and patrons went to tell Nathan of Hester's presence, but the man squirreled himself away before performances. They did not understand his nerves. Nathan could break wind on stage and the audience would think it was a song from the sweet hereafter.

Nathan did not hear his phantasmic cohorts. He stood in meditation in a coat closet backstage.

The crowd flooded through the gilded doors and into the wallpapered hall. They walked under dusty chandeliers and a gold-flecked, tin ceiling. Some rushed the grand staircase for balcony seating.

Ushers guarded the front rows on the ground floor and directed lesser patrons to standing room in the rear.

Hester put her leg braces on, stowed her wheeled chair in a closet, and haltingly walked to her seat near the front of the stage. She heard constant dead chatter from every angle of the Watchbird. It was not a welcoming building. Every other corner had some fat cherub or angry gargoyle keeping its eye on you. She was soaked in saltwater.

Hester angered at the finery of the folk filling the theater.

Her son had nice things.

His people had nice things.

Nathan of her namesake, of her blood. The little bastard that didn't die in the oven, didn't die in the orphanage, didn't die in the damn bookshop. He would die tonight and she'd shove him in the trick box and gain back her dead sight. Maybe she'd become the grand dame medium of the world and she'd be the one with nice things.

It was swagger and smugness that made Hester decide to kill Nathan in a crowded theater on the last night of his farewell to Boston. Graham had tried to convince her otherwise. He spouted horseshit about her new limitations. Hester did not tolerate limitations. She wanted to hurt Nathan and the people that adored him. She wanted to do it quickly. Efficiently. She had a pistol. She would use it.

She sat where an usher guided her, in front of the orchestra pit. There were three shivs, a club, rope, and her knucklebuster-gripped knife under her skirt, in case the pistol faltered.

The dead shouted warnings. They rattled the closet door. Nathan stood still with his hands clasped and eyes closed.

The Watchbird shook the floorboards beneath him.

Nathan continued to meditate.

The dead watched Hester guardedly and debated how to murder her without harming anyone who sat around her.

They did not want to damage Nathan's career.

CHAPTER FIFTY-EIGHT

BOSTON, MASSACHUSETTS, 1884

MOLIÈRE'S NOSE JABBED Hennet in the ear when he rested his head on the wall. Every wall, hell, even the stage front, was littered with literary carvings.

Previously, the only theater Hennet saw involved gals flashing knickers. He was pleased that entertainment hadn't changed. Once the crowd settled in, an actor complained about making deals with devils. Hennet didn't give a damn. His attention was on the broads in the background, painted and draped with barely a stitch of britches.

The crowd was tense. Hennet could feel that. It wasn't from the bawdy show either. They squeezed forward as much as possible. Black-laced women, misery-soaked men, morose little ones, and anxious others shoved for clearer views. Above him, balcony railings were intermittent at best. All it would take was one sneezing asshole and you could go teetering off the edge. Yet, people leaned. Even the high-and-mightys that afforded the front row inclined forward.

Most of the attendees were dressed in mourning. They came wondering about their dead friends, dead family. It made Hennet whistle at the unceasing sorrow Nathan hauled. Considering the witch-haired woman the boy came from, he wasn't a fraud either.

Hennet surveyed the stage (ten foot lamps wide), searched for exits (auditorium doors behind him and a side door stage right), and assessed his surroundings.

He saw her.

A dead bluebird flew into Hennet's chest and pecked at his heart. Hennet mistakenly thought that this skipped beat was for love.

She sat at the front of the stage by the orchestra pit. The man to her right did not notice that he was being pickpocketed. There were twigs in her hair. Hennet didn't need to see her face to know it was her.

Hennet wanted a son and a wife by night's end.

Walleye noticed Hennet noticing Hester Garlan. Every haint around Walleye jawed on about her. *Watch her, what's she doing here, keep her still, don't let her near him.* Not knowing what to do, Walleye did nothing. Didn't warn Hennet 'cause his warnings went sour anyways. He itched his elbow stump and watched the ladies on stage.

The final strains of music burst from the orchestra pit, the actor took a bow, the living statues glided away, and a short man and a thin man flipped and somersaulted onto the stage.

Chapter Fifty-Nine

Boston, Massachusetts, 1884

SARAH SAT IN a chair in the wings.

Nathan came behind her and rested his hands on her neck.

"Darling," she said and nuzzled into his wrist.

"By my count, my lovely, we are to depart in less than four hours," Nathan whispered. "And once we are in our compartment, I am going to rip the front of your dress open."

Sarah feigned shock. "But sir! My buttons!"

"And nibble what is underneath."

Sarah made a small "Mmmm" and wished time would move forward.

Zip rolled his eyes. He would spend the whole journey hiding under the bench from their nakedness.

"Are you prepared?" Sarah asked.

"As much as I can ever be. The first fifty had their requests boxed, but I expect the crowd to be riled and shout questions."

"You will do splendid and I will watch it all from right here."

Sarah clapped as Rarely and Fence finished their acrobatics and the curtain closed. The men nodded at the couple as they left the stage.

Grimm went on stage. He carried a man on each of his shoulders.

Nathan felt a tug.

Several tugs.

There was a toddler at his knee. The half-headed boy pointed. Nathan looked past Sarah into the crowd. He paled.

The dead shouting had not been heard. The Watchbird's subtle quaking garnered no attention. So neighborhood apparitions and ghostly guests made a blue tower of babel above Hester Garlan's head. Graham had warned Hester of this, but she threw salt to quiet him during the acrobatic activities.

Nathan recognized the woman.

"What is it?" Sarah asked.

"My mother."

Sarah stood and balled her fists.

"Whoa, darling, whoa," Nathan said and held her back.

"Where is she?"

"She is the wild-eyed one with the excellent posture near the orchestra pit."

Sarah frowned at the woman as she peeked around the stage curtain.

"Do you think she is here to make amends?"

"Doubtful."

"What do the dead say?"

Nathan stopped to listen. A murmuring of clubs, knives, past transgressions, and hidden pistols filled his ears.

"She wouldn't dare assassinate me in front of a full house of onlookers. She is not suicidal."

"She has weapons?"

"Yes."

"Nathan! Throw her out! Resell the seat!"

"I will announce her from the stage and demand her egress."

Zip growled his disapproval.

"Are you mad? Why not do it quietly?"

"Because she appears old and I am feeling cruel." Nathan ran his fingers through his hair and rubbed the small dent on the side of his head.

Sarah did not say anything. She wasn't sure what to say. She did not like that Nathan wanted to humiliate this woman—a woman who looked only slightly older than herself. But Sarah had not been abandoned and repeatedly stabbed by her either. She picked up Zip and petted him to ease her mind.

Grimm did five push-ups on stage with a man standing on his back who held his wife in his arms.

Nathan judged his mother. There were streaks of grey in her hair. Her dress was out of style and rode a little bit high in the front. It revealed the braces on her legs. He did not dismiss her as weak, but she surely did not appear as imposing as in previous years.

The dead in the Watchbird dispersed above Hester. Their charge had seen her. But they did not settle. They paced back and forth causing a breeze in the theater.

Chapter Sixty

Boston, Massachusetts, 1884

By the end of the strongman act, Hester had snagged two billfolds, a pearl bracelet, and a butterfly hatpin. She had grown bored with pilfering and now examined the carving in front of her.

Hester felt a distinct sensation. She was watched. It was a mistake to think it was only Graham Johnson.

Graham pushed himself upon Hester.

"Mr. Johnson, get out of my hair."

"I like you from behind, my corrupt buttercup," Graham whispered. His impending death filled him with a lust for life.

"Don't talk as if you've had anything from behind."

"You would treat me better were you to know what I know," Graham said. He had heard dead whispers that Nathan's father was in attendance.

Hester kept her eyes on a carving.

"It's Euripides," Graham said.

"I don't care."

"He wrote a play about a woman who set fire to her children and felt righteous for doing so. You would enjoy it."

"Go away," Hester said.

"Pardon?" asked the man to Hester's side.

"Wasn't talking to you, was I?"

The man turned away in a huff.

"There is someone here who would interest you, other than your son," Graham said. Hester would never say she needed or wanted anyone, but the tall, dark outlaw suited his brawling bawd. Graham wouldn't mind sharing with a man like that.

Hester threw a dash of salt over her shoulder. It hit Graham and a man that sniveled into his sleeve over losing his best friend to a riverboat brothel wreck.

Grimm took two bows and left the stage to roars of applause.

Graham glared. Fine. He would sit quietly. She would kill her son. She would kill him. Ye gods, he hoped whatever came next was restful and devoid of women.

Hester's neck prickled and so did behind her knees. Her body vibrated in want of Nathan boxed and in her pocket.

The curtains shuffled back and mournful violins played. A table and two chairs were revealed to the crowd. On each side of the stage was a standing candelabra.

Sarah kept watch on Nathan's mother.

She could not tell Grimm. He had exited on the other side of the stage.

"You do have a plan, do you not?" Graham asked.

Hester did, but she did not answer. She ignored all the dead chatter around her. Knew that her body was lined with extra wards, extra salt.

Nathan Garlan walked on stage.

The crowd roared.

Everyone leapt to their feet.

The Watchbird groaned. It felt too full. Arrol had oversold the room.

Arrol rolled his chair by the front doors. He did not want to watch Nathan's final performance.

Hester stood with the rest of the crowd.

"Greetings, my friends," Nathan said.

Applause covered him.

The clapping turned to foot stomping. Turned to shouting. People tried to push closer to the stage. The floor became a pit of shoving. Hats were crushed. Chairs toppled over. Women gave and got sharp elbows. Shoes were stained. Everyone had a question full of wonder or want. Arms and handkerchiefs waved at Nathan Garlan.

Nathan took two steps backward. He'd never had such a strenuous welcome.

Sarah dumped Zip to the ground.

Hester pressed against the edge of the orchestra pit. It was small. There was barely enough room for the three violinists. She worked her arms upward, away from her sides. Her pistol was in hand. She would gut-shot Nathan, get on stage, slice him open, shove him in the box, and then live a full, fancy life.

Hennet was in the middle of the room, ten feet from his son. The floor was uneven with debris.

Ghosts congregated upon the stage with waves of requirement and warning. They sleeve-tugged. They ear-whispered. It was hard for Nathan to see the audience through the many spirits that sauntered around him. The living assumed a fan to be offstage. Why else would Nathan Garlan be windblown?

Sarah reached into her clutch and pulled out a pearl-handled revolver. She did not trust Nathan's mother.

Walleye wandered away from Hennet and found Zip. He petted the dog.

Graham Johnson paced by the foot lamps. Impatient. He picked at his
nails. He spit. He didn't like that Garlan looked well-read. As a rule, Graham
didn't support murdering bookish-types.

"My friends, calm yourselves," Nathan said. "I have an announcement."

The crowd did not calm. It roared.

"When will I die? Where is my mother? Who killed my Matthew Ryan?
When will the Lord return? Should I buy the property in Louisville? Is my
husband a cheat? Is there a Hell? Mort's in Heaven, eh? What color are God's
eyes?"

Hester's shooting hand was unencumbered.

"Friends! People! My mother is in attendance tonight. Let us turn our
attention to her."

Nathan looked down at Hester.

The audience followed the medium's gaze.

Nathan mirrored Hester's smirk.

Hester was struck by how much Nathan Garlan looked like her.

Then she shot him.

The audience went quiet.

The dead went silent.

Nathan reached for his guts.

Hester smiled.

Nathan fell to his knees.

The crowd stood still. No one moved. It had to be part of the show.

Sarah sighted Nathan's mother. Hester pulled herself onto the stage.
Sarah pulled the trigger. Her hands shook.

Sarah's shot had gone high. Hester yowled and fell near Nathan.
Hester's collarbone was shattered and she hadn't seen who shot her.

The violinists were the first to run.

Arrol and Grimm opened the auditorium doors, the front doors, and the side exits. There'd be a brief recess. The Night Watch would take the rowdy ones. The show would go on.

Or not.

A dead wind gusted betwixt Nathan and Hester. Hester could not elbow through it.

Nathan felt like he'd been bitten in half by an ogre.

The crowd took a communal breath and held it.

The Watchbird howled. Its boards rustled violently. It sent audience members lurching. Graham Johnson stumbled over several foot lamps.

The foot lamps fell into the orchestra pit.

"Get the hell out of my way!" Hennet yelled and pushed to the stage.

Nathan heard the man.

The dead muttered, "Father, sire, conceiver, daddy."

Nathan watched the man jump over the orchestra barrier. He had a father who had a hard face but kind eyes.

Hester took a short length of saltwater monk's rope off her thigh. She knotted it and lassoed it around her son and self.

The dead wind that gusted between Hester and Nathan disappeared. It circled and pushed outside the ring. The rope didn't move. Hester was untouched. Nathan bled at her feet. The wind tapped lightly at the rope. It tempested against it. Nothing. It could not enter the circle.

Sarah aimed and fired. The bullet should have hit Hester in the face, but the dead wind that probed the monk's rope inadvertently skewed it. Hester's leg brace busted instead.

Nathan kicked at his mother.

At the exhalation of their joint breath and the report of the third gunshot, the crowd realized that everything had gone terribly awry. This was not a dramatic presentation. How had this happened? All they wanted was answers and now a gale blustered through the theater and there was a fire in the orchestra pit and people screamed and the fire licked up the curtains and people fainted and the fire crept to the edges of the balcony and people pushed backward and the fire moved quick and the balcony creaked and people fainted out of it and the room was hot and smelled of sweat and sulfur and smoke stung their eyes and how could they get out if they couldn't see the exits and what were they stepping on, they were stepping on people.

Everyone panicked.

People streamed out of the auditorium. Grimm and Arrol were smashed against separate walls. Smoke billowed out of the front doors. A bucket brigade was called together by the acrobats, comedians, and nearby shop owners. Flames unfolded from the back of the Watchbird like wings.

Hennet made it on stage. It was cluttered with audience members who searched for side exits. They scurried a wide circle around the bleeding mother, her son, and the zephyr that whirled around them. The candelabras fell and set the stage further to flame.

The dead wind whipped back and forth. It could not break through Hester's monk's rope.

People trampled each other to leave the room.

Walleye kept Zip from being flattened.

Nathan vomited blood.

Hester fell on her son.

Graham cheered Hester on.

Sarah and Hennet pushed from opposite sides of the stage through frenzied flocks of people.

Graham grabbed Hennet and wrestled him to the ground.

The balcony, engulfed in flames, crashed to the floor. It crushed those underneath it. It blocked the central exit.

The crowd ran. There were no doors. There were no windows. There was no way out. The air smelled like burnt meat. Blood smeared spats. Char smudged faces. People cowered in corners not yet burning.

The dead wind slammed itself against the monk's rope. It backed up, knocked over Sarah and thirty others, and crashed forward again.

The monk's rope did not move.

Sarah climbed over people and on to her feet.

Nathan pulled a pistol from his jacket pocket.

Hester raised her knife.

Nathan vomited more blood and the gun slipped from his red grip.

Sarah saw Hester's hand raise. Nathan saw Sarah. The knife came down. It dropped deep into Nathan's chest. His eyes locked on Sarah's.

Hester followed her son's stare. She saw a small woman in a singed, sophisticated, sea-green gown.

Graham rode Hennet's back. He busied the outlaw with every ass-poking, eye-gouging dirty trick he had. Graham would not have any man kill Hester before Hester could kill her son.

Walleye calmed Zip.

Sarah raised her gun.

With a quickness that astounded even her, Hester sawed into Nathan's chest. Broke his ribcage. Exposed his heart.

Nathan saw the trick box. Knew what it was. He grabbed the grounded pistol and put it to his head. He had to leave before she had him in the box.

Hester howled in protest.

So did the dead.

The Watchbird shook the stage.

Hennet's pant leg caught on fire.

Walleye put the dog on his shoulder and smacked the fire out.

Nathan smiled at Sarah.

He mouthed, "Go west."

Sarah cried out.

Nathan pulled the trigger.

Hester shoved the box into Nathan's chest.

Sarah emptied her revolver into Hester Garlan.

A slight, blue shimmer left Nathan and entered the trick box.

The dead wind cycloned the room in a rage. Fiery corpses were flung at the catwalk and walls. Those still breathing were belted at the remains of the balcony. The stage was cleared of all but Nathan's family and lover.

Zip howled and leapt from Walleye's shoulder.

Hester's heart exploded, followed by the left side of her head. A chunk of cheek and bone landed before Zip—who nosed them into a fire patch.

Before she died, Hester thought, "You are goddamn wrong if you think I'm going."

Sarah and Hennet rushed to Nathan.

"He's my son," Hennet said.

Sarah did not ignore the tall, dark man. She did not hear him. She grabbed the box and tucked it into a dress pocket. When she did this, two silver toads fell out. Sarah threw herself on Nathan. The two toads tumbled betwixt blazing stage boards, unnoticed.

The room crackled. Moans came from fleshy heaps of wreckage.

"And where is my death?" Graham kicked Hester's bloody body.

"Shut your mouth," Hester said from behind him.

Hester noticed the brown-eyed outlaw mourning Nathan. Her black heart blushed. Death put Hester in a foul mood and seeing the outlaw made her sulk further. Graham threw his arms around her. Every other Watchbird ghost—and there were now quite a few panicked newlydeads—hissed at the two of them.

Hester hissed back. She stomped around the Watchbird in search of a way out. Graham followed. He noted feasible titles for the evening in his journal. *Filicidal and Flaming Death for Famed Medium!* or *Eyewitness Account: Anguish! Fire! Fatalities! at the Watchbird Theater (by the Keats of Current Events, Graham Johnson).*

The hall stank like a chamber pot dropped down a chimney. The room was black smoke and crimson conflagration.

Walleye stood over his brother's hunched shoulders. Felt sorry for Net. Couldn't do nothing.

Zip licked Nathan's wounded head.

"He was my son," Hennet said again.

Sarah did not hear this either. Her sobs were too loud.

Outside, Arrol, Grimm, and the gathered crowd saw the Watchbird Theater's roof collapse.

Chapter Sixty-One

Boston, Massachusetts, 1884

THE BUCKET BRIGADE focused their efforts on wetting down neighboring buildings.

Grimm climbed over rubble in the alley. He would search for Nathan. For Sarah. For others that had not made it out.

He stopped when the side entrance burst outward.

Sarah limped out of the distorted doorway.

She was followed by a dark-eyed man.

The man carried Nathan slack in his arms.

Sarah dazedly walked forward.

Her arm brushed past a faded broadside that read THE REV. DR. ENTON BLAKE'S CORRESPONDENCE CURES! POPULARLY PRICED PHARMAKONS AND PHYSIKS!

Grimm picked Sarah up.

She let him.

He nodded at the dark-eyed man in the hat.

Hennet didn't nod back. He gripped Nathan tighter.

They met Arrol at the mouth of the alley. He sat on a crate. His rolling chair had been destroyed in the mayhem.

With a whimper, the rest of the Watchbird fell.

Chapter Sixty-Two

Boston, Massachusetts, 1884

1,012 PEOPLE ENTERED the Watchbird for Nathan Garlan's final performance.

144 made it out alive.

Chapter Sixty-Three

Boston, Massachusetts, 1884

SARAH WAS ON the midnight train to San Jose. Well, not directly to San Jose, but to a carriage that would connect her somewhere else and eventually she would be in Chicago then on another train and in another carriage.

She wanted to be away.

Grimm would attend to the funeral. Arrol told her to leave.

She would not bury Nathan. He was not in his body. She had Nathan with her. He was in the box. She had seen a shimmer. Nathan.

But how did she get him out?

The other passengers gave Sarah wide berth. She stank of rot, sweat, and smoke. Did this train have standards or not? It was a despicable form of capitalism to let someone so filthy on board, even if she had a private compartment. You could smell her through the door, for goodness' sake.

People talked.

Sarah Winchester did not care.

She was used to people talking.

Zip curled around the box on her lap.

Sarah looked out the window and knew that sleep would not come.

CHAPTER SIXTY-FOUR

BOSTON, MASSACHUSETTS, 1884

HESTER COULD GET no further from the Watchbird than one step out of the smoldering front doors. She sat with Graham Johnson before the entry. Hester stabbed an indecipherable bodily stain on the boardwalk with her knucklebuster-gripped knife. Graham Johnson sketched article illustrations in his journal. He captured a cadaver-crowded, horse-drawn ambulance, a weary shop owner (with a handkerchief tied around his nose and mouth), and a cluster of specters that overlooked their own bodies, piled under a tilted lamppost.

The building was still on fire behind Hester and Graham. The bucket brigade watered all that it could.

"Darling Lady Death," Graham said to Hester.

"This is bullshit," Hester said more to herself than Graham. She poked at her chest and head gashes.

"Indeed."

"Never once caught a break in my whole damn life. Why should I get one now?"

"You are whining, my cerulean strumpet."

Hester wailed in a way that made her not recognize herself. She flailed, threw her knife, and kicked at smoke. She fell onto her back and sobbed.

Graham sketched Hester's boot and stockinged leg.

Should Hester have tried, she would've found that she could have, once again, sent spirits to the Something After. Being dead, she could see the dead and the old words were still inside her. But she did not think. She did not try. Hester brooded.

It was here that the Reverend Doctor Enton Blake found them. He was late. His nap had gone long.

In the last year, Enton had gained back his hearing of the dead. It took some doing. Took some adventuring, some bribing, some calling in of favors and hard-learned words, but Blake heard the dead and Hester Garlan made more ruckus than any of the hundreds of others who lost their lives in the rubble and char that was the Watchbird Theater.

Hester opened her eyes to see the Reverend Doctor Enton Blake standing before her.

"Blake," Hester whispered. Her dead throat was sore.

"I'd say gay to see you, Hester, but you stole my sight, didn't you?"

"You want the trick box."

"Yes."

"My son's woman has it. I can help you find her. Unbind me," Hester said. Nothing would make Hester happier than to kill the woman who killed her, though she didn't know the mousy murderer's name.

"Unbind you? Ridiculous," Blake said.

"Do you want to find the box before you die, or not, old man?" Hester asked.

"Tactful, as usual, Miss Garlan," Enton said.

Graham put down his pencil nub and journal. "Hello, Enton."

"Graham?"

"Yes, sir."

"I have missed our book discussions."

Graham sighed. "I, as well."

"Can we get on with it?" Hester fumed.

"With what?" Enton played coy.

"I will tell you the damned words," Hester said.

"What words?" Enton asked.

"The words you want to know, old man. The words you've always wanted to know."

"You will tell me how to send the dead to the Something After?"

"Yes."

"Proceed."

Hester, seeing no other option, whispered the words and technique into Enton's ear.

He nodded.

"Thank you, Miss Garlan. That will be most useful."

He pinned the words close to his heart.

Hester spit on Enton's shoe.

Enton's foot grew cold. He said, "Graham, I cannot give you a true death without seeing you."

"Can you unbind me from Hester's corpse?"

"Absolutely."

"I should like to walk the world. Please, make it so, Doctor."

The Reverend Doctor did.

Something in Graham's chest felt like sugar dissolving in tea. Like a letter meeting a match. Like a torrent of water washing him clean.

Graham said, "Goodbye, Hester. You have been a bitch and a bother, and, I want to be alone now."

Hester bit her thumb at the bastard.

Graham shook his head and strolled away. He had spent too much of his life dedicated to someone else's ambitions. He knew a place with an indigo chase he could write on.

"I told you the words, Doc."

"You did," Enton agreed.

"Unbind me."

The Reverend Doctor Enton Blake took a stone from his pocket. He threw it where he thought Hester to be. She felt pulled to the stone. Enton Blake threw several more stones, these taken from the edge of a white desert. Hester felt further pushed at the first stone. Enton spoke in a language Hester did not understand.

She cursed a streak so crude a blue cloud formed around her as she was sucked into the first stone.

The Reverend Doctor Enton Blake put the faintly weighty stone in his jacket pocket.

He did not immediately leave the Watchbird.

144 people needed a doctor. Perhaps more would be found in the wreckage.

He would find out who Nathan's woman was.

He would find the trick box.

He would find his father.

First, he was needed here.

Enton Blake asked a yellow-vested man directing the bucket brigade how he could help.

Chapter Sixty-Five

THE FIRST PERSON the yellow-vested man directed Enton Blake to was Hennet C. Daniels.

Corpses lined the boardwalk. Hennet sat among the stiffs. His head was in his hands. His clothes were blackened. He was bleeding. He didn't know from where.

Walleye walked on the corpses. He made them belch and fart.

"Sir, let me assist you," Enton said.

Hennet didn't answer.

"Sir, you have burns. You are bleeding," Enton tried again.

"I got a dead brother that follows me around. I got a son that died tonight. I got a woman I loved who killed him. What the hell are you gonna do to fix that?"

"Your deceased brother pursues you?" Enton repeated.

"Yes."

"What is his name?"

Hennet nodded at a belching corpse. "Name's Walleye."

"Walleye," the Reverend Doctor said.

Walleye looked his way.

"Walleye, do you want to stay with your brother?"

"Net?"

"Yes, Net. Do you want to stay with Net?"

Hennet stared at the old man.

"Nah. Tired of him. He's tired of me."

"Well, Walleye, I can make it so you don't follow him around. Would you like that?"

Walleye bobbed his head yes.

After a pause, Enton said, "Walleye, you must use words. I cannot see you."

"You can make it so I go anywhere?"

"Yes, Walleye, I can."

"I want that," Walleye said.

The Reverend Doctor Enton Blake released Walleye from Hennet.

Hennet stayed silent and sitting throughout.

Walleye didn't feel any different, or maybe he did. There was a knot in his stomach that loosened and let go.

"You do it?"

"You may go anywhere you please, Walleye."

"You tell Hennet I say so long?"

"Most assuredly."

Walleye started to walk away.

"Doc," Hennet said.

"Yes?"

"Ask him where he's headed."

"Walleye?" the Doc inquired.

"Gonna live on the hill with Mule."

"What'd he say?"

"He's going to live on a hill with his mule."

"Anything else?"

"So long."

Hennet pressed his fists into his eyes and then let his hands fall to his sides.

"May I tend your wounds?"

Hennet nodded.

It'd give him time to figure out his next step. He sure as shit didn't know what a person did when they were old and alone in the world.

Maybe go someplace warm. Someplace with possibility. Someplace like California.

EPILOGUE

PART ONE

SAN JOSE, CALIFORNIA, 1884 – 1906

THE FIRST YEAR that Sarah lived in San Jose, she mourned. She did not go out. She did not sketch. She lived in hotels. She slept through great swaths of her days. She carried the trick box everywhere—no matter that the spirits it made her see and hear were needy and gave her migraines. She often wept so violently that she vomited on the dead that crowded her.

The second year that Sarah lived in San Jose, she demanded of herself to stop wallowing. She put the trick box in a safe. Sarah looked at her aging hands and wanted more than memories of a dead child, a dead husband, and a dead lover.

There was still time to start again.

In 1886, Sarah Winchester bought a comfortable eight-room farmhouse on roughly one hundred and sixty acres.

It did not stay eight rooms for long.

It had to be large enough for herself, her servants, visiting family, and especially her niece—Isabelle's Daisy, who called on her often enough to become her companion.

Sarah built because she had the ideas and money to do so. She had volumes of scratch pads filled with dormers, floor patterns, sweeps of steps, custom cabinetry, shades of paint, intricate porch spindles, banisters, and thousands of other odds and ends.

Sarah built because she had time.

The bustle and haste of sketching additions, obtaining special order materials, hiring craftsmen, beginning an orchard, investigating first-rate fruit dehydrators, avoiding the Neighbors, and maintaining excellent relations with the gardeners filled her days with something more than loneliness.

Sarah missed Nathan most when she looked at his books. His uncommon, beautiful books. He read everything from technical occult texts with diagrams so detailed that they made your eyes twitch to the latest by Twain.

In a fit of fierce sorrow, for frozen-faced, wall-watching still occurred from time to time, Sarah had burnt all that had been in Nathan's steamer trunks and the trunks themselves…but not Nathan's books. Zip had eaten part of the ashes before she could stop him.

By 1890, Sarah had a full bucket of guilt. The trick box had been in her safe for five years. Nathan had been confined for longer than that. She had moved on, but he could not. It was a cruel arrangement.

Sarah searched Nathan's esoteric tomes for assistance in releasing him from his confinement. Most of the volumes were in bygone and obscure languages.

The trick box came out of the safe.

Sarah learned dead languages by talking to the dead.

It was no longer maddening or migraine-inducing, and it was absolutely nothing like being hemmed in by William or Annie. There was nothing intimate or vicious about what she experienced. These spirits were clear about what they wanted. They asked for assistance. Sarah gave it when she could. She directed them elsewhere when she couldn't. She held regular séances to appease their requests. She rang bells at midnight three days a week to signal conversation openings. It did not have to be midnight. It was midnight because Sarah did not like the Neighbors.

"That mad woman," the Neighbors said, long before Sarah ever started with the bells. "She ruined that house. Have you seen the latest addition? No? Of course not. She built that hedge. Blocked any decent view. She had a baby that died. And a husband! My housekeeper said that Winchester's carriage driver swears she was there at the Watchbird disaster."

Sarah had built a hedge. She didn't like gossips. She didn't like most people. She had tried inviting the Neighbors over when she first moved in and it had…not gone well. There had been rude, untrue editorials in the paper. Now, Sarah only ever invited children over for iced cream socials in the summers—not their parents.

When she rang her bells, the dead came for palaver and patronage. In exchange for aid and attention, apparitions taught Sarah the lost languages of Nathan's books. She then searched his volumes for unbinding words.

She never found them.

What Sarah found was that walking her orchards pleased her. She grew plums, apricots, and walnuts. She dried them and sold them at market under her own label.

Emancipating Nathan was more than a leisurely diversion, but it was not her life.

Two years into her reading, the same year Ellis Island became a reception center for immigrants to the United States, Sarah Winchester became a summoning post for the dead.

After reading a booklet entitled *Eternal Imprisonment: An Oral History of the Trick Box, Its Functions, and Its Agonizing Application to the Unliving* (a booklet Sarah could not recall seeing in Nathan's collection before, written by a man named Graham Johnson), she mastered how to briefly beckon non-regional spirits to her.

Johnson outlined that if you placed a trick box in a recently built window or door and you uttered several old words a specter would appear. There was no controlling who came or how long they would stay. Most spirits would be whisked to the Something After in a matter of moments.

Graham Johnson speculated that even a spirit held within a trick box could be summoned forward. This was pure conjecture, but it was Sarah's only lead in years of research.

If Sarah could bring Nathan forth, she could send him off.

Sarah was capable of building a great many doors and windows.

For true, Sarah's home grew large.

She designed each addition herself, usually on paper scraps, tablecloths, or in the dirt with her workmen looking on.

What was once eight rooms turned to one hundred sixty. It was seven stories. She had a fine bell tower. She had a ballroom with stained glass windows that quoted Shakespeare. She had a door that led to a twenty-foot drop on the front of the house because she'd always intended to make a balcony, but never came round to finishing it out. She had short stairs that made it easier on her arthritis. She had a washboard built into her sink.

Laborers at the Winchester house found Sarah to be omnipresent. One moment she would be detailing instructions for the parquet, the next she would be in the storage shed respectfully reprimanding a worker who used four screws he had not noticed were gold-plated on a mundane project.

When the last nail or hinge went on a door, when the last bit of frame cornered off a window, Sarah would place the trick box in the entry point and say words that her workers never quite heard. She met many fine and ferocious phantoms—including that of Louisa May Alcott, Mary Ann Cotton, and the Middlebush Giant—but never did she see Nathan.

Sarah grew old.

Sarah kept building.

By 1906, she was sixty-seven and no longer built at an aggressive pace. She now placed the trick box in windows and doors because there was beauty in ritual. She thought old women deserved hobbies more vital than tatting lace and knitting.

EPILOGUE

PART TWO

SAN JOSE, CALIFORNIA, 1906

THE REVEREND DOCTOR Enton Blake made it to Sarah Winchester's home at 4:45 a.m. on Wednesday, April 18, 1906.

Many tragedies and disasters had stood in his path.

Enton was one-hundred-and-six years old. He was blind in one eye. He walked in short, slow steps with a cane.

It had taken him many years and all of his strength to get to the widow's home, but he had and he wasn't knocking at a side entrance.

The porch was large.

The house intimidating.

There had been a hedge, a gate, a long carriageway, and several steps his old knees did not delight in.

Enton Blake did not care to wait for society's judgment of a reasonable hour. He was keenly aware that his right foot was in the grave and his left foot wanted to follow.

He lifted his cane and pounded on the front entrance of the Widow Winchester's home. White lady or not, rich lady or not, he would have what was his. That trick box. His father. He knew the words to send a spirit to the

Something After and there was no way he was shuffling fatigue-footed from the world until his kin could, too.

By the third bout of cane pounding, a servant peered through the art glass and shook his head at Enton Blake.

Shook his head no.

Enton would have none of it.

He hit the glass with his cane. It rattled until his arm became sore.

The servant shook his head again and pointed to the side of the house.

The Reverend Doctor Enton Blake was tired.

Tired of life.

Tired of trying.

Tired of being treated like the dog instead of the doctor.

He was twelve breaths from death. He sure as hell was not going to huff over to a side entrance.

The servant disappeared.

Enton would've bellowed displeasure, but he had not had more than a whisper in him for years.

He missed his patter. His shouting. His days of prodding crowds. He slumped against the door and allowed his friends to bang upon the entry for him.

The dead woman with the knitting needles pounded the hardest.

"Thank you," he said.

His six friends nodded and circled their Enton.

The ghosts of the Winchester house peered out of the windows. Those on the manicured lawn near the front of the house had the best view.

A servant in a billowing robe strutted onto the porch.

"What are you doing?" he asked and put his hands on his hips. He had one slipper on. His nightcap was askew.

"I would speak with Mrs. Winchester," Enton said.

"No."

"I would speak with her or I will cause damages."

"No, and I am about to send for the authorities."

"I would speak to Mrs. Winchester," Enton repeated. "She has my property." His voice was hoarse. Barely there. He did not feel well. His heart. It did not feel strong.

"Leave now and you will not spend the rest of your filthy, brief life behind bars."

Enton Blake took two steps to the servant. "I would speak with Mrs. Winchester."

Enton's friends surrounded the servant.

"If you will not leave the premises, I will take your ancient arm and force you off."

Enton sighed.

The sigh was not deep.

He was light-headed.

He knew what would happen next.

Enton took another step to the servant. It was with his left foot.

He fell to the porch and breathed his last.

His friends did not move. They were shocked. They did not actually think that the Reverend Doctor Enton Blake would ever leave them.

The servant straightened his cap and gave his own sigh. He would have to send for the authorities for certain, now.

Enton Blake did not leave his friends.

He joined them.

His last thought was "Oh no, not with my father half a minute into that house."

The Reverend Doctor Enton Blake went haint.

And he loved it.

Oh, he was still old, still rickety, and he found it disconcerting to be a partial mist, but he had not moved so elegantly in decades.

"Friends," Enton said to the six ghosts that followed him for a lifetime. His friends circled around him.

"Please guard my cadaver. There is a gift for the widow in my pocket."

All nodded.

"I do not think we will meet again," Enton added. "I would have you know that I love you."

He need not unbind them. They were already free.

Before there could be tears, Enton walked through the front door.

The house was large. Miles of hallways. But it was not hard to find the widow.

She was awake.

She sat in the Daisy bedroom.

She drank tea to soothe herself after a dream of screams, fire, and blood. Sarah sat with the trick box on her lap. She was about to put it aside and once again lay her old bones down, but a shuffling came through the door.

"You, woman," Enton Blake called out to Sarah as she sat in her favorite high-backed chair with a knitted lap blanket.

"Who are you?" Sarah asked.

"The Reverend Doctor Enton Blake's my name, dearest lady. I have been tracking you for a biblical age."

Enton swaggered to her. He had missed his sway. He put his hand in his pocket so that he would remember to tell her of the pocket on his body.

"I have not a clue who you are. You have not been to my house before."

Sarah's fingers defensively tightened on the box. It was hard to do. Her arthritis was worse and worser.

"Darling woman, spirits talk of you the way they did of Nathan Garlan—cordial, honest, indulgent, and intelligent," Enton began.

A crackle of remembrance came upon Sarah.

"You son of a bitch," she interrupted.

"How have I given offense?"

"You sold me a defective cure," Sarah said.

Enton Blake was taken aback.

"I would do no such thing."

"You did," Sarah said. She shook the trick box at him.

"I did not."

"You did. Years ago, I bought stones to burn. They were to cleanse the air of the spirits in the room. I knew it was a temporary twelve-hour banishment, but it did not work. It did not work at all. All it did was give my parlor the stench of pigs rotting in a ditch. I demand reimbursement."

Sarah was a rich woman and she spent mightily, but she was one for a bargain and getting what she was owed.

Enton Blake frowned. He had a sharp memory of Graham Johnson bashing his head against iron and not paying attention to the mail-order requests he fulfilled.

"I apologize. I do recall the mistake you speak of. I assure you, Mrs. Winchester, if you had written for a reimbursement, I would've provided one. For now, I have a larger proposal."

Sarah was intrigued.

"What do you want?"

The lamps around the room flickered as random specters whisked their heads through the wall to listen in.

Out front, Sarah's servant awaited for the authorities to arrive to cart away the old man's body.

"Mrs. Winchester," Enton started.

"Call me Sarah. I do not like to be called Mrs. Winchester."

"Sarah," Enton said. He sat down in her vacated chair.

Sarah leaned on the edge of her bed.

"Sarah, you have a trick box in your hands."

"I do."

"It contains your lover."

Sarah did not blush. She was not ashamed.

"It does."

"It also contains my father."

This was not what Sarah had expected.

Enton Blake did not let her get further into her thoughts.

"I want to release him. No. I want to release *them*."

Sarah's mouth opened to speak.

Enton swept onward, for he thought this woman to be reasonable. "If I discharge my father from that trick box, your lover will also be emancipated. The door cannot be opened for one and not the other."

"I—did not know of your father."

"You would have no way of knowing such a thing. Honestly, my kind and good woman, I am tired. I had a love and she died six years back. I had a business and it was sold. I was done with life and I finally died. I am not going to live this afterlife longer than I have to. I want to release my father. I *will* release my father. Then I will adventure to the Something After."

The Reverend Doctor Enton Blake collected the words he had put close to his heart.

"You can do that?" Sarah asked. "You can break Nathan from this box?"

"I can."

"And if he wants to leave, you can help him…move on?"

"Yes."

"Please, do it. Please." Sarah offered the Reverend Doctor the box.

"I warn you, there will be no goodbye."

"None?"

"I will say one set of words and those in the box will be called out. I will say a secondary set of words and we will all be unbound from this world."

Sarah offered the box again.

The Reverend Doctor Enton Blake reached his hand out of his pocket to take it. He paused.

"Sarah, you must check my body's pockets."

"Body? Where?"

"Near your front door. Check my jacket for a smooth, black stone. It has a crude toad carved onto one side."

Sarah's eyes went wide. "Who does it hold?"

"Nathan's mother."

"Ugh."

"Do what you think is fair with it."

"I don't know what I could do with a woman like that. I do not want her anywhere near me."

"You are resourceful. You will form a fitting end for Hester Garlan."

Sarah reluctantly nodded in assent.

Enton took the box.

He disappeared from Sarah's sight. So did the droves of dead that peeked through the walls.

The trick box floated in the center of her room.

Enton Blake held the box. He pictured his father. He felt the air thrum around him. He felt his import grow. He felt the world bend to his will.

He said the words.

The floorboards shook. The walls swayed. The ghosts kept them from breaking. A roaring noise. Paintings fell. Dishware clattered and cracked downstairs. A tree collapsed on the front lawn. The brick chimney broke apart. The room tilted. Sarah scrambled onto her shaking bed and hid under her quilt.

It was 5:12 a.m. when the trick box broke open.

"Do not be a coward," Sarah said to herself and peered above the covers.

The room held only the dim light of a turned-over candle.

She did not see when a handsome man with glasses appeared in the room. He had a chest wound and strong eyes similar to Enton Blake's.

She did not see when Nathan Garlan appeared in his black velvet tailcoat and teal paisley cravat. There was a small hole at his right temple and a large hole behind his left ear. His chest was a bloody mess.

Nathan smiled at his Sarah. How beautiful her grey hair framed her head. He walked to her. He kissed her eyebrow. Touched her cheek.

Sarah's face tingled and grew cold.

Enton took his father's hand and laid his free hand on Nathan's shoulder. Nathan nodded at the Reverend Doctor. He would not haunt Sarah.

The ceiling of the Daisy room collapsed.

So did the observation tower.

Three of the house's seven stories flattened.

The Reverend Doctor Enton Blake said his last words.

Enton, his father, and Nathan went to the Something After.

Sarah screamed as the world fell down around her.

The ghosts that had held the walls steady during the earthquake—for the entire western seaboard had quaked at the breaking of the trick box—left the room.

When the world stopped shaking, Sarah was trapped. The door was jammed. The window was too high for a gorgeous old girl like her to climb out of. Parts of the ceiling had caved in.

Sarah cried.

For love.

For deliverance.

For her ruined home.

For the chance to rebuild.

She waited to be found by her servants.

The next morning, Sarah saw the devastation.

The earthquake had been monumental.

She was not intimidated.

She made a list of business to attend to.

Her first requirement was quickly fulfilled.

The servants found Enton Blake's body.

Sarah found the toad stone.

It did not take her more than a quarter of an hour to bury Hester Garlan three feet deep at the base of her oldest apricot tree. It was a tree that Sarah allowed a nearby orphanage to pick fruit from.

The afternoon felt fresh and Sarah's heart felt full.

She was not worried about filling her days.

She would do the thing she loved.

Sarah would continue to build.

Acknowledgements

OH. MY. GEEZ. Writing a book is hard and there are a helluva lot of folks to thank after one gets done. Here's the shortlist of those that brought me continual coffee and confidence.

Amanda Camino

Mort Castle

C.S.E. Cooney

Amal El-Mohtar

Everyone at the Mount Prospect Public Library

Shotgun Shawna Flavell

Moosher Helwig

Sara Johnson

Nicole Kornher-Stace

Jerome "Silver Fox" Ludwig

Mom

John O'Neill

Caitlyn Paxson

Nida Prukpitikul

Julia Rios

Tim Scheiman

Frankenmonster Stascik

Sally Tibbetts, Kitchen Witch

Ysabeau Wilce

AFTERWORD

THIS BOOK CAME about because of a road trip with my mom. We shucked off Midwestern dust and went California-way. Along the drive, we stopped at the Winchester Mystery House™ in San Jose. After exploring the gorgeous Victorian mansion that a supposedly mad, haunted widow built nonstop for near thirty-eight years, I wanted to know more.

When I began writing, there were no reputable books on Sarah Winchester. I spent a marathon session in the California room of the San Jose Public Library...and with my notes, my mother's notes, the internet, and ambition, *There Is No Lovely End* was written.

What it boils down to is this: Sarah Winchester was real. She was not a sorrowing hysteric. If she was haunted, it was probably by memories. She ended up with about 50% ownership of the Winchester Repeating Arms Company and made roughly $1,000 a day before income taxes. (This is over $20,000 a day, adjusted to inflation.) She had free time, extended family, and money. Her hobby was architecture.

Sarah Winchester had a sound mind for business and was philanthropically good for her community and country. Her home became her work, her art, and her legacy to the world.

For more information on Sarah Winchester, I strongly recommend reading *Captive of the Labyrinth* by Mary Jo Ignoffo. It admirably separates gossip from history.

As for *There Is No Lovely End*...it is a novel of historical fantasy. I took many, many creative leaps. The following will help you identify fact from fancy.

Did Sarah Winchester exist in real life?

Yes.

Did her child, Annie, die as an infant of marasmus?

Yes.

Did her husband, William Wirt Winchester, die of tuberculosis?

Yes.

Did Annie and William turn into hideously behaved ghouls that haunted Sarah Winchester?

Who knows?

Did Abraham Lincoln go shooting with Christopher Spencer and William Wirt Winchester on the White House lawn?

Yes, he went shooting. Yes, it was on the south lawn. No, Winchester and Spencer weren't there. Lincoln was with William Stoddard, his personal secretary, and it was the summer of 1861. They used an early Henry rifle and a modified Springfield rifle-musket.

Did Nathan Garlan exist?

No.

One of the legends behind Sarah Winchester states that a Boston medium was the reason she moved from New Haven, Connecticut, to San Jose. This medium told Sarah that she was cursed and haunted by all of the folks killed by Winchester rifles. The only way to appease these spirits was to move out

West and build a home big enough for all of them. If she ever stopped building, she would immediately die.

I was intrigued by the medium. He (or she) was a wild card whose name was forgotten by time, if the person ever existed at all. This gave me tremendous license to make the medium into whoever I wanted.

Wait, Hester Garlan, Hennet C. Daniels, and Graham Johnson aren't real either?

Nope. Totally made up, and yowza, those terrible bastards were fun to write.

And the Reverend Doctor Enton Blake?

Was made up. Enton was inspired by my love of medicine shows and the absolutely fabulous photography book *Reflections in Black: A History of Black Photographers 1840 to the Present* by Deborah Willis.

PATTY TEMPLETON is roughly 25 apples tall and 11,000 cups of coffee into her life. She wears red sequins and stomping boots while writing, then hits up back-alley dance bars and honky tonks. Her stories are full of ghosts, freaks, fools, underdogs, blue collar heroes, and never giving up, even when life is giving you shit. She won the first-ever Naked Girls Reading Literary Honors Award and has been a runner-up for the Mary Wollstonecraft Shelley Award. *There Is No Lovely End* is her first novel.

64232089R00252

Made in the USA
Middletown, DE
10 February 2018